Keep You By

By

Callie Langridge

For Jenny, Ethel & John,
With love, always x

Prologue

The day had dawned to a perfect spring morning. Just as the announcer on the wireless had predicted, an unbroken arc of blue stretched across London. But through the open window of her small upstairs flat, Gertie only vaguely registered the warmth and the chatter of her neighbours on the street below. She sat, transfixed by the contents of a letter which had landed on her doormat earlier that morning.

Outside, crockery chinked, and women and girls laughed while they laid places at the trestle tables arranged down the middle of the road. A group of boys shrieked, their shoes slapping on the pavement, charging up and down in a high-spirited game of British Bulldog. Up on ladders, men whistled and joked, calling instructions to each other as they strung out bunting, connecting each red-brick semi to its neighbour and its neighbour's neighbour. After six long years a cloud had lifted from the world and today was a day for celebration. A day to look to the future, not to the past. Or so Gertie had thought that morning when she woke early, so eager to prepare her contribution for the party that she hadn't bothered to dress.

While still in her dressing gown and slippers, she had cracked two precious eggs into a week's ration of butter and flour and beat it to a fluffy yellow batter. She had been halfway through dividing the mixture between two greased tins when the letterbox rattled in the shared hallway downstairs.

Now the mixture for her sponge cake sat pale and wet and raw, half in the mixing bowl and half in a tin. The kettle she had boiled to make a cup of tea had long since gone cold. For the last hour, she had not moved from her chair. She held a sheet of paper in one hand and clutched a small photograph in the other while, on the table, a tiny wilted flower lay beside the cracked eggshells. Once again, she read the single page written in the hand of the man in the photograph.

She put her hand to her neck and felt the pulse in her throat. She had never expected to see him again. Now here he was. In her kitchen. Captured in a spilt second in time, his cap tucked neatly beneath the epaulette of his uniform, his head thrown back, mid-laugh. He looked even younger than she remembered.

The grind of a key turning in the lock downstairs brought her back to her senses. Hastily, she folded the letter and forced it back into the envelope with the photograph and flower. Gripping the edge of the table, she eased up from the chair, the sound of the footsteps on the stairs hastening her progress. She clutched her stomach and shuffled as quickly as she was able through to the small parlour. She took a box of matches from the mantelpiece, fumbled to strike one and, as it sparked, she took a final look at the handwriting before putting the match to the envelope. As the flame licked around the edge of the stamp, the front door to the flat opened. In the same moment, a crippling pain in her stomach made Gertie bend double and she sank to her knees on the hearthrug, still gripping the envelope.

Part 1

Chapter 1

'Oi, London!' a voice yelled from the back row of the school coach. It was followed by a crushed Ribena carton, which narrowly missed Abi's head, and landed on the empty seat beside her. A dribble of purple soaked into the faded orange fabric. Abi grabbed her satchel and pulled it onto her lap.

Less than a week at her new school and she already had a nickname. She wasn't even from London. Not that Thug would take any notice, even if she could be bothered to explain that she was from Middlesex. The massive boy in her year with hair like a brown Brillo pad had about as much in the way of brains as the stinking cow muck that filled his dad's fields.

'Where's your apples and pears?'

It was a girl's voice this time. Tracey Evans – the only girl in Thug's gang. She was almost as big as Thug, with peroxide highlights that looked like a bird had perched on her head and messed all down her greasy ponytail.

Everyone on the back row laughed like Tracey had told an award-winning joke. Didn't they know that apples and pears meant stairs? There was nothing funny about that. Abi really, really wanted to turn around and tell them all that they were a bunch of country bumpkins, and if they thought that wearing their school ties so only the thin end showed was cool, then they were completely tragic. Instead she slumped down in her seat. Making an enemy of the school bully and his gang was probably not the brightest idea. Not if she was going to have to spend the

3

next few months with them on the stinking coach that bussed the farm and village kids to and from school each morning and afternoon.

'Oi, Squirt!' Thug shouted. Abi glanced across the aisle at the first-former with a pudding-bowl haircut and blue-rimmed NHS specs. Staring straight ahead, he hugged his plimsoll bag like it was a teddy bear.

'Squirt,' Thug shouted again, 'I'm talking to you. What have I told you about respecting your elders?'

The look on the poor kid's face said everything. Abi was in no doubt that he'd rather put on a PE skirt and play for the girls' netball team than do anything Thug asked of him. Slowly he peered around. No sooner was his head beyond the safety of the manky seat than he was showered with chewed up paper pellets blown through empty biro tubes. Thug and his mates did an impression of a pack of hyenas.

'You all right?' Abi mouthed across the aisle. Squirt shrugged before pulling his anorak hood over his head and tucking his knees to his chest.

Abi rubbed a hole in the condensation dripping down the window. She stared out at the fields stretching for miles in a patchwork of squares. If she were at home now – Twickenham home, proper home – she would be walking back from school with Nisha and Sarah, sharing a ten pence mix-up from the newsagent. She had written to them twice a week for the last six weeks. They had replied once; a short Christmas card, hastily scribbled as they were on their way out shopping. The highlight of Abi's Christmas holiday had been a trip to the school outfitters in Dorchester. While Nisha and Sarah had been rummaging through *Chelsea Girl* and *Top Shop*, she had been standing in her bra and knickers behind a curtain suspended between the Girl Guide blouses and Cub Scout jumpers, listening to Mum and Nan bicker because Mum wanted to buy everything on the school uniform list but didn't want to borrow the money from Nan. In the end, Nan made Mum accept by agreeing that the money was a loan, which

Mum could pay back when her new catering business started to make a profit. With that sorted, they kitted Abi out in an horrific assortment of grey, along with five pairs of navy belly-warmer knickers that weren't even on the list.

Something made a splat on the window just above Abi's head. A blob of chewed up paper slipped down the glass in a trail of spit.

'Got off lightly there, London,' Thug shouted. 'Wouldn't want to spoil your shiny new blazer. Or should that be *shitty* blazer. Was that satchel your best Christmas present?'

The hyenas on the back row erupted again. Only first-formers had new blazers and satchels, not fifth-formers. Mum should have painted a target on her forehead and been done with it.

The coach stopped on a narrow country road, framed on both sides by tall bushes, stripped of their greenery by winter. Abi grabbed her duffle coat and satchel and got down from the coach. As it pulled away, she heard the sound of the hyenas knocking on the back window. She yanked her satchel onto her shoulder, hugged her coat for warmth, and turned into the lane leading from the road. The lane was barely wide enough to drive a car down. Although Mum had managed to squeeze the Cortina through on the first day of the Christmas holidays. It was the first time Mum had driven down to Dorset. Not that she had any choice; Dad had spent the entire journey in the passenger seat, barely able to stare out of the window.

Abi kicked a clod of dried mud. It shattered into pieces. She walked slowly downhill and pushed open the gate at the end of the lane. As she stepped onto the gravel path, the view opened up before her. Grass swept down to the cliff edge. The only thing separating the grass from the coastal path and the cliff edge beyond was a low white wooden fence. Way down below, foamy waves lapped at the pebbly beach and further along the coast, waves crashed against a rocky outcrop. All around, birds hung in the grey sky. A seagull swooped low over the angry waves. At the very last moment, when it looked like the wave might rise up to pull it under, it caught a breeze and floated higher and higher until it soared above the cliffs, its wings outstretched. Higher it went, skirting the very edge of the horseshoe bay, swooping over the fields undulating like a giant green roller coaster all the way round towards Bridport.

Abi watched the seagull float over the fields of cows and sheep until it was just a speck in the distance before she turned towards the whitewashed cottage perched high above the bay. Cliff Cottage. It was miles from its nearest neighbour or the closest village. Abi had always thought it looked like a group of cottages had gone for a day out at the beach and left one of their little cousin cottages behind.

Making her way around the back, Abi found the kitchen door open a crack. With the range belching heat, it was often too hot to keep the door closed. She was about to step inside when she heard voices. Nobody talked about anything that mattered in front of her any more. Tip-toeing towards the door, she paused just short of the step so that nobody inside could see her.

'Do you think we can cancel the order for that side of salmon?' She heard her mum say. 'I don't want to end up stuck with it now the christening's been cancelled.'

'Couldn't we cut it up and put it in the freezer?' Nan said.

'I can't afford to pay for it. I was counting on the money from the buffet. I can't keep the deposit. Not when the baby's ill.'

'Let me pay for it. I can treat the girls to some nice salmon sandwiches at our next bridge night.'

Mum sighed. 'You can't keep bailing me out. If I'm going to make a go of this catering business, I've got to do it properly.' There was a pause and Abi strained to hear. 'Why am I even bothering? It's a disaster from start to finish.'

'Now listen to me, Rose,' Nan said. 'I won't have you talking like that. You're doing a wonderful job. I couldn't be prouder of how you're coping.'

'Coping? Hanging on by the skin of my teeth, you mean.'

'You know it's only your hard work that's keeping your family together, don't you? Look at me. A frown doesn't suit you. That's better. I'll have a word with Jim at the fishmongers. See if he won't cancel the salmon order. His mum does the church flowers with me. He's a good lad.'

'Don't go paying for it behind my back.'

'Don't be daft.'

Abi peered through the gap between the door and the frame. She watched Nan reach across the kitchen table and take hold of Mum's hand.

'Some days I feel I'm only just clinging onto sanity, Mum. I sometimes think Mick's not the only one going round the...'

'What did the doctor say yesterday?'

'He's got to carry on taking the pills. He's been referred to the psychiatrist at the hospital. The GP said it will take time... Time doesn't pay for Abi's new school uniform, does it? It doesn't put food on the table... and it doesn't bring back our home and friends and...'

'I know, love.'

'Abi worked so hard to get into St Margaret's. Got the headmistress's prize for art at the end of term awards.'

'Don't do this to yourself, Rose.'

'What was the point in any of it now she's at that awful comp? She's got her O-levels in a few months. She should have her desk in her room back home, not shoved up in that old attic bedroom... Oh Mum, I'm sorry, I don't mean to sound ungrateful after you've taken us in–' Abi's mum sobbed, and Abi took a step back.

'You stop right there, Rose. Who else could you turn to but your old mum, hey?' Nan smiled and rubbed Mum's hand. 'I couldn't be more thrilled to have you all here. It's been so lonely since your dad... well since then. Don't go worrying yourself about Abi. She's a good girl. She'll do well wherever she goes to school. Just so long as she's got you and Mick.'

'But she hasn't got Mick, has she? None of us have got him.'

The gravel cracked beneath Abi's shoes. With the precision of a meerkat, her mum looked towards the door.

'Abi, is that you?'

There was nothing for it. 'Yeah, Mum, it's me.'

'"Yes", not "yeah",' Mum said as Abi stepped into the kitchen. 'Why haven't you got your coat on? It's freezing out there.'

Abi shrugged and dropped her satchel to the floor.

'How was school?'

Abi shrugged again.

Nan got up and circled Abi in a hug. Abi rested her chin on Nan's shoulder. Her creamy white hair felt so soft. She smelled of *Yardley's* talcum powder, coal tar soap, and freshly baked bread. At least some things didn't change. Nan gave her a final squeeze and pulled away. Looking her up and down, she smiled. 'You're okay, aren't you, love, now there's a good girl.'

Abi nodded.

'I got you those batteries today for your cassette Walkman thingy.'

'Thanks.'

'Have you made any friends yet at school?'

Abi thought of Thug and Tracey. 'Not really.'

'You will. A lovely girl like you. Are you hungry? Fancy a quick sandwich before tea?'

Abi nodded. 'Ham, please. If that's okay?'

'Of course it's okay. This is your home, you can have what you like, when you like.' Nan kissed Abi on the cheek and busied herself with a loaf of bread, a tin of ham, and the butter dish. 'This is just like when your mum used to come home from school. Always starving, she was. Working that brain all day. Not like me – I was a terrible student! You're so like your mum was at your age. Two peas in a pod. All gangly arms and legs.'

Abi looked at her mum. She was gripping the tablecloth. The dark shadows under her eyes were getting darker. Back home Mum wouldn't be seen in public without mascara. Her fair hair, usually styled, was pulled back in a limp ponytail. Her eyelashes were so pale they were barely there. A tear slipped down her mum's cheek. Abi looked away. She kicked at the floor tiles. The scent of warm soapy suds wafted from the washing machine wedged in beside the stone sink under the window. In the corner, the fridge buzzed away like a swarm of bees had been trapped inside. Nan's modern appliances, uprooted from her fitted kitchen in Southall a year earlier, looked so out of place. They belonged in a kitchen with wall-to-wall lino, a built-in dishwasher and an eye-level electric oven, not squeezed into this kitchen on wonky red quarry tiles. A kitchen that didn't even have cupboards, just shelves lining the walls, some covered by yellow and white checked curtains but most with their contents on show – pans, crockery, packets and jars of preserved fruit. There wasn't even a proper cooker, just the range belching away like an old steam train.

'Here you go then,' Nan said, handing Abi a plate.

Abi went to step outside.

'Where are you going?' Mum said.

'I thought I'd eat outside.'

'You'll catch your death.'

'Rose,' Nan said. 'Let her go.'

Mum's shoulders sagged like a deflating balloon. 'Put your coat on,' she said. 'And thank your nan for the sandwich.'

Abi placed the plate on the table and pulled on her coat. 'Thanks, Nan,' she said.

'You are very welcome, my love.' Nan smiled and nodded to the door.

Outside, Abi struggled with a glass filled to the brim with Nan's sweetly-sour homemade lemonade and a plate piled with enough ham sandwiches for three men. She followed the smell of cigarette smoke into the back garden. She found her dad sitting on a deckchair in the doorway of the shed at the end of the garden, staring out to sea. It's where he had spent every day since they arrived. Only the low fence separated him from the sandy coastal path and the sheer face of the cliff beyond.

'Dad, I've brought you some food,' Abi said and stood beside him. She counted ten cigarette stubs in the grass outside the shed. He took another cigarette from the packet balanced on his thigh and put it between his lips.

'It's your favourite,' Abi tried again. 'Ham.' She thrust the plate and glass at him. *Please, Dad. Please eat. You can't live on just fags and tea forever.* He patted the pocket of his parka. Abi placed the glass and plate on the ground, took the box of matches from the ground, and handed it to him. He struck a match, lit his cigarette and drew in so deeply that his pale stubbly skin sank beneath his cheekbones. He flicked the spent match into the bushes rattling in the breeze and blew the smoke out in a single long line.

'I'll leave your sandwich here then,' Abi said. 'In case you change your mind.'

Avoiding the kitchen door, Abi made her way back to the front of the house where the path was edged by painstakingly pruned flowerbeds. The clematis she had helped Granddad plant last spring was in hibernation around the porch above the front door. He would be so proud of how it had taken. Correction, he would have been proud. Abi sank to the step. Clutching her legs to her chest, she balanced her chin on her knees. She picked up a stone and ran her finger along the jagged edge before lobbing it at the Cortina. It hit the tyre and bounced off. She picked up another and was about to throw it when she felt something nudge her leg.

'Cyril!' she said and gathered Granddad's Jack Russell into her arms. His coat was damp and sticky and he reeked of salt, but Abi didn't care. He wriggled with excitement and dropped his tennis ball so he could treat her to a thorough face wash. His breath smelled of ham. Abi laughed and ruffled the fur on the top of his head. 'At least someone enjoyed Dad's sandwich.' Cyril squirmed until he could reach his ball. He grasped it between his teeth then turned and dropped it in her lap.

'What? You want to play?' Abi put Cyril on the step and made a show of getting up slowly before setting off at a sprint towards the back garden. Cyril chased close at her heels. 'Come on, slowcoach,' she shouted and ran in the direction of the coastal path.

Chapter 2

Gertie walked swiftly up the quiet street and came to a stop on the pavement outside a large grey building. She unsnapped the clasp of her handbag and took out a letter. The number on the letterhead matched the number picked out in gold above the door. Easing up the sleeve of her blouse, she checked her watch. She was an hour early. She folded the letter, slipped it back inside the envelope, and retraced her steps to a tearoom she had passed on her way from the Underground. She looked in through the white tape criss-crossing the window. It seemed decent enough; with tablecloths and waitresses in black dresses with crisp-looking aprons.

As Gertie pushed open the door, a bell rang above her head. A waitress greeted her with a brief 'Good morning.' She seated Gertie at a table in the window and took her order for tea.

'There's no cake,' the waitress said. 'There might be some toast.'

The nerves that had been brewing in Gertie's stomach since she had telephoned to make the appointment the week before bubbled in her stomach. 'Just tea, thank you,' she said.

The waitress relayed the order to a woman behind the counter and soon returned to place a pot of tea, a small jug of milk, and a teacup and saucer on the table. She retreated and joined the woman at the counter. They looked in Gertie's direction. She turned away. Did they know? Could they tell? Perhaps women like her regularly took a seat in the window for a cup of tea while waiting for their allotted time in the grey building further along the street. In Gertie's mind, the women were gossiping about her. In reality, they probably cared as little about her affairs as they did about the business of the scraggy pigeon puffing out its feathers and pecking at the cracks in the pavement outside.

Gertie placed the tea strainer over the cup, poured the tea, and picked up the milk jug. In years gone by, she would have drowned the tea in milk. But now any indulgence when it came to the precious commodity of food would have drawn a frown or a shake of the head from a beady-eyed onlooker. Asking for sugar would have been akin to Eve asking a causal passer-by to pluck a juicy apple from an overhanging branch.

With just a splash of milk, the tea turned to a rusty orange colour. Gertie picked up the cup and blew across the top. A young couple passed by the window: he smart in his blue RAF uniform, she as fresh as the first bloom of spring, her cheeks pink and her neat figure in a pretty sunshine-yellow dress. Arm in arm, they smiled at each other, at the world. How happy they looked. Needing nothing more. Needing nobody more.

Gertie placed the cup carefully back in the saucer. The china chinked, and the surface of the tea trembled. Once upon a time, a very long time ago, she had been just like that girl. Had it really been eight years since that afternoon in St James's Park, just a few streets from here? Eight years since she had been stepping out with Sid for six months.

Every Saturday afternoon during their courtship, Sid took her to the pictures 'up west' and then for tea at the Lyons Corner House in Piccadilly. And every week, she stuffed the violet creams he bought her down the sides of the chairs in the various picture houses – she hated the floral taste but didn't have the heart to tell him.

That particular Saturday in December, instead of taking her to a picture house, he took her to see the glittering Christmas window displays on Bond Street. Afterwards, they sat on a bench in St James's Park, watching the ducks slide across the frozen water.

Sid rested his arm along the back of the bench, his hand around Gertie's shoulder, pulling her close. 'If you could live anywhere in the world,' he said, in a cloud of warm breath, 'where would it be?'

Gertie didn't have to think for long. 'In a house by the sea.'

'Not Hollywood then, like in those magazines of yours?'

'I live in my father's vicarage, silly. Where would I find the money to pay the rent on an apartment in the Hollywood Hills?'

'An apartment is it? Sounds fancy. What about those dreams of sailing across the Atlantic and seeing New York.'

'I've no money for that, either. The only thing I'm ever likely to do is help my mother sort through donations of clothes for the poor and serve tea to all the callers to the house. They ring the doorbell at all hours of the day and night, you know. Mother says I should always be ready to serve tea. I sometimes think my hands will one day stick to that big old tea pot.'

'You have other skills, too.'

'Like what?'

'Like being the most beautiful girl in London.'

Gertie felt her cheeks colour. 'Now I know you're teasing,' she said. 'My only other skills are annoying Ruth and disturbing Father when he's trying to write his sermons.'

'Don't do yourself down. You wouldn't look out of place stepping out with any one of those dashing Hollywood actors you love so much.'

Gertie slumped back against the bench. 'Just because I read magazines, Sidney Smith, and go to see pictures, it doesn't mean I'm a daydreamer, you know. You sound like my family. Perhaps you should be courting Ruth. She's more your own age. And she's a teacher. You might prefer the serious sister over the silly heart.'

Sid smiled. 'Tell me about your house by the sea, then.'

'I'm not sure I want to now.'

Sid squeezed her shoulder. 'Go on, Gert.'

She could never stay cross with Sid for long. And this was one of their favourite subjects of discussion. 'Only if you promise not to laugh at me,' she said.

'Promise,' Sid said solemnly.

'I'd live every day as though it were a holiday. Imagine waking every morning to breathe in clean sea air.'

'Would anyone else live in this house by the sea with you?'

'Well… a dog,' she teased. For as long as she had known him, Sid and his family had kept Jack Russell terriers. They were good for ratting in the grocery shop his father owned.

'Anyone else?' Sid asked.

'Some children. Perhaps.'

'Some?'

'Lots,' Gertie said, barely containing a grin. 'And they'll run down to the beach every day and make sandcastles and swim in the sea until sunset. They'll be as free as birds without a single care in the world. I won't even mind if they don't like school. As long as they're happy.'

'I see.' Sid smiled at her and in the process managed to knock his gloves from the bench to the ground. He stooped to pick them up and Gertie watched the ducks on the pond.

'Look at that silly thing!' She pointed and laughed at a duck sliding across the ice, its wings outstretched, quaking as it went. When Sid didn't laugh, Gertie turned back and found him still down on the ground. He had removed his hat and was twisting the brim through his fingers.

'What are you doing down there?' she laughed.

Sid placed his hat on the bench and winced.

'What's wrong? Is it your leg? Oh, Sid, get up before you do yourself a real mischief.'

'Gertie, I–'

'You know what the doctor said. You've to be careful. That ulcer's flaring. Get up off your knees before–'

'Please, Gertie!' Sid interrupted. 'I'm sorry. But won't you give a man the chance to speak?'

Gertie was too surprised to offer any kind of reply. Sid took a deep breath and took her hands in his. 'Gertrude Alice Brown,' he paused and took another breath. 'Will you do me the honour…

that's to say, will you do me the greatest honour… of letting me come to live with you in your house by the sea? Gertie, will you be my wife?'

Sid produced a small box from the pocket of his overcoat. He snapped it open to reveal three tiny rubies mounted in a gold band. 'It's not exactly the crown jewels, but I thought you might like it.'

For the first time in her life, Gertie was lost for words. She looked from Sid to the ring and back again.

Sid shifted on his knee. 'Are you going to make me stay down here forever?'

'No. Sorry. Oh, Sid. Yes. My answer is yes. Yes, Sid. I'll marry you!'

Sid sprang to his feet, as though the instruction from his doctor to mind his ulcerated leg had quite vanished. Gertie removed her gloves and Sid's hands shook as he fumbled to slip the ring onto her finger. He was smiling at her like a man who had won a jackpot on The Derby. He took her in his arms and held her close.

'I promise to love you forever,' he whispered into her hair, his breath warm against her cool skin. When he kissed her, she felt sure that Sid's was the sweetest kiss in the whole world.

***

'Will that be everything?'

'Sorry?' Gertie snapped to attention. She tried to place her body in the situation in which she found herself. She was in a tearoom. On Harley Street. With a waitress staring at her.

'Do you want more tea. Or some toast?' the waitress asked.

'No, thank you.'

Gertie took just a sip of the cold tea. She fished a coin from her purse and placed it on the table.

Outside, the warmth of the pavement came up to meet her. She made her way back to the grey building and paused to look at her watch. It was time.

'May I help you?' the prim receptionist asked without a smile. Gertie unclasped her bag, took out the letter and handed it across the desk. The receptionist gave the letter a cursory glance before handing it back.

'Take a seat, please.'

Gertie's heals clicked as she crossed the marble floor. She sat on a chair beside the cold fireplace. The sun streaming in through the large window warmed the side of her face. Just like it had the day… no, she wouldn't let another memory elbow its way in. Today was about looking forward. Not picking over the past and pining and… *Think, Gertie, think.* Corned beef. That's it. Corned beef. If she could get a tin of corned beef, she would make a pie for tea. Topped with a spot of mash. She sat up straighter in the chair. There was a smell. A familiar warm and spicy scent. Looking towards the mantelpiece, she saw the source: a vase of white lilies.

Lilies, lilies, lilies…

Her mother placed a vase containing two pink lilies on the chest of drawers in Gertie's room. Mother and Ruth helped her dress and when she was almost ready, Ruth left to go to the church to arrange the flowers. Mother sat on the bed beside Gertie.

'Now,' she said, patting Gertie's knee. 'I have something for you.' She took hold of the locket at her neck and eased it over her hair. 'This was my mother's. My father gave it to her on their wedding day. She gave it to me on mine and now I want you to have it, Gertrude.' Gertie's mother slipped the oval locket over Gertie's head, adjusted it at the collar of her dress and smiled. Gertie ran her finger over the tiny rosebud engraved into the surface of the gold. This was more than just a wedding gift. It was a sign. Her mother had finally forgiven her for having a head full of dreams. In her nineteen years on Earth, her mother had never treated her like a grown up before. Gertie put her arms around her mother. 'Thank you, Mama. I shall treasure it always.'

Her mother gently patted Gertie's back. 'You are going to make a wonderful wife and mother. You have so much love in your heart and I'm so very proud to call you my daughter, Gertie.'

The spring sun shone through the stained glass of Father's church and Gertie stood beside Sid in a pool of multicoloured light. She wore a cream dress with a matching hat and Sid looked so handsome in a dark suit with a pink carnation in his buttonhole to match her posy. Ruth was her bridesmaid. After the service the whole party went to Sid's parents' for the wedding breakfast and Gertie experienced her first taste of champagne. The bubbles tickled her nose and made her so giddy.

She could hardly wait to reach the hotel in Dorset to start their honeymoon. Every time she looked at Sid beside her, she grinned. They were to spend a night in a hotel in Dorchester from where they would travel on to the holiday cottage owned by one of her father's university friends. It was called Cliff Cottage and was apparently high up on a horseshoe bay with magnificent views across the sea. They would have the cottage all to themselves for a whole week. She would cook Sid eggs and bacon for breakfast every morning, just like Mother had taught her. They would walk every day along the cliffs. The breeze would make her cheeks so ruddy and full of health that Sid would be unable to resist keeping his lips from hers.

Eventually they waved goodbye to their family and friends and travelled to the station by cab to catch the train. With a carriage all to themselves, Sid kissed her all the way to the coast and when they arrived at the hotel, they went straight to their room, missing supper. This was what she had been waiting so long for. Not the ocean liners or dashing Hollywood actors. But Sid.

When they returned from their blissful week by the sea, they moved into two rooms in a house in Streatham. It was nothing fancy. A bedroom and a living room with a kitchenette, two chairs by the fireplace and a small dining table. The wallpaper was dark and the curtains heavy, but Gertie cheered it up with new lace curtains, a white tablecloth and two pink cushions. Each morning she laid their breakfast table with the tea service Sid had bought her as a wedding gift. It was decorated with a cheerful design of a yellow cottage with a red roof up on the top of a pea green hill.

'It's only from Woolworths,' Sid had said as she unwrapped it. 'But every time you use it, you can remember that house I promised you. By the sea with lots of children.'

Soon after they moved in, Gertie found a position as a filing clerk at a firm of solicitors on The Strand. She took two buses to work every morning, but each evening was home in good time to have a meal on the table for Sid. And each evening, with the washing up cleared away, Sid helped her with her homework. Mrs Eves, the office supervisor – a spindly woman with round glasses on the tip of her pinched nose – said if she gained an understanding of legal terms then one day she might be proficient enough to become a secretary. So, Gertie borrowed a stack of books from the library and tried to learn case law and procedures. Whenever she pushed the books away, prepared to give it all up, Sid was there to slip his arms around her waist and pull her onto his lap.

'Fill your brain with all that clever stuff and you'll bring home more money,' he'd say. 'And we'll have that house by the sea all the quicker.' Then he'd kiss her and her reward for working hard was to spend the night with him beneath the pink bedspread his mother had given them as a wedding gift.

It hadn't taken Gertie long to get used to that side of married life. Sid was gentle and patient, and she grew to long for the feel of his hands on her. The feel of him on her. The way he moaned because of her.

***

'Doctor Carter will see you now,' the receptionist said.

Gertie gripped her handbag. She crossed the marble floor and opened the door to a room. A doctor with neat grey hair and wearing a white coat, told her to take a seat. She looked around the room at the heavy shelves stacked with leather-bound books, a cabinet with brass handles, a sink in the corner with a bar of green soap in a porcelain dish, and a white towel folded neatly on the side. In the brief time it took Gertie to survey the room, the doctor finished consulting his notes.

'Go behind the screen,' he said with a wave of his hand. 'Take off your clothes below the waist and lie down on the table. Let me know when you're ready.'

Gertie did as she was told. She went behind the white screen in the corner of the room, removed her stockings and skirt and underthings. She lay on the table and waited a few moments before saying, 'I'm ready.'

The examination was swift and perfunctory. All the while, Gertie bit her lip and stared at a brown damp stain on the otherwise pristine white ceiling. When the doctor was done, he left her alone to dress. She emerged from behind the screen to find him washing his hands at the sink.

'You menstruate regularly, don't you?' he said over his shoulder, while Gertie rearranged her petticoat and took a seat.

'Yes.'

'And you enjoy relations with your husband?'

'I…'

'There's no need to be coy, Mrs Smith.'

'Yes.'

She enjoyed it all right. Perhaps she enjoyed it too much. Perhaps she'd damaged herself inside. She stared at the aspidistra in a china pot by the window.

'There's absolutely nothing wrong with you,' he said as he wiped his hands on a towel and sat behind his desk. 'Eat plenty of red meat, if you can get it, and take a regular glass of stout. Liver. Get liver if you can. Good day to you.'

Back out in the lobby, Gertie handed an envelope to the receptionist. It contained the fee for the consultation. A fee Gertie had withdrawn from their savings account without telling Sid. Mercifully, he trusted her to manage their accounts.

Out on the pavement, Gertie stood and let the sun warm her face. That doctor had said nothing the doctor she had visited five years previously hadn't. Eat liver. Was that it? She had served up so much liver over the years that she should by rights own a butcher's slab.

She walked slowly away from the building. At the Underground station, she passed a pile of sandbags in the entrance. Sand spilled onto the pavement from a rip in one of the bags. As she rode the escalator down, she gripped the handle of her handbag. When she boarded the train, she balanced her handbag in her lap and dug her fingernails into the arms of the seat. Was every object – every single thing – in this world conspiring to dredge up memories to taunt her? The sea and sand took her back not only to their honeymoon, but to the Whitsun weekend the year before the Saturday she stood at the altar in her father's church.

Each year Mother raised funds to send a group of the older children from the congregation on a hiking trip to the coast. Ruth had chaperoned the trip for years, and Mother and Father reluctantly agreed that at eighteen, Gertie should help her. It had been a weekend full of walking and singing and cooking sausages over campfires, and paddling in the waves at Southend-on-Sea. Of sleeping in the hayloft above a barn with the girls while the boys and their male chaperones slept in tents in the field. There had been two male chaperones. One was Father's mild and ineffectual verger, Henry. He was hapless and hopeless. The dozen East End eleven-year-old boys ran rings around him. And then there had been Sidney Smith. Gertie hadn't thought about him in years. She seemed to remember someone saying he'd gone to live Brixton way as an apprentice plumber. When he'd turned up on the train, he looked nothing like the little Sid Smith who used to whiz up and down the streets of Bethnal Green on his bike, making deliveries for his family's grocery shop. Always with his little terrier running by his side. He'd been roped into the role of chaperone by his father. There was nobody better qualified to keep his charges in check. Once upon a time he had been one of those East End boys.

Gertie could barely keep her eyes from him. Someone had stolen the skinny lad and replaced him with a man. Sidney Smith had even grown into his ears. He had a sweep of dark hair and muscles that Gertie sneakily watched every morning when he washed and shaved in a bucket in the farmyard, his top half bare and his braces hanging around his knees. He was handsome – not film star handsome, he was a little too stocky to be Clark Gable – and there was something about him that made her sorely tempted to climb to the hayloft and tip a bucket of water over his head. But for once she didn't give into the temptation of her naughty side.

She did, however, make a point of walking beside Sid whenever possible. He limped slightly on account of an injury he got when he sat too close to the steaming water escaping a boiler he was working on. But, as Gertie decided, everyone needed at least one fault. It wouldn't do to be without imperfection.

Gertie emerged from the Underground at Embankment Station. She walked through the gates of Victoria Embankment Park and looked out over the river. Above the water and towards the docks, giant barrage balloons hung in the sky, their casings taut like giant swollen bellies. Gertie roughly smoothed down her skirt. She unclasped her bag and took out the packet of cigarettes she now kept in there. She held the cigarette between her lips and lit the tip with a match. She drew the smoke deep down into her lungs.

How many more family meals would she have to endure during which her relatives' expectant looks turned to disappointment when no announcement came? Whenever she visited Mother and Ruth at the vicarage, she walked through streets of women who had more children than they knew what to do with. Children with dirty hair and no shoes. Children who slept three to a bed. She didn't have a fortune but the nest egg in the Post Office account that she religiously added to each week was enough to clothe a baby, feed a baby, and let it sleep between clean sheets every night. Even Ruth had beaten her to it. Five whole years after Gertie married Sid, Ruth married Henry and within a year they had a baby boy. The beautiful, bouncing Arthur, with a shock of red hair, just like his father. But Gertie could barely enjoy her nephew because whenever she walked into a room the lively conversation and cooing over Arthur turned to stony silence. But worse than that were the pitying smiles.

She hadn't told Sid about her previous visit to a different doctor on Harley Street and she wouldn't tell him about this one. If he was disappointed in her he didn't let it show. But seven years. Seven long years she had waited. All the while, deep inside, a doubt grew, spreading like an ink stain. It would never happen. She would never hold her own baby in her arms. Never feel a pair of chubby hands touch her face or watch the rise and fall of a tiny chest as it slept warm and safe in a crib beside her. She moderated her dreams. One baby. Just one baby would be enough. Each month she clung to the hope that the dull ache in her stomach was a new life, shaping and forming. She dreaded looking in her underwear because each month it was the same: a tell-tale dark stain followed by a hollow desperation rattling in her empty belly. Nobody saw the tears she cried for another baby that wasn't to be. Bit by bit, the house by the sea and the children running down to the beach had begun to fade into a mist, as though it were someone else's dream.

Chapter 3

Abi – Thursday 23 January 1986

While everyone else piled from the coach, Abi sat rooted to her seat. Squirt was first off, his plimsoll bag held above his head as a shield against the shower of chewed up paper pellets raining down on him. The back-row dwellers were the last to lumber down the aisle, each one punching the back of Abi's seat as they passed.

Abi was in no rush to enter the gloomy grey concrete box that was West Hill High, with its classrooms painted salmon-pink and snot-green. It was only when the driver turned around to check the coach was empty that Abi grabbed her satchel and trudged down the steps.

After morning registration, Abi stood in the corridor trying to fathom the directions on a map of the classrooms, battered on all sides by kids yelling in an accent she could barely understand. The sixth-form boys were as tall and broad as grown men. There had been no boys at St Margaret's, never mind boys with moustaches and voices like the baritones from St Aiden's who had joined the girls for choral concerts in the chapel of St Margaret's twice a year. The teachers and prefects from St Margaret's would have a field day here; dishing out demerits to all the kids not walking down the corridor in an orderly manner. Abi shrank towards the wall. Her new form tutor, Mrs Croxley, had told her to try to make friends. She glanced up from the map at everyone barging along the corridor. All the kids in her year had been friends for at least five years, they were about as interested in her as they were in the teacher yelling at them to slow down before someone fell and cracked their skull open.

Eventually, Abi located the art class as much by the smell of poster paint and PVA glue as by the squiggles on the map. The other kids pushed and shoved for the seats at the back of the class. Abi sat on an empty stool at a high bench at the front.

A man appeared from a store cupboard in the corner of the room. He made a beeline for Abi. 'Abigail Russell, I presume?' he said.

Abi looked him up and down. He was wearing jeans with his shirt and tie. And he smelled of cigarette smoke. He was like no teacher she had ever known.

'Yes, sir,' Abi said, staring at the silver stud in his ear. 'I'm Abigail. Abi.'

'You can call me Mr Munro, Abigail, Abi,' he said with a smile. 'It's good to have fresh blood in the class. But I'm afraid you have the misfortune of being lumbered with my attempt to teach art this year.' He dropped a sketchpad down on the bench. 'Write your name in the top right-hand corner. And guard it with your life. Things have a habit of going AWOL around here if they're not nailed down.'

Mr Munro walked to the front of the class, rolled up his sleeves, and grabbed a piece of chalk. 'Right, you horrible lot, sit down and listen up.' Somehow, he succeeded in getting everyone into a seat. He kept the class quiet for long enough to explain the basics of perspective, demonstrating on the board how every line radiated from a single, central point.

'Got it?' he asked, looking over his shoulder at the class, when he had completed the outline of a room. There were a few murmurs. 'I'll take that underwhelming response as a "yes". Good. Look guys, don't forget you've got to turn in your O-level projects in a couple of months. Do this well and this could be one of them. Now take out your pads and draw me your dream room. It can be anything. Let your imagination run wild. It could be a room on a space station. In a forest. How about in a long-forgotten chateau buried in the darkest recesses of a volcano? But,' he added when a group of boys started sniggering, 'keep it clean. No handcuffs or whips. And yes, Adamson, I'm talking to you.'

While everyone else laughed, Abi took up her ruler and 2B pencil and opened the new sketchpad. She put grey pencil to crisp white paper and soon there was a picture of a bedroom taking shape with everything radiating strictly from the central point of the window. In her room she had a bed, a wardrobe and a chest of drawers with a television on top. And on the walls, striped wallpaper. If she got the chance to colour it in, the wallpaper would be red and white. And there was a desk in the corner. The lead in Abi's pencil snapped as she pushed it into the page. She sharpened her pencil before pressing on with the drawing, working so quickly that she was already putting the finishing touches to the curtains when Mr Munro came to look over her shoulder.

'Good work, Abi. Very good.' He leant against the high bench and crossed his arms. 'I've seen your report from your last school. Top of your art class, hey. We'll have to make sure we don't let you down, won't we? Do you have your O-level project work for me to check over?'

'It's at home, sir.'

'Bring it in to the next class. I'm looking forward to seeing it. I hear you won the prize for art in your last school. You could be my ticket to the only A grade in this class.'

Mr Munro flicked a piece of chalk towards the back of the class and started shouting as he followed the chalk. Abi hid a smile in her palm. Maybe, just maybe, that place at art college wasn't going to be a daydream after all.

Ten minutes before the end of the lesson, there was a knock at the classroom door. The school secretary came in and told Mr Munro that the headmaster wanted to see him.

'Right,' he said, handing a piece of chalk to a girl with jug ears and braces. 'Michelle is in charge. If she hears a peep out of any one of you, then she has my full authority to write your name on the board. I'll deal with any troublemakers when I get back. Got it?'

Mr Munro closed the door behind him and the class managed to last for all of ten seconds before erupting, leaving Michelle, chalk in hand, utterly bemused.

Abi didn't care about the noise; she was way too busy lining up the angle of the grain in the pine of the wardrobe to be bothered what anyone else was doing. She was just putting the finishing touch to a knot in the wood when her arm was pushed from behind. A dark grey line scraped through the centre of the page, splitting her room in half.

'Do you fancy Munro, London?' a voice said. 'Got the hots for him, have you?'

Abi took the rubber from her pencil case and scrubbed at the grey line.

'Did you hear me?' the voice said again.

Abi kept scrubbing at the pencil line. Maybe Thug had a really bad life at home. Maybe that's why he was so angry all of the time. If she ignored him, he might go away. She felt the rubber grabbed from her hand. Or maybe not. *One, two, three...* She stared at the wardrobe in her drawing, wishing that it would open up and suck her in, reminding herself that Nan had always taught her to count to ten before she did anything hasty.

'Oi, London,' Thug sneered. 'Don't you want this back?'

She nodded but didn't look up.

'What's the magic word then?'

She didn't answer.

'Are you deaf? I said what's the magic word?'

'Please,' she said quietly.

'Please what?'

'Please can I have it back?'

'What? I can't hear you.'

'Please can I have it back?'

'Have what back?'

Only an idiot wouldn't guess that Thug wanted her to say the word 'rubber', so he could make some joke about johnnies to embarrass her. 'Keep it,' she said.

'So you don't want your *rubber* back. D'you hear that everyone? London says I can keep her *rubber*.' He laughed, and it sounded like the whole class was laughing with him.

'Why don't you just leave me alone?' Abi said, still looking at the wardrobe.

'Ah, poor London.' Thug spoke like he was talking to a baby. He took a step back and when he next spoke, his voice was loud, like he was on stage, addressing an audience. 'Do any of you know why she's here? Why she left posh London to come down here? Do you want to tell them, London?'

Abi gripped her pencil and stared at her wardrobe. There was the sound of stools scraping across the floor as the other kids left their seats.

'Her dad went round the twist,' Thug said. 'He lost everything. His business and their house. And they had to come and live in an old holiday cottage with her nan. That's right in't it London? You all live in an old holiday cottage. Not even a proper house.'

Abi felt her cheeks burn. She could sense the crowd moving closer like an audience at a gladiatorial tournament.

'Say it's not true,' Tracey said. 'Go on.'

'You don't know what you're talking about,' Abi said quietly.

'Oh yes I do,' Thug said, his voice full of what sounded like glee. 'Your nan does the flowers with my nan at the church. And your nan told my nan *everything*. What happened to your granddad then?'

Abi began to shake.

'Go on, tell us,' Tracey said and pushed Abi's shoulder. 'What happened to your granddad?'

One, two, three…

'Him and your nan had been living there how long?' Thug said 'Two months? Three months? He was digging in the garden and…'

From the corner of her eye, Abi saw Thug clutch his chest. He made a choking sound and stumbled backwards. The class erupted again.

'Ah, poor London,' Tracey said. 'Did Granddad die there in the mud?'

Thug righted himself and leant in close to her. 'Who'd want to retire to that house anyway? Your family must all be mad. Are you mad, London? Are you mad like your dad and your granddad and—'

In a single move, Abi chucked down her pencil and was up on her feet. She spun around, put her hands on Thug's chest and pushed. Hard. Thug didn't see the attack coming. He stumbled, tripped, and fell, taking two stools crashing to the floor with him.

For a second, the world seemed to stop turning. The whole class gasped, and Abi stared down at Thug. As stunned as she was, it came nowhere close to the look of utter shock on Thug's face. He stared up at her, like he couldn't quite believe what she had done. All too soon, he came to his senses. His eyes widened. He clenched his fists. But as he started to scramble to his feet and Abi looked around for an escape route, a shout went up.

'Munro's coming back!'

Everyone ran to their seats and took up their pencils. Abi righted her stool, sat down, and stared at the board, her heart pounding so she thought it might burst out of chest. Just as she was thinking it couldn't get any worse, Michelle turned to the board and wrote, "Alan Jones" and "New Girl".

Mr Munro was going to come back and see her name on the board and be so cross to think he'd wasted his time with her. An excuse. She needed an excuse. But as she was wracking her brain, a girl ran forward. The girl grabbed the board rubber and wiped out "New Girl". She turned around, gave Abi the thumbs up, and was back in her seat just before Mr Munro pushed through the door. He looked at the board.

'Jones. I might have known. If I were a betting man I'd have put money on you. You are as predictable as the atomic clock. See me after class.'

'But it wasn't just me…' Thug protested.

'Shut up and sit down, Jones.'

'But…'

'But nothing. Sit down or go and meet my old friend the athletics track. Your choice.'

Thug muttered something. Abi chanced a glance over her shoulder but instantly regretted it. Thug slumped down on his stool and Tracey Evans looked directly at her. She slid her finger along her throat. 'You're fucking dead meat,' she mouthed.

Abi looked back to her picture. The wardrobe door was still closed.

At lunchtime, Abi sat alone at a table in the reference section of the library. She crossed her arms on the table, making a nest on which to rest her head. Anything. She could have done anything. She should have asked for her rubber back to give Thug his cheap thrill. But oh no, she had to pick a fight with Thug and Tracey Evans. They were going to kill her. She parted her arms and banged her head on the desk.

The door to the library opened. Abi grabbed her satchel and was preparing to make a run for it when a face peered around the corner of a bookshelf.

She slumped down in the seat. The girl who had rubbed her name off the blackboard sat down next to her.

'Hello,' the girl said. She pulled a sketchpad from her bag and opened it at her picture from class. 'You're good at this perspective stuff. Can you help me?' She swirled her finger over the page. 'The lines are all wrong. Look, everything's wonky. I'm rubbish at art.'

Abi looked at the drawing. The angle of one of the lines from the window was wrong, which meant the shape of the bed was out. 'I'm not a teacher. Ask Mr Munro.' She stood to leave but the girl touched her arm.

'Sorry,' the girl said, pulling her hand away. 'Please don't go. I wanted to say something else. It's just that my dad plays cricket with Thug's dad. If you want me to, I can get him to have a word with Thug's dad about what he did to you. He'll go mad if he knows Thug's picking on girls. If you think Thug's big, you should see his dad.'

Abi looked into the girl's wide brown eyes. She didn't seem mad. Abi pulled her satchel into her lap anyway. This could all be part of a bigger plan to catch her off guard. Maybe this girl was a friend of Thug and Tracey. Maybe her job was to lull Abi into a false sense of security and then bang! Thug and Tracey would appear and not because they had developed a sudden urge to consult the Encyclopaedia Britannica. Or maybe there was a more straightforward explanation.

'Did Mrs Croxley put you up to this?' Abi said.

The girl looked puzzled. 'No. You're from London, aren't you? I love London. My mum and dad took me there last year. We saw all the sights, Big Ben, Madame Tussauds, Harrods.'

'That's nice for you.'

'It was. I bet living in London was way more exciting than living here. It's *so* boring. Everyone around here thinks anywhere further away than Dorchester is abroad.'

The girl smiled at Abi. Either she was really stupid and didn't know when someone was being sarcastic, or she was genuinely nice. But why would this pretty girl in trendy patent shoes want to be nice to a nerd kitted out in regulation school grey with a leather satchel?

'I didn't actually live in London. It was just outside.'

'Well that's close enough. So anyway, I thought, you know, if you wanted to, maybe I could give you a tour of Bridport. On Saturday if you're free. We don't have Harrods, but we do have a few shops and a burger bar. And then we could do some revision at the library. But only if you want to.'

Abi wanted to say that she would love a tour of Bridport. Every Saturday so far in Dorset had involved filling sandwiches and vol-au-vents for Mum's catering jobs. 'I don't think I can,' she said.

'Oh…'

The bell for afternoon registration rang and the girl pushed her sketchpad back into her bag.

'I'll try and get out of it,' Abi said. 'But in case I can't, thanks, you know, for what you did earlier, rubbing my name off the board.'

'That's all right.' The girl smiled as she pulled her bag onto her shoulder. 'I can't stand bullies. I'm Penny. Are you in geography next? I could walk to class with you.'

Abi sat in geography thinking about Penny's offer of a trip into Bridport. It probably wouldn't happen; Mum didn't really like her going anywhere with anyone she didn't know and hadn't vetted. In maths class, all thoughts of a potential trip evaporated. Abi spent the whole lesson wishing it would last another hour. All too soon the bell rang. She walked slowly from class to the coach and took a seat right behind the driver.

Thug probably had hundreds of fights every day. He'd probably forgotten all about a girl pushing him over in front of the whole art class.

'Hurry up you lot,' the driver said and started the engine. A gang of kids pushed and shoved each other up the steps. Abi leant in closer to the window and watched their reflections as they crowded in the aisle beside her.

'If it isn't Munro's little bitch,' Tracey said and punched the seat above Abi's head. 'Thinking you're better than us in that blazer and with that satchel. When your family haven't got two pennies to rub together.'

'Hey!' The driver looked in his mirror and shouted, 'I don't want any of your trouble on here. I'll tell the head if you start anything. Don't think I won't.'

'I don't know what you're talking about,' Tracey said in a sickly-sweet voice, 'I was just saying hello to my new friend, isn't that right, Abigail?' She stretched a blob of pinky-grey gum between her teeth to make a bubble and popped it. Tracey's spit landed on Abi's cheek.

'Do you think I was born yesterday?' the driver said. 'Any more from you and you're off. D'you hear?'

Thug dug his hands deep in his pockets. 'Leave it, Trace. She's not going anywhere. We can sort her out later. Come on.' He lumbered to the back with the rest of his gang trailing behind him.

But Tracey hovered for a moment longer. She leant in so close that Abi could smell her. She stank of cigarettes and something like sour milk. Abi turned towards the window.

'Don't think this is over,' Tracey said and punched Abi in the shoulder.

***

As soon as she got back to Cliff Cottage, Abi changed out of her uniform and made her bed. She peeled the potatoes for dinner and offered to iron the sheets Nan and Mum had washed that day. Dad only came inside when it was time to eat. Midway through carving his chop, he balanced his knife and fork on the side of his plate.

'I've been doing some thinking,' he said, without looking up from his plate.

Abi looked at Nan and Mum. They looked back at her. All three of them looked at her dad. He rested his elbows on the table and pressed his fingertips together.

'I'm going to dig over Sid's old veg patch,' he said. 'Ready for planting in the spring.'

There was a pause.

'Well I think that sounds like a fine idea, Mick,' Nan said with a smile. 'What do you say, Rose?'

Abi watched as Mum put down her cutlery and dabbed her mouth with her napkin.

'Dad would have liked that,' Mum said. There was even the hint of a smile when she reached and covered her husband's hand with hers. For the first time in weeks, he didn't flinch when touched. He picked up his knife and fork and started to cut his chop again like nothing monumental had just taken place.

Abi looked at her mum, there was no time like the present. 'Mum,' she said. 'I met a girl in class today. She's invited me to go into town on Saturday. She said she'd take me to the shops and show me around. I just wondered, since the christening was cancelled–'

'I think that sounds like a lovely idea,' Nan interrupted. 'Abi could do with making a friend or two.'

Mum picked up her napkin and laid it back in her lap. 'I'm not sure I like the idea of you traipsing around town with a stranger.'

'She's not a stranger. She's really nice. She's called Penny and she stuck up for me–'

'She did what? Why would you need someone to stick up for you?'

'It was nothing. Just, well, someone was teasing me. That's all. And Penny was like, really nice.'

'She was either nice or she wasn't,' Mum said. '"Like" doesn't come into it.'

'She was nice,' Abi said. 'And she said we could do some revision at her house.' Chucking in anything to do with schoolwork often helped influence Mum's decisions.

Mum shook her head. 'It's not a good idea. I need to go over to Lyme Regis to meet a woman about catering a retirement party. I can't take you to Bridport too.'

Without missing a beat, Nan jumped into the conversation. 'Abi can get the bus. She's old enough. The bus stop is only down on the corner.'

'No, I don't–'

Nan reached into her handbag beside her feet. 'I'll treat her,' she said waving her purse. 'She deserves it for all the help she's given us around the house. Don't you think, Rose? Did you see how well she folded those sheets today?'

Abi crossed her fingers under the table.

'No,' Mum said.

Abi uncrossed her fingers. There was as much point in trying to change the direction of the wind as there was in attempting to change her mum's mind when it was made up. Abi kicked the leg of the table.

'And you can stop that behaviour, young lady. Haven't I got enough to deal with without you playing up?'

Dad's chair creaked.

'It's not fair,' Abi said under her breath.

'Life isn't fair.' Her mum's voice took on a familiar haughty tone. 'The sooner you learn that, the better. Do you think this is what I had planned for my life? Well, do you?'

Abi wanted to say that she never asked to come and live in this stupid old house in the middle of nowhere. She hadn't asked to leave her friends, who still hadn't written or phoned. She hadn't asked to go to a school where she was bullied. Instead, she picked up her glass. Her hands must have been slippery from the grease from the chop, because the glass slipped through her fingers. She tried to catch it, but it was too late; the glass crashed to the floor and shattered.

For a moment everyone was silent. The first voice to speak was sharp and high-pitched.

'You stupid, stupid girl! You did that on purpose, didn't you? Smashing things because you don't get your own way. And now I'll have to replace it. Do you think I've got money to burn? You don't give a thought to anyone but yourself. Isn't it bad enough that we've lost everything? I rue the day that—'

'Rose!' Nan cut Mum off mid-flow.

'I'm sorry,' Abi said. She leapt from her chair and grabbed the dustpan and brush from beside the back door. Desperately she began to sweep the shards into a pile.

Abi was still on her knees when she heard her mum say quietly, 'What am I doing?'

Abi looked up. Her mum had scooped her hair back from her face. She was gripping her scalp.

'Abi. Go to your room please,' Nan said, without taking her eyes from Abi's mum.

'But the glass.'

'I'll sort that out. Just go to your room. Now please, sweetheart.'

Abi lay face down on her bed and thumped the mattress. She screamed into the pillow. She should never have answered back. Speaking up never worked. Spinning over, she kicked the bed frame and stared up into the eaves. She dragged herself up from the bed and rested her head on the window. Down in the garden, Dad was sitting in a deckchair just outside the shed. His cigarette smoke swirled in the light of the lamp inside the shed. His shoulders sagged, making his brown jumper look like a crumpled paper bag. Maybe she was too much like him. Scruffy, with mousey hair stuck somewhere between dirty brown and dark brown. Even the long arms and legs she'd inherited from Mum weren't quite right. They were gangly, not slim and graceful. Perhaps that's why Mum hated her; she reminded her too much of Dad.

'Knock, knock,' a voice said gently from the doorway. 'All right if I come in?' Abi nodded. The floorboards creaked as Nan crossed the room. She sat down on the bed and patted the spot beside her. Abi sat down, and Nan took her hand and placed it in her lap.

'Now, sweetheart,' she said, 'I know this has all been a shock. Coming to live here. One thing you have to remember is that your mum and dad love you very, very much. They're just going through a difficult time at the moment. You're old enough to understand that bad things happen to good people.'

'But the glass. I didn't mean to…'

Nan let go of Abi's hand and slipped her arm around her shoulders. She pulled her close. 'Just give her time.'

Nan rocked her gently from side to side. 'You mustn't keep it bottled up. Even when you were a small thing, you took things to heart. You can always talk to me. Let me take on your troubles. My shoulders are broader than yours.'

A hot tear forced its way down Abi's cheek. Nan was the only person who could make her cry.

'Here,' Nan said. She let go of Abi and pulled a small green box from her pocket. She prised it open and in spite of everything Abi felt a tingle of excitement. Nan's locket was a treat usually saved for birthdays and Christmas. Nan took the locket from its velvet cushion and placed it over Abi's head. The chain felt cool against Abi's skin. She fingered the ridges of the rosebud engraved into the surface of the gold oval.

Nan smiled. 'Keep it on for now and come downstairs. I think your mum would like to see you.' She patted Abi's knee, slipped a hankie into her hand, and with a puff, hauled herself up from the bed. She stopped in the doorway. 'I want my smiley Abigail back. The girl with all the quips. I know it's hard to believe, sweetheart, but this wrinkly old woman was once a slip of a girl. I was full of fun, just like you. And I understand more than you know. Oh, is that a grin I see?'

It was. Just a little one. Abi kept her smile in place until she heard the stairs creak. She had read somewhere that a fake smile was easy to spot. It disappeared as quickly as it came.

Ten minutes later, Abi stood in the kitchen doorway. There was no sign of the glass. Or the dinner plates.

'Sit down then.' Nan smiled. 'You're making the place look untidy.'

Abi pulled out a chair and took a seat at the table. Nan poured her a mug of tea.

'What was that you were saying about Saturday, Rose?' Nan said as she stirred a spoon of sugar into Abi's mug.

'I suppose it's not such a bad idea,' Mum said into her tea. 'But I want you home by three. I don't want you getting that bus on your own in the dark.'

'I promise,' Abi said.

'What you need,' Nan said, pointing to Abi's red tracksuit bottoms, 'is a new pair of trousers. Those are half-mast. A new pair of denims. That's what you need.'

'Jeans, Nan. They're called jeans,' Abi smiled.

'That's what I said,' Nan said with a wink. 'I can fair see your ankles in those.'

Chapter 4

Rose – Wednesday 21 August 1963

Femur, patella, tibia, fibula, tarsal, metatarsals, phalanges. Rose wiggled her toes, sending a light flurry of sand onto the tartan travel blanket. She brushed it off, marvelling yet again at what an outstanding feat of mechanics the human body was. Hundreds of bones – 206 to be precise – connected to thick muscle by tensile cartilage, beneath a spider's web of capillaries, fed by arteries pumping blood straight from the heart.

She stretched her legs beyond the edge of the blanket and watched the long quadriceps expand just below the surface of her sun-browned skin. Warmth passed from the smooth pebbles into her heels. In biology class, Miss Millicent had explained the process of nerve endings transmitting messages to the brain rather like that of an operator connecting a call at the telephone exchange.

'But, girls,' she had said, looking at the class over the top of her half-moon spectacles, a note of warning in her voice, 'in the same way that an operator might plug a caller into a stranger to speak at cross purposes, so an incorrect message might be sent from the brain down the spinal cord. Generally, such a misdirected message might elicit an involuntary spasm. But, in severe cases, after a traumatic accident for example, then the messages may be permanently interrupted, leading to long term or life-long paralysis.'

In spite of the heat of the day, Rose shivered. She was quite glad of the distraction when someone shouted her name. 'Rose! Rose! Come on in. The water's lovely.'

Shielding her eyes from the midday sun, Rose looked towards the shore. Her mother was paddling in the shallow water, wearing a bright yellow bathing suit and tortoiseshell-framed sunglasses shaped like a cat's eyes. Her father was next to her, sporting a pair of checked swimming trunks, his body as solid as an ox. Nothing would keep her parents from their daily dip in the sea. It was an essential part of their holiday. Just a few days in Dorset and they had both taken on the colour of boiled lobsters.

Rose picked up her book and waved it. She made a show of flicking through the pages. Her mother took the hint and turned back to her father. Rose watched them over the top of the pages, chatting away happily as though in over thirty years of marriage they hadn't had every conversation it was possible to have. Dorset had that effect on them. At the first hint of warm salty air wafting through the open windows of her father's Morris Minor, her parents transformed into children again. Somehow between mortgage payments and gas bills, her father had always managed to put enough into his firm's savings scheme each month so that in Rose's eighteen years they had never once missed their annual fortnight in the crooked old cottage on the cliff. At least they were happy for the moment. In a few weeks, when they waved her off from King's Cross Station, they would need a stack of hankies. Rose had replayed the impending scene in her mind hundreds of times and it was never pretty.

The rumble of a motorcycle engine echoed around the high walls of the bay. It stopped on the cliff top, on the road just above the cottage. It could mean only one thing. Rose crossed her legs at the ankles, held her book in one hand and looked intentionally occupied. But soon she heard heavy boots crunching through the pebbles towards her.

'Aw'right, Rosie-Posie.'

'It's Rose,' she said, keeping her eyes firmly on her book. 'And yes, I'm fine. Or I was until you disturbed me.'

Arthur dropped his black leather jacket and slumped down beside her. He snatched the book from her hands. 'What's this, couz? Trying to look all academical are you?'

'I think you mean academic. And reading can be for pleasure, in case you didn't know.'

Arthur turned the book over. '*The Composition of the Human Skeleton*?' he read in a silly voice. 'Sounds riveting.'

Rose grabbed the book from him. 'Shut up, Arthur.'

'Oooh. Pardon me for breathing. And look at you in that red bathing suit. What are you supposed to look like? Brigitte Bardot or something?'

She didn't answer straightaway. She had to plan a smart reply. She looked down at him resting back on his elbows; his skinny legs stretched out like two blue matchsticks in his jeans. That was too obvious a target. 'Hasn't Elvis asked for his hair back yet?' she said.

Arthur laughed and ran his hand through his red quiff. 'I'll give you that one. See, even you can be a human being when you try. Now budge up. These stones are cooking my backside.' He shoved her roughly across the blanket, and laid back again, eyes closed, face turned up to the sun. 'I'm as stiff as a board thanks to you. A few nights on that lumpy sofa have played havoc with my back.'

'I did offer to sleep in the parlour. You're welcome to the bed in the creepy old attic, if you want it.'

'Oh yeah, and where would you put all your *stuff*? I ask you, what does a person need with so many clothes? And all those rollers and pots of cream and slap and Lord only knows what else.'

'I wouldn't expect someone like you to understand anything about personal grooming,' she said.

'What do you mean, someone like me?'

'Someone who's happy to go around stinking of oil with black mess under his fingernails.'

Arthur held up a hand and examined it. 'The old girl had engine problems,' he said, wiping his hands on his jeans. 'Lucky for me I bumped into a couple of blokes who work in a garage in town. They helped me put her right. Hey, they said there's some kind of dance in town on Saturday night. Fancy it?'

'No,' Rose said, imagining a barn full of locals in gingham dresses, skipping around a bale of hay.

'I could treat you to a lemonade,' Arthur smiled.

'I said no.'

He was treating her like a little girl to goad her. Well she wouldn't rise to it. She picked up her book and had just opened it when something moved in front of them and blotted out the sun. It was her mother, wrapped in a towel, dripping seawater. Rose curled her toes and pulled her legs onto the safety of the blanket.

'Auntie G!' Arthur said, jumping to his feet. He went to give her a hug then took an exaggerated step back. 'Whoa. On second thoughts I don't want you soaking my threads.'

'You cheeky so-and-so,' Rose's mother said and tapped him on the arm. 'Don't think you're too old to get a clip around the ear. I was just about to ask whether you wanted some lunch, but I don't think I'll bother now.'

Arthur gave her one of his cheeky grins. 'Don't be like that, Auntie G. I'm famished.'

'That's what I like to hear. What about you, Rose?'

'What are you making?'

'Pilchard and cucumber sandwiches.'

Rose grimaced. 'Isn't there any cheese?'

'No. But I could open a tin of ham.'

'I think I'll wait for dinner tonight.'

'You sure? You know you should eat something.'

'Mother, I'm not a child.'

'So you keep telling me. And like I keep telling you, it doesn't matter to me how old you are, you'll always be my little girl.'

It took all of Rose's effort not to scream. Why did her mother insist on treating her like she was still a little girl who needed to have her hand held to cross the road? She was eighteen. Not eight.

'Well,' her mother said, 'I'll make you a sandwich anyway. In case you change your mind.'

Arthur sat down again, and Rose waited for her mother to be comfortably out of earshot before saying, 'I won't.'

Arthur dug his bony elbow into her ribs. 'You know you wanna be a bit nicer to your mum. She's all right.'

'Thank you, Arthur, but when I need advice on how to handle my relationships, I'll be sure to let you know.'

'Oi, missy. Don't you go getting all hoity-toity just because you've managed to fool someone that you've got brains. You're no better than you ought to be.'

'I've never said I was.'

'Good. Just you remember that. Don't forget, I knew you when you was a little girl sitting on this very beach eating sand sandwiches. Not so clever then were you?'

'I suppose not.' Rose smiled. Arthur made it impossible to stay cross with him for long.

'Anyway, you should think yourself lucky that Auntie G and Uncle Sid have got some gumption. Not like mine.' He nodded dismissively over his shoulder to his own parents sitting on deckchairs further up the beach. Auntie Ruth was wearing a cotton dress, covering her from neck to ankles, and her pale skin was hidden under a wide-brimmed straw hat. Beside her, Uncle Henry wore a shirt and tie. His only concession to the heat of the day was that he had rolled up his trouser legs to his knees. Not for the first time, Rose wondered how such a serious and conservative couple had produced a son like Arthur. But one look at Uncle Henry left little doubt of Arthur's parentage. Arthur had inherited Uncle Henry's hair. And his freckles. And his knobbly knees.

'Stuffed shirts,' Arthur said, curling his top lip.

'Don't be cruel. Your parents can't help it if they're disappointed in your choice of career.'

'Don't you start too.' He frowned. 'I've committed one too many mortal sins for God to want me in the family business. Bedsides, dog collars don't suit me.'

Rose sighed. 'You really are hopeless. Do you ever take anything seriously?'

'Not if I can help it. Life's too short to go around worrying all the time. And you could do with relaxing a bit too. Take a tip from your cousin Arthur and calm down. Not everything in life needs to be planned out and ordered and sorted into neat little boxes. Just jump on and enjoy the ride.'

'They do have a point, though. You are twenty-four. Isn't it about time you stopped messing about with motorbikes and got a proper job?'

'Excuse me,' he said, his eyes widening. 'A mechanic is a proper job. And for your information, Miss-Know-It-All, I've got an iron in the fire when it comes to my future career.'

'Really? What?'

Arthur tapped the side of his nose. 'You'll have to wait and see. So, this dance on Saturday? Shall I get you a ticket?'

'No. I'm washing my hair.'

'Your loss.' He jumped up and brushed the sand from his trousers. 'I'm off to get my nosebag. Coming?'

'In a while.'

'Suit yourself.'

Arthur crunched away through the pebbles, leaving Rose to twist a tassel of the blanket around her fingers. Was Arthur right? Was she really too serious about everything? Should she be a bit more like him and let life happen rather than plan every aspect of her future in minute detail? She just couldn't help it. Where Arthur thrived on chaos, she needed order. Was he right about her becoming some kind of terrible snob? After all her parents had done for her, was she somehow betraying them? They had always made sure that she had everything she needed, even if it meant they had to go without. When they were saving to send her on the school trip to Paris, her father had gone without his weekly trips to the British Legion for a couple of months. When she grew out of her school uniform, her mother took in washing to earn the money to pay for a new skirt and blazer.

'No daughter of mine will ever be second best,' Rose's mother said while she ran the iron over the white shirt of the bank manager who lived up the road. And if it was possible, her parents had been even more thrilled than her when the letter arrived from Edinburgh. Her father had grabbed it from the doormat and handed it to her.

Her parents stood to one side, waiting for her reaction. And when she opened the envelope and smiled, they smothered her with kisses. But while they were gushing over their 'brilliant daughter', Rose slipped one sheet of the letter into her blazer pocket. Her parents didn't need to know that a full scholarship wouldn't cover all of her expenses at university. Besides, she had it all worked out. She had eighteen years of birthday and Christmas money in a savings account in the Post Office, which would give her a weekly allowance. If she lived frugally and found a part-time job, then she could cope.

Her mother and father had made her believe that she could be anything she wanted to be. They had encouraged her to work hard to get a place at grammar school and then to stay at the very top of her class. Why had she spent whole weekends indoors, tackling pages of long division or memorising the photosynthetic equation while her friends met in the park, if not to better herself? Now she wanted the rewards. She wanted to be successful and to buy her clothes from John Lewis on Bond Street, not from the stalls on Southall market. She wanted a modern house furnished with smoked glass tables from Heals on Tottenham Court Road, not dusty old hand-me-downs from the houses of long-dead relatives. She wanted to buy her groceries from Selfridge's food hall, not to pull potatoes and carrots from a veg patch in the garden. And she wanted a brass plaque on a consulting room door: 'Dr Rose Smith'.

She looked up and saw that her father was still on the beach, shaking sand from his shoes. He leant down to pull them on, but the scar below his right knee made bending a bit of a struggle. Apparently, the original burn had reached all the way through to the muscle in his calf – the tibialis anterior. It had happened years before Rose was born but the hair over the scar had never grown back. It still had the appearance of a half set blancmange. When she was a little girl he had let her practice her bandage skills on his leg. He was a very obliging patient and would sit in his armchair by the fire, sipping his tea while she carefully dressed his wound in a crepe bandage borrowed from her mother's first-aid tin. 'Oh, that feels much better,' he would say. 'I do believe you are the finest doctor in the whole wide world, Miss Rose Smith.' And her reward was always to take a barley sugar from the little dish he kept on the sideboard.

Rose dropped her book, jumped to her feet and ran across the hot pebbles towards him. 'Dad! Dad! Wait for me,' she called.

He turned around and smiled. 'Whoa there. Where's the fire?'

'Nowhere,' she said, catching her breath. 'I just wanted... I just wondered... Am I doing the right thing? Edinburgh is so far away and–'

Her father put his hand out to stop her. 'You, my love, are the brightest, most beautiful young woman in the world. You can be anything you want to be. Do anything you want to do. The world is out there for the taking. And you're going to be a brilliant doctor. If anyone ever tries to tell you otherwise then they'll have me to deal with. Okay?'

'Okay.'

He held out his crooked arm. 'Come on. Let's go and see what your mum's rustled up for lunch. All this swimming has made me ravenous.'

Rose slipped her arm through his. His arm was strong and warm, and she rested her head against his shoulder. 'Thanks, Dad.'

He patted her hand. 'You don't need to thank me, love. I'm your dad. It's what I'm here for.'

Chapter 5

Early on Saturday morning, with a ten-pound note from Nan folded in her pocket and her school books in her satchel, Abi took the bus from the village into town. At eleven o'clock, she stepped down outside the library.

'Hello!' Penny said, waving madly. It was a grey winter's morning but with a smile that beamed from ear to ear, Penny seemed to carry her very own ray of sunshine around with her. She wore a furry jacket and a scarf with matching furry pompoms at each end. Her hair was pulled into a perfect French plait. Abi looked down at her own grey duffle coat. She forced her hands into the pockets of her beige cords and pushed down, trying and failing to force down the inch or so they were lacking in length. If Penny noticed that Abi looked like she was dressed from the cast-offs from a jumble sale, she didn't say anything.

'I like your plait,' Abi said.

Penny ran her fingers along the dark ridge. 'My Mum won't let me leave the house until she's done my hair and checked what I'm wearing. She thinks I'm a Sindy doll or something. Mums, hey. So what's first? Library for revision or shops?'

Abi tried not to look at her cords. 'Shops,' she said. 'My nan gave me some money to buy some new jeans.'

'Oh good! I'll take you to my favourite place!'

Abi followed Penny to the High Street, Penny chatting constantly, pointing out highlights of the town; the Town Hall, cafés, the little cinema. Finally, she stopped at a clothes shop. The luminous knitted jumpers suspended in the window – pinks, greens, oranges – were exactly the type of clothes that would have made Abi's mum grimace and pull her further up the street.

'They look brilliant!' Penny said when Abi emerged from the changing room in a pair of stonewashed jeans. 'I wish I was tall like you. Your legs go on forever.'

'Should I get them then?'

Penny nodded. Abi paid for the jeans and after telling the shop assistant she would keep them on, she shoved her cords and satchel into the carrier bag. If she walked around town with a carrier bag from this trendy shop rather than her satchel, maybe, just maybe, anyone looking at her wouldn't think she was so much of a nerd.

Penny's next stop on her tour was a stall in the market square selling make-up. She chose a pink lip-gloss from a little wicker basket. 'You should get this,' she said handing the lip-gloss to Abi. 'Pink suits pale skin. I know *all* about hair and make-up. If you ever need a haircut, let me know. My mum owns *Shirl's*, the beauty salon down by the bay. Are you getting this then?'

'I'm not supposed to wear make-up.'

'What, *no* make-up? None at all?'

'Well, no. I mean not for school or anything.'

'But for special occasions.'

'Of course,' Abi forced a sort of laugh. 'I mean, special occasions are okay.' She handed forty-nine pence to the stallholder and stuffed the lip-gloss in her pocket. If Penny thought not wearing make-up was weird, it was probably best not to mention the even longer list of Mum's absolutely forbidden things – pierced ears, staying out after dark, unsuitable friends, doing anything other than your absolute best at school, swearing, boyfriends... 'Let's go to the library,' Abi said.

They had only taken a few steps away from the stall when Abi felt herself grabbed and pulled into a gap between two stalls.

'What the...'

Penny put her finger to her lips. She pointed to the market area. Abi pressed closer to the stall, the cold metal of the frame as cold as the chill running through her.

Thug and Tracey and the rest of their gang were messing around in the market square, pushing each other into stalls, picking things up, putting some of the items back, and sneaking others into their pockets.

'It stinks in here,' Penny whispered, covering her nose. She was right; the smell of raw meat and blood wafted from the butcher's stall beside them. Without warning, something was thrown from the side of the stall into a box by their feet. It was pink and squidgy and bleeding. They both screamed and grabbed each other.

'London!' A call came from across the square. Abi looked up. Thug and Tracey and their gang were heading straight for the butcher's stall.

'Run!' Penny said. She grabbed Abi's hand. Together, they set off through the network of passages created by the stalls.

'Oi! London!' A call came again.

Abi gripped Penny's hand. They jumped over boxes of stock – apples, carrots, wool – and dodged sacks of potatoes and a crate of swedes. More shouting came from behind. 'They're catching us!' Abi yelled. Slipping on what looked like fish guts, she dropped her carrier bag. Penny scooped it up. 'Come on,' Penny said. Still gripping Abi's hand, she took a sudden turn. 'This way,' Penny yelled without slowing down.

They emerged onto the High Street as a bus pulled into the bus stop. Yanking Abi's arm, Penny dragged her onto the bus. Abi looked back as Thug and Tracey emerged from the stalls. They turned this way and that. Tracey's eyes locked on Abi's. She pointed and shouted and soon she and Thug were running along the pavement. Penny dumped a handful of coins in the driver's tray. The doors closed as Thug and Tracey reached the bus stop. They yelled and banged at the door.

'I don't think so,' the driver said as he pulled away from the stop. 'You in trouble, girls?' he said over his shoulder.

'We're… fine… thanks,' Penny said between breaths.

Abi collapsed onto a seat at the front. She doubled over trying to stop her lungs burning. Penny fell onto the seat beside her.

'That… was… a… close… shave…' Penny managed to say.

They looked at each other and collapsed, half laughing, half catching their breath.

Ten minutes later, Abi stepped down from the bus. They had come to a modern estate of houses on the edge of town, with cars on the drives and well-tended lawns. Like the estate in Twickenham. Like home home.

'Are you okay?' Penny said.

'What?'

'You've stopped.'

'It's my shoelace.' Abi stooped to tie the lace of her trainer. It was already tied in a double knot. 'Shall we go back to town? Thug and Tracey have probably gone home.'

'We're here now,' Penny said. 'Come on.' She let them into one of the houses. 'Mum and Dad are working,' she said. 'Let's go to my room.'

Abi followed Penny up the stairs, her trainers sinking into the thick cream-coloured carpet. She stood in Penny's bedroom, clutching her carrier bag, while Penny went downstairs to get snacks. When Penny returned with an armful of cans of pop, bags of crisps, and sweets, Abi was still standing in the middle of the room staring at the fitted wardrobes, the television *and* video, the shelves lined with statuettes of dancers and trophies, and the desk with a pen pot and neat pile of books.

'You can sit down,' Penny laughed.

Abi sat on the very edge of the pink and white striped duvet cover.

Penny laughed again. She dumped the food on the bed. 'You can put your bag down.'

Abi placed the carrier bag on the floor. Her arms felt empty. 'You like to dance then,' she said.

'My *mum* likes me to dance,' Penny corrected. 'Tap and ballet. Since I was four. Do you dance?'

It was Abi's turn to stifle a laugh as she remembered the day the dance teacher had told her mum that her daughter's talents may lay elsewhere. 'Not really,' Abi said.

'Oh well… Do you like *Top of the Pops*?'

'I love it.'

'Have you seen this week's?'

Abi shook her head. She hadn't seen this week's, last week's, or the week's before. Nan had said she could watch it on the black and white portable in the parlour, but mum thought the music might disturb Dad if he decided to come in from the shed.

Penny jumped from the bed. She switched on the television and hit play on the video. 'I've got the last few months' episodes on here.'

The opening music started and Abi felt like an old friend had burst into the room. Penny leapt onto the bed. She arranged the pillows and cushions and patted the spot beside her. Abi shimmied up the bed and nestled in beside Penny. While they watched episode after episode, Penny kept Abi topped up with chocolate and pop and kept her entertained with a running commentary on the choreography. Every so often, Penny reminded Abi of slipping through the fish guts. They laughed so hard that Abi nearly snorted cola out of her nose, which made Penny laugh even harder. From time to time, while the music played, Abi looked across at Penny, snuggled up beside her. She wanted to pinch herself.

They had just shared a third Kit Kat when there was a knock on the bedroom door. Abi wiped her mouth and sat up straight.

'Muuuum. Daaaad,' Penny yelled. She lobbed a cushion, which hit the door and landed on the floor. 'How many times? You're supposed to knock and wait to be invited.'

'Sorry, love.' A man pushed the door open. It was clear where Penny's dark hair and dark eyes had come from.

'You're supposed to be working,' Penny said.

'We popped home for lunch,' he said. 'And less of the cheek, young lady.' He smiled as he spoke.

'You must be Abi.' The lady behind him stepped into the room. 'Penny's been so excited about today. It's been Abi this and Abi that.'

'Muuum,' Penny whined.

'Sorry, darling.'

Abi had never seen a lady as perfectly presented as Penny's mum. She wore white jeans and a pink blouse held in at the waist by a white belt. Her nails were painted a sort of burgundy, matching her hair and her stiletto sandals.

Remembering her manners, Abi scrambled from the bed. 'It's nice to meet you, Mr and Mrs Raymond.'

'Oh dear,' Penny's mum said, shaking her head. 'Two things you need to know about us, Abi. One – we don't stand on ceremony. Any friend of Penny's is welcome here any time. And two – call us Tony and Shirl. "Mr and Mrs Raymond" makes us sound so old and stuffy.'

Penny let out a huge sigh.

'Ignore her,' Tony said to Abi. 'Our little Penelope can be a bit of a stick in the mud sometimes. Now, I do believe there is a young lady in here in need of a lift home later.'

'I don't want to be any trouble,' Abi said. 'I can catch the bus.'

Shirl smiled. 'We wouldn't hear of it, darling. Tony'll give you a lift home. Just pop down when you're ready. No rush. Come on, Tone,' she said and shooed Tony out. 'Let's leave these girls to their fun.' But before she left, Shirl peeked back inside and grinned.

Penny slammed the door behind her parents. She scooped up a cushion and held it to her chest. 'God, I'm so sorry. They are *so* embarrassing.'

'They're not that bad. Wait till you meet mine,' Abi said. But as she imagined that unhappy event, a chill ran down her spine.

***

At just before three o'clock, Tony turned his car off the main road. Abi had tried to convince him to drop her at the end of the lane, but he insisted on a 'door-to-door service'. He looked in the rear-view mirror, shaking his head. 'I still can't believe you live at Cliff Cottage, Abi. I knew this place when I was a kid.'

Penny nudged her. 'How many times is he going to say that?'

'Oi,' Tony said. 'Mind your manners, young lady. Honestly, Abi, I bet you're not this stroppy with your parents, are you?'

Penny folded her arms across her chest and huffed as Tony brought the car to a stop by the fence. He got out and stood with his hands on his hips, looking up at the cottage. 'Bloody hell. It's hardly changed at all.'

Abi and Penny got out of the car, Penny apologising yet again for her embarrassing dad. The front door opened.

'Hello,' Mum said and walked down the path towards them. 'Thank you so much for bringing Abigail home. There really was no need. She had the bus fare.'

'It's really no troub–' Tony started. But as Mum approached, his arms dropped to his sides. 'Rose!' he said. 'Rose. It is you, isn't it? My God. Who'd have thought it?'

Mum stopped and stared at Penny's dad. 'Tony?'

Tony laughed. 'Good God. I can't believe it. What a blast from the past. Come here.' He put his arms around Mum and pulled her close. Mum stood with her arms glued to her sides. Penny made a noise like she was trying to spit out a wasp. Abi looked from Mum to Tony. This was mad. Penny's dad knew her mum.

Tony took a step back, shaking his head. 'I can't get over it. Rose Smith, as I live and breathe. You haven't changed a bit.'

'It's Rose Russell now,' Mum corrected.

'If I'd known you'd bought the old place, I'd have come down sooner. So this young lady must be your daughter then.'

'Yes. Abigail's my daughter.' She untied her apron, rolled it up, held it tight. She brushed her fringe from her eyes. 'The house belongs to my mother. My father died last year so we moved down here to look after her.'

'My condolences.'

'Thank you.'

There was a pause as Mum looked at Tony. He smiled at her.

'Hello there,' Abi's dad called, walking towards them, shifting his muddy trowel into his left hand. He wiped his right hand on his trousers and offered it to Tony. 'Mick Russell,' he said.

Tony took Dad's hand and shook it firmly. 'Tony Raymond. Good to meet you, Mick. I was just reacquainting myself with your wife. I knew her when we were kids. What was it, Rose? Twenty-odd years ago?'

'Something like that. Tony was friends with Arthur when we came down here on holiday.' Abi's mum took a step towards Dad. Dad pointed his muddy trowel at Tony's car.

'Jag, very nice.'

'It's not a bad run-around. A bit thirsty, mind. If you're ever in the market for a new motor, Mick, come and see me. I have a car dealership just outside of town. Raymond's Autos.'

'The showroom on the bypass with the Porsche on the forecourt?' Dad said.

'The very one. And I can always arrange a good deal for a friend.'

Dad laughed. 'Thanks for the offer. But the old Cortina's still got a few years left in her. And we're a bit financially embarrassed at the moment.'

Abi thought she saw Mum wince. Since Dad had taken to speaking again, he had developed a habit of saying whatever came into his mind, despite Mum's constant reminders to filter his words for appropriateness first.

'The offer's there if you change your mind,' Tony said.

Abi stood in the garden waving to Penny until the back of the car disappeared up the lane. When she stepped through the front door, she jumped.

'God, Mum,' she said, clutching her chest. 'You scared the life out of me. What are you doing there?'

'So Penny is Penny Raymond,' Mum said, holding back the curtain from the small window beside the door, staring up the lane.

'Yeah. Did you know her dad well?'

'Not very well. He was my cousin's friend.'

'Where's Nan?'

'In her room. Spring-cleaning her wardrobe.'

'But it's winter.' Abi hesitated, waiting for Mum to tell her to stop being cheeky and to begin the interrogation into what she'd bought, where she'd been, what she'd done. But Mum didn't say anything. She just stood there, clutching the curtain, her neck flushing a deep pink.

'I'm going up to see Nan. Okay?'

'Yes. Okay.'

It was like talking to a statue. She would never understand how her mother's mind worked. Leaving her mum to her curtain, Abi ran up the stairs to find Nan to model her new jeans and find a suitable hiding place for her contraband lip-gloss. It was only when she was halfway up the stairs that she remembered her schoolbooks hadn't left her satchel all day.

Chapter 6

At half past three, Gertie stepped from the offices of Miller and Miller onto The Strand with her handbag and the jacket of her brown suit draped over the crook of her arm. She paused to waft cool air onto her neck before turning right and heading in the direction of Trafalgar Square.

The end of the working day hadn't come a moment too soon – it was her half-day off. From the way Mrs Eves had been glaring at her all day over a mountain of legal papers, anyone would think it was her fault that they'd lost the second filing clerk in as many months. But who could blame Doreen for moving back to her family in Worthing when it seemed that half of London had had the same idea? If for one moment Gertie thought that Sid would leave the city, she would go directly to Victoria and book two tickets on one of the crowded trains heading for the south coast. But there was as much chance of Sid abandoning London as there was of prising the cigar from between Churchill's fingers.

Even now, the memory of joining the long queue outside the butcher's last Saturday made her shudder. Mrs Green from number twelve had just begun to tell Gertie how her sister's children were expected back from Wales, when she was interrupted by a noise like a mechanical bee high in the sky. Everyone in Brixton Market stopped what they were doing to look up and, as one, watched the silver drone emerge from the clouds, a flame shooting from its tail. Only once it had passed overhead, did everyone look back down and carry on with their business.

'Better that those kiddies stay in Bridgend at this rate,' Mrs Green had said, clutching her shopping bag tight to her body. 'Nobody should have to live like this. 'Specially not children.'

Gertie glanced quickly up to the sky while waiting for a bus to pass on St Martin's Place. When the road was clear, she crossed. Doodlebugs. It was such a sweet-sounding word for such a terrible weapon. At least the bombs dropped from planes piloted by men seemed to have some kind of identifiable targets. With the doodlebugs, the whole of London was on tenterhooks, watching the skies and waiting for that blasted noise – even in broad daylight.

Trafalgar Square seemed quieter than a normal summer's day. A few chaps in suits sat on the benches; ties loosened, eating sandwiches from paper wrappings. Groups of office girls sat around the edges of the drained fountains with their skirts pulled up to their knees and their faces turned up to the sun. Gertie crossed the square and sat on one of the empty benches. She took her cigarettes from her bag and lit one. Folding one arm across her waist, she rested her elbow on the back of her other hand as she smoked. Before the war she would never have dreamt of smoking alone in public but now, well, who would really care?

She drew in deeply, blew out a single long grey line then checked her watch. It didn't matter what time they arranged to meet, Ivy was always ten minutes late. Gertie looked down Whitehall, half expecting to see Ivy tottering along on her high heels. It was empty save for a bus. She had never asked what, precisely, Ivy had left Miller and Miller to do at the Ministry of Information – careless talk and all that. No doubt her father – who was something high up in the Home Office – was behind the move. From what Ivy had said, he had always thought working in a solicitor's office beneath the education he had paid a king's ransom for. But from Ivy's silk stockings and never-ending supply of lipstick, it was obvious she still received an allowance from her father and that she had absolutely no intention of letting anything as dull as rationing curb her love of luxuries. Ivy's only concession to the war was to convert her soft spot for minor members of the European aristocracy into a fondness for Yank officers.

Gertie eased her foot from her shoe and looked at the heel of her stocking. It could do with darning again. She couldn't help but smile at the picture in her head of Ivy with a darning mushroom in one hand and a needle in the other. Ivy was extravagant and unpredictable but at least these weekly meetings gave Gertie something to look forward to. Although she was adamant that she would not repeat her mistake of last week. Today she would absolutely not let Ivy talk her into visiting the little drinking club in a basement just off Charing Cross Road. And she would not drink glass after glass of gin and lime as though it were lemonade.

The bus journey home was still somewhat of a blur and how she had managed to sober enough to make Sid's supper was a minor miracle. Thankfully it had only been leftovers of a heavy pie of carrots and cabbage with a potato crust and Sid hadn't even noticed that it was barely warm. He ate the food like he always did now, in silence and with little enthusiasm. He didn't even talk about his day at the dinner table any more. 'There's some things not fit for a lady's ears,' was all he'd say, if he said anything at all.

Gertie took another long drag of her cigarette and, as she blew out, a thought crossed her mind. She tried to quiet it, but it just wouldn't go away. It was the question that kept her awake at nights and crept in to disturb every quiet moment. Might it have been better if Sid had been able to enlist? He'd tried. God only knew how hard. The air attacks on London had barely begun when Sid presented himself at the army recruiting office in Brixton. The selection process had gone well, right up until the point Sid dropped his trousers. The doctor had taken one look at the scar on his leg and declared him unfit. He tried a second time to enlist at the Streatham recruiting office and a third, going all the way to Hoxton. But each time the result was the same. As soon as each doctor saw his leg, they put a large cross through the papers on their clipboards. Sid repeated the third doctor's comments to her word-for-word. 'Too much of a risk, I'm afraid, old chap. The old wound might open up, leaving you vulnerable to infection. You would be a liability to any man serving beside you. And we wouldn't want that now, would we? Shame, you're as strong as an ox otherwise.'

At first Gertie had been relieved. Sid would stay at home. What a lucky woman she was. She wouldn't have to worry about him every minute of every day. And with him in their bed every night there was the chance, no matter how slight... How stupid she had been. She had watched Sid gradually lose enthusiasm for everything, for life it seemed. He stopped going to the pub and not long after that had stopped wanting to do what husbands and wives do in bed.

She should never have suggested he volunteer for the National Fire Service. With his plumbing experience and physical strength, the NFS had seen past the issue with his leg. If a problem developed, then they could simply send him home to sit out the rest of the war. He had given up plumbing altogether to work full time in the Fire Service. For four years he had volunteered for every shift and duty, even on his rostered days off. He worked so long and so hard that when he came home to Gertie – his eyes red-rimmed, his face and hands thick in grime and oil and soot – she hardly recognised him. His duty had become an obsession. Like he had something to prove.

Gertie dropped her cigarette and ground it out under her shoe. A group of American servicemen sauntered across the square, sending pigeons fluttering in their wake. In their smooth uniforms with cigarettes dangling from their lips and caps at rakish angles, they looked to Gertie like a troupe of matinee idols. The girls by the fountain clearly thought so too. They gave the soldiers coquettish little glances and giggled into their palms. *Make the most of it*, Gertie thought. *Enjoy it while it lasts.* She opened her handbag, took out her compact and lipstick – a hand-me-down from Ivy – and had just applied a fresh coat to her bottom lip when someone stopped right in front of her.

'Is that perch taken?' a man asked. From his accent Gertie assumed he was one of the Americans.

'No. It's free,' she said rubbing her lips together. She snapped the compact shut and dropped it into her bag along with the lipstick. The bench dipped as it took the soldier's weight.

'It's a beautiful day, eh?' the man said.

'Pardon? Oh, yes. I suppose it is.'

'And here was me thinking it always rained in England. I guess you can't believe everything you see in the movies.' He thrust his hand at her. 'I'm Aaron.'

For a moment she was unsure of how to respond. The brashness and confidence of these young servicemen still took her by surprise. But where was the harm in passing a few minutes in conversation while she waited for Ivy? She took the soldier's hand. 'Mrs Smith. Mrs Gertrude Smith,' she said. And that's when she noticed the boxy shape and rough khaki fabric of the soldier's jacket and the folded cap tucked under the epaulette at his shoulder. The final clue that this was not one of the Americans was the 'CANADA' patch stitched onto his sleeve.

'I wonder if you might help me, Mrs Smith,' the solider said and released her hand. 'I was looking for Buckingham Palace, but I don't have a clue which way to go. They seem to have taken all the signs down.'

Gertie tried not to smile. 'It's Buckingham. Not Buck-Ing-Ham.'

'Oh, I see.'

She looked into his face. He had close-cropped blonde hair and blue eyes with long eyelashes so fair they were barely there.

'So? The Palace?' he asked again.

'Oh yes, sorry,' Gertie said and pointed to the road leading away from the square and towards Admiralty Arch. 'Go through there and you're on The Mall. Walk all the way along and you'll find Buckingham Palace at the very end. It's the big white building. You can't miss it.'

'Thanks. You're a regular Good Samaritan. So, Mrs Smith, what brings you out on this fine day? Do you work local?'

'Not far. I'm a secretary for a firm of solicitors on The Strand. I'm waiting for my friend. We're going for tea.'

'At least the movies got something right then.'

'Sorry?'

'That you English love your tea. You drink it morning, noon and night. Am I right?' He smiled, and his eyes seemed to turn just a bit bluer.

Gertie didn't know whether to laugh or be offended. So she laughed. Cheeky so-and-so. She had dresses in her wardrobe older than him. She tried to keep a straight face when she nodded towards the American soldiers who were now sitting amongst the girls.

'I'm surprised to see one of you out on your own. I thought your kind only travelled in packs.'

'What?' A frown creased the bridge of his nose. It took a moment but then he laughed, and it was deeper than Gertie imagined it would be. 'I guess that's a fair point. But you see, I tied on one too many when we arrived in town last night. Or maybe two too many. Anyway, when my pals set off to do it all over again this morning, I thought to myself, "Aaron, don't waste all day looking at the inside of a pub, go and do a bit of sightseeing in beautiful London Town".'

Gertie glanced around Trafalgar Square, at the signs pointing to the nearest air-raid shelter, to the hoardings advertising War Bonds that obscured the bronze relief panels depicting sea battles at the base of Nelson's Column.

'I'm afraid there's not much to see,' she said. 'Everything pleasant seems to be hidden away.'

'Oh, I don't know,' he said. 'It all looks pretty spectacular to me. Where I come from a new barn is about as exciting as it gets.'

Gertie followed his gaze, from the National Gallery, across to the steeple of St Martin's and then back up to Nelson standing on his column high in the sky. Maybe this young solider was right. Even with sandbags piled up around doorways, posters carrying stark warnings of the perils of speaking to strangers, and every window taped against blast, there was still beauty in London. Perhaps you just had to look harder to see it now.

'Take that place. Where I'm staying,' he continued, nodding over his shoulder to the imposing grey building of the Canadian High Commission on the corner of Cockspur Street. 'They call it the Beaver's Club. It's like putting up in some mansion house. I've never stayed anywhere like it. Except for the mansion they have us bunked in out in Berk-Shire.'

He pronounced it as if the name of the county rhymed with 'shirk' with a breed of working horse tacked on the end. Gertie didn't even attempt to hide her laugh this time. 'Bark-sher,' she corrected.

'Bark-sher,' he repeated slowly then sighed and shook his head. 'I tell you what, it's a good job I bumped into you. Otherwise I might have made myself look stupid what with saying my words all wrong. Thanks, Mrs Smith.'

'Gertie. Call me Gertie.'

He performed an exaggerated bow from his waist. 'Well it's a pleasure to make your acquaintance, Gertie. Aaron Dukszta at you service.'

Gertie laughed as much at his sweet attempt at chivalry as at his unusual name. 'That's quite a mouthful. How do you say it again? Duck-star.'

He grinned. 'I guess I'm not the only one that needs lessons in pronunciation. It's Duck-*zhtar*. I'm Scottish on my mom's side and Polish on my dad's.'

'Oh,' she said. 'I'm sorry.'

'That I'm Polish or that I have an almost unpronounceable name?'

'Polish. Sorry, I don't mean to say that I'm sorry you're Polish. I'm afraid that I have a tremendous gift for putting my foot in it. It's just that with Poland and everything that's happened there…'

Aaron held up his hand. 'It's okay, really. I know what you're trying to say. And thank you. But most of my immediate family are back home in Alberta. My grandparents emigrated to Canada when my dad was just a baby. But we still have family in Warsaw. Only… we haven't heard from them in a while.' For the briefest moment, his voice faltered and he looked down to the ground. He quickly looked back up at Gertie. 'But at least I'm here, doing my best to set things straight, right? Like my grandpa always says, you have to take whatever life throws at you and turn it into a positive. If life gives you lemons, make a big batch of lemonade.'

'That's a good attitude to have in the circumstances.'

He shrugged. 'What's the alternative? If you dwell on things, they fester and eat away at you. And where does that get you?'

'Nowhere, I suppose.' Gertie smiled. 'Your grandfather sounds like a very sensible man.'

'He is. Between you and me, he thinks of himself as a bit of a philosopher. He has a saying for just about every situation. And talking of positives,' Aaron said, dipping his hand inside his jacket, 'would you like to see a picture of my girl?'

Without waiting for a reply, he pulled a photograph from his breast pocket and handed it to Gertie. She took it and looked down into the face of a young woman sitting on a blanket surrounded by grass. The fringe of her long, dark hair was pinned back from her face. In a summer dress with a scalloped collar and with one slim leg crossed over the other, she smiled for the camera.

'She's very pretty. What's her name?'

'Margaret,' he said. 'But everyone calls her Peggy. Her folks own the farm next to ours, so I've known her my whole life. But it was only last year that she finally gave in and agreed to go steady with me. I'm a lucky guy. Peggy's the prettiest girl in town.'

'I don't doubt it.' Gertie handed the photograph back and Aaron tucked it safely back into his breast pocket.

'Before I left home last fall, I helped my dad dig foundations for a house in the meadow where that photograph was taken. Peggy just loves that place. It's full of wild flowers and crickets and bees. When I get back, I'm going to build such a fine house for us so we can get married right away and I'll work on my dad's farm.

I did think about studying to become a doctor, I got my High School Certificate and I volunteered at the local hospital for a few semesters. But I figure that'll all take too long and anyway, my dad says I'm a natural with cattle.'

'Can't you study and marry in a few years?'

'Oh, you don't know Peggy,' he said with a little raise of his eyebrows. 'She's desperate to set up home and start a family. Got her heart set on two boys and two girls. If I leave it too long she might just go and find someone else. Anyway, I'm a medic in my unit. I figure by the end of this I'll have had my fair share of fixing people up.'

Gertie decided not to point out that if this girl loved him as much as he appeared to love her, then she would wait for him to follow his dreams before settling down. Not only was it none of her business but he probably wouldn't thank her for sticking her oar in. She chose the safe path along the conversation. 'You must miss Peggy and the rest of your family terribly.'

'I do. It's funny, you don't really appreciate your friends and family till they're not there every day, do you?' He pointed to her left hand. 'So what about you? Is your husband overseas?'

'My husband?' She looked down at finger, at the two rings that had been a fixture for so long that she hardly noticed them anymore. 'No, he's a fireman. So he's home. Some of the time.'

'A fireman!' Aaron made an impressed noise by sucking air through his teeth. 'We saw all about the firemen in London on the newsreels back home. They sure are brave men. Going into burning buildings to save people while the bombs are still dropping all around them. And with just a jerkin and a tin hat for protection. Your husband must be quite a man to face that night after night. Real brave.'

'Yes. Yes, I suppose he is.'

'I was still in grade school when we saw the films of the Blitz. It was people like your husband and the soldiers coming off the beach at Dunkirk that inspired me to join up as soon as I was old enough. It seemed wrong that you were all suffering so much over here and there we were, eating popcorn and watching Mickey Mouse, halfway across the world.'

'You were still in school at the start of the war?'

'Yes, ma'am.'

'How old are you exactly?' she asked.

'Nineteen. Last May.'

'Nineteen?' She struggled not to sound surprised. 'You're incredibly mature for your age.'

'My mom says I've got an old soul. According to her I came into the world knowing just a little too much about everything but not quite enough about anything.'

Gertie thought she saw his neck flush as he kicked at the ground. He bent forwards slightly and rested his elbows on his knees before twisting to look at her.

'Can I say something?' he said. 'And I hope you won't be offended. It's just… well, when I saw you from across the square you looked lost in your thoughts, like you had something weighing on your mind. You've been so kind, listening to me talk about myself. And I really don't like to see people glum. I'm a good listener, you know, if you want to talk. A problem shared… right?'

Gertie looked into his face, into his blue eyes and to his mouth that was formed into a small, encouraging smile. In that moment she was tempted. The relief of unburdening to this sweet, sensitive boy with an old soul would be immense.

'I'm fine,' she said finally.

'Really?'

'I'm just tired. The raid kept me awake last night and I've been busy at work today. It's just the normal things.'

'And what else are normal things?' he asked. His eyes held hers until a voice sent Gertie shuffling away across the bench.

'I say,' Ivy called, heading across the square, waving enthusiastically. She stopped before them and stood with her hands on her hips. 'Made a friend have we, Gert? Aren't you going to introduce us?'

'What. Oh yes, of course.' Gertie stood up and Aaron got to his feet beside her. He was a good head and shoulders taller than both her and Ivy. 'Ivy Chappell, this is Aaron Duck-shtar.' She said it carefully, making sure to pronounce Aaron's name correctly. From the corner of her eye she caught his smile.

'Delighted to make your acquaintance, Mrs Chappell,' Aaron said and performed another of his little bows.

'It's *Miss* actually. And likewise, I'm sure,' Ivy said, in what Gertie knew to be her seductive voice.

'Well,' Aaron said, slapping his thighs. 'I guess two's company and three's an inconvenience. I should really let you ladies go and get your tea. But before I go, would you mind?' He put his hand into the pocket of his trousers and pulled out a camera. 'I like to send photographs home to my folks. So they can see what I've been up to.'

Ivy stepped forward. 'Give it here,' she said. 'I'm a dab hand with a camera. You should see the snaps I took in Biarritz in the summer of thirty-eight. I'd give Cecil Beaton a run for his money.' While she directed Aaron to stand by the lions, shooing him this way and that, Gertie took the opportunity to observe his face in profile. When a pigeon swooped down to land by his feet, he laughed with his head thrown back. It was this laugh that Ivy caught with a click of the camera.

'Thanks, Miss Chappell,' he said when she handed the camera back to him. He returned the camera to his pocket before shaking her hand. Then he turned to Gertie. 'And thank you for the directions and the company, Mrs Smith.' He lowered his voice, took her hand in both of his and shook it. His grip was strong and the skin of his hands soft. So unlike Sid's hands with dark tufts of hair on each finger and countless scars and scratches and blisters. 'Remember,' Aaron said, 'what to do when life gives you lemons.'

'Make lemonade.' Gertie smiled.

'Precisely.' Aaron smiled back and let her hand slip from his.

Ivy took a step closer to Gertie and Aaron gave them a small salute before turning and heading away. Together they watched him walk across the square towards The Mall, his hands pushed deep into his pockets.

'I say,' Ivy whispered and slipped her arm through Gertie's. 'What a sort.'

'You can put your eyes back in their sockets, Ivy Chappell. He's only nineteen years old *and* he's promised to a young girl back in Canada.'

'Shame. Nineteen is a bit young. Even for me.' Ivy pouted. 'And what's all this about lemonade?'

'What? Oh, nothing. It's just a saying his grandfather has.'

Ivy laughed. 'What a funny titbit to share. Come on,' she said, pulling at Gertie's arm. 'We're going to The Ship. There's a Yank lieutenant that I've got my eye on and I'm reliably informed he takes a tipple there every afternoon.'

Gertie let Ivy guide her up the steps towards the National Gallery and while they waited for the traffic to clear, Ivy chatted away about a darling new hat that she'd bought. As they crossed the road, Gertie took one last look over her shoulder. But Aaron had already gone.

***

When Ivy's Yank officer failed to appear, she tried to talk Gertie into helping her drown her sorrows. But Gertie allowed herself only two halves of stout before heading off to catch her bus. She arrived home at just before six o'clock and prepared a small supper of a nub of cheese and a slice of bread, which she ate in the armchair while listening to a Strauss concert on the wireless. She would have preferred something jollier: a big band show, Harry James perhaps or Glen Miller. But the waltzes were lively enough and at least they filled the flat with music. At just after eight o'clock, she secured the blackout blinds, drew a bath and enjoyed a soak. She towel-dried her hair and was considering turning in for the night with a good book when the wail of the air-raid siren cut through the night air. With a sigh she put on her nightdress, pulled on her overcoat, and slipped her feet into Sid's old gardening shoes. At the bottom of the stairs she collected the gas lamp and a box of matches, locked the front door and traipsed down the driveway into the back garden. Darkness was falling but she didn't need to light the lamp to make the journey she had made hundreds of nights before.

Pulling back the sacking cover from the entrance to the shelter, Gertie found Sally already inside. She was kneeling down, settling a mussy-haired Brian into the bottom bunk while struggling to balance baby Rosemary in the crook of her arm. 'It's like an oven in here tonight,' Sally said. 'Just look at the walls. They look like they're sweating.'

Gertie adjusted the sacking, sealing them into the tin dome with the musty smell of dried earth. 'It's better than that night we had to bail it out,' Gertie said, squeezing into one of the two deckchairs. 'Do you remember? It was raining stair rods and we had to sit in here with our feet up on the chairs.'

'Don't remind me.' Sally sat heavily in the chair beside Gertie. 'I had to put Brian in the top bunk and I didn't dare sleep in case he fell out and drowned.'

Sally's lamp was already lit and hung from the hook Sid had fixed into the ceiling. Gertie put her own lamp on the dusty floor. 'Ted at the factory tonight?' she asked.

'As always,' Sally said. 'It's fire watch duty tonight. He was...' Her words were drowned by the boom of anti-aircraft guns sounding in the distance. She flinched and pulled Rosemary closer. 'I don't know why we bother coming out here. If one of them bombs was to fall on us, I'd rather we was all tucked up in our own beds. At least we'd be having one last good sleep. And we wouldn't be any the wiser.'

Gertie rubbed Sally's knee. 'Come on now,' she said. 'Chin up. We promised Sid and Ted we'd always come out here. There's not a shelter with more earth on top of it in the whole of London. Do you remember that day they put it up? You said it looked like they were digging down to Australia.'

Sally smiled briefly and adjusted the white shawl over Rosemary's chubby legs. 'I know you're right. But sometimes it gets me down. That's all.'

'I know,' Gertie said. But she also knew it would take more than a few empty words of encouragement to take Sally's mind off the noises overhead. She smiled. 'Stop me if you've heard this before, but did I ever tell you about my light-fingered old landlady?'

Sally grinned, leaning forwards. 'Oh I love that story. Go on, Gert, tell me about the tight old cow.'

So, while the guns pounded in the distance, Gertie began to tell Sally her tale. In truth, she liked to tell her stories just as much as Sally liked to hear them. There was something reassuring in the familiarity and at least, if only for a few minutes, it took them both away to a place and time when they weren't camped out in a tin hut in the back garden. This tale about the landlady who owned the rooms she and Sid had rented before they came to live upstairs from Ted and Sally was a particular favourite. How she'd thought for weeks that either Sid was tucking into all their food or they had an incredibly hungry mouse making merry with their bread and sugar (that always got a laugh from Sally), until one day she came home early from work to find the landlady in their pantry with a saucer, helping herself to their butter.

Gertie was just getting to the part where she talked Sid out of calling the police when a drone overhead made her stop. In the faint lamplight, Sally's eyes followed the path of the noise. And then, somewhere close by, it stopped. After a short moment of silence, when neither of them breathed, a terrific explosion rattled the shelter. Earth fell through gaps in the tin, the lamp swung sharply on its nail, casting shards of light onto the bunks which moments before had been in shadow. Brian squirmed under his blanket and Gertie put her hand up to stop the lamp. When it finally came to rest and the shadows returned to their rightful places, she saw Sally clutching Rosemary even tighter.

'Oh, Gertie. When will this all end? The papers said it would be over once we got into Europe. What was the point in all them boys going over to France when it's worse now than ever?'

'Sid says it's just Hitler having one last pop.' Gertie raised her voice to be heard over the clatter of bells on a nearby street. 'It'll be over by Christmas. Just you wait and see. And we'll all sit together and have a toast that we got through it, safe and sound.' She said it with as much conviction as she could muster and then took Sid's hip flask from the pocket of her overcoat. 'Here. Have a nip. Calm your nerves. Let me take Rosemary.'

She held out her arms and took Rosemary from Sally while Sally took the flask from her.

'She's putting on weight,' Gertie said, smiling into the little sleeping face.

'Don't I know it,' Sally said, unscrewing the cap of the flask. 'She sups me dry and I can hardly keep up with the amount of stewed apples she can get through.' She took a long sip then wiped the back of her hand across her mouth.

'There'll be plums and pears on the trees at the end of the garden soon enough,' Gertie said, gently squeezing Rosemary's chubby knee. 'Come harvest time, I'll help you bottle them for her if you like. They should keep her in stewed fruit all through the winter.'

Sally sighed. 'What would I do without you around, Gert? You're a true friend. Really you are.' She went to hand the flask back, but Gertie indicated for her to take another sip, which she did. Calmed a little, Sally said, 'Do you still want to come and meet us in Lewisham on Friday? My sister's looking forward to seeing you again. She said we could meet in the café in Woolworths if that suits. I know it's a bit of a trek, so I'll understand if you've changed your mind.'

'Nonsense. I wouldn't miss it.' A trip on the Underground and the bus was a small price to pay to spend time with Sally and the children. Especially Rosemary.

'Lovely.' Sally smiled. 'We'll meet you there. I'm taking the kiddies tomorrow to stay for the night to give my sister a break from looking after Mum.'

'I'm looking forward to it already. Now come on, why don't you crawl in with Brian and get some sleep. You look done in. I'll sit with Rosemary for a while.'

'Now you mention it, I could really do with a kip. She refused to go down for her sleep this afternoon so I didn't get mine either. But are you sure? I don't want to lumber you.'

'Of course. Now come on. Get in.'

Without any more encouragement, Sally eased from the chair onto the bunk. She curled around Brian and pulled the blanket over them both. She looked up from the pillow. 'She adores you, she does,' Sally whispered. 'And you're so good with her. You should have a baby of your own, you're a born mother.'

Gertie arranged the shawl to best see Rosemary's face and brushed her pink cheeks with the tips of her fingers. 'One day,' she said. 'Now go on, you close your eyes and get some sleep.'

All through the raid Rosemary slept peacefully in Gertie's arms as though the pounding of the ack-ack guns were a lullaby. In a way they probably were. In her six months of life she had known nothing but this. And while Rosemary slept, Gertie had Sally's words for company.

'You should have a baby. You're a born mother.'

'One day.'

She had said it so many times that she could almost believe it herself. Almost.

Long after the all-clear had sounded, after the birds had struck up their dawn chorus in the trees outside, and the first fingers of pale daylight had begun to break through the gaps between the sacking and corrugated metal, Gertie let her companions sleep on. She should have woken Sally to take her little family back to the comfort of their own beds. But if she let them go, she would have to return to the emptiness of her own.

The sound of a vehicle on the street woke Rosemary and she began to grizzle. Gertie took a bottle from Sally's bag on the floor and offered it to her. She watched Rosemary's tiny bud-like lips suck at the teat and listened to the little satisfied noises of guzzling milk. Once she had drained the bottle, Gertie gently prised the teat from her mouth and placed the bottle on the ground. She held Rosemary over her shoulder and rubbed her back. When she brought her back down into her arms, she rocked her until her eyelids closed. Something about the way Rosemary's fair eyelashes fluttered as she drifted into sleep, made Gertie think of the boy, Aaron. The memory of him made her smile. How pleasant it had been to talk to him, one human being to another. A conversation not about war or bombs, but about him and his hopes and dreams. She was once like him: full of optimism for the future. What she wouldn't give to be that girl again. To believe in a dream where she could live in a house by the sea. A house filled with children. To have Sid pull her into his lap and kiss her and then crawl beneath the pink bedspread and feel wanted. Instead she lived this half-life, spending hours alone watching the clock, terrified that each night was the night a fire-wracked building would collapse and take Sid from her. Even when he came home he wasn't really there. With no energy left, he collapsed into bed and immediately fell into a deep sleep while she lay awake beside him, waiting for the nightmares to start. The nightmares that made him scream into the darkness shouting about trapped people. It was all she could do to whisper to him and tell him everything would be all right.

Damn this war, this stupid, bloody war. Would Sid ever come back to her? And if he did, would he be the same person? Her Sid?

It took all of Gertie's effort not to shout out. Instead, she pulled back the shawl and rested her cheek against Rosemary's face, glad of the familiar, warm baby scent. 'I just want to know there'll be a future,' she whispered. 'I just want to feel alive. Is that too much to ask?'

Chapter 7

Abi tipped the juice of five lemons onto the mound of sugar in Nan's cut glass jug. She pounded at the concoction with a wooden spoon, making the kitchen table wobble on the uneven tiles. Her pounding fell in time with the loud tick of the clock above the cooker – *tick (pound), tock (pause), tick (pound), tock (splat)* – building to a rhythm as the hands moved too quickly toward the hour.

Why did Mum have to go and stick her oar in when everything had been arranged? By all rights she should, at this very second, be on the bus into town to spend another day at Penny's, eating Kit Kats and watching more *Top of the Pops* in colour. Not standing here counting down the minutes to disaster – *tick (pound), tock (pause), tick (pound), tock (splat)*. She could have lied to Mum and told her that Penny had refused the invitation. But the truth was that Penny had grabbed her in the middle of geography class and jumped up and down saying, 'I'd love to come! I can't wait!'

So that was that. While Abi had walked around under the shadow of her very own cloud all week – when she wasn't dipping into classrooms or sitting at the very front of the school coach to avoid Thug and Tracey – Mum had talked of little else but Penny. Did Abi think that Penny would like a Victoria sponge or perhaps she would prefer a chocolate cake? And what was it that Penny's mum did for a job again? What was their house like? Did Penny have any brothers or sisters?

Abi grated the zest of one of the lemon halves into the jug. What did Mum want? A report from Tony and Shirl's bank manager?

And what did it matter what kind of cake Penny liked when she would probably never get to taste it? She would take one step inside Cliff Cottage, see how they lived, and then chase her dad's car back up the lane, begging him to take her straight home. Back to their house with cream carpets and colour televisions. And far away from the wonky old cottage with curtains instead of kitchen cupboards, Nan's collection of fish-shaped copper jelly moulds staring down from the kitchen walls, and the portable television balanced on an old wooden table in the cramped parlour with a white doily placed on the top. If nothing else, it would give Penny a laugh and she could tell everyone she knew about the lucky escape she'd had from the Munsters who lived in the crazy house up on the cliff.

Abi continued to pound at the jug, gradually adding water until, on the dot of ten, the doorbell rang. She heard a movement in the hall and then the kitchen door opened. Penny came in first followed by Mum who was holding a bunch of pink carnations wrapped in paper.

'Wotcha.' Penny smiled.

'Wotcha,' Abi mumbled to Penny and then to Mum, 'What are the flowers for?'

'They're from me,' Penny said. 'Mum said to bring then to say thank you to your mum for having me.'

'But you've only just got here. What if you don't have a good time?'

'Don't be silly, Abigail,' Mum said and squeezed past her. She took a vase from under the sink and turned on the tap. 'Why on Earth wouldn't Penny have a nice time?'

'Because,' Abi whispered, under cover of the running water.

'What are you making?' Penny asked peering into the jug.

'Lemonade.'

'Homemade lemonade? I didn't know there was such a thing. I thought it just came in bottles or cans.'

Abi wished their lemonade was clear and full of bubbles and in a bottle from the supermarket, not green and made from Nan's old recipe. Penny picked up the grater and grated some zest into the jug. Abi glanced at her mum. She was holding the vase under the running tap but was too busy looking over her shoulder at Penny to notice that water was gushing out of the vase, soaking the sleeves of her blouse. Her eyes flicked from Penny's face to her hair to her legs and feet, and all the way back up again. Why did her mum have to be so weird? Was she trying to find something wrong with Penny so she would have an excuse not to let Abi go into town again?

Abi dropped the spoon into the jug. The sticky concoction splashed over the table. She grabbed the grater from Penny and slammed it down. 'Come on,' she said. 'I'll show you my room.' She pushed Penny out into the hall and looked back to find her mum resting against the sink, clutching the carnations in one hand and the vase in the other. She was staring at the back of Penny's head. Abi slammed the kitchen door behind them. Wasn't it bad enough that Dad was having one of his 'off' days and was hiding out in the shed to avoid the fuss? Was it too much to ask to have just one normal parent? Abi practically pushed Penny up the two flights of stairs. Penny wanted to stop to look at everything; the twisted spindles of the banisters, the tiny window on the first-floor landing which looked out over the bay, Nan's collection of thimbles arranged on a shelf beside her bedroom door. When Abi prodded Penny inside the attic, she thought Penny might actually wet herself.

'You've got a fire! In your bedroom!' Penny ran to the fireplace. She held her hands out to the flames of the fire Abi's dad had been up to lay to take the chill off the room. On any other day, Abi would have been expected to make do with two pairs of socks, an extra jumper and a pile of blankets to keep warm. But not today. Oh no, today, Mum had insisted that they could spare a bucket of coal. Just the one, mind.

Penny brushed her fingers along the black cast iron. She sank to her knees and peered into the flames. 'It's just like the children's room in *The Phoenix and the Carpet* and look...' She got to her feet and rushed to the window. 'It's like a porthole on ship.' She peered out at the view for all of two seconds then jumped on the bed, making the old metal frame creak like a hibernating creature had been woken from its slumber.

Abi watched from the doorway, chewing the skin around her thumbnail. *Please don't notice the peeling wallpaper. Please don't think all the blankets on the bed is weird.* She waited... waited...

'Your house is soooo brilliant!' Penny said with a huge smile. 'It's all so... magical. Have you ever seen *Bedknobs and Broomsticks*?' She fiddled with one of the brass orbs. When it wouldn't budge, she scanned Abi's drawings tacked to the walls. 'You're really talented. Look at that seagull. I really believe it could fly. Oh, and that dog. It's just *too* cute.'

Abi took her thumb from her mouth. She took a step towards the bed. 'He,' she said. 'He's a he. His name's Cyril.'

'Cyril,' Penny said, trying the sound of his name. 'I love dogs. I love all animals actually. My mum won't let me have a pet, of course, not even a gerbil. She says she's allergic and that her whole head would swell up if we had one in the house.' Penny stopped talking abruptly and frowned. 'You know what, I don't think she's allergic at all. I reckon she's made it up, just so she doesn't have to clean animal hairs off the carpet.'

Abi sat on the edge of the bed. '*My* mum won't let Cyril in the house today. Just because she cleaned the kitchen floor this morning. We can go out and see him in a bit. I mean, if you like.'

'If I like? I'd love. Everything is brilliant here. I've never been anywhere like it. And I...' Penny stopped. She looked down into her lap. 'Sorry. My mum says I talk too much when I'm nervous.'

'Why would you be nervous?'

Penny stared at her lap as though there was something fascinating decorating the legs of her jeans. 'I used to have a best friend, you know. Gillian. Her family emigrated to New Zealand last year with her dad's job. We'd been best friends since infants, but since... Mum's always going on at me to make new friends. She doesn't get it that I just don't have anything in common with

anyone at that school.' Penny squirmed. 'I thought that maybe…
maybe, you'd want to be my… You probably think I'm an idiot
or something and… Please can I use your phone? I want my dad
to come and get me.'

At last Abi felt she could smile. 'You know that thing your
mum said about talking too much?'

'Am I doing it again?'

Abi nodded. 'I don't want you to leave.'

Penny looked at Abi from beneath her fringe. She smiled a
small smile. 'Thank you for inviting me. I can't wait to come here
again. It's so much better than my house.'

'Oh yeah, right,' Abi laughed so much that she snorted. 'I
mean, why would anyone want a video and colour telly in their
bedroom?'

Penny laughed with her and Abi wanted to pinch herself. Was
this really happening? Penny liked Cliff Cottage. She liked the crazy
attic room. She even seemed to like her. Maybe Penny had just the
right screw loose, which meant she couldn't see the craziness of Abi's
family and their life out in the wonky house by the sea.

For what was left of the morning, Abi lay next to Penny,
snuggled beneath Nan's tartan blanket, listening to music on her
radio cassette – one of the few possessions she had refused to part
with. It had made the car journey from Twickenham to Dorset
on her lap. They sang along with the songs and when Penny
wasn't giving Abi the who's who of everyone at school, she flicked
through Abi's sketchbooks making so many appreciative noises
that Abi felt herself blush.

The fire eventually died down, so they left the rapidly cooling
room and made their way back down the stairs. They pulled on
their coats and slipped out into the garden. Cyril was busy digging
out the roots of one of Nan's azaleas.

'Does he like Polos?' Penny asked.

'He's a dustbin. He likes everything,' Abi said.

Penny took a packet of mints from her pocket. She had barely
ripped the paper when Cyril was at her feet, offering his paw.

After having his fill of mints, Penny spent the next ten minutes chucking a tennis ball down the garden for him to fetch. Abi stood by, watching. Every now and then she intercepted the ball and she and Penny descended into a fit of giggles when Cyril tried to dig it out of whichever pocket she hid it in. Abi had just hidden it in her back pocket when a voice called out.

'Girls!' Mum shouted from the open kitchen window. 'Lunch!'

In the kitchen, Abi made Penny sit with her back to the sink while they ate their cheese and pickle sandwiches. Her mum was hovering by the draining board, watching them, wiping a tea towel around the rim of the same glass again and again. Penny hadn't finished chewing her final mouthful of sandwich when Abi grabbed their plates of cake. 'Come on,' she said, standing up. 'We'll have this in the parlour.'

Abi placed the plates on the carpet and sat heavily on the sofa. She huffed loudly. 'God, I'm so sorry about my mum,' she said, curling her legs beneath her. 'She's so embarrassing.'

Penny sat beside her. 'Why?'

'Oh, nothing. She just is.'

'She can't be all bad if she made this chocolate cake.' Penny picked up one of the plates and took a bite of the slice of cake. She closed her eyes and murmured. Between mouthfuls, she nodded to the mantelpiece lined with framed black and white and colour photos; Abi's mum and dad cutting their cake on their wedding day, Mum in a frilly dress when she was a baby, Mum on her first day of school with ribbons in her white-blonde hair, Nan holding Abi on her christening day, Granddad helping Abi open presents one Christmas morning. 'Your family likes photos then,' Penny said.

'My nan says she likes to have her family around her all the time.'

Penny put her plate down and headed for the fireplace. She picked up a photograph in a silver frame. 'Was this taken here?'

Abi unfurled her legs and joined Penny. She looked at the black and white photograph of a group of people arranged around a bench – two sitting down, two standing behind, and two kneeling on the ground.

'Yup. That's my mum's family. They used to come here on holidays when Mum was young. That's why Nan and Granddad bought the cottage when they retired.'

'Is that your mum?' Penny asked, pointing to the teenage girl in a dark bathing suit, kneeling on the ground, smiling for the camera, her hair tumbling to her shoulders. 'She's so beautiful. My mum said she met your mum when they were younger and she remembered she was pretty. She could be a model.'

Keen to divert attention from her mum, Abi pointed to the scrawny chap kneeling beside her. 'That's Arthur, my mum's cousin.'

'Look at his quiff! Who does he think he looks like? John Travolta?'

'You should see the photo my Nan has on her dressing table. Arthur's wearing huge flares and has a parrot on his shoulder. Nan says he travelled all around the world when he was in the Merchant Navy. Apparently, he ran off and joined up not long after that picture was taken. He married a woman in Brazil and they've got loads of kids. But Nan says his parents never forgave him for running off like that.' Abi shuddered as she looked at the lady in an old-fashioned long dress, buttoned to the chin, her hair pulled back in a bun and the man beside her, sitting as straight as a poker in his socks and sandals. The severe look in the eyes of her Great Aunt Ruth and Great Uncle Henry had always given her the creeps, as though, somehow, they were reaching through the years to tell her off for something.

'Do you ever think about going away like Arthur did?' Penny asked. 'You know, going off to see the world?'

'Dunno really. Do you?'

'All the time. I… oh, you'll think I'm stupid if I tell you.'

'No I won't.'

Penny lowered her voice as though afraid someone might hear them. 'As soon as I've finished my A-levels, I'm leaving. I'm going to spend the summer in Europe. You can get a train ticket that lets you travel all around Europe. It doesn't cost much. And you can stay in youth hostels and campsites. I've read all about it. My mum and dad can't stop me. I'll be eighteen. I've been saving my birthday money for years, so I won't ask them for a penny. And when I get back, I'm going to study English Literature at UCL in London. I can't wait.'

'You won't study dance then?'

'No!' Penny half laughed and half choked. 'I only keep going to dance classes to keep my mum off my back. It's not what's in here.' She pointed to her chest. 'It's not me. What about you? What do you want to do when we leave school?'

Abi picked up a cushion from the armchair and held it to her stomach. She had never told anyone her dream before. Should she...? 'This probably sounds stupid because I'm not even sure that I'm good enough... but I've always thought that maybe, well, I'd like to study art.'

'Where will you apply?'

Penny said it so casually, as though there was no question that Abi was good enough. Before she could stop herself, Abi said, 'There's a college called Saint Martin's School of Art in London–'

'London! It's fate. We can share a flat somewhere like Camden or Carnaby Street. It will be so brilliant. Say you'll come to Europe with me too.'

Abi stared slack-jawed. A few short hours ago, she was standing in the kitchen waiting for Penny to run screaming from the cottage and now here she was, with an invitation to travel to Europe and go back to London. 'Okay,' she said, her cheeks beginning to ache from smiling. 'Why not? I'll come with you.'

Penny smiled back. 'Good,' she said, before turning back to the photo. 'So who are they?' she asked about the final two people standing at the back of the group; a woman in a sleeveless dress decorated with sunflowers, her wavy hair held back from her face by a pair of sunglasses shaped like a cat's eyes, and a man, one arm around her shoulders, the other hand resting on the back of the bench, his shirtsleeves rolled up, a cigarette tucked behind his ear.

'My nan and granddad,' Abi said. She nudged the armchair beside the fireplace with her knee. Should she tell Penny that, sometimes, when she sat in Granddad's favourite old chair with its threadbare arms hidden beneath lace doilies, that she was sure she could smell the sweet apple scent of Old Holborn tobacco?

'Is it true…' Penny said gently. 'What Thug said… about your granddad, how he…?'

Abi dug her fingers into her palm. 'Yes.'

'Oh, Abi, I'm sorry.'

Abi shrugged but all the while, her mind played out the scene in their old home in Byron Avenue. Her mum answered the phone out on the stand in the hall. There was a scream so loud, so terrifying. Dad rushed from the living room. Abi rushed from her bedroom. Halfway down the stairs, she saw her mum collapsed on the floor. The vicar's voice was saying 'hello' on the receiver that dangled from its cord, swinging backwards and forwards. He had called as Nan was in shock and unable to speak.

'And your dad,' Penny said. 'Is he okay?'

The scene in Abi's mind changed. The 'For Sale' sign in the front garden of Byron Avenue. Mum telling her friends they were moving so they could look after her mother following her father's death. Dad sitting in the living room. Smoking. Just smoking. Not eating. Surrounded by boxes that Abi had helped Mum pack as Dad couldn't even bathe, let alone do anything physical. The Cortina stuffed with boxes. Everything else sold through small adverts in the paper and what couldn't be sold, taken to the charity shop. That was the real reason for decamping to Dorset. The collapse of the hardware shop that had been in Dad's family for generations. There had been arguments. So many long nights of rows. Dad had secretly remortgaged the house in an attempt to pay wages and keep the shop afloat. Granddad's death had been the most inconvenient convenient excuse to hide behind for the move.

'Abi?' Penny said and placed the photograph back on the mantelpiece.

'My dad's on pills,' Abi said quietly, dropping the cushion back to the chair.

With no warning, the parlour door flew open. 'Well, who do we have here then?' Nan said, a huge smile on her face and a carrier bag in her hands. She grabbed Abi's hand and gave it a squeeze. One of her squeezes that said *everything is going to be okay*.

'This is Penny,' Abi said.

'Penny, Penny, Penny,' Nan said. She put her arms around Penny and gave her a huge hug, her carrier bag rustling. She took a step back. Keeping hold of Penny's arms, she looked her up and down. 'What a smasher you are, Penny. You've really cheered up our Abi.'

Penny giggled, but she didn't seem to mind. 'Thank you,' she said.

'Oh, and these are for the two of you. I popped into the village shop after arranging the flowers for tomorrow.' Nan handed the bag to Abi. 'Go on, then. Have a peek.'

Abi reached inside and pulled out a tin of Quality Street. They only had Quality Street as an extra special treat at Christmas.

'Now,' Nan said, 'get that lid off and you girls tuck in. I'm going to bother your mum for a cuppa and see what your dad's up to out in that shed. He's supposed to be potting up some seeds for me.'

'They're all for us?' Abi asked.

'Every single one.' Nan placed one warm palm on Abi's cheek and the other on Penny's. 'It's not every day you find a new best friend.' She gave each girl's cheek a squeeze. 'Oh, you are just so delicious. I could eat you both up.'

***

The next Saturday, Mum excused Abi of her chores and allowed her to go to Penny's again. The Friday after that, Mum said she could invite Penny to sleepover at Cliff Cottage.

They were sitting together on the coach outside school, noses in a textbook, revising for a test on the French Revolution, when a commotion at the front made them look up.

'Well, if it isn't the lezzers,' Tracey jeered, squeezing through the aisle towards them. She formed a slit between two fingers and flicked her tongue between them, making a disgusting slurping sound. Penny dropped the book and jumped to her feet.

'Don't,' Abi whispered and tried to grab Penny's arm, but Penny pulled it away. Since Tony had had 'a word' with Thug's dad, the bullying had stopped, except for the odd rough tackle by Tracey in hockey or a shove in her back when Abi was alone in the corridor. The last thing she needed was it starting up again.

'If you've got something to say, Tracey Evans, then say it to my face,' Penny said.

'Oh, don't worry about that, Miss Goody-fucking-two-shoes, I will.'

Penny didn't flinch. 'Go on then,' she said. 'We're waiting.'

'I'm not,' Abi said under her breath.

'What's this,' Tracey sneered. 'Upset your girlfriend, have I?'

'You really are pathetic,' Penny said, her voice calm. 'Just because you haven't got any friends, it doesn't give you the right to make fun of people that have.'

'Friends! With her. You wanna be careful who you go around with. You might end up with some of what's owing to her.'

'Which is?'

'She knows. Don't you, London? You know what's coming your way.'

Penny lowered her voice. 'If anything happens to Abi, we'll all know who's to blame. Won't we?'

Thug and the rest of his gang had boarded the coach behind Tracey. Abi saw a look pass between him and Penny.

'Move it,' Thug said, shoving Tracey in the back.

'You what?' Tracey turned to face him. 'Have you forgotten what she did to you?'

'I said, move it.' He shoved her again. This time Tracey did what he said but not before taking a parting shot at Abi. 'This ain't over. You won't always have your bodyguard around to protect you. Remember that.'

As Thug and his gang barged to the back, Abi grabbed Penny's arm and pulled her into her seat. 'What did you say all that for? She's going to kill me.'

'No she's not. She's all talk.'

'It's all right for you. What if she tries to cave my head in when you're not around?'

'Best make sure you're never on your own with her. I told you, I hate bullies. They're all cowards really. You just have to stand up to them. Come on,' she said picking up the textbook. 'Where were we? Ah, that's it. Robespierre.'

Abi looked at Penny. She looked so sweet with her curly brown hair and big brown eyes, like butter wouldn't melt.

***

From that Saturday, Abi and Penny spent alternate weekends in town at Penny's and at Cliff Cottage. At Cliff Cottage, Penny sat at the kitchen table like she belonged; shelling peas, filling tart cases with jam, helping to make mountains of egg sandwiches for buffets. Mum still hovered around but thankfully the staring business eventually subsided.

When they weren't helping in the kitchen, they walked Cyril on the beach. They sat at the kitchen table, warming their feet by the range, passing the long winter evenings chatting or reading or refining their European escape route. They had a map of Europe, which they spread out on the table to circle destinations. At any sound of someone approaching the kitchen, they hid the map under a pile of books. Weekends in town always included a trip to the library and it was on one of these visits that Penny, egged on by Abi, snuck a copy of *Hollywood Wives* past the elderly librarian. She almost gave the game away when she fumbled and dropped her library card on the floor, but the ancient librarian was too either too embarrassed or too short-sighted to say anything about what was tucked between *Jane Eyre* and *North and South*.

Back at Penny's they wedged the chair from her dressing table under the handle of her bedroom door and barricaded themselves in with a family-size bag of Revels. But the chocolates stayed in the bag when they flicked through the dog-eared pages.

'Do you think this is really what *it's* really like?' Penny asked, turning the colour of a post box.

'If it is, I'd rather not,' Abi said.

'Me either.' But neither of them suggested putting the book down.

Penny was so much a part of the family that she was at the kitchen table when Abi's dad made his announcement.

'It's only part time,' he said and cut into his sausage. 'They need some extra help in the power tools section. They think my experience will come in handy.' He said it as though being offered a job at a DIY superstore was nothing. He hadn't even told anyone that he was going for an interview.

Nan passed around the teapot in celebration and Mum smiled. 'I think that's wonderful news.'

Chapter 8

Rose held the curtains back from the parlour window and breathed a sigh of relief as the back end of the Morris Minor disappeared up the lane. Mother and Auntie Ruth had spent most of the morning trying to talk her into squeezing into the back of the car between them for a day trip to Lyme Regis. It was only when her father intervened, telling them that she was old enough to make up her own mind, that they had given up and packed a picnic just for four.

Rose let the curtain fall. For the first time in days, Mother and Auntie Ruth weren't in the kitchen squabbling over something – that morning it had been the most efficient way to wrap a sandwich in greaseproof paper. Father and Uncle Henry weren't in the parlour with their newspapers, reeling off the cricket scores and speculating on where the gang that had robbed the Glasgow to London Royal Mail train might have gone to ground. Even Arthur had pulled on his jacket and roared away on his motorbike directly after he had finished his bacon and eggs.

After listening to the blissful silence for a second, Rose grabbed the travel blanket from the back of the sofa, hurried through the kitchen – shedding her shorts as she went – and stepped out of the back door in just her bathing costume.

She crossed the lawn, the morning sun warming her hair. At the end of the garden, she spread out the blanket and lay down, stretching out her legs. The grass was as soft and as warm as a hearthrug beneath her heels. She closed her eyes, and rested her head in her palms. With no hint of a breeze and with the sun gently warming her eyelids, Rose thought about the textbooks she still needed to buy; whether she had withdrawn enough from her Post Office account to see her through the first two weeks in Edinburgh; would a black turtleneck sweater make the right impression at her first lecture? Bit by bit, her mind went blank of these thoughts and focused on the soft shush of waves on the pebbles below, the squawk of a seagull high overhead, and the buzz of a bee hovering around the foxglove beside her. She drifted into a light sleep, imagining that at any moment the bee's tiny wings would come to a stop as it disappeared inside the trumpet-shaped bloom to have its fill of pollen. Instead, the buzzing grew louder, so loud that she sat up and shielded her eyes to look around for the source of the noise.

It took a few seconds for her sleepy brain to put two and two together and realise that the buzzing wasn't a bee at all, but a petrol engine pulling up outside the cottage. She lay back down and screwed her eyes tight shut. It was clearly too much to ask to have a single morning of peace.

The noise of the engine cut out and Rose kept her eyes closed. She didn't stir, not even when she heard the squeak of the front gate and felt the vibration of boots crossing the lawn.

'If you think I'm making you lunch, then you've got another thing coming,' she said.

The boots came to a stop just beside her head and the shadow crossing her took the heat from the day.

'It's a good job I'm not hungry then,' a voice said.

Coming instantly to her senses, Rose jumped to her feet. The voice spoke not in Arthur's cockney twang but in a deep Dorset drawl. Rose grabbed the blanket and pulled it around her. At the same time, she tried to make out the man's face. With the sun behind him, he was nothing more than a featureless shadow. Rose took a step back. Okay, there was a strange man in the garden. She was wearing little more than her underwear.

'My dad's in the house,' she said. She could have kicked herself for the shake in her voice and the way her fingers fumbled, refusing to tie the blanket around her. What kind of surgeon was she going to make if she couldn't even get her fingers to do what she told them?

'So that wasn't your dad I saw driving off up the road then?' the stranger said.

Rose took another step back and felt her pulse quicken in her throat. 'This is private property you know.' Where was Arthur? The one time she really needed him and he was nowhere to be found. She looked towards the house, sizing up the distance to the back door. Her calf muscles twitched, but as she was about to make her move, she felt something touch her arm. She looked down. It was the man's hand.

'I'm sorry if I startled you, I didn't mean to,' he said. 'I was looking for Art. I helped him out yesterday. When his bike broke down in town.' His hand rested just above her elbow. He wasn't grabbing or holding her back. If she moved, his hand would simply slip away.

'You know Arthur?' she said, the beat in her neck slowing slightly.

'Yes,' the man said. 'Skinny guy, red hair, funny accent.' He released her arm and stepped into her field of vision. Finally, and without the sun behind him, Rose could make out the detail of his appearance. He was dressed just like Arthur, in blue jeans, a white T-shirt, black leather jacket and heavy-soled boots. But any similarity to her cousin ended there. Because where Arthur was short, slight and pale, this man – which was what he was, Rose guessed he had to be at least twenty, maybe twenty-one – was tall and broad-shouldered. His tanned skin made him look like a European. He wore the fringe of his thick, dark brown hair long so that it fell over his eyes. And what eyes they were. So brown that they verged on black, with eyelashes longer than Rose had ever seen, even on a woman.

'You must be Rose,' he said, pushing his fringe back from his eyes. It immediately fell forward again. 'Art said that his cousin was here on holiday with him. It's a pleasure to meet you.' He held out his hand and she took it, gripping the blanket tight beneath her armpits. She made sure her handshake was strong and business-like, just as her father had taught her. But this man held her hand for longer than her father ever had. When he eventually released her, he dug around in the pocket of his jeans and pulled out a small metal bolt. He pressed it into her palm. 'I promised I'd drop this off for Art.'

'Oh, I see. He's not here,' she said. 'Arthur. He's gone out.'

'Shame. But will you give it to him when he gets back?'

'Yes, of course. And I'm sorry. I mean, that he wasn't here. That you've had a wasted journey.'

The man smiled, and Rose noticed how his mouth rose on one side causing a dimple to form in his right cheek. 'I wouldn't say it's been a completely wasted journey. But I suppose I shouldn't outstay my welcome. You'll be wanting to get back to your sunbathing.' He nodded to the patch of flattened grass.

'Yes, I suppose I will.' Rose closed her fingers around the bolt. It was still warm from his pocket.

'Well, it was good to meet you, Rose. Maybe I'll see you around.' The man smiled again before heading back up the garden. Rose stood and watched him. He walked with his hands dug deep into the pockets of his jeans and with each step, the buckles of his jacket jangled as though he was wearing a belt made from bells. It wasn't until he was about to disappear around the side of the house that she suddenly remembered her manners. 'Who should I say called?' she shouted after him.

He stopped and turned back to look at her. 'Ray. My name is Ray.'

***

'You want me to take you where?' Arthur rocked back on the kitchen chair. 'You've changed your tune.'

Rose grabbed his empty plate and teacup from the table, turned back to the sink and submerged them in the frothy bubbles. 'Don't make more of this than there is,' she said, scrubbing hard at a smear of salad cream. She heard the feet of the chair thud to the floor before Arthur joined her at the sink. He picked up a tea towel, plucked a plate from the draining board, and gave it a half-hearted swipe.

'Correct me if I'm wrong,' he said, placing the plate on the side. 'But I could have sworn I heard *someone* say that after eighteen years, she had seen everything there was to see in Bridport. That she had no intention of going there ever again because what would she want with penny arcades and shops selling fossils and candyfloss?'

Rose could tell from Arthur's voice that he was smiling. She took a scouring pad from the draining board and began scrubbing between the prongs of a fork. 'Don't bother then. Not if it's too much trouble.'

Arthur sighed. 'Don't be so bloody touchy. I'll take you to the coffee shop if that's what you want.' He plucked another plate from the rack. 'It's not such a bad idea. Ray often pops in there of an afternoon and if we bump into him I can thank him, proper like, for dropping off that part.'

'Really. Oh, yes, I suppose you can.' Rose turned her back to Arthur, partly to collect the teapot from the table, but mainly so he wouldn't see her grinning.

Half an hour later, and after much shouting up the stairs for her to get a move on, Rose stepped out into the afternoon sun. She closed the kitchen door behind her, walked around to the front of the cottage, and found Arthur already sitting astride his motorbike. 'At last,' he said, thrusting a silver pudding bowl of a helmet at her.

'I'm not wearing that thing.' She frowned. 'Why should I? You don't wear one.'

'That, my dear,' Arthur said, rapping a knuckle against his brow, 'is because I have a skull made of steel whereas you – as a mere mortal – have a bonce made of bone. It's up to you, but no helmet, no ride. Sid'd kill me if I let anything happen to his little princess.' He shoved the helmet at her again and she begrudgingly accepted it. With great care she placed it over her freshly brushed hair and secured the strap under her chin.

'Hurry up. We haven't got all day,' Arthur said. 'I still don't know why you wasted all that time changing your clothes. You were fine as you were. Well, as fine as *you* can be.' He looked over his shoulder just in time to catch her frowning at the seat. 'Bloody hell, Rose. What do you want? Cinderella's pumpkin carriage? You could eat your dinner off that. Now get on or I'm going without you.'

'All right, all right,' she said. It was either get on and risk an oil stain on her white Capri pants or spend the rest of the afternoon at Cliff Cottage with no chance of... well, no chance of anything even remotely interesting happening. She climbed up behind Arthur and slipped her arms around his scrawny waist. 'I just hope you spend as much time cleaning this thing as you do tinkering with its innards,' she said.

'Philistine! I don't tinker, I tune. This engine is a finely honed, streamlined beast. You just wait and see.' To prove his point, Arthur stood up in his seat and kicked down sharply on the pedal. The engine roared to life, vibrating beneath her and rumbling all around her. 'Ready?' Arthur shouted over his shoulder.

'Ready,' Rose shouted back.

'Hold on tight.'

Arthur revved the engine and set off up the lane at such a speed that Rose struggled to keep hold of him. The bushes on either side rushed by in a blur of green and she tightened her hold around Arthur's waist and buried her face in the back of his jacket. The smell of leather and oil filled her nostrils until finally she plucked up the courage to twist her head to take in the view, still keeping her cheek pressed firmly to Arthur's back. The sky and sea flashed by as two streaks of blue. Cows and sheep were reduced to indistinct smudges of brown and white. The wind rushed past her face so fast that she had to fight to keep her eyes open. Nothing in her life, not even riding the Waltzer at the May Day fair in Greenford Park, had been as fast as this and she didn't know whether to scream or to laugh. She had certainly screamed when she rode the Waltzer. And the more noise she and her friends made, the harder the fairground worker had pushed their carriage so that the world whirled around them in a haze of electric fairy lights and loud music. While her friends shrieked with delight, Rose had screamed in terror. What if the bolts holding the car sheered? What if the force pinning her head back to the seat damaged a vertebra? What if Marjorie sitting beside her actually needed to use the paper bag her mother made her carry on every bus journey on account of her weak stomach? When the ride finally ground to a halt and her friends clanked down the metal steps, laughing and stumbling into each other, all Rose had been able to do was thank her lucky stars that her feet had once again made contact with solid ground.

Racing through the Dorset countryside with the roar of the engine in her ears and the breeze buffeting her face, she was teetering on a knife-edge. At any moment catastrophe could strike. A car coming from the other direction might veer off course and crash into them. A patch of oil on the road might make them skid out of control. But unlike the time on the Waltzer, today Rose had an overwhelming desire to shriek with delight. She was almost disappointed when they began to slow on the approach to the outskirts of town.

They slowed further still to navigate the traffic on the roads in Bridport and finally slowed to a crawl to pull up outside the Town Hall. Arthur manoeuvred into a parking space at the end of a row of other motorbikes. The engine shuddered to a stop and Rose felt her cheeks stiff from smiling so much. With the roar of the engine still ringing in her ears, she got down from the bike, unfastened the helmet, smoothed down her hair, and paused to check her reflection in the mirror of one of the parked motorbikes. Her cheeks were pink and her eyes looked even bluer than normal.

'Don't crack it,' Arthur said and swung his leg over the saddle. Rose chose to ignore him. She was still enjoying the sensation of flying too much to let anything, including Arthur, annoy her.

Arthur seemed in no mood to hang around amongst the crowds thronging the pavements – shoppers making their way to the stalls of the midweek market outside the Town Hall, holidaymakers struggling with uncooperative deckchairs and windbreaks – and, after pulling a comb from his back pocket and running it through his hair, he chivvied Rose towards the coffee shop.

The first thing that hit Rose as she stepped through the door of Alberto's was the smell – a rich, intense, warm smell; delicious, like chocolate only more chocolatey – followed by the din from the people packing the tables. Children shouted and bickered, a baby in its pushchair cried because its mother was trying to wipe something resembling jam from its face, men and women talked loudly, all trying to be heard over each other's conversations and the music coming from a jukebox in the corner. Rushing between the tables and booths was a small army of red-faced waitresses in black skirts and white blouses. They scribbled orders and delivered plates of cream cakes and pastries, and all the while a large moustachioed man barked orders from behind the counter where he held court at a huge, frothing chrome machine.

Rose looked around from occupied table to occupied table. Arthur barely had the patience to wait for a kettle to boil, never mind hang around for a table to become vacant. What if he decided to give up and drag her back to the cottage? She was about to suggest they take a walk to the market to buy some flowers for their mothers when a family in a booth began to collect up their belongings. While the woman was still helping a little boy and girl clamber down, Arthur slipped into the seat. 'Don't mind me,' he said. Rose smiled an apology but wasted no time in slipping into the booth opposite him, and almost as soon as they had taken their seats, a waitress stopped and balanced a tray on the edge of their table.

'Well if it isn't little Mary,' Arthur said, handing her a plate containing the sticky remnants of a half-eaten rum baba. She took it from him.

'Less of the little if you don't mind.'

He held up his hands. 'Hey, sweet stuff, don't hold it against me. Like they say, the best things come in small packages.'

'Bloody cheek.' She smiled. 'I didn't expect to see you again so soon. Twice in one day, you must really like the coffee.'

'What can I say? It's the best in town. But it wasn't me that wanted to come. It was my cousin, Rose here, what wanted to sample the delights of Alberto's. Otherwise I wouldn't have bothered.' He winked at Mary, making her laugh. Rose looked from one to the other and suddenly everything fell into place. Why Arthur had agreed to bring her into town with no argument. Why he had rushed her to get ready. And why he had been so careful to comb his hair after the ride.

'It's a pleasure, I'm sure,' Mary said to Rose. Her features were petite, matching the rest of her, and she wore her auburn hair back from her face in a red Alice band.

'Likewise,' Rose said and put a cup and saucer onto the tray.

'Thanks, lovey. He's driving me up the wall today,' Mary said, nodding over her shoulder to the moustachioed man while she gave the table a wipe with a cloth. 'He'd give bleedin' Mussolini a run for his money. If I didn't need the money, I'd tell him where to stick his lousy job.'

'Just say the word,' Arthur said, forcing himself back into the conversation. 'And I'll sort him out.'

'Oh, Art.' Mary grinned. 'My hero.' She took a pencil and a pad from the pocket in her apron. 'Come on then. I'd better look busy. What can I get you?'

'Does it have to be off the menu?' Arthur asked, waggling his eyebrows suggestively.

Mary laughed and turned to Rose. 'He's on form today, ain't he?' She pointed to Arthur with the end of her pencil. 'I've known him all of two days and he's as forward as you like! Is he always like this?'

Arthur didn't give Rose the chance to reply. 'Not always,' he said. 'It's you what brings it out in me, Mary.'

'Well if I bring it out of you, then you can put it straight back in.' Mary laughed again. It was a sweet laugh and made Rose smile. She liked Mary. It wasn't every day she met someone who could give her cousin as good as he gave.

Arthur finally stopped flirting for long enough to place their orders and Mary made her way back to the counter with an extra wiggle that Rose knew wasn't for her benefit. Arthur was watching Mary like a puppy might look at a juicy marrowbone in a butcher's window; his eyes glazed and his tongue practically hitting the table. On an ordinary day, Rose would have seized on this unexpected chance to rib him. But on an ordinary day she wouldn't have had a little voice in her head reminding her of what it was that people in glasshouses shouldn't do.

After Mary delivered their orders and disappeared through a door behind the counter, the old Arthur returned. He blew across the top of his coffee and began to regale Rose with a thrilling tale of the time he had been entrusted with the task of servicing a Rolls Royce. While he spoke, Rose looked over his shoulder at the row of parked motorbikes. There were eight. No less than when they had arrived, but no more either.

'There'll be no coffee taste left at that rate,' Arthur said eventually.

'Pardon me?' Rose looked quickly from the motorbikes to her cousin.

'I said there'll be no coffee taste left,' he repeated. 'That's the third sugar you've put in.'

'Is it? Oh, I know it is. It's how I like it.' She placed the glass sugar pourer back on the table and picked up her spoon. She stirred the murky brown liquid, tapped the spoon on the side of the cup, and placed it in the saucer. She took a sip and tried not to wince when she realised that she had, in fact, succeeded in making the coffee too sweet rather than less bitter. How disappointing to discover that the taste of coffee didn't live up to the promise of its chocolatey scent. She would much rather have a cup of her mother's tea or a glass of her homemade lemonade.

'I should have got you a glass of milk.' Arthur plucked his tiny cup of extra strong black coffee from its minuscule saucer. He held it by the rim rather than the handle and knocked it back in one.

He smiled and breathed out with a contented sigh. 'So, like I was saying, we're not so different after all.'

'Sorry?'

'I was saying that I had to bleed a sump the other day and how car mechanics isn't really all that different to surgery. Only what I do with oil and steel you'll be doing with blood and bones.'

'Oh, right.'

He returned his cup to its saucer. 'Have you heard a single word I've said?'

'What? Of course.'

'Hmmmm.' Arthur frowned. 'I compare your precious surgery to fixing a car and you don't bat an eyelid. Here was me thinking you wanted to spend some time catching up with your old cousin but you've hardly said two words. And whatever is going on over my shoulder must be really interesting.' He pointed to her cup. 'Another?'

'No. Thank you.'

'Perhaps the little girl would prefer a strawberry milkshake.'

Rose folded her arms across her chest. Just when she had been on the verge of apologising for not paying attention, Arthur had to go and make her so cross that rather than saying sorry, she wanted to give him a swift kick in the shin. She did what she always did when he annoyed her; she wrinkled her nose and stuck out her tongue. Arthur looked at her and laughed.

'I don't care what anyone else thinks,' he said. 'You ain't got me fooled. You're nothing but a big kid.' He was still laughing and shaking his head when the door to the street opened.

Over Arthur's shoulder, Rose saw two men stumble in, laughing and pushing each other. But it wasn't until a third man followed them inside that she realised her tongue was still sticking out. She sucked it back in. But it was too late. Ray had already caught her eye and he was smiling.

'What's that racket?' Arthur said turning around. When he saw the source of the commotion, he smiled. 'Lads. Lads,' he shouted and beckoned. 'Over here. Come and join us.'

Rose stared at the pool of coffee that had collected in the bottom of her saucer. She listened to the jangle of buckles approach and the slap of hands on the back of leather jackets. 'Rose,' Arthur said, 'come on, budge up and make some room for the lads.' Instead of budging up, she jumped up.

'I'm going to put some music on,' she said and almost bumped into the neighbouring table in her rush to get away.

Rose pressed her hands to the glass covering the jukebox. What had she been thinking? Why on Earth had she asked Arthur to bring her here? And why, when she was supposed to be a grown up, had she stuck her tongue out? Maybe she should ask Arthur to take her home. Yes, that's what she would do. She would choose a record and then with her shoulders back and her head held high, she would walk back to the table and tell Arthur that it was time to leave.

She took a coin from the change purse in her pocket and forced it into the slot. She tried to focus on the list of songs but the words seemed to blur into one, a side effect of the awful coffee no doubt, which might also explain the sick feeling churning up her insides. What did it matter which song she chose when she would be out of the door before it was even halfway through. She hit a random button and watched the arm select a record then rotate to lay it on the turntable. The needle dropped into the grooves and after a slight crackle, the opening notes and words of a song that she recognised from the radio came from the speaker.

'You like The Beatles then?' a voice said over her shoulder. Rose felt her face burn as though all of the blood from her body had suddenly been redirected to her cheeks. It was all she could do to keep her legs from shaking as she watched the record spin around and around under the glass.

'I don't... I suppose so.'

'John Lennon's a genius. Don't you think?' Ray said.

'I'm not... yes.'

There was a pause filled only by the music. 'Are you going to stare into that jukebox all day?' Ray said.

Oxygen, that's what she needed. More oxygen in her blood to slow her pulse. After two deep breaths she turned around.

'Have I got something on my face?' he asked.

'Pardon me?'

'It might explain why you can't bring yourself to look at me.'

Gradually Rose let her eyes travel up. She swallowed as she saw the straight line of his collarbone beneath the cotton of his white T-shirt. Further up she went and took in his clean-shaven chin, the dip between his top lip and nose, which she struggled to remember the name of. Just as she remembered it was called the philtrum, her eyes settled on his brown eyes, and the name of it slipped from her mind again.

'That's better. I like to see who I'm talking to.' Ray reached past Rose and leant against the jukebox. His arm was so close to her face that she could smell the leather of his jacket and feel the warmth radiating from him. 'I never expected to come in here and find you. Arthur said something about you not wanting to come into town. Something about you having seen everything there is to see here. Apparently, Bridport holds no surprises for you.'

'It doesn't. I mean… it didn't.'

'Until now?'

'Yes, until now.'

'So what changed your mind?' As Ray spoke, Rose watched the dimple appear in his cheek.

'I don't know.'

'I can't say I blame you. There's not much in this dull town apart from this place. Unless you fancy a tea dance or an afternoon concert in the church hall.'

'Do you? Go to the afternoon concerts I mean?' As soon as the words left her mouth, Rose wished she could grab them and put them straight back in. Because Ray laughed. Not a loud laugh or a nasty laugh but enough to make her feel stupid.

'I can't really see me sipping tea and tucking into a slice of Battenburg with all the old duffers, can you? I suppose that's not something you have to worry about, living in London. I bet you have your pick of clubs and dancehalls. I hear Soho and the King's Road are the places to be. You don't know how lucky you are. The monthly dance at the Town Hall is about as good as it gets around here.'

Rose composed a sentence in her head and decided to risk opening her mouth again. 'So you go then? To those dances?'

'Sometimes. There's one on this Saturday. I hear there are still some tickets left, if you feel like dragging yourself into town again that is.' Ray smiled down at her. 'Anyway,' he said, running his fingers through his fringe, 'me and the lads have to be off. We've got a new set to rehearse for Saturday.'

'Rehearse?'

'For the dance.'

'You're in a band?'

'Yeah.' He nodded to his friends still horsing around with Arthur. 'Ian over there's on drums and Gary's on bass. I'm on guitar and I sing.' He hovered over her for just a moment longer before pulling away and standing up straight. 'Anyway. I'd better go. We've only got the rehearsal room booked for an hour. I'll see you on Saturday then. Maybe.'

'Yes. Maybe.'

Rose watched Ray walk slowly back to the table. He paused to shake hands with Arthur and when he nodded, Ian and Gary jumped up to follow him. Rose was still watching him when he pushed open the door. He didn't look back. Not even a glance.

***

A sliver of moon hung low in the sky and Rose watched it disappear briefly then reappear from behind a thin trail of cloud. She stood in darkness with her forehead against the attic window but dared not move from the spot. Since Arthur had mentioned their excursion into town, Rose's mother had pursued her for a blow-by-blow account of the trip and Rose had only avoided the subject by feigning tiredness and heading for bed. A creaking floorboard would provide Mother with the perfect excuse to climb the staircase with a hot milky drink and restart her interrogation. Trapped in the heat under the eaves, Rose needed a cup of cocoa even less than she needed to discuss her day.

She watched the ghostly reflection of her eyes stare back at her from the dark. It felt impossible that they were the same eyes that had looked out at her from the mirror that morning when she brushed her hair. They could never have guessed that they would not, in fact, spend the day reading the pages of a medical journal but find themselves taking in the sights of an Italian coffee shop and a pair of brown eyes.

Rose moved her head, trying to find a cool spot on the glass. She wrapped her arms around her waist. This was ridiculous. She wasn't the person he thought she was. She had never stepped foot inside a club in Soho or the King's Road. And he had only said those things to be polite because she was Arthur's cousin. He had been friendly, that's all. Any other interpretation of their conversation was simply wishful thinking. She shouldn't be thinking about him at all, wishful or otherwise. She should be focusing on the fact that in less than a week, she would be crammed in the back of the car heading back to Southall and soon after that she would be boarding a train to take her to her new life. With all of that to focus on – all of the planning and preparations – why did her mind insist on dragging her back to the events in the coffee shop, replaying the scene in minute detail, over and over again like the record revolving in the jukebox?

She turned from the window and picked her way carefully across the floorboards to the bed. It was far too hot to get under the covers so she lay on top of the bedspread. But even lying perfectly still, sweat collected in the creases of her elbows. Using the darkness as a canvas, she visualised a cross-section of human skin; subcutaneous tissue, dermis, epidermis, hair shafts, pores, sweat glands. The diversion from her thoughts was short lived. She found herself imagining skin covering the ridge of a long, straight collarbone hidden beneath a white cotton T-shirt. Closing her eyes, she ran her fingertips along the length of her own collarbone.

Chapter 9

Abi – Thursday 20 March 1986

'Right, you horrible lot! Are you ready to party?'

Mr Munro's voice boomed through the speakers set up on a temporary stage at one end of the gym. When the guitar riff blasted, all the girls did exactly what Prince said, and went crazy. From every corner they flooded the basketball court, their every movement caught in the disco lights flashing on the stage. The boys stayed around the edges of the gym, leaning against the walls.

From her position up in the tiered seating, Abi was almost level with the swags of crepe paper criss-crossing the ceiling and the giant cardboard Easter eggs suspended from the basketball hoops. She took a sip of the orange squash she had bought from the prefects' refreshment table and coughed it back into the cup.

'This is disgusting,' she said to Penny sitting beside her. 'It's weak and warm and why the hell does it taste of soap?'

'"Love Cats",' Penny shouted into her ear.

'What?' Abi shouted back.

'The Cure. That's what Mouldy Munro's going to play for them.' She pointed to the goths standing in a huddle of serious black on the opposite side of the court.

'"Tainted Love",' Abi said, putting the plastic cup down on the floor while simultaneously yanking at the front of the pink boob tube she was wearing. Maybe if she had more than a couple of pimples for a chest the stupid thing would stay up. 'Why did I let you talk me into borrowing this?'

'Because you look fantastic,' Penny said.

'No. *You* look fantastic in sequins and spangles and shit. I look like a freak.' Abi ruffled her hair and a shower of glitter hairspray fell onto her jeans. Her mum would have a fit if she knew she had let Shirl curl her hair, let alone put lip-gloss and blusher on her. No make-up and no pierced ears until she was eighteen, those were the rules. There was no specific rule about boob tubes, but she was pretty sure Mum wouldn't like them either. There was way too much skin on show. Showing skin was a definite no-no in Mum's rulebook.

'Mum asked me to check if your mum and dad are coming to their Easter drinks party?' Penny said, taking a sip of her orange.

Abi brushed the glitter from her collarbone. 'I don't think so. Mum's got a big do on at the Town Hall that day. She said she was going to send your mum a card to say they couldn't come. It's probably in the post.'

'Oh, okay,' Penny said.

Abi hated not telling Penny the whole truth. It *was* true that Mum was catering a party in the afternoon, but she'd be finished way before seven o'clock when Tony and Shirl's party was due to start. Mum's excuse this time was that she'd be too tired. But Abi knew it was just another excuse. She hadn't accepted any of Tony and Shirl's invitations to their drinks evenings. She could have made an effort, just this once.

'This is disgusting,' Penny said, wiping her mouth on the back of her hand. She dumped her cup on the floor and grabbed Abi's arm. 'Come on.'

'I don't want…' Abi protested. Penny yanked her arm harder.

The heaving crowd on the dance floor buffeted Abi as she shuffled self-consciously from one foot to the other.

'Nobody's looking!' Penny shouted. 'Just let yourself go.'

'I can't.'

'You dance in my room, don't you?'

'That's just in front of you. Nobody else can see me. I'll look stupid.'

'Nobody cares. See?'

Abi looked around. The floor was packed with groups of girls all laughing and dancing. Nobody was looking at anyone else; they were too busy having fun with their friends. Nobody was bitching or judging or poking fun. First-formers danced next to third-formers, second-formers with fourth-formers. Nobody seemed to notice they were dancing beside kids who they wouldn't even look at in the corridors tomorrow. It was like the normal rules of school had been suspended.

The intro to 'Into the Groove' came through the speakers and Penny grinned. 'Come on. I showed you the moves to this one. It's Madonna,' she said, as though Abi hadn't heard every beat and key change a hundred times on the radio. There was no point arguing with Penny, so Abi fell into step beside her. Some other girls joined them to form a circle and copied Penny's moves too. After Madonna, they danced to so many songs that Abi lost count. Their circle grew even bigger when some boys joined them for 'Baggy Trousers' and stayed for 'The Birdie Song' and 'The Hokey Cokey'. Mr Munro was even generous to the goths. He played 'Tainted Love', 'Love Cats' and 'Eloise', and Abi and Penny stayed on the dance floor for every song.

Nobody was looking at Abi. Nobody cared about her boob tube or her glittery hair. She didn't even mind when a bunch of clumsy boys bashed into her. Penny was right. It really was fun. She could have carried on dancing all night. But all too soon the sound of a slow saxophone came through the speakers. When George Michael began to sing the words of 'Careless Whisper', the floor emptied. Abi stood beside Penny in the row of girls lining up along one wall with the boys lining up opposite. Gradually individual boys crossed the floor to pick out girls to dance with. While she was considering making a break for the loo, Abi spotted someone crossing the floor towards them. She nudged Penny. 'Look.'

'He won't ask me.'

'I bet you fifty pence he does.'

Dean Henry, the captain of the football team, all six foot of him in a white shirt and jeans, was heading their way, his eyes fixed on Penny just like they had been over the Bunsen burner in chemistry for the last few weeks. He stopped and whispered in Penny's ear and she turned to Abi. 'Will you be okay?'

"Course. I need a wee anyway.' She moved in a bit closer so that only Penny could hear. 'And you owe me fifty pence.'

Penny wrinkled her nose before Dean took her hand and led her to the dance floor. Abi watched Dean slip his arms around Penny's waist and Penny reach to put her arms round his neck. They started to sway in time to the music. Or rather Penny swayed in time while Dean looked like he had a broom handle stuck up his back. Well, he was tall, good looking and the best footballer in the school, it wouldn't be fair if he was good at everything.

Abi turned to head for the loo but found her path blocked.

'All right, London?'

Oh, great. 'Fine,' she said. She tried to sidestep Thug but he stepped into her path again.

'Is it something I said?' he asked, leaning in closer so that she was nearly knocked sideways by his smell.

'Did you actually have a bath in your dad's Old Spice?' she said wafting her hand in front of her nose.

'Got to make a good impression for the ladies.' He popped the collar of his pink T-shirt. Abi burst out laughing. Other girls might have fallen for him since he'd sorted out his hair and started to dress better, but to her, he was and always would be, Thug.

'You know, you scrub up all right, London,' he said. 'Play your cards right and I might just dance with you.'

'What?'

'Oh, go on then, since you insist.' He reached for her hand but she snatched it away.

'You are joking, right?'

'Ah, come on, London. Don't play hard to get.' He smiled from the corner of his mouth. He'd had his braces removed too. 'You know you want to.'

'Have you gone psycho? I wouldn't dance with you if you were the last person on Earth.' She waited, expecting him to say something just as horrible back. But he didn't. He just looked down at her and even in the dark she could see triangles of colour bloom in his cheeks.

'Yeah,' he said, kicking at something on the floor, 'course I was joking. As if I'd dance with a fucking loser like you. Are you mental?' He turned his back on her and began pushing his way through the crowd towards his mates on the other side of the gym.

Abi watched him go. He couldn't be serious. Penny got to dance with the best-looking boy in school and she got Thug. It had to be a bet. Yes, that's what it was. His mates had put him up to it. That's why he was pissed off. Because he'd have to go back to them and tell them he'd lost the bet. What a freak.

Still trying to work out Thug's game, Abi headed for the girls' changing room. Her footsteps echoed around the empty corridor.

She was finishing up in a cubicle when the volume of the music rose and fell as the door to the changing room opened and then closed. She unlocked the stall and was heading for the sinks when she sensed someone behind her.

'Well if it isn't lezzer. And without her girlfriend to hold her hand.'

Abi froze. *Keep calm, leave quickly with no fuss.* Without lifting her eyes from the floor, she turned and headed for the door.

'I don't think so, do you, London?' Tracey leant against the door, her arms folded across her chest. 'You,' she said staggering forwards so that Abi had to take a step back, 'are a fucking slag. I've always hated you. But tonight...' She stumbled and had to right herself. 'Tonight I really fucking hate you.'

The heel of one of Tracey's white stilettos was missing its rubber cap and it tapped on the tiles as she moved forwards, forcing Abi to back away towards the row of sinks. 'And what the fuck do you think you look like? All that glitter. Do you think you're a fucking fairy or something?'

'No,' Abi said. The cold sink pressed against her spine where the back of the boob tube had ridden up.

'Well who the fuck do you think you are then?'

'Nobody,' Abi said. Maybe if she said what Tracey wanted to hear she would back off. Tracey's eyes narrowed and her pupils slid around under her eyelids.

'That's right. You… are… a… nobody.' With each word, she dug a sharp nail into Abi's bare shoulder. 'So why the fuck did you ask Thug to dance with you?'

'I didn't, he–'

'Don't lie! He told us you begged him.' Tracey's face was so close that Abi could see the blue mascara gloop in the corner of her eyes and smell the booze on her breath. Before she realised what was happening, Tracey grabbed her face. She gripped so hard that Abi felt her own teeth dig into the inside of her cheeks.

'Get it through your thick skull. Thug is mine. He wouldn't look at you. Understand?'

Abi couldn't speak so she tried to nod, and Tracey caught her looking towards the door.

'No point looking for your girlfriend. She's not coming to save you this time. She's dancing with that fuckwit, Henry.'

Abi squirmed. Tracey smiled. 'Oh, hit a nerve, have I? Jealous, are you, that your girlfriend's found herself a boyfriend? Ah, poor little lezzer.'

Abi squirmed again and Tracey dug her fingers in harder. 'It's just you and me, London.' Tracey grinned. 'So, what are were going to do with you?'

Abi had a good idea what Tracey wanted to do with her and had no intention of hanging around for it. It was now or never. Summoning all of her strength and courage, she raised her arms, pressed her hands to Tracey's chest and pushed, hard. Tracey clearly wasn't expecting the challenge because she stumbled backwards. Abi seized the opportunity to barge past her but on her way to the door she heard an almighty crash. She spun around and saw Tracey stumble. The metal tip of her shoe scraped along the tiles, leaving a long white line like chalk on a blackboard as she disappeared into a cubicle. And then it went quiet.

Abi paused with her hand on the door. A voice in her head told her to run. Another told her to stay. Tracey might be hurt. She couldn't just leave her. She might have cracked her head on the toilet. She might throw up and choke on her own sick.

Abi tiptoed back to the cubicle, peered inside and found Tracey wedged between the toilet and the wall, her skirt hitched up so that the pale, flabby skin at the top of her legs was on show along with her grubby pink knickers.

Abi tried not to look at her knickers as she nudged Tracey's leg with her foot. 'Tracey... Tracey... Are you okay?' When she didn't respond, Abi nudged her harder. Suddenly Tracey jerked to life, her arms flailing, babbling something that sounded like, 'Fucking kill you.' She didn't look capable of getting up never mind starting anything, but Abi wasn't prepared to risk it.

By the time she had run the length of the corridor, the crowds were spilling through the gym doors.

'Abi! Abi!' Penny called from the middle of the throng, waving and pushing her way towards her. Penny smiled. 'Dean's asked if we want to go to Burgerillos with him and his friends.'

'Yeah sure. Burgerillos,' Abi said, still trying to catch her breath. She grabbed Penny's hand and dragged her towards Dean and his mates who were hanging around by the doors.

'What's the rush?' Penny laughed.

'I'm starving. Come on.'

'What's happened to your face? Are those scratch marks?'

Abi put her hand to her face and rubbed her cheek. 'I'm just hot. Come on. You don't want to keep Dean waiting.' She gripped Penny's hand tighter and pulled her out into the cold night air.

Part 2

Chapter 10

Gertie – Friday 28 July 1944 – Morning

Gertie woke early. She pulled back the kitchen curtain and opened the window to a beautiful summer's morning. A warm breeze brought with it the green scent of fresh-cut grass. Gertie took a stub of bread from the cupboard, tore off a small chunk, crumbled it between her palms, and sprinkled the crumbs onto the windowsill. While she waited for the kettle to boil, the resident blackbird flew down from the poplar tree to peck at the crumbs, his orange beak and glossy black feathers glorious in the sunshine.

It hardly seemed a fair trade. Each morning he gave her the gift of his song and all she had to offer in return was a handful of stale crumbs. The loaf may be two days past its best, but she would get into terrible trouble if someone saw her and reported her for wasting food.

The kettle whistled making the blackbird fly away. Gertie poured the steaming water onto a spoon of leaves in the teapot. When this war was over, she would go down into the garden every morning and scatter fresh cake all over the lawn for the birds to feast on, and sod the prying eyes of Mrs Lane at number twenty-two.

Between sips of her tea, Gertie prepared a plate of food. Just a bit of boiled tongue and a couple of cold potatoes, which she wrapped in a clean tea towel so that it wouldn't spoil. It was highly unlikely that Sid would make it home from the fire station at lunchtime as planned since he had warned her the night before that he had volunteered for an extra shift. But she prepared the food anyway, just in case; she didn't like to think that Sid might come home to find no meal on the table.

Forgoing breakfast since Sally's sister, Enid, had said there should be a scone or two to be had at Woolworths if they got there early enough, Gertie headed to the bathroom where she quickly bathed in a finger's depth of tepid water. In the bedroom, she dusted powder on her nose, rubbed some Vaseline into her eyelashes, and applied just a small amount of Ivy's hand-me-down red lipstick.

As a special treat, Gertie dressed in one of her prettiest dresses – a short-sleeved shift dress in a blue and white checked fabric. She fastened the tiny blue buttons, which ran all the way from the hem to the collar, and secured the blue belt around her waist. As an extra special treat, she took a cardboard box down from the top shelf of the wardrobe. Her best shoes usually only saw the light of day for birthday parties, weddings and Christmas. But why shouldn't she wear them today when they were going to have a lovely tea and then go to the park for Brian to run to his heart's content so that she, Sally and Enid could chat and coo over baby Rosemary? Sally and Enid always made an effort to look nice and she might not have another occasion to want to feel glamorous for some time.

To get to Lewisham for ten o'clock, Gertie had to take the Underground to London Bridge and a bus from there so, at just before nine o'clock, she turned from her street onto Brixton Road, enjoying the click-clack the heels of her tan suede court shoes made on the pavement.

At Stockwell station she bought a ticket and rode the escalator down to the platform as a train whistled down the tunnel. It was a short journey to London Bridge, where she emerged once again into daylight. There were a few clouds gathering in the sky out towards the east but nothing significant, and certainly not enough to spoil their plans for the day. Gertie waited only a few minutes for a bus to arrive and took a seat on the lower deck.

'All aboard!' The conductress called and rang the bell. 'So where are we going today?' she asked Gertie. 'New York, Monte Carlo, Paris or Plaistow?'

Gertie smiled and handed the conductress her fare. 'I should be so lucky. Just Lewisham High Street for today please. And would you mind letting me know when we're there? I'm not too familiar with the area.'

The conductress punched a ticket and handed it to Gertie. 'Don't worry, lovey,' she said. 'I'll give you a nod when we're a few stops away.'

The conductress moved off down the aisle, swaying in perfect time with the motion of the bus and expertly manoeuvring through the narrow aisle; no mean feat since her backside was almost wide enough to touch both rows of seats at once. She stopped to share a joke with an old lady and the volume of her laughter gave the rumble of the engine a fair run for its money.

Gertie settled back into her seat, popped her purse into her bag, and pulled out her knitting. Freeing the needles from the spool of red wool, which until last week had been one of Arthur's little waistcoats that he had outgrown, she spread the body of a tiny cardigan out in her lap. One sleeve was already attached and Gertie counted the rows on the needle. If she worked quickly, there was a chance she might finish the second sleeve in time to stitch it to the body before the bus arrived in Lewisham.

Her needles soon fell into a rapid *tip-tap*, *tip-tap* and by the time the conductress came and took hold of the strap above Gertie's head, she had cast off the sleeve.

'Three more stops and we'll be there,' the conductress said, swaying as the bus turned a corner. She pointed to the knitting. 'Ahh that's a bonny thing. For your little one is it?'

'No,' Gertie said, running a finger over the ridges of the tiny cuff. 'It's for my friend's little girl. I was hoping to surprise her with it today.'

'Oh isn't that sweet. I've got a scarf on the go for my granddaugh–' the conductress began. Her words trailed away as the sound of a mechanical buzz overtook the rumble of the bus. She looked up. 'It's all right, lovey. You know what they say, it's only when the racket stops that you have to worry.'

Gertie held her breath. The old lady sitting at the front of the bus looked up. So did the man who had taken a seat across the aisle from her. Even the driver in his cab leant forward, craning to see into the sky. Gertie said a rushed, silent prayer. *Please don't let it stop. Please let it carry on. I promise to be a good person from now on if you'll just let it fall somewhere far away from here and far away from any other people.*

The metal casing of the bus muffled the path of her words to heaven. The buzzing stopped. The brakes of the bus let out a terrific screech. Gertie was thrown forward like a rag doll in the grip of an angry child. She closed her eyes, thrust out her hands, desperate to brace for the impact. Before she could make contact with anything, a brilliant white light filled the bus. It penetrated her eyelids. She was lifted clear from her seat. She floated briefly, suspended in air, before crashing down. She landed back in her seat and something very large and very heavy fell on top of her.

In the seconds that followed, there was nothing. Blackness. Silence. Complete and utter stillness. As though all of the air had been sucked from the world. Was this it? Was she dead? Was her soul being drawn from her body? As soon as the thought crossed Gertie's mind, the world came hurtling back, bringing with it the unmistakable cries and moans of injured people.

Gertie tried to move. But she was trapped, pinned to the seat by whatever had landed on her. She felt no pain, just a rising sense of panic. Each breath came shallower than the last; her chest crushed by the heavy weight. She tried to cry out. It came out as nothing more than a wheeze. Her heart raced.

And then as if he were present, Sid's urgent, steady voice came into her head. *'If you ever get trapped, don't panic. Stay calm but fight to get out and don't stop fighting till you're free. Don't give up. Whatever you do, do not give up.'*

With the encouragement of Sid's words ringing in her ears, Gertie filled her lungs as far as she could. She twisted from side to side. The small movement was just enough to free first one arm and then the other. She groped around, trying to work out what it was that had fallen onto her. Blindly she ran her hands over the object. Her fingers came across something hard and cold with a leather strap attached to it. She followed the strap and found what felt like shoulders. With every ounce of strength she had left, she pushed. The weight fell from her and slumped to the floor.

Dazzled by the sudden return of daylight and gasping to catch her breath, Gertie saw that every window in the bus had shattered. The floor was littered with glass. Some large shards had even embedded into the cushions of the seats. Pulling herself hastily together, she sank to her knees beside the conductress who had come to rest on her back in the aisle.

'Miss… Miss. I'm sorry. You were crushing me.' Gertie took hold of the conductress' hand. Her fingers snagged on something sharp. She turned the hand over. The chubby flesh was peppered with splinters of glass. Gertie rested the conductresses' arm across her stomach. It was then that she noticed the dark pool forming around the conductress' head and trickling into the wooden grooves of the bus floor.

'Oh God. Oh no. Please someone help!' Gertie yelled. She looked around, hoping that another of the passengers would hear and come to her aid. Instead she saw the man across the aisle slouched in his seat, clutching his neck and making an awful rattling noise. The old lady had fallen from her seat and was laying in the aisle with one of her legs at a terrible angle, the contents of her handbag – an identity card, a ration book, a handkerchief and a small black purse – spilled out across the floor.

'Please,' Gertie shouted again. 'There are people in here that need help.'

A pair of heavy boots thudded onto the back of the bus. 'Anyone injured in here?' a man called.

'Over here, please,' Gertie said. A man wearing a tin hat made his way to her, his boots crunching on the glass littering the floor. Another man followed him onto the bus and ran up the stairs to the upper deck, taking the steps two at a time.

Gertie held onto the back of the seat and pulled herself to her feet but not before she straightened the conductress' skirt so that her pink petticoat was no longer on display. The man knelt beside the conductress. His examination took just seconds.

'She's gone,' he said and ran his hand over her face to close her eyes. He removed his hat and briefly held it to his chest before returning it to his head. He stood up and secured the strap under his chin. 'Are you all right?' he asked Gertie.

'Yes, yes, I'm fine. She fell on me and…'

The man puffed out his cheeks. 'You should thank your lucky stars. Looks like she took the brunt of the blast and the glass. If it wasn't for her…' He looked Gertie up and down. 'Well, anyway, you best go to the ARP station in the park. They'll patch you up there.'

He moved off towards the old lady and another man in a tin hat boarded the bus. Gertie moved aside to give him access to the man clutching his neck. She grabbed her handbag and stumbled from the bus.

People filled the road, running in every direction. They were shouting, pointing, yelling. Debris was scattered across the ground, glass, dust, broken roof tiles. An ARP man pushed through the hysterical crowd. He took hold of Gertie's arm. She looked back at the bus. Apart from the shattered windows it appeared relatively unscathed.

'How?' she said. 'If a bomb fell on it.'

'The bomb didn't fall on it,' the ARP man said as he guided her through the crowds. 'It was the blast wave what blew the windows out. It fell on the High Street. Doodlebug, it was. Direct hit.' He pointed, and Gertie followed the direction of his finger to a plume of smoke rising high in the sky just a few streets away. The clatter of bells of two fire engines and an ambulance racing down the street made Gertie flinch.

'Come on, dear, let's get you seen to,' the ARP man said.

'But my friend and her children. And her sister. They're waiting for me. I have to get to them.'

'Where are they, dear? If they're close by we might be able to take you to them.'

'Woolworths. They're waiting for me at Woolworths.'

She saw a look pass over the man's face. 'Come on, dear. Let's get you a cuppa and get you patched up.'

She let him guide her into a park where a crowd had gathered just inside the gates.

'That's right,' a woman said. 'Marks and Sparks and Woolies. Both gone.'

Gertie stopped. She pulled her arm from the ARP man. She ran to the woman. 'Did you say Woolies?'

'Yes, love. My lad just cycled from there. Thank God he works just off the High Street. He said it's all but razed to the ground. Whole bloody lot of it gone. Reckons there's little chance of any survivors, what with the state it's in.'

Gertie didn't hear anything else. She turned and stumbled back through the gates and out onto the road.

She pushed through the crowds towards the High Street. But a policeman was stopping anyone heading in that direction. She looked around. Nothing was familiar. Everything was odd. There was no Sally, no Brian, no Rosemary.

Gertie sank to the pavement with her feet in the gutter. More people filled the road. Some came from houses to sweep up glass and broken roof slates, others ran from the direction of the High Street. They all talked so loudly. They gawped at the smoke rising high into the sky. An ambulance screamed past. Gertie slammed her hands over her ears to block out the tales of limbs lying in gutters or blasted up in trees. The world had turned into a gruesome carnival parade.

A mobile WVS canteen arrived in the park and the ARP man and a woman from the van came and sat on either side of her.

'Come on, drink this,' the woman said and held a mug of tea to Gertie's mouth. The man tried to convince her to go to the first-aid station, but she refused to be moved. When a bus eventually arrived, already packed with passengers, they helped Gertie to her feet and the ARP man insisted the conductor squeeze her on. A man stood to let her sit and she rode back to London Bridge where she boarded the Underground. Other passengers kept looking at her and a few asked whether she needed help.

'No, I'm perfectly fine,' she replied. She didn't need help. There was nothing wrong with her. Not like that poor conductress whose eyes she could still see looking up at her, like the empty eyes of a doll. If she hadn't fallen and landed on her then... Gertie fumbled to light a cigarette and when the train pulled into Kennington she changed to the Waterloo branch of the Northern line.

Emerging from Charing Cross station into the daylight, she blinked, unsure why she had made the journey to the office on Friday when it was closed. She thought about taking the bus to her parents but decided against it. There would be fussing and questions.

Overwhelmed by the need to sit down, she walked to the end of The Strand. She crossed the road and a taxi beeped angrily when she forgot to look both ways. She sank onto a bench in Trafalgar Square. Sally and the children wouldn't have been in Woolworths, would they? She crossed her arms around her waist and held herself tight. Her teeth began to chatter in spite of the heat of the day. She had no idea how long she had been sitting there when someone spoke to her. 'Gertie... Gertie... it is you.'

The bench dipped as someone sat beside her.

Chapter 11

On a full moon night, Cliff Cottage stood alone in the path of a spring storm. The wind whipped around the house making it creak like a boat tossed on the sea. Even the windowpanes rattled in their frames.

Abi was so used to the changing sounds of the seasons that she barely noticed the wind howling down the chimney as she sat on the rug in the attic, hunched over an open textbook, surrounded by the debris of a Friday night English lit revision session: balled-up sheets of paper, a half-eaten packet of chocolate chip cookies, the crumbs of a family-size bag of cheese and onion crisps, and four empty cola cans. But after two hours of trying to fathom why God would want a crow to say the word 'love', the only thing she had succeeded in working out was that Ted Hughes had clearly been on something when he wrote it.

'I love this view,' Abi heard Penny say. Abi stopped chewing the end of her pencil and looked up. Penny was standing at the window, her forehead resting against the glass, her nightdress shifting slightly in the breeze that crept around the ill-fitting frame. She had one bare foot crossed over the other and her dark hair hung loose over her shoulders and down to her waist. 'It's so romantic here. Like something out of *Wuthering Heights* or *Jamaica Inn*.'

Abi snapped her poetry book shut. 'You're soft in the head.' She stretched her arms above her head, clicking each vertebra back into its proper place. 'This is a creaking old house in the middle of nowhere. There is nothing, repeat, nothing, romantic about that.'

Penny sighed and flopped down on the bed making Cyril, who was tucked into a perfect nose-to-tail circle, rise and fall as if he were riding a wave. She grabbed a magazine and flicked through the pages before sighing and chucking it to the floor. Then she arranged her books into a neat pile, shuffled her papers into order and placed them on the floor before wiping some biscuit crumbs from the blanket, plumping up a pillow, and sitting back.

'What's wrong with you?' Abi said running her bare toes along the matted fringe of the rug. 'You've been in a funny mood all night. I've never seen Miss Swot of the Year 1986 give up on revision before. Especially not English.'

It was meant as a joke, but Penny didn't smile. She yanked a blanket from the end of the bed and wrapped it around her shoulders so that her head poked out like a tortoise peeking out from its shell. 'Tell me again what we're going to do when this is all over?' Penny said, nodding to the books and folders and pens and pencils strewn across the floor.

'Well I thought I might brush my teeth and wash my face and—'

'Funny. Not!' Penny pulled a face and stuck out her tongue. 'You know what I mean.'

'Oh, you mean what are we going to do in about a billion years, when we've finished A-levels?' Abi pushed her poetry book away. 'I wouldn't get your hopes up. I'll be lucky to scrape Ds and Es in my O-levels. They probably won't even let me stay on for sixth form in September.'

Penny sighed again. She crossed her legs, rested her elbows on her knees, cupped her chin in her palms, and chewed her bottom lip; a sure sign she was thinking about something else.

'Oh cheers. Thanks for your vote of confidence,' Abi teased.

'What? Oh, don't be stupid. Of course you'll pass your O-levels. Anyway, I'm not talking about exams. It's just… well… and don't bite my head off, but I mentioned Europe to my mum today. And before you say anything, I know I shouldn't have bothered but she was driving me mad. And do you know what she said? She said that it wouldn't happen in a million years. She said if I couldn't be trusted to get myself up in the morning, how could I ever be trusted to look after myself travelling around Europe on a train for a month.'

It was Abi's turn to sigh now. 'God, Penny. What did you go and do that for? They're never going to agree to us going off on our own.'

'I know, I know, but I wanted to prove that I can make my own decisions. She's still bugging me to do that ballet recital even though I told her I need to revise for my exams. She said I should be able to do both.' Penny paused to flick her hair over her shoulder. She puckered her lips, warming up for one of her impressions of Shirl. '*Real life is about juggling priorities, Penelope. The sooner you learn that, the better. Do you think I became a successful business woman by keeping just one ball in the air at a time?*' She sighed and balanced her chin in her palms again. 'Why can't she accept that I'm not a little kid any more? I feel like telling her to stick her ballet lessons up her... well, her you-know-where. Why should I carry on with stupid dancing for her when she won't let me do anything *I* want to?'

Abi couldn't bear to see Penny so miserable, not when it was in her power to make her best friend smile again. She reached for the tourist map balanced on a stack of books beside the fireplace and unfolded it on the bed, resting it against Penny's legs. 'Look,' she said, tracing the blue felt-tip pen line across the map of Europe with her finger. She stopped at the north of France. 'In two years' time it'll be first stop, Paris for the Eiffel Tower, the Arc De Triomphe and the Louvre. Then on to Rome to see the Trevi fountain and the Coliseum.'

'And then,' Penny said, finally smiling as she grabbed Abi's thread, 'onto Germany to spray some graffiti on the Berlin Wall and visit the Brandenburg Gate. Then to Amsterdam to ride a bike beside the canals and see Anne Frank's house. Oh, and the windmills, don't forget the windmills.'

'We'll spend every morning seeing the sights and every afternoon, you'll sit in pavement cafés, drinking coffee and reading your boring Oscar Wilde and Virginia What's-her-face novels and I'll set up my easel and sketch portraits of people to make us a few francs or lira or marks or… what's the currency of Holland again?'

'Guilders.' Penny grinned and gripped the blanket around her neck. 'And then when we get back, we'll go to uni in London. You'll study art at Saint Martin's and I'll read English at UCL. We'll share a flat and we'll meet loads of fantastically interesting people.'

'Precisely. And look.' Abi took a black metal box down from the mantelpiece and handed it to Penny.

'What am I supposed to be looking at?' Penny asked, eyeing up the gold and red decoration depicting pagodas and Chinese ladies.

'Duh! Don't the leaves they're picking and the teapots in their hands give you a clue?'

'Okay,' Penny said and shoved the metal box back at Abi. 'So it's an old tea caddy. What's so special about that?'

'My Nan gave it to me. I'm going to save up all my birthday and Christmas money and keep it in here. It'll be my Europe fund. I'm going to hide it under that loose floorboard under the rug so that even if someone robs the house, they won't find it.'

'That's brilliant. I want a tin and a Europe fund too.'

Abi laughed. 'Princess Penny doesn't need a crappy tin to keep her money in. All she has to do is ask her dad and he'll buy her a gold piggy bank decorated with diamonds and fill it with a thousand–'

'Shut up.'

'Shut up yourself, spoilt cow.' Abi laughed again. 'Anyway,' she said, flicking the edge of the map, hoping to look like she couldn't care either way, 'I was thinking how you've probably changed your mind about coming to Europe with me. I mean, you probably want to stay here and get married to Dean and have loads of babies. I can always find someone else to go with.'

Penny's face dropped. 'You do know you're not even funny, don't you? Promise me right here, right now, that we're going to Europe – *together* – and then to London. I'll die if I have to stay here all my life.'

'Won't Dean mind you running away?' Abi tried her best not to grin.

'It's not running away. And he can come and visit us in London. You won't mind, will you?'

'Not fussed,' Abi said. She grabbed the crisp packet, dug her hand inside and ran her finger around the bottom. 'So,' she said, pulling her hand free and sucking the crumbs from her finger, 'where's he taking you on your hot date tomorrow?'

'It's not a hot date. We're only going to the cinema. Come if you want.'

'And play the gooseberry? No fear.'

'Dean could bring one of his friends.'

'Err, no thanks.'

'Ed said he would go out with you, if you wanted.'

'Ed with the spots and hair like pubes? Thanks a lot.'

'Not Ed then. Don't you fancy any of Dean's friends, not even just a little bit?'

'Well, if you could wave a magic wand and turn one of them into Rob Lowe...'

'Seriously, Abi.'

'I am being serious.'

Penny folded the map and placed it on the floor. 'Dean's friends are all right. You could do a lot worse, you know.'

Abi rolled her eyes. *Here we go again*, she thought. Penny trying to fix her up. Why was it so hard for Penny to understand that she just wasn't interested? Not in Dean's mates or any other boy at school. They were immature idiots who spent all their time trying to ping girls' bra straps or cop a feel in the playground. Besides, she didn't need a boyfriend when she had Penny.

'I just don't see what the fuss is about. All you get out of having a boyfriend is holding hands and having a snog, and I can get a snog any time I want from Cyril. Can't I boy?' At the sound of his name Cyril raised his head and Abi offered her nose to him. He dutifully gave her a lick before tucking back into a ball.

'You really are the most gross person I have *ever* met.' Penny laughed. 'But I tell you who *does* want to snog you.' She leant over the edge of the bed like she was about to share a secret. 'Thug!'

As soon as the name left Penny's lips, she pulled the blanket over her head to hide from the pencil Abi grabbed and launched at her.

'Get lost!'

'Oh, come on,' Penny laughed, emerging from the blanket. 'You must have seen how his tongue hits the floor every time you walk past him. And he's not that bad now he's had his hair sorted. My dad says he's been picked to play for the seniors' team at the cricket club.'

'If you like him so much why don't you go out with him?'

'Duh. Because I'm going out with Dean. Anyway, Thug's not in *lurve* with me.' Penny laughed again.

'Well you should go out with Thug. You'd be a perfect match. You're both idiots. And even if I did like him – which I don't – have you forgotten that he belongs to Tracey Evans?'

Penny's smile dropped. 'I still can't believe you won't let me tell anyone about what she did to you at the disco. The headmaster should know at least. She can't go around threatening to beat people up and getting away with it. You should have told me at the time. I'd have gone into those toilets and… well I don't know what I'd have done. But it would have been something.'

'Why do you think I didn't tell you? I was lucky to get out of there without getting my face pushed in. Anyway, you should be thanking me for saving you from seeing her knickers. Gross!'

'But it's just not right. Her walking around school like Lady Muck because she got away with bullying you.'

'I was the one that got away with it. I'm lucky she was drunk and can't remember that I pushed her over. She'd kill me if she knew.'

'*Maybe* she does know.' Penny grinned. 'But *maybe* Thug has warned her to back off. He wouldn't want to see the face he loves getting all mashed up, would he?' Penny lay back on the pillow and began to hum before singing, '*Abi and Alan sitting in a tree. KISSING.*'

'Shut it, stupid. I wouldn't touch him with yours,' Abi said. It just made Penny sing even louder so Abi jumped to her feet and headed for the stack of books by the fireplace. Finally, Penny stopped singing.

'What are you doing?' she asked.

'None of your beeswax.'

'Tell me.'

Abi looked back over her shoulder. 'If you must know, I'm looking for that Jackie Collins book we borrowed from the library. I want to check what it is you should be doing with Dean. Remember? What those people got up to in the swimming pool and in the trailer and in the hotel room?'

Penny grabbed the pillow and chucked it at Abi, but it fell short and landed by her feet. 'Abiiii! I can't believe you said that. You're disgusting and dirty and evil.'

'Me?' Abi laughed, and dragged the pillow back to the bed. 'I'm not the one going out with Dean Henry. And you need to be ready for when he tries it on. You wouldn't want any nasty surprises.' She sat down on the edge of the bed and gripped the pillow to her stomach.

'He wouldn't dare try it on,' Penny said, tugging the pillow from Abi. 'He knows I'm not that kind of girl.'

Abi watched Penny plump the pillow, lay down, and crawl beneath the blankets. She couldn't help smiling. Dean was no threat. Not really. Boys didn't like nice girls like Penny, who didn't do *it*. Even nice boys like Dean. And when he dumped Penny – which he would – Abi would be there to pick up the pieces of Penny's broken heart. They would run off to Europe and then to London. Just the two of them.

Penny threw back the blanket. 'Get in! It's freezing in here.'

Abi clambered under the covers and lay facing Penny. They were crammed so close in the single bed that their noses almost touched. Penny pulled the blanket up and tucked it around their shoulders but when her feet made contact with Abi's, she shrieked. 'Your feet are like blocks of ice!'

'Warm them for me then,' Abi said and felt Penny's warm feet rub against hers. 'We will go to Europe, you know,' she said. 'We'll be eighteen. We can do what we want. No one can stop us.'

Penny smiled. 'Promise me something else. That no matter what happens in the future, we'll always be friends.'

'Of course, stupid. Who else would come and eat snails and frog legs on Champs Elysees with me?'

'Or bratwurst in Berlin.'

'Or pizza in Rome.'

'Or... or... actually I don't know what they eat in Holland.'

'Cheese,' Abi said. 'Edam.'

Penny freed her hand from the blanket and held up her little finger.

'Aren't we a bit old for this?' Abi said. But Penny thrust her crooked little finger at her again.

'Pinky promise,' Penny demanded.

'What am I promising?'

'That we'll be friends forever.'

Abi gripped Penny's finger. 'Pinky promise that we'll be friends forever.'

'To the ends of the Earth and back again?'

'To the ends of the Earth and back again,' Abi repeated.

Satisfied, Penny released Abi's finger and settled into the pillow. Abi listened for a few minutes to Penny's attempts to explain why a crow might say 'love'. Gradually her words trailed away so that the only sound in the room was the whine of the wind outside. Penny's long, dark eyelashes began to flutter. Abi waited, watching. Once she saw the blankets rhythmically rise and fall with Penny's soft breath, she eased back the covers and slipped from the bed. She crossed the room. A floorboard creaked. Penny murmured. Abi stood perfectly still. When Penny settled, Abi slipped her sketchbook from her satchel. She sat cross-legged on the rug and looked up at the bed.

Penny was facing her with eyes closed. Abi flipped open the pad and picked up her favourite pencil. Working quickly, she sketched the sleeping form of her best friend. Her face, her dark hair spread out on the white pillow, the way her body was contained in a small patch of the bed. Penny always slept curled up, like a small creature sleeping beneath the leaves in a forest.

With a final flick, Abi added the curl that tumbled from the pillow and hung down the side of the bed. She put the pencil aside and took a moment to leaf through the other sketches in the book. It wasn't her normal sketchbook. It was her secret sketchbook. Her heart raced a little faster as she relived the drawing of each picture. Penny in the garden playing with Cyril. Penny studying at the kitchen table. Penny curled up in Granddad's chair, looking into the flames of the fire in the parlour. Each moment had been captured without Penny realising. She had refused every one of Abi's requests to sketch her. She was bashful about posing. But with no need. She was so very beautiful.

Abi pushed the sketchbook into her satchel. Carefully picking her way across the room, she slipped back into bed. Cyril made his way stealthily up the bed to lie in the slight dip between Abi and Penny's legs. The movement made Penny stir. Abi waited for her to settle. She stroked Cyril's ears, fighting the urge to put her fingertip to Penny's eyelashes to find out whether they felt as soft as they appeared. She reached to switch off the lamp and tucked in behind Penny.

Closing her eyes, she listened to Penny's soft breath in the darkness. Penny's warm body felt as familiar to her as her own. With images of canals and cafés floating through her mind and Penny's hair brushing her cheek, she drifted into a peaceful sleep. And all the while the spring storm raged outside the house.

Chapter 12

Rose – Saturday 24 August 1963

From her position halfway up the stairs, Rose looked down at Arthur. He was resting with his back against that wall, the tip of one of his highly polished shoes balancing on the skirting board. He looked uncharacteristically smart in a suit with a thin black tie and was keeping himself occupied by twirling the keys for the Morris Minor around his index finger. Rose managed to descend a few more steps without being noticed and couldn't resist a little joke at his expense. 'So how long exactly did you spend in front of the mirror greasing your hair?' she asked.

'For your information, Miss Know-it–' Arthur started. But when he turned and looked up the stairs, the keys fell limp in his hand. He put his thumb and forefinger in his mouth and let out a shrill wolf whistle, bringing Father and Uncle Henry from the parlour, and Mother and Auntie Ruth from the kitchen.

'Oh, Rose!' her mother said, holding a tea towel to her face. 'You look so beautiful. Look, Ruth! Look at my little girl all grown up. It doesn't seem five minutes since I was plaiting her hair and now look at her. I can't believe it. Her first proper dance.' A tear hovered on her mother's eyelashes and Auntie Ruth handed her a hankie before turning her attention to Arthur's foot.

'Arthur! Get your shoe down from that wall. You'll ruin that wallpaper,' she said, a frown knitting her eyebrows together.

'I'm not a child,' Arthur mumbled under his breath. He moved his foot anyway.

'Less of your lip,' Uncle Henry said. 'Have a bit of respect for your mother and for other people's property.'

Arthur tutted and moved aside bumping into Rose who, despite the crush in the hall, had made it down the last few steps. She stumbled and had to steady herself by holding onto the banister.

'Come on now,' her father said, putting himself between Rose and the rest of her family. 'Give the girl some space.' He tucked his newspaper under his arm and took Rose's hands in his. 'Lovely,' he said quietly, looking her up and down. 'Absolutely lovely.'

Rose smiled. Of all the people in the world, she knew she could trust her father to give her an honest opinion. He was as incapable of telling a lie as he was of going a single day without checking the newspaper for England's cricket score. She put her arms around his neck and kissed him on the cheek. 'Thank you, Dad.'

'Careful now,' he laughed. 'You don't want to go and crease your posh frock now, do you?'

'I don't care.' She rested her head on his shoulder. He smelled of Brylcreem and Old Holborn. He smelled of Dad. After giving her an awkward sort of pat on the back, he took a step away, coughed and fumbled in his pocket. He pulled out his wallet, took out a note and handed it to Arthur. 'Here,' he said. 'Have a good time. But not too much drinking. I want you to bring her back safe and sound. You hear?'

Arthur folded the note, tucked it into his breast pocket and gave a little salute. 'Aye, aye Cap'n'.' He crooked his arm and offered it to Rose. 'Come on then m'lady. Your chariot awaits.'

***

Rose stood beside Arthur in the queue outside the Town Hall, looking around at the people thronging the market square. It was still light, and the evening air was thick with the warm scent of summer mixed with sweet perfume and the sharp tang of vinegar from the fish and chip shop across the road. The men in the queue for the dance all looked so smart in suits and ties and the girls so pretty in their best dresses. The square was alive with their chatter and with music floating through the open windows. Rose felt like she was standing in the very heart of Bridport. Perhaps that's why her own heart was beating so rapidly. In competition. She felt for the pulse in her wrist. It was far quicker than it ought to be at rest.

'Good night for it.' She heard Arthur say and looked up quickly to see to whom he was talking. But it was nobody she recognised.

'Not much chance of a seat,' Arthur shouted into her ear when they finally made it through the surging crowd into the dark function room. 'I said we should have got here earlier.' He craned his neck and surveyed the room while Rose fanned her face with her hand. All of the chairs at the tables circling the packed dance floor were occupied and the people without seats milled around in large groups, smoking cigarettes, drinking, smiling, leaning in close to each other to make themselves heard over the records a man up on the stage at the far end was playing.

'Drink?' Arthur asked. He pointed to the bar running along one wall which, apart from the candles on the tables, provided the only light in the room.

Rose nodded. 'Something with lots of ice. It's so hot in here.'

'You want to try wearing this.' Arthur tugged at the collar of his jacket. 'Wait here for me. Okay? I don't want you going AWOL in this mob.'

'Okay.'

Arthur began his push towards the bar and with nobody to talk to, Rose turned her attention to the dance floor. There was a row of girls lined up along one side with a row of boys lined up opposite; looking for all the world like pawns on a chess board. When it seemed as though nobody would ever make a move, a boy suddenly plucked up the courage to break the stalemate. With his shoulders back but his face turned down to the floor, he manoeuvred through the dancing couples and came to a stop before a pretty girl with straight, black hair. He leant towards her and whispered into her ear. It took a little encouragement and nudging from her friends, but finally the girl nodded and followed him on to the floor to join everyone else in The Twist, swinging their hips from side to side while twisting their arms in the opposite direction. Rose looked back along the row of chaps. She looked at the fair-haired, the red and the dark; the tall, the short and the fat. *Stop looking,* she told herself. *You're here with Arthur.* Bedsides, it was still early.

Eventually Arthur returned and shoved a wide, shallow glass at her. 'Here,' he said and wiped his forehead with the cuff of his shirt. 'It's worse than the terraces at Upton Park on Dockers Derby day in there.'

Rose plucked a cocktail stick from the drink. 'What's this?'

Arthur raised his eyebrows. 'What does it look like, Rose? An elephant?'

'I can see it's a glace cherry, *Arthur.* I meant what's the drink?'

He grinned, a silly grin, which instantly put Rose on her guard. 'Babycham,' he said. 'It's just like lemonade. But with a little extra.'

Rose peered into the glass.

'Bloody hell, Rose. Live life on the edge for once, won't you?' Arthur nudged her elbow. 'Do you really think I'd poison you?'

She ran that idea around her head for a moment before taking a deep breath, raising the glass to her lips, and taking a tentative sip. The bubbly liquid tasted sour and smelled faintly of the white spirit her father kept in the garden shed to clean his paintbrushes. But after the initial shock, and much to her surprise, Rose's taste buds decided they were actually intrigued rather than repelled by this new taste and demanded another sip. She raised the glass to her lips for a second time and Arthur laughed.

'See,' he said. 'You should trust your old cousin. You'll have to learn to hold your grog if you're going to be a student. Those smart Alecs up in Haggisland'll be expecting you to down more than just one glass of sweet sherry of an evening. There's no time like the present to get some practice in.' He chinked his glass to hers. 'Down the hatch, couz.' He took a large mouthful of the dark brown liquid in his glass and swilled it around his mouth before swallowing it down.

'What's that?' Rose asked. Arthur held the glass up and swirled the liquid around, making a muddy-coloured wave wash around the inside of his glass. 'This, my dear, is rum. A proper man's drink. You'll need a few more hairs on your chest before you can handle this.' He smirked and took another sip. Rose was about to dig him in the ribs when she heard someone calling their names.

'Rose! Art! Oi. Art!'

Rose only had to look at the silly grin on Arthur's face to know to whom the high-pitched voice belonged. 'There she is,' he shouted as Mary elbowed her way towards them. With her hair piled up on top of her head and tottering on high heels, she was a good four inches taller than Rose remembered. Her dress, the colour of Chinese jade, was cut rather more tightly over the bust than her coffee shop uniform.

'Bloody Nora,' Mary said, puffing out her cheeks when she finally made it through the last line of people. 'I thought I was a goner in there.'

Arthur leant down and kissed her on the cheek. 'You look knockout, doll. Absolutely knockout. Drink?'

'Oh, ta. Gin and It, please.'

Arthur handed his glass to Mary and eased back into the scrum. She took a large swig then pulled a face and stuck out her tongue. 'Urgh, rum,' she said. 'I thought it was only pirates what drank that muck.'

Rose smiled and pointed to Mary's hair. 'I hardly recognised you.'

'D'you like it?' Mary said, patting the back of her head. 'My friend Shirley did it. She's training to be a hairdresser. She's ever so good. Half an hour of backcombing it took to get it all the way up there and almost a whole can of spray. Anyway, forget about me. Look at you. In't that the dress from *Maiden Heaven's* window.'

Rose ran her hand over the full skirt. 'I decided to treat myself.'

'Bloody hell. That's a treat and a half.' Mary eyed up Rose's dress like it was made from real gold rather than yellow satin. 'It looks even better on you than it did on the mannequin. Bet it cost a pretty penny though. *Maiden Heaven* ain't cheap.'

Rose hid her smile by taking a sip of her drink. She had only gone into the boutique the day before out of curiosity; to see what a clothes shop in Bridport had to offer. Somehow the saleslady had talked her into taking the dress into the changing room. How could she have known that the pencil thin straps, each decorated with a row of tiny white daisies, would have fitted so snugly over her shoulders, and the nipped in waist of the full skirt would have circled her so perfectly. When she had emerged from behind the curtain the saleslady had taken a step towards her and straightened out the skirt, saying that it could have been made for her and that nobody else had looked quite as pretty in it. It was that revelation that saw Rose pop into the Post Office and hand her passbook to the postmistress behind the counter.

Rose put her hand to her shoulder and ran her finger along the raised ridges of one of the tiny daisies. Yes, it was an extravagance. But living off nothing but baked potatoes for the first two weeks in Edinburgh would be worth it. Besides, she had saved money by wearing the white court shoes she had brought from home and borrowing a small white shoulder bag from Mother. She took another sip of her drink. Arthur emerged from the crowd and was about to pass a glass to Mary when she rushed forwards, almost knocking it from his hand. He jumped back, narrowly avoiding the gin splashing from the glass.

'It's Shirley!' Mary shouted, standing on tiptoes, waving her black handbag above her head. 'Oi, Shirl! Shirl, over here!' Rose followed the direction of Mary's waving and saw a woman making her way towards them. Unlike Arthur and Mary, this woman didn't have to use her elbows to force her way through; the crowd seemed to part for her. She placed one foot very precisely in front of the other, rather like a cat, and the eyes of the men who moved aside to let her pass fixed on her swaying hips as though they were magnetic. As she got closer, Rose saw that her close-fitting, black dress was trimmed at the strapless bodice and hem with red taffeta. With her dark hair pinned up high on her head in a series of intricate swirls held tightly in place, she gave the impression of a starlet painted on the side of an aeroplane in old Hollywood war film.

'This,' Mary said smiling broadly when she reached them, 'is my friend, Shirley.'

'All right?' Arthur said and held out his hand. 'I'm Art. Pleasure to meet you.'

Shirley took his hand and her eyes seemed to smile when she said, 'So you're the famous Art that's got our Mary all hot and bothered.'

'Shirl!' Mary said. Even in the darkness, Rose could see she was blushing. Arthur grinned and seized the opportunity to slip his arm around Mary's shoulders and pull her close.

'What can I say?' he said. 'She's only human.'

Shirley laughed – a deep laugh, which rumbled somewhere down in her ribcage. 'Looks like you've got yourself a right charmer there, Mary,' she said and tapped Arthur on the arm.

'So what about you?' Mary asked Shirley. 'Did you have to come on your own in the end?'

Shirley's smile dropped to a pout. 'What do you think? Mr Unreliable said he'd see me later. He wants to be careful. I had five blokes invite me tonight. One of these days I might just take one of them up on it.'

'You wouldn't!'

'I might,' she said, a wicked sort of smile returning to her lips.

'No you wouldn't.' Mary turned to Rose. 'You should see them together. If ever a couple was meant to be together it's the two of them.'

'That's what I'm talking about,' Shirley said, adjusting one of her concrete swirls. 'That's what he thinks too. And that's why he keeps me dangling like I was put on this Earth to be at his beck and call.' She turned to Rose. 'Don't know about you, love, but I reckon we'd all be better off without men.'

'Oh,' Arthur said, raising his eyebrows, pretending to be offended. 'Don't mind me, will you?'

'Sorry, darling.' Shirley's eyes flashed. 'Present company excepted.' She touched Arthur's arm again and Rose smiled. This Shirley was fun. A bit brash, but fun.

Arthur took his cigarettes from his breast pocket and offered them around. Both Shirley and Mary accepted. They huddled around Arthur's lighter, the flame illuminating their faces like they were warming their hands over a glowing brazier. Rose wiped the perspiration from her chest. It was certainly hot enough to believe they were standing around a burning dustbin.

'You don't smoke?' Shirley said to Rose. A plume of smoke hovered around her cherry-red lips before she sucked it down.

'I've never tried.'

'Good for you. It stunts your growth, so my old mum says. Not that it's done me any harm.' She thrust out her cleavage and her laugh rumbled up from her ribs again. 'So what do they call you then?'

'Rose.'

'Oh,' she said, dragging out the word to at least double its normal length, 'so *you're* the doctor that Mary's been telling me all about. Well, I'm pleased to make your acquaintance, Doctor Rose.'

It was Rose's turn to blush now. Nobody apart from Arthur had ever called her Doctor Rose and he only ever did it to annoy her. 'It'll be a while before I'm entitled to call myself that. But thank you. And it's a pleasure to meet you too, Shirley.'

Shirley flicked her wrist and a tube of ash floated to the floor. 'Call me Shirl. There's no need to stand on ceremony. Not now we're friends.' She took Rose's hand. 'Oh, look at me. I feel cleverer just touching you. Come on, I want to introduce my brainy new friend to the rest of the gang.'

Rose let herself be led through the crowd. Shirley may have felt cleverer just touching her but, with her hand in Shirley's, Rose certainly felt more popular. They stopped at a table beside the dance floor and Shirley pulled her forward. 'This, ladies and gents,' she announced in a break in the music, 'is my new friend, Rose. And this delectable creature,' she said, pointing to Arthur, 'is her cousin, Art. Mary's new beau.'

Arthur wasted no time in going around the table, introducing himself properly. He shook hands and cracked jokes making the chaps and Shirley laugh and the other girls giggle behind their hands. When Shirley left Rose to join Arthur, Mary stayed by her side. 'Just look at him,' Mary said. 'Isn't he dreamy? That accent makes me go weak at the knees. And all those freckles are like little drops of melted chocolate. I could just lick 'em off.'

Rose peered at Arthur and tried her hardest to see him through Mary's eyes. It was no good. All she saw was her silly cousin Arthur, messing around and acting the clown. When he came to the end of his one-man comedy show, Arthur drew some more chairs to the table and Shirley had him squeeze one in beside a chap in spectacles and a yellow turtleneck sweater.

'There you go, you sit there, love,' she said to Rose. 'Phillip here's just like you. Got brains coming out of his ears. You don't want to get lumbered with the rest of us. We haven't got two ounces of sense to rub together. You'd be bored in minutes. That's right isn't it, Phil? You'll keep an eye on Rose.'

Rose had barely taken her seat when Phillip took her hand. He shook it just a bit too enthusiastically and when she prised her hand from his grip, he introduced himself as a law student. He was home for the summer holiday and seemed very keen that she should hear all about his collection of antiquarian first editions and the boat his father kept in the harbour.

'I can take you out for a turn around the bay while you're here if you fancy it. I'm studying for my first mate's exam,' he said.

Rose smiled politely. Phillip was pleasant enough and if he noticed her constantly looking over his shoulder to the main door, he was too much of a gentleman to say anything. When Arthur returned to check on her, she grabbed his wrist. 'Won't you sit with us?' she said. 'Just for a few minutes. Phillip can tell you all about his father's boat.' But Arthur just laughed and placed another drink on the table in front of her.

'What?' he said. 'And deprive everyone else of my witty repartee. Sorry, Rosie, but no can do. I've got a room to work.'

Rose had no choice but to return to Phillip's take on where Britain had gone wrong in relation to the Suez crisis while the other couples gradually drifted from the table to the dance floor. Marooned with Phillip, Rose punctuated his seemingly bottomless pit of opinion with sips from her third glass of Babycham and she was just enjoying the sensation of the bubbles popping on her tongue when Phillip unexpectedly leant towards her.

'Do you want to dance?' he shouted and pushed his spectacles further up the bridge of his nose. 'I'm afraid I'm a bit of a clodhopper but I'm prepared to give it a whirl if you are.'

Rose leant back in her chair, trying to hide the fact that she was wiping his spittle from her ear. 'Thank you, but I think I'll sit this one out. Actually…' She looked towards the door, imagining how someone coming in might get the wrong impression of Phillip looming so close to her. 'I was thinking that I might go outside to get some air. It's so hot in here. Don't you think?'

Phillip rose from his chair and smiled. 'Splendid idea.'

'Oh, no,' Rose corrected him quickly. 'I was thinking I would go alone.'

'Oh, I see,' he said. 'A drink then. Let me get you a drink for when you come back. What was it? Babycham?'

'You don't have to,' Rose said. She stood up, grabbed her bag and yanked it onto her shoulder. If he bought her a drink, then she would be obliged to come back and listen to more of his opinions. She was about to leave when Phillip sat down heavily; his shoulders sagging like a sail on a windless day. He frowned, rested his elbows on the table and balanced his chin in his hands. Rose paused. 'I'm sorry,' she said. 'Thank you. A drink would be lovely.'

It was still light outside and the square was full of people – men with their collars open, eating bags of chips; groups of girls laughing and flirting with groups of boys. Rather than stay amongst them, Rose headed off to find a quiet spot of her own. She made her way to the edge of the Town Hall and stopped beside an alleyway leading down to the back of the building. She leant with her back against the wall and looked towards the fish and chip shop opposite. Earlier that evening the bulbs forming a border around the sign above the door had given off individual spheres of light. Now Rose could only make out a single white blur. She squinted but it didn't help. She closed her eyes to see whether she could clear the image and start again but as soon as her eyelids met, she had to prise them apart. Why, when she knew full well that she was standing on solid ground, did she feel like she was swaying? Like the pavement beneath her feet was a swelling wave? It must have been all that talk of boats and harbours and first mates and...

'Shepherd's delight,' a man said quietly into her ear.

Rose jumped, her heart pounding like it was trying to punch its way free of her chest.

'The sky,' Ray said. He raised his arm to point to the pink hue in the sky and the leather of his jacket brushed Rose's bare shoulder. 'Red sky at night, shepherd's delight,' he said. 'You probably don't bother with old farmers' sayings like that up in London.'

Rose's fingers sought out the locket at her neck. She threaded it along the chain and stared straight ahead. 'No. I mean... yes, we do,' she said.

Ray leant against the wall beside her and from the corner of her eye she saw him reach inside his jacket. He pulled out a crushed cigarette packet, shook it and offered it to her. She looked down at the two cigarettes standing proud of the others but shook her head. She watched Ray take one and light it. He inhaled deeply as he returned the packet to his pocket.

'So,' he said, speaking and exhaling smoke simultaneously. 'What are you doing out here on your own?'

'I wanted some air. I was hot.'

'Right.'

'And you, I mean, what are you doing out here? Shouldn't you be rehearsing for later?' She was trying to keep her voice steady, but it wasn't easy when Ray shrugged and she felt his shoulder move against hers.

'Nobody in there'll notice if we play a few bum notes,' he said. 'And I like to take a breather before I go on stage. To collect my thoughts.'

Rose prised herself away from the wall. 'So I should go then and leave you on your own.'

Again, Ray drew deeply on his cigarette and a long, straight plume of smoke passed by the side of Rose's face.

'Did I ask you to leave?' he said.

'No, I suppose not.'

'Well then.'

She settled back against the wall and took hold of the locket again.

'That's a nice bit of gold,' Ray said. Still holding the cigarette between his fingers, he pointed at her necklace.

'It's my mother's,' she said. 'She lets me wear it on special occasions.'

'So a dance at the Town Hall is a special occasion?'

Rose let the locket fall back to her chest. Was that a laugh in his voice? Was the necklace too much? Did Ray think she was overdressed? If he thought that her mother's locket was over the top then what would he say if he knew about the makeshift beauty parlour Mother had set up in the attic to get Rose ready for the dance? All the fussing with heated rollers and make-up and the ceremony where her mother had opened the small box and placed the locket around her neck.

'It's not such a special occasion,' she said still looking ahead, trying to sound casual. 'But you know what mothers are like.'

Ray took another drag on his cigarette before flicking the stub into the gutter. It bounced twice before disappearing down the drain. 'We could go somewhere,' he said. 'When I've finished my set. The Anchor Inn down on the beach at Seatown is quiet. We can talk.'

'I couldn't... Arthur. He'd miss me.' Rose made to touch the locket again but her hand was intercepted on its way to her neck. Ray's fingers clasped hers. His hand was warm, his grip sure. He moved from his position against the wall to stand in front of her. Rose looked down at the ground but could sense his eyes on her.

'Arthur's got his hands full with Mary,' he said. 'He won't notice if you slip out for half an hour. I can have you there and back before he even realises you've gone. I want to get to know you better. There's something special about you, Rose.'

Rose felt the blood rush to her cheeks. 'No there's not. I'm not special at all.'

Placing the index finger of his free hand beneath her chin, Ray gently tipped her face up so that she had no choice but to look at him.

'Oh yes you are,' he said. 'You're incredibly special. And beautiful.'

He looked at her with such intensity that Rose couldn't bring herself to turn away. Before she had time to react, he leant down and pressed his lips to hers. She should have protested that she wasn't the kind of girl that let a man she barely knew take advantage of her. Instead, she closed her eyes, relishing the taste of salt and smoke on Ray's lips. Her head began to swim again. But this time, instead of fighting the sensation, she rode the wave. And she didn't want it to end. Ever. But all too soon, Ray pulled away.

'Meet me here after the set,' Ray said, his face just inches from hers, his voice heavy with breath. 'I want to see you alone, Rose. I need to see you.'

Ray slipped down the alley to enter the building through a backdoor and Rose made her way slowly back round to the front. Every so often she put her fingertips to her lips and smiled. Ray had kissed her, and she had let him.

On her way over the threshold into the Town Hall, she stumbled, making herself giggle. Imagine being so giddy from a kiss that she couldn't even control her feet! This was turning out to be a week of firsts. Her first ride on a motorbike. Her first drink of Babycham. Her first kiss.

Once inside, Rose decided against heading back to the table. She lingered in the lobby. It was a shame to think of a cold glass of Babycham going to waste but enduring even one more of Phillip's stories would be too high a price to pay for another drink. Or was it? She imagined the bubbles popping on her tongue and was weighing up whether it would be rude to rush in and snatch the glass from the table when a cheer went up. Instantly everyone in the lobby wanted to be in the function room. Rose waited for the rush to die down before making her way to the door to look over the heads of the crowd to the stage. Ian came on first and took up his position behind the drums followed by Gary with his bass. And then, from behind a black curtain, Ray appeared. He walked slowly across the stage, a leather strap around his neck, his guitar balanced against his hips. He stopped at a microphone stand in the centre of the stage, nodded and, as one, Gary and Ian joined him in the opening chords of a song. In response to Ray's deep voice, everyone in the room got to their feet and danced and cheered and sang along. But Rose found that she was suddenly incapable of movement. She watched, dumbfounded, as Ray's fringe fell into his eyes and stayed there. Those fingers strumming the strings of the guitar were the same fingers that only minutes earlier had held hers. The lips forming the words of the song were the same lips that had pressed to hers. The man up on the stage – the popular, talented, gorgeous man – liked her. *He* liked *her.*

Rose was so engrossed in the spectacle on stage that she only realised the set was over when Ray left the stage and a stream of people began pushing their way back out into the lobby. This was it. She was going to do it. She was going to meet Ray outside, climb on board his motorbike and go for a drink with him. But not before she had checked her make-up.

The 'ladies' was wall-to-wall with girls jostling for position at the long mirror above the row of sinks. A queue stretched out into the hallway. Above their heads, a fug of cigarette smoke hung in the air and the chatter was almost louder than the music in the hall. While Rose inched her way along the queue towards the cubicles, she watched a group of girls unravelling a roll of toilet paper, handing wads of it to a girl standing by the hand towel. She was sobbing so hard that mascara inched down her cheeks like two spindly spiders.

'He's not worth it,' one of her friends said, wiping the girl's face. 'They're all bastards.'

Not all, Rose thought and smiled as she nipped into a vacated cubicle. She slid the latch across, took a compact from her bag, and fished around for her lipstick. Making an 'o' with her lips, she carefully applied a fresh coat of pink before examining her reflection in the little round mirror. Did she look older now, wiser? She should do. Now that she had been kissed she was a woman. She smiled at her reflection and snapped the compact shut. She was returning it to her bag when a familiar voice rose above the general din beyond the door.

'So he showed his face then,' Mary said.

'Finally,' Shirley replied. 'But notice how he didn't bother to come and say hello? Just got up there on the stage. He spends more time fiddling with that bloody guitar than he does me. If you get my drift.'

Mary giggled. 'You're terrible! But you've got to admit he did look good.'

'And doesn't he bloody know it. I tell you something though, he better make it up to me or that's it. And I don't just mean a Cherry B and a fumble round the back of The Red Lion this time. For once he better make it up to me proper. Or we're over.'

'Yeah and that's Pinky and Perky flying through the window.'

Rose stood with her hand on the lock. She would have sat on the floor and stayed in the cubicle until the very last person had left if somebody hadn't bashed on the other side of the door. 'What's taking you?' an angry voice shouted. 'Have you fallen in?'

Reluctantly she slid the latch and had taken only one step outside the cubicle when the girl barged past her. 'About bloody time,' she said.

Rose stared at the floor tiles. All she had to do was get out of the toilets. Just a few short steps…

'Well if it isn't Doctor Rose,' Shirley called. 'We were wondering where you'd got to.'

Shirley was looking at Rose in the mirror, as she puckered her lips and applied a fresh coat of lipstick. Mary took hold of Rose's hand.

'Oh, Rose,' she said. 'Where have you been? Art's been ever so worried. He thought Phillip might have upset you. I told him that Phillip's not capable of upsetting anyone but I don't think he believed me. He's protective, your Arthur, isn't he?'

'What? Yes, he can be,' Rose said. She was responding to Mary's question but couldn't take her eyes from Shirley. 'So your... boyfriend. He's here?'

Shirley wound down the lipstick, slammed on the lid and handed it to Mary. 'If you can call him that.' She rubbed her lips together then dabbed at the corners of her mouth with her little finger.

'Don't be daft,' Mary said and dropped the lipstick into her bag. She turned to Rose. 'They're always like this. Running hot and cold. But they're meant to be together, mark my words. Like Liz Taylor and Richard Burton, they are.'

'Or Bill and Ben.' Shirley laughed and hoisted up the front of her dress. Rose stared at Shirley's reflection; at her red lips and her cleavage like two ripe apples pressed beneath the chiffon. Every other girl at the mirror paled beside Shirley. She was like an orchid in a field of dandelions. A question hovered on Rose's lips. She wanted to swallow it down but her brain insisted on sending a message instructing her vocal chords to ask it.

'What's his name?'

'What's whose name?' Shirley asked, rubbing her finger across her front teeth.

'Your boyfriend. What's his name?'

Shirley stopped rubbing her teeth and frowned. 'If you mean the good-for-nothing ratbag, waste of space, that I have the misfortune of being lumbered with, then I'd call him Pig. But if you ask anyone else that then they'd call him Ray.'

Rose felt the room begin to spin around her. She stumbled and Mary caught her. 'Are you all right, Rose?' Mary said.

'She's had one too many, that's all,' Shirley said. 'I did say to Art that she looked a bit on the young side to handle so much. Don't worry, love, we've all been there. Get your mum to do you a great big greasy fry up in the morning. That'll see you right. Nothing like a couple of thick rashers and a bit of fried bread to soak it up.'

Rose clutched her stomach. The sour taste of bile rose to the back of her throat. She felt Mary's hand press against her brow. 'I'm not so sure, Shirl,' Mary said. 'She don't look too good. You all right, Rose? Rose? I'll go and get Art. He'll know what to do.'

Chapter 13

Abi pulled the plug from the kitchen sink and looked out of the window. The storm had cleared overnight into a perfect spring Saturday. There wasn't a single cloud in the endless expanse of blue. The blind at the window barely rattled in the soft breeze coming in through the open kitchen door. It was days like this that made living at Cliff Cottage worthwhile. Almost.

Abi dried her hands on a tea towel and sat down at the table. 'Done?'

'Nearly.' Penny patted a stack of foil-wrapped parcels. 'Two cheese and tomato sandwiches and two apples.' She took two fairy cakes from the pile cooling on a wire rack and placed them onto a fresh sheet of foil. 'Are you sure your Mum won't mind? Aren't they for the beetle drive tonight?'

'She said we could have one each.'

'If you say so.' Penny crunched the foil around the cakes to form another neat parcel, which she handed to Abi. 'So where's everyone run off to?'

'Mum's gone to meet someone about a catering job,' Abi said and shoved the parcels into a carrier bag, not nearly as carefully or as neatly as Penny had wrapped them. 'Dad's gone into work to help with a stocktake and Nan's down at the church hall putting up decorations for this evening. She's spent all week making these crazy beetle things out of egg boxes and pipe cleaners, like you'd make at playschool. Look,' she said, pointing to a black smear on the table. 'She found an old tin of paint in the shed and gave them all a coat of it.'

'I bet you helped her.'

'Might have.'

'You're both big kids.'

'Oi, I'll have you know that my beetles were very professional, not like Nan's weirdos.' Abi curled up her arms and stuck out her tongue in an impression of a squashed beetle.

Penny laughed. 'Right. I'm going to get my revision notes to take to the beach. Shall I get your folder too?'

'You want to study? *Today?*'

'I think *you* should. What did Mrs Bennett say yesterday?' Penny pretended to adjust a pair of glasses on her nose and dipped her head as though looking at Abi over the top of thick bifocals. 'Abigail Russell, it is not enough to excel in one subject alone. Where will pretty drawings and paintings get you without a creditable academic record to support them? Nowhere young lady, that's where.'

Abi frowned. 'Can I help it if I'm not a genius like you? How am I supposed to know why a stupid crow wants to say "love" or why the ghost of some old bloke wants to wander around on a turret just to scare his son?'

'If it was Mouldy Munro giving you advice you'd be like "Oh, Mr Munro. Of course, sir. Anything you say, sir. Three bags full, sir."'

Abi felt her cheeks colour. 'No.'

'Yes,' Penny laughed. 'But don't worry, I won't tell anyone that you dream of having Mouldy's babies.'

Before she'd even finished her sentence, Penny was out of her seat and in the hall. She narrowly avoided the soggy tea towel Abi lobbed in her direction.

'Silly moo!' Abi shouted after her. But Penny was already halfway up the stairs, the steps creaking beneath her as she ran to the top of the house.

Abi collected the tea towel and sat back at the table. She only did what Mr Munro said because she needed a good grade in art. There was nothing wrong with that.

Penny's footsteps thudded back down the stairs.

'I hope you're not spreading rumours about me and Mouldy because–' Abi started but the phone ringing in the hall stopped her mid-flow.

'I'll get it!' Penny shouted. 'Hello... No sorry she's not here... No, neither is she... No, I'm her friend. Okay, yes, I'll get her. Hold on.'

Abi wandered out into the hall and Penny held the receiver out to her, her hand covering the mouthpiece. 'It's your dad's boss,' she whispered.

'What does he want?'

'Don't know. He didn't say.'

Abi took the phone. 'Hello.'

'Is that Abigail?'

'Yes.'

'Abigail, it's Mr Rees. I manage the shop where your dad works. Now, you're not to worry, but your dad's had a bit of an accident. He was up on a ladder counting compost bins and he fell off. We called an ambulance and they took him to hospital but I'm sure it's just a precaution.' He paused. 'Are you still there?'

'Yes,' Abi whispered, her throat dry.

'You need to find your mother and go to the hospital. I'd go myself only I've got the whole shop to stocktake before the end of the day, and with a man down now. Is that okay? Can you find your mother and tell her?'

'Of course.'

'Good. Let me know how he gets on, will you?'

The dialling tone sounded but Abi still cradled the phone. Penny put her armful of folders on the floor and took a step closer. 'Is everything all right?'

'It's my dad. There's been an accident. He fell off a ladder and he's at the hospital. I have to find Mum. His boss said it wasn't serious but why would the ambulance take him to hospital if it's not serious?'

Penny took the receiver and replaced it on the cradle. She slipped her arm around Abi's shoulders. 'When my dad sprained his ankle at cricket, the ambulance took him to hospital in case it was broken. They just do it to be on the safe side. I'm sure your dad'll be okay. Who was your mum meeting?'

'I don't know.'

'Come on then.'

Abi followed Penny into the kitchen where Penny consulted Mum's calendar. 'That's weird.'

'What?'

'I thought you said she had a meeting about a catering job.'

'She has.'

'There's nothing written on here.'

Abi looked at the calendar. Penny was right. The only thing against today's date was *WI CAKES*. 'I don't understand. She always writes down her appointments.'

'Not this time. She must have forgotten.'

'Mum *never* forgets anything.'

'Are you sure she didn't tell you and you just can't remember?'

'No. She went off on her bike as soon as Dad left, while you were in the bathroom. But she didn't say anything about where she was going. How am I going to find her, Penny?'

'She can't be far if she went on her bike. Why don't you go to the church hall and see if your Nan knows who she was meeting? I can stay here. If your Mum comes back I'll tell her what's happened.'

'On your own?'

'I won't be on my own,' she said and nodded to Cyril who had jumped on a chair and was nosing in the carrier bag on the table. Penny scooped him up and tickled him behind his ears. 'I'll phone my dad to pick me up in a bit. You'll want to go straight to the hospital when you find your mum. I can always cancel my date with Dean tonight if you want me to stay here and wait for you all to get back.'

'No. You go. I'll phone you later or tomorrow.'

Abi ran out of the open back door and down to the shed. She pulled her bike free of the folded deckchairs, jumped on and pedalled back up the garden. Penny was standing on the step with Cyril in her arms.

'See you later,' Abi called as she cycled past.

'Not if I see you first,' Penny called after her and waggled Cyril's paw like he was waving.

Abi had never pedalled so quickly down the twisting lanes. The fields and hedges trailed by in a blur of green. It was two miles to the village but if she pushed hard, she could do it in less than ten minutes. She stood up on the pedals and forced the bike up the steep road to the summit of the cliff. The image of Dad in the back of an ambulance kept her legs pumping when they began to burn. Soon she was up on the exposed road at the top of the cliff and, with the wind behind her, she picked up speed. If she kept up this pace, she might make it to the church in just a few minutes.

She was already passed the turning to the cliff top car park when her brain caught up with her eyes and realised they had seen something pushed into a hedge further back. Pulling on the brakes, she dragged her feet along the tarmac and came to a sharp stop. She pedalled back, dropped her bike to the ground and grabbed the handlebars of a bike that had been shoved deep into the hedge. She pulled it free and saw a line of black electrical tape running the length of the saddle. It was the repair she had helped Dad make last week after Mum snagged the saddle on an exposed nail in the shed.

Abi felt the blood drain from her legs. Had Mum been in an accident? Had a car knocked her off her bike on the way to her meeting and the ambulance men had abandoned the bike in the hedge when they rushed her off to hospital? Abi quickly looked over the rest of the bike for any sign of damage. There were no new scratches that she could see. No twisted spokes or bent wheels. The lights and reflectors were intact.

In an attempt to work out what was going on, Abi tried to put herself in Mum's shoes. Mum had been stuck in a boring meeting for the last hour, discussing mushroom vol-au-vents and profiteroles. She was on her way home when she saw the turning for the car park and thought; *'I know, I'll stop and go for a walk'*. Bingo! That was it. Mum's favourite thing to do in good weather was to go for a long stroll along the beach.

Satisfied that Cagney and Lacey couldn't have done a better job of solving the puzzle of the bike in the hedge, Abi balanced Mum's bike against the branches, picked up her own bike and balanced it against Mum's, and set off down the sandy track.

There were two vehicles in the car park; a white car with an old couple inside – a flask and two cups balanced on the dashboard between them – and a red van. A man stood at the back of the van, holding the door open for a Labrador to jump inside. Abi was about to run past but when the man slammed the door she spotted a third vehicle tucked away in the far corner of the car park; a silver Jaguar with a Christmas tree shaped air freshener hanging from the rear-view mirror.

She could have fallen to the ground and kissed the dirt. At least now when she found Mum they could track Tony down. He wouldn't mind giving them a lift to the hospital. They could even pick up Penny on the way.

Just beyond the car park, the path split in two. Abi took the turn towards the viewing area. From there you could see for miles along the coast towards Cliff Cottage and to Bridport in the distance. If she was lucky she would spot Mum somewhere down on the beach.

After running the length of the path, she slowed to a trot to take the spur down to the viewing area, fully expecting to find it empty. What Abi saw made her stop in her tracks. Mum was sitting on the bench looking out to sea, holding the hand of the man beside her. They were so close that their legs almost touched. And they were so deep in conversation that they didn't notice Abi behind them.

A sick feeling churned in Abi's stomach. She sank to her knees behind a gorse bush. Why was Mum sitting on a bench with Tony, holding his hand?

Part of her wanted to run away but an even bigger part kept her rooted to the spot, watching through the branches as Tony listened to Mum talk, his shoulders sagging.

And then, as if it couldn't get any worse than Mum holding his hand, she put her hand to the back of his head and ran her fingers through his hair. In response, Tony turned to look at her. He put his palm to her cheek and they sat there, staring at each other until Tony leant forward and kissed her. It wasn't a long kiss. It was worse than that. It was soft. With their eyes closed.

***

Only snippets of the next few hours embedded into Abi's memory. She remembered stumbling back to her bike. She remembered pedalling hard and arriving at the church hall and falling through the doors to tell Nan about Dad. She remembered feeling sick in the back of Father Pearson's car.

'It'll be all right,' Nan said, holding Abi's hand. 'Don't worry.'

By the time Mum pushed through the doors of accident and emergency, Dad was being discharged. His right arm was in a cast from his wrist to his elbow, a sling holding it against his chest. Mum dashed to him and made a tremendous fuss, brushing her hand though his hair.

'I got such a shock when I got back to the house and Penny told me. Oh, you silly bugger,' she said to Dad. But when she kissed him, Abi looked away. She knew where Mum's hands and lips had been just hours before.

***

On the way home from the hospital, Mum stopped the car at the chip shop and Nan treated them all to a fish supper, which they ate from the paper at the kitchen table. Mum cut Dad's fish into bite-size chunks as though he was a baby. Dad held his fork awkwardly in his left hand. While he ate, he told them how he had come to topple from the ladder.

'The bloody thing gave way under me and there I was, hanging onto the shelf for dear life.' He dipped a chip into his ketchup. 'I shouted but they were all out back, having a crafty fag. I hit the floor like a sack of spuds. Laurel and Hardy eat your heart out,' he said and popped the chip into his mouth.

Mum and Nan laughed. Abi couldn't laugh. She sat with her hands in her lap and stared at her plate. 'Please may I be excused,' she said.

'Of course, love,' Mum said. 'You must be exhausted cycling all that way today.'

Out in the hall Abi could still hear the voices in the kitchen.

'Is she all right?' Nan asked. 'She looks pale. She was in a terrific state when she got to the church today. Looked like she'd seen a ghost.'

'I expect it's the shock,' Mum said. 'She'll be fine after a good night's sleep.'

Abi couldn't sleep. She lay awake in the darkness listening to the sounds of the house. The creak of the floorboards, the groan of the roof buffeted by the gathering wind, the squeak of the springs as she turned from one side to the other and back again.

If only she'd gone straight to the church hall without looking back she'd never have seen Mum's bike and she wouldn't have these horrible pictures in her head. When she closed her eyes, they came back – Tony with his hand cupping Mum's cheek, Mum with her hand in his hair, Tony and Mum with their lips together. And then she pictured Mum rushing through the hospital doors, so concerned for Dad.

It all twisted around in her head until it didn't make any sense. She kicked off her sheets and gripped the pillow to her face.

***

The good weather didn't even last a day. The next morning a strong wind pushed the clouds across the grey sky. Before anyone else was awake, Abi let Cyril out of the back door and followed him down to the beach.

She walked along the edge of the surf, the dirty brown foam seeping into her trainers, the drizzle soaking through her jeans. She sat on a boulder and looked out at the sea. What was she supposed to do? Should she tell Nan or Dad what she had seen? What about Penny and Shirl? Or should she just keep it to herself?

She picked up a stone, flicked her wrist and watched it skim three times across the surface before sinking. She skimmed another stone and another and watched each disappear. If only she could join them – sink and never come back. All she had to do was walk into the water until the waves reached her waist, carry on a bit further until they reached her shoulders, and then the sea would do the rest.

She had no idea how long she'd been sitting there when Cyril nudged her leg. 'All right,' she sighed. 'You want your breakfast. I get the hint.' She got to her feet and followed him slowly up the beach; back to the last place on Earth she wanted to be.

The house was silent except for the tip-tap of rain like a thousand tiny needles on the kitchen window and Cyril snorting as he wolfed down a whole tin of dog meat. It was midday but it was dark enough outside to be night.

Abi lobbed the empty can into the bin. As she chucked the fork into the sink, the back door flew open, the sudden rush of wind blowing the pages of Nan's newspaper on the table.

'What a day!' Mum said, holding her handbag over her head. She slammed the door shut and shook the rain from her bag. 'I've just dropped your dad at The Red Lion for a couple of pints. He wants to get everyone to sign his cast. I just hope he doesn't let them write anything too filthy.' She laughed but didn't seem to notice that Abi didn't laugh with her.

'I'm picking your Nan up from Stella's at three. You can come for the ride if you like. Now, I fancy a nice bowl of warming soup. What about you?'

'No.'

'Oh well, I'll heat up a whole can anyway in case you change your mind. Did you eat breakfast?'

'No.'

Mum shrugged off her coat and hung it on the hook behind the door. She unhooked her apron and pulled it over her head. 'What's wrong with you, Miss Grumpy Pants? Did someone get out of bed on the wrong side?' Mum looked her up and down. 'And look at your jeans! They're soaking. Here, take them off and I'll put them on the clothes horse in front of the range.' She held out her hand as though to help. Abi pushed it away.

'Abi!' Mum said and pulled her hand away. 'What are you playing at? I don't know what's got into you but you can snap out of it. Quick smart.'

Abi felt something like a flame rise in her belly. She wasn't playing at anything. It was Mum playing at… 'I saw you,' she said.

Mum took hold of the ties of her apron and passed them around her waist. 'Saw what? What are you talking about?'

It was clear that Mum had no idea what Abi was talking about. Maybe that was for the best after all. Maybe she should just keep her mouth shut. Maybe she hadn't really seen what she thought she had. There was a chance, no matter how small, that she had jumped to conclusions and made a terrible mistake. She should go to her room, get changed, eat a bowl of soup and forget everything. And she was going to do it; really, she was, until Mum had to go and open her mouth.

'For heaven's sake, Abigail,' she said, angrily trying to fasten the apron at the front of her waist. 'I don't have time for your silly games today. If you have something to say, just spit it out.'

And there it was, the tone she always used when she wanted to put Abi down. *Not today*, Abi thought. She wouldn't be made to feel stupid today.

'I saw you on the beach yesterday,' Abi said. 'With Tony.'

The ties dropped from Mum's hands and her apron flapped open. Her arms dropped to her sides and she stared at Abi. Her lips moved like she was trying to decide what to say. Surely that was wrong. Surely the words to tell the truth didn't need to be thought about because they were already there. When Mum gave up and turned her back on her, Abi knew.

'Abigail, I really don't know what you're talking about,' Mum said, her voice trembling as she took two bowls from the draining board and a can of soup from a shelf. She fumbled to open the can. 'I won't tell you again. Go and take those jeans off before you catch a chill. That's all I need. Nursing you through a cold with everything else I've got on.'

Abi couldn't move. She couldn't move and couldn't speak. Mum turned to face her with the can opener in her hand. 'Listen, young lady, I don't know what fantasy you've concocted in that overactive imagination but I can tell you that you've got it all wrong.' She grabbed the saucepan. The soup made a thick glugging sound as she emptied out its contents.

'What have I got wrong?' Abi said. 'That you were on the beach or that you were with Tony?'

Mum dropped the can in the bin and gripped the edge of the worktop, the rigid line of her shoulders screaming at Abi to back off. But she wouldn't, not this time. Mum was so busy protecting her horrible secret that she couldn't even see the pain she was causing her own daughter. Did she even care?

'There are things you don't understand,' Mum said slowly.

'Like what?'

Mum's shoulders slumped and she sighed. 'Please, Abi, just drop it.'

'Why? What is it? Tell me. I'm not a child.'

Mum laughed, a sad laugh and picked up the pan. 'But you are. That's the point.'

'I don't understand. Why were you there with Tony, Mum? Why?'

'We were discussing a bit of business.'

'Do you always kiss people you do a bit of business with?'

Mum slammed the pan down on the draining board and the orange-coloured soup slopped over the sides. 'This conversation is over.'

'Why?'

'Because I said so. Things aren't always as simple as they seem. You'll realise that one day.'

'Is that why you go on so many walks on the beach on your own? To meet *him*?'

Mum spun around. 'Just drop it, Abi. I mean it.'

Abi saw the look of warning flash across Mum's eyes but she couldn't back down, not now.

'I saw you with my own eyes. You were kissing him.' She forced herself between Mum and the range. 'Why were you kissing Penny's dad? Why Mum?'

Cyril, clearly disturbed by Abi's raised voice, started to bark. He ran to her, leaping frantically up and down and Mum used the distraction to push Abi. Whether it was to get past her or to get her out of the way, Abi didn't know. But Abi lost her balance and stumbled over Cyril. He yelped and she grabbed out, desperately grasping for anything that would keep her on her feet. The last thing she saw was the door of the range rushing towards her. There was a bark. A shout. A crack. A pain like a shard of ice driving through her eye.

And then... nothing.

Chapter 14

Rose – Saturday 24 August 1963

Rose sat on the bench in the back garden. The airless atmosphere cloaked her as though she was locked in a tiny, windowless room. Everything – the grass, the shrubs, the shed, the little gate at the end – was covered by a blanket of night. She closed her eyes and listened to the swish of waves on the beach far below. All she wanted was to sleep, to forget that this night had ever happened. The world behind her eyelids began to spin again. It wasn't quite as bad as it had been earlier, she no longer felt sick, but it was bad enough to make her open her eyes and grip the edge of the seat.

Looking up to the sky, she picked out one of the thousands of tiny pinpricks glinting like a torch shining through a giant sieve. From somewhere deep in her memory she dredged up what little she knew of astronomy. That star – that bright shining light – was all that remained of a long-dead sun. It was a ghost. A swansong. The final flourish of a disappearing world.

Putting her fingertips to her face, she massaged her brow. She should never have let herself lose control like that. Life only made sense when everything was in its rightful place. She stood up and wrapped her arms around her waist. How dare Ray treat her like that? How dare he kiss her and fool her into believing that he had feelings for her when all along he was probably laughing at her, thinking that she was a stupid little girl in a yellow party dress playing at being a grown up?

She paced along the edge of a flowerbed. What was he to her anyway? She knew nothing about him except that when he smiled, a dimple appeared in his cheek. He could sing a bit. When he kissed her, he tasted of cigarettes and his lips were soft and… Rose dug her fingernails into her palms and swallowed down a scream. That's all she needed; to scream out loud and watch the lights appear in the upstairs windows. It was bad enough that she would have to prepare a heavily edited version of the evening to satisfy Mother's curiosity at the breakfast table tomorrow, never mind waking her now and having to rustle up a story of a wonderful evening on the hoof.

Rose's stomach churned at the prospect of a plate of Auntie Ruth's fried bread, oozing dripping, when a dull rumble in the distance made her stop pacing and look up. Out across the bay the headlight of a motorcycle traced a path like a firefly along the dark coast road. Arthur. When he had driven her back to the cottage earlier she had insisted he go back to the dance. Whether he had believed her fib that her headache was a result of the loud music rather than the booze, she would never know, but after she said she didn't need a nursemaid, he had dropped her outside the cottage, exchanged the car for his motorcycle, and headed straight back in the direction of town. There was little point in ruining his evening too.

Gradually the light wound its way along the road. It grew ever larger as it got closer. It crossed Rose's mind to let herself into the cottage and creep up the stairs. But the prospect of hiding away in the stifling attic was enough to make her have second thoughts.

As the rumble of the engine cut out at the end of the lane, Rose kicked off her shoes, stashed them under the bench, and set off at a pace down the lawn. Out on the coastal path, the soft grass gave way to sharp sand littered with hazardous pebbles. She waited for her eyes to adjust to the moonlight before picking her way carefully down the steep path, keeping one hand against the cliff wall as though it were a rocky banister. Once at the bottom, she navigated the warm pebbles and the ghostly-grey line of boulders standing sentry along the length of the beach. She came to a boulder with a scoop in its surface, perfect for nestling into. She sat down, brought her knees up to her chest and pulled her dress down to cover her legs.

The sea crashed against the shore, dragging the pebbles backwards and forwards, backwards and forwards. Rose balanced her chin on her knees and looked out to the moon hanging low over the horizon. She would head back inside soon. Once she was sure that Arthur was safely tucked up on the sofa in the parlour. She closed her eyes and was enjoying the sensation of the sea breeze ruffling her hair when she heard a noise over the sound of the waves. Footsteps. Crunching through the pebbles behind her.

'Arthur,' she sighed. 'What are you doing here? I told you to go back to the dance.'

The footsteps stopped. 'It's not Arthur.'

Rose jumped to her feet. She briefly lost her footing on the shifting surface. 'What do you want?'

'You.' Ray took a step towards her, his face half in shadow. Rose stood for a moment, curling her toes around the pebbles. What should she do? Run back to the house? But why should she when *she* had done nothing wrong? *He* was the one who had kissed *her*.

Rose pulled back her shoulders and raised her chin. 'Well I don't want to see you. I was having a perfectly nice time *alone*, thank you very much.'

'You said you were going to meet me and you didn't.'

'How did you know I was down here anyway?' Rose said, folding her arms across her chest. 'I could have been asleep for all you knew. I should be asleep.'

'I took a chance and it paid off, didn't it? When I pulled up, I saw you running across the garden. I waited for you. Outside the Town Hall, like we said. And when you didn't show up I went and found Art. He said he had to bring you home. Something about a headache. I'd have brought you home if you'd said.' Ray took a step towards her; she took a step back.

'You shouldn't have come.'

'What was I supposed to do when you ran off without saying anything?'

'I didn't run. For your information, I left because I wanted to. And as far as I'm aware, I don't need to ask your permission.'

Ray made to touch her wrist but she kept her arms firmly folded and twisted so she was just beyond his grip.

'Are you angry with me?' he said, pulling his hand away. 'Have I done something to upset you?' He paused, presumably waiting for a reply. He didn't get one. 'If I've done something wrong, then you should give me the chance to put it right.'

Again, Ray took a step towards her. This time she stood her ground. Her instinct told her to demand that he leave, to deal with the situation calmly and to salvage at least a shred of dignity. Instead three words blurted out before she could stop them. 'What about *Shirley*?'

He shrugged. 'What about her?'

'I'm not in the habit of stealing another girl's boyfriend. I'd never have let you–'

'Boyfriend?' Ray laughed. 'Is that what she's been saying? I'm not her boyfriend. Listen, Rose, if that's what this is all about then you can forget it. I've known Shirley since we were at school. We went out for a while but it's over. She just can't accept it. That's hardly my fault.'

Rose's head began to swim again. It was all so confusing. Shirley had seemed so certain. 'Just leave me alone,' she said and turned to walk away. Ray put himself in her path.

'It's all just a stupid misunderstanding. Stay.'

'So you can make a fool out of me again? You must think I'm really stupid.' Rose looked into Ray's face, trying to read what he was thinking.

He looked down at her and said softly, 'Stupid? How could I ever think you're stupid? You're intelligent, interesting and…' His voice trailed away but his gaze didn't falter. He didn't even blink.

'Didn't your mother ever tell you that it's rude to stare?' she said triumphantly. She waited for him to come back with a smart response. Instead, Ray shoved his hands deep into his pockets. He looked down at his boots and kicked the ground.

'Well?' Rose said, buoyed by the novelty of wrong-footing him. 'Cat got your tongue?'

'Actually no. I... It's just that... well, my mum didn't have much to do with shaping my manners. She...' He seemed to be finding it difficult to finish his explanation. 'I don't want sympathy or anything. It's just that I never really knew my mum. She died when I was three.'

Rose felt ever vestige of wind and bluster sucked from her sails. 'Oh, Ray.' She put her hand to her mouth. 'I'm so sorry. If I'd known I never would have said... I'm so very sorry.'

He shrugged. 'It was a long time ago. But manners weren't exactly top of the list of what my dad and my older brothers taught me.'

'Oh, Ray. There's nothing wrong with your manners. I shouldn't have said that. It's just... it's just. Oh Lord, I'm so sorry.'

'Don't be. It's not your fault.' He finally looked up. 'And don't look so sad, it doesn't suit you.'

'Sorry.'

'Stop saying sorry.'

'Sor–'

He smiled and shook his head. Rose watched the dimple appear in his cheek. Poor Ray. There were days when she would gladly have been free of her own mother's fussing and worrying. But to lose her forever? It was an unbearable thought. Was it possible Ray was telling the truth about Shirley? How could such a smile hide a lie? She knew girls at school who mooned over boys, when it was quite clear the boy wasn't in the least bit interested. Perhaps Shirley was one of those girls.

Rose touched Ray's wrist. He pulled his hands from his pockets and clasped hers.

'Are we friends again?' he asked.

She nodded and looked down at his fingers around her own.

'I'm glad. So, will you sit out here with me for a while and keep me company? Now that I've come all the way out here, it seems a shame to go back into town right away.'

Rose looked up at the dark cliff. 'I'm not sure. It's late. I should really go inside.'

Ray slowly traced a circle on each of her palms. 'Nobody knows you're here. Arthur's still at the dance. There were no lights on when I came past the house.'

A shiver ran through Rose. 'All right,' she said. 'But just for a minute.'

Ray freed her hands. He slipped off his jacket and laid it on the ground. Rose sat down, willing him to take her hands again and trace circles on her palms. Instead he sat beside her, legs bent, elbows resting on his knees. He picked up a pebble and chucked it towards the waves. It splashed in the water. 'So…' he said.

'So…'

'What do you want to talk about?'

Rose laughed. 'I don't know.'

Ray reached into the lining of his jacket and pulled out a small hip flask. Unscrewing the cap, he took a sip before offering it to her. She shook her head. The sea air had finally stopped the world from spinning. The last thing she needed was to jump back on the merry-go-round. Ray replaced the cap and slipped the flask back into his pocket.

Rose looked at the side of his face. If it was possible, he was even more handsome in the moonlight. The dark shadows clung to the angles of his face and made him look like a matinee idol.

'You know, it's weird,' he said, looking out to sea once again. 'I can't believe I actually know someone who's going to be a doctor. That's a proper job.'

'Being a mechanic is a proper job too.'

Ray picked up another stone and threw it towards the water. 'I guess there are people destined to wear white coats and stethoscopes and others destined to wear greasy overalls and have their heads stuck under bonnets till they draw their old-age pension.'

'You could do something else. If you wanted to. You could go to college. You could train to be whatever you want to be.'

Ray laughed. 'People like me don't go to college.'

'What do you mean, people like you?'

'Rough people. Stupid people.'

'You're not stupid.'

Ray laughed and turned to look at her. He flicked his fringe from his eyes. 'I'm not fishing for compliments. And I'm not complaining. I do all right. I've got money in my pocket and a roof over my head. And I've got my music and ambition. I'll make something of myself one day, you just wait and see.' He took hold of her hand. 'There's only one thing missing from my life.'

'What's that?'

His grip tightened around her fingers. 'She's sitting right beside me.'

Rose felt his free hand on her cheek. She gave in to his gentle pressure, turning her to face him.

'Do you know how beautiful you are?' he said.

'I'm not at all beautiful.' She tried to look down, but Ray tipped her chin up to him again.

'Yes,' he said, 'you are. I feel like the luckiest man in the world right now, sitting here with you. I know it's only been a few days but when I'm not with you, I can't stop thinking about you. I've never felt like this about anyone before.' He pressed her palm against his ribs. 'See, Rose. That's what you do to me. Whenever I see you I swear I feel fit to burst.' He pressed her hand harder to his chest. Beneath the thin white cotton, she could feel his heart pounding.

'You shouldn't talk like that,' she said while the warmth of his skin seeped through his T-shirt into her palm. 'You hardly know me.'

'Tell me you don't feel the same about me.'

'I don't… I can't… It's too quick.'

His grip on her fingers tightened. 'You're leaving in a few days. I might never see you again. If we've only got tonight then let's not waste it. I want to show you how much you mean to me.' With every word, he inched closer to her. 'Please, Rose,' he said and kissed her softly. He put his arms around her and pulled her close. He kissed her again. Rose didn't resist when he laid her down.

He was over her, kissing her neck, her shoulders, her earlobes. He ran his fingertips along her collarbone, down her arms and up the inside of her legs. Every touch, every warm breath, sent a thrill through Rose. The world was moving so fast. Spinning and swirling. It felt so good to be in Ray's arms. To feel so warm. To feel alive. To feel wanted.

'Rose,' Ray breathed into her ear. 'I want to tell you something.'

'Yes,' she said, surprised by the breathiness in her own voice.

'My name's not Ray.' He looked down at her, his fringe hanging in his eyes. 'Everyone calls me that because my surname's Raymond. My real name's Tony. I just wanted you to know that.'

'Tony,' Rose said and brushed his fringe from his eyes. 'It suits you.'

'Do you like me, Rose? Really like me?'

'I really like you, Tony Raymond.' She looked at his lips, wanting them to press against hers again.

'And you know we don't have to do anything you don't want to.'

'I know.' She cupped the back of his head and pulled him back down to her.

Chapter 15

Apinpoint of light flashed in Abi's eyes. Warm fingers pulled at her face. There would be a scar but it should fade. She was young enough to heal.

The doctor smiled. He was kind and his voice was soft and calm. Abi wished he would say she had to stay in hospital. He didn't. He sent her home. Home. The word sounded so hollow.

Nobody questioned that it was an accident. Abi had tripped over Cyril and cracked her head on the door of the range while Mum was making lunch. Abi didn't bother to put anyone straight. What was one more lie?

***

Up in the attic Nan fussed with the blankets and plumped Abi's pillow. She handed Abi a glass filled to the brim with lemonade. 'Come on, drink up. It's full of goodness. We'll have you right as nine pence in no time.'

Dad, who was sitting on the edge of the bed, lifted up his arm to show off his cast, freshly decorated with red and blue felt-tip squiggles like tattoos. 'Two Russells in two days. That A&E doctor will think we're re-enacting the battle of The Somme down here at Cliff Cottage.' He chuckled and slapped his thigh with his good hand.

Nan dipped a flannel into a bowl of water on the mantelpiece and pressed the damp fabric to Abi's eye. She worked carefully. Because she avoided the gauze covering the line of stitches running from the corner of Abi's eye to the tip of her ear, it didn't hurt her at all.

'Steak,' Dad said. 'That's what boxers use to take the swelling down. And our Abi here looks like she's gone ten rounds with Henry Cooper.'

'Mick,' Nan laughed. 'You'll give the girl a complex.' She kissed Abi on the forehead. 'It's not that bad, sweetheart. You're still my beautiful girl, even with a black eye.'

Abi took a drink of the lemonade and handed the glass back to Nan. There was a knock at the door and Dad got up to open it.

'Mmm, someone's being spoiled,' he said, looking over the tray Mum carried in. 'Soup *and* a cheese toastie with a slice of Madeira and a glass of Lucozade. You'd better be quick or I might just polish it off myself.'

Mum placed the tray on the bed. 'Come on, sweetheart, eat something. You need to keep your strength up.'

Abi turned over to face the wall.

'Why don't we leave her for now, Rose?' Nan said. 'She'll get her appetite back once she's had a sleep.'

'I don't know… she's had a nasty knock on the head. Shouldn't we sit with her?'

'Gertie's right,' Dad said. 'Let's leave her to rest.' Abi felt the tray lifted from the bed. 'You heard what the doctor said. There's nothing to worry about. A few days in bed and she'll be as good as new.'

'If you think that's for the best.' Mum didn't sound sure. 'I've got your nan's brass bell here, love,' she said to Abi. 'I'll leave it on the floor, right here by the bed. Ring it if you need anything. Anything at all.'

Abi listened to the footsteps and the creak of the door being pulled to. She heard Dad's voice out on the landing. 'Hey, come on now, Rose. Worse things have happened at sea. She'll be her old self in no time, demanding cherryade and marshmallows, just like she did when she had chickenpox when she was six.'

Abi stared at the wall, pulled the blankets up over her shoulders, and put her hand to her face. She pressed the swelling around her eye and winced. She ran her fingers over the gauze, feeling the bumps of the stitches beneath. There was only one thing she wanted, and it wasn't chicken soup and Lucozade or cherryade and marshmallows, it was an explanation. Mum's refusal to admit or deny what Abi had seen could mean only one thing. She was having an affair with Tony.

For the three days and nights Abi spent in bed, it was this thought that kept her company. Even when she slept, there was no escape. Every time she woke, it was to a throbbing in her face and the memory of one of two nightmares. In the first, the scene on the beach was played out over and over again. Only now Mum and Tony weren't just kissing, they were laughing and joking; happy with themselves that they had succeeded in fooling everyone. In the second, unable to lie any longer, Abi revealed the truth about Mum and Tony and about her 'accident'. But as the words left her mouth, she watched Dad wither, his skin turning grey as he crumbled like a leaf in autumn. Nan cried and cried until she disappeared into a lake of her own tears and Penny and Shirl tumbled hand in hand down a helter-skelter with no end.

Abi wasn't stupid, she knew these nightmares were caused by her brain trying to make sense of what had happened. But still, they left a sick feeling in her stomach. Were they in some way a warning? A sign of what would happen if she ever did tell the truth?

If the nightmares weren't bad enough, she spent every waking moment on edge; waiting for Mum to find yet another excuse to come up to the attic. She hovered in the doorway like a ghost, watching, waiting, even when Abi pretended to be asleep. Countless times a day she crept in with a tray of food or a magazine or a glass of water for Abi to take her tablets. On the second day she removed the gauze from Abi's face to let the air get to the wound and help the healing process. She insisted on cleaning around the stitches with a cotton bud soaked in TCP, even though Abi flinched from her touch. And all the while, she babbled on about who had phoned to wish Abi well, what treat she could have when she was well enough to get up and go shopping and how there shouldn't be a scar. Hadn't the doctor said that she was young enough to heal?

Abi hoped there would be a scar. She wanted Mum to look at her face every day and see it. Because cooking her favourite food and making promises of treats didn't fool Abi; she knew Mum was trying to buy her silence. *Look at me*, she was saying. *I'm kind and generous. Don't tell anyone. I'm not that bad.*

But she was that bad. And Abi hated her mother for making her an accomplice in her secret. With each passing hour that nub of hate grew; spreading like a patch of mould, seeping deeper and deeper until Abi could feel it like a black spot in her core. She would keep Mum's secret. Not for her sake but for Dad and Nan and Penny and Shirl. But her silence wouldn't come for free. Before she shut her mouth on the subject forever, she would have her revenge on Mum in the single way that would destroy her.

***

On the Tuesday following the accident, Abi left her untouched tray of shepherd's pie and apple crumble on the floor, and for the first time in three days, got dressed. She picked her way down the stairs in her socks and while everyone was eating dinner in the kitchen, she slipped out of the front door, pulled on her trainers and, like a burglar, crept into the garden and took her bike from the shed.

She cycled a mile inland to a dairy farm set back from the road amongst a scattering of barns. The farmhouse crouched black against the fading light of the evening sky, its low roof like the spine of a hunched animal.

Abi balanced her bike against the fence and a chill wind rattled through the crops in the fields, whispering around her bare legs. She took a book from her pocket and pushed through the gate, the hinges creaking. A dog barked somewhere behind the house. Abi paused just inside the yard. This place was so strange. She felt dizzy and the side of her face ached from where the scab was tugging at the stitches. Maybe she should just give this up as a bad idea.

She couldn't.

She walked quickly across the yard and didn't stop until she was standing in the square of light flooding from the front door. She adjusted her hair to cover the side of her face. *Okay. Now.* She pressed the doorbell and it rang in a far-off room. A muffled voice shouted. And then silence. She raised her finger to press the bell again but pulled it away at the sound of a woman's voice in the hallway. 'Am I the only one that gets the door in this bloody house?'

A chain rattled and the door opened, releasing the smell of frying mince. A short, wide woman filled the doorway.

'Yes?'

'Is Alan in, please?'

The woman squinted at her. 'Who wants to know?'

'My name's Abi. I'm in Alan's class.' She held out the book. 'I was supposed to give him this at school but I forgot. Can I see him please?'

Thug's mum smiled and the skin around her eyes creased into deep ridges. 'Alan with a book! You sure you got the right house, my love?'

Abi nodded.

'If you say so.' Thug's mum laughed and her whole chest wobbled. 'Alan get down 'ere now,' she shouted up the stairs. 'There's a girl 'ere says she's got a book for you.' The woman gave Abi a final bewildered look, shook her head and walked back up the hall, still laughing.

Heavy footsteps pounded down the stairs and Thug appeared in the hallway. When he saw it was her, he smiled. He leant against the doorframe, crossed his arms and looked down at her.

'Well, well, well. What've we got here then, London?' He smirked and pointed to her face. She knew how bad it looked; the row of stitches like barbed wire zigzagging across the purple-green bruise. 'I hope you gave as good as you got,' he laughed.

'Come outside. I want to talk to you.'

'Is that why you ain't been in school, then?'

'Just come outside.'

He snatched the book from her hands. '*To Kill a Mockingbird*. What would I want with this?'

Abi snatched it back. 'Forget about the book. Just come outside and close the door. I need to ask you something.'

Thug smiled, stepped outside and pulled the door to behind him. 'Say what you came to say then. But hurry up, my tea's nearly ready.'

This was it. There was no going back once the words she'd been rehearsing all day were out of her mouth. She stood on tiptoes and whispered into his ear. 'I want you to fuck me.'

Thug took a step back. 'You what?'

'You heard.'

'Is this some kind of joke?' He looked over her shoulder towards the gate. 'Is your mate waiting out there to take the piss out of me?'

'No, it's just me. Look I'm not going to ask again. But if you don't want to…'

'I didn't say that.'

Abi followed Thug to a barn where bales of straw and sacks of feed were stacked up to the ceiling. In the farthest corner, he stood with his hands deep in his pockets, staring at the floor, kicking at one of the bales.

'Where?' Abi asked.

'Where what?'

'You know. Where do you want to…?'

'Oh…' He emptied the contents from an open bag of feed into a wheelbarrow, dropped it to the ground and kicked it flat. 'All right?'

Abi looked from the plastic bag to Thug. 'You have done this before, haven't you? You're not a virg–'

''Course I have,' he snorted. 'Loads of times. What do you think I am? Gay or something?'

Before she could change her mind, she sat down on the bag. Hitching up her school skirt, she slipped her knickers down her legs, kicked them away, and lay back. She parted her legs and, knowing exactly what Thug could see, she buried her face in the crook of her arm. This was mad. She should get up and run away. Before she could make a move, she heard the crack of straw underfoot, followed by the sound of a zip and the chink of what sounded like a belt buckle hitting the ground. She squeezed her eyes shut, bit down on her lip, and waited.

Thug was soon over her; his hands pressed to the ground either side of her head, his bare legs warm against hers. He tried to kiss her.

'No,' she said and turned away. 'I don't want to.'

He didn't try again. Instead his knuckles dug into her thighs as he adjusted himself.

She had rehearsed this scene so many times that she could see them as clearly as if she was hovering in the rafters looking down. Thug was on top of her, her arms and legs sticking out from beneath him like the legs of a turtle. She was there but not really there. But when Thug tried to force himself into her, she tumbled from the safety of the rafters and slammed back into her body.

She cried out and tried to sit up. Thug pushed her back, shoving his hand over her mouth.

'Shut up,' he hissed. 'Someone'll hear. It's not even in yet. What's wrong with you? It won't go in.' He kept his hand over her mouth, pushed harder and finally forced himself fully inside her.

She hadn't wanted to feel anything. Not pleasure, not pain, just numb. But each time Thug pushed into her, she felt her insides being ripped open. He grunted in her ear, keeping his hand over her mouth so that his fingers pressed against her teeth. Her legs scraped against the concrete floor. The cattle snorted outside and rubbed against the corrugated metal walls of the barn. It was all too much. She wanted it to stop. But just as she tried to squirm free, Thug's whole body went rigid. His hand forced her head back against the floor. He let out a loud groan, shuddered and collapsed onto her, his weight crushing the air from her lungs.

She was pinned to the ground unable to move or breath. Without any warning, Thug prised himself free. A pain ripped through Abi but this time when she cried out, Thug ignored her. He was busy getting to his feet and fastening his jeans.

She pulled herself up onto her elbows. Her arms and legs felt like the bones and muscles had turned to mush. With a great effort, and keeping her legs together in an attempt to stem the pain, she dragged herself up into a sitting position. She felt something damp between her legs and looked down to find milky-coloured blood leaking from her. She retched and managed to scramble to her knees just in time for her empty stomach to force a pool of bile out onto the plastic bag. She retched again and clutched her stomach.

Somewhere in the distance, Thug's mum called him in for his tea.

Chapter 16

'Come on then,' Dad called up the stairs. 'The traffic on the bypass is murder at this time of day. And don't get too used to this chauffeur service. Once those stitches are out, it's back to the coach for you.'

Abi stood in the attic, dressed for school, her satchel in one hand and her stained knickers from last night in the other. It was laundry day today. She was supposed to put her knickers in the hamper in the bathroom for Mum to find.

'Chop chop,' Dad called again. 'I can't risk driving too fast with this cast on my arm.'

In the kitchen, Abi found Nan at the sink drying up, and Mum at the range busy pushing some bread around the frying pan. Nan looked over her shoulder and smiled. 'There she is. The walking wounded.'

'How do you feel?' Mum asked without looking up from the pan.

Abi shrugged.

'That glass of juice is for you and I'm making you some eggy bread. Sit down and I'll serve it up.'

'I'm not hungry.'

'Here,' Nan said, taking a roll of silver foil down from the shelf. 'Why don't we wrap it in this? She can take it with her and have it at playtime.'

'I won't be hungry then either.'

'Don't be silly. You need to eat something…' Mum turned to look at Abi but her smile dropped. 'Oh Abi, look at your skirt.

171

I only ironed that on Sunday, why is it so creased? It looks like you've slept in it.'

Mum balanced the spatula on the side of the frying pan and tried to touch Abi's skirt. Abi pushed her hand away. 'I don't care about my stupid skirt. And I said I'm not hungry. Why won't any of you listen to me?'

'Abi!' Dad had come into the kitchen and was standing behind her. 'What's got into you? Your Mum and Nan are trying to be nice. They don't deserve to be spoken to like that.'

'Don't worry, Mick,' Nan said and laid a sheet of foil on the table. 'She's tired and grouchy. I feel like that some days. You're probably not looking forward to school today. Is that it, sweetheart? Don't worry, if anyone is mean about your face, you just tell them they'll have all of us to deal with.'

Mum took up her spatula again and nudged the bread onto the foil. 'As long as she doesn't go hungry today, I'll be happy. I just wish there was time to run the iron over that skirt.'

Abi sat in the front seat beside Dad, the eggy bread warm in her satchel against her legs.

'If anyone gives you a hard time about your face then you just tell a teacher,' Dad said. 'If there's any trouble, I'll come up to the school myself.'

Abi stared out through the windscreen, hoping her face was the only thing people would pick on her for today. She had barely slammed the car door when she found out it wasn't.

As soon as Dad pulled away, the taunts began. 'London loves Thug! London loves Thug!', 'What was it like then? In a barn, you dirty cow!', 'Did you "milk" him then. Ha ha ha ha.'

Abi pushed her way through the crowd at the gates. She was on her way to the side doors and the relative safety of the library, when someone grabbed her arm and dragged her into the dingy alley behind the canteen.

'Is it true?' Penny said. 'What they're all saying. Is it true?'

Moving away from the huge metal bins, which stank of rotting cabbage, Abi plastered on the blank expression she had prepared specially for this moment. 'Is what true?' she said.

'You do know Thug's going round school telling everyone that you went to his house last night and asked him to… asked him to…' Penny lowered her voice, '…fuck you.'

'And?'

'Oh my God.' Penny covered her mouth. 'It is true. You do know it's rape, don't you? You're only fifteen. It's not your birthday for another two months.'

'It's not rape if I asked for it.'

'It actually is. How could you, Abi? With *him*.'

Abi shrugged.

'But you hate him. Why would you do *that*, with *him*? I told everyone he was lying. I said you would never do that in a million years. How could you let me find out like that? You should have phoned me. I would never do anything like that without telling you.'

'I don't have to tell you everything.'

'What?'

'I said I don't have to tell you everything.'

'Thanks a lot,' Penny said, clearly hurt. She pointed to Abi's eye. 'I phoned you know, but your Mum said I couldn't speak to you because you were in bed. She said that I shouldn't come out to see you because you needed peace and quiet after your accident. And all the time you were creeping around behind my back seeing *him*. He obviously means more to you than I do.'

Tears hovered on Penny's eyelashes. Abi had to fight the urge to put her arms around her.

'Why do you even care what I do?' She looked down and kicked a mouldy potato peeling into the gutter.

'What?'

'You've got Dean now. You don't need me.'

'I don't understand what you're saying,' Penny said, tears inching down her cheeks. 'Nobody's more important to me than you. Abi, you're my best friend.'

'*Was* your best friend,' Abi corrected.

'I…? What…?' A sob choked Penny's words. 'But you promised… We're going to be best friends forever. We're going travelling and going to uni in London. We're getting a flat and…'

'That was never going to happen. It was all just a stupid daydream. Go to uni with Dean if it means that much to you. Anyway, I'm going now.'

Summoning all of her courage, Abi turned her back on Penny and walked away down the alley.

'Abi. Abi…' Penny called after her. 'Please, Abi, I don't understand. If I've done something wrong then I'm sorry. Please, Abi. Please talk to me. I'll finish with Dean if that's what you want. Please, Abi, don't go.'

Abi didn't look back. After running the barrage of taunts in the playground, she pushed through the door into the girls' toilets.

She wanted to be alone; instead she found Tracey standing at a sink. When she looked up and saw Abi's reflection in the mirror, Tracey spun around.

'You fucking slag!' she said, her eyes bloodshot, mascara running down her cheeks. For the briefest moment Abi felt sorry for her. Until Tracey launched herself across the room and grabbed her arm.

'You fucking bitch. I should rip your fucking head off,' she yelled in Abi's face. But it was when she tried to twist Abi's arm behind her back that something inside Abi snapped, like a rubber band wound one too many times. With a sharp jerk, she yanked her arm free.

'No, I should rip your fucking head off,' she said, pushing Tracey away. 'I shagged Thug, Tracey. What are you going to do about it?'

'I'm gonna fucking kill you.'

Abi took a step back and pointed to her cheek. 'Go on then. Hit me. You've been waiting ages to do this. Give it your best shot.' Tracey didn't make a move, so Abi grabbed her fist and put it to her cheek.

'Do it!' she yelled. 'Hit me. Give me another black eye. I want you to hit me.'

Tracey pulled her hand free and backed away. 'You've gone mad,' she said, wiping her nose on the back of her hand.

'Come on, Tracey. Don't tell me you're full of shit like the rest of them. Hit me. Cave my head in. Because I don't fucking care. Do you get it? I don't care. Kill me if you want.'

Tracey stared at her. 'You fucking freak,' she said backing away. She grabbed her bag from the floor and barged past Abi, out into the corridor.

With her heart pounding so hard that she could hear it in her ears, Abi slammed into a cubicle. She kicked the door, making it swing on its hinges. She kicked it for a second and a third time so that it banged against the frame and made the whole cubicle shake.

She slammed the toilet lid, sat down, and held her head in her hands. Why hadn't Tracey beaten the shit out of her? She deserved it. She didn't care about Thug. He was just a means to an end. Everyone in school knew how much Tracey fancied him. Abi squeezed her eyes shut and kicked the back of the door. She would do anything to reach into her head and replace herself with Tracey in the memories of last night. The dirt, the sound of the cows rubbing against the metal barn, the blood.

She opened her satchel, pulled out her balled-up knickers, and chucked them into the sanitary bin. How was she ever going to get revenge if she couldn't even bring herself to put her knickers in the laundry for Mum to find? This had all been to hurt her so-called mother. Losing her virginity before she was sixteen. She couldn't even see the plan through. And how was she ever going to cut herself off from Nan and Dad when she had failed at the first attempt? She was supposed to have started the process that morning by being mean to them and making them hate her. Instead they made excuses for her behaviour and were nice to her.

The only thing she had got right so far was hurting Penny. She pictured the look on Penny's face – the tears and the confusion

– and kicked the door again. What else was she supposed to do? Tell the truth? Tell Penny that she had slept with Thug to punish Mum for having an affair with Penny's dad? Tell her that she was breaking off their friendship because she would rather break her own heart than Penny's?

A tear dripped onto her skirt. It was followed by another and another. Everything in Penny's life was the same as it had been on Saturday. But there wasn't a single part of Abi's life left untouched by what she had seen and now done. Her life could never be the same again. And she *had* to cut herself off from everyone because if she didn't, she ran the risk that at any moment she might let the truth slip out and destroy all the people she loved. But first she had to stop crying. She had to learn how to be alone. She curled her hand into a fist.

'Toughen up,' she said and punched herself in the thigh. 'Toughen up.'

Chapter 17

Gertie – Friday 28 July 1944 – Afternoon

'Gertie? Gertie. What's happened to you?'

Gertie felt a hand touch her shoulder and turned to see a pair of blue eyes, full of concern, looking back at her.

'Gertie, it's me,' he tried again, shifting along the bench towards her. 'It's Aaron. We met here a couple of days ago. Remember?'

With her arms still wrapped around her waist, Gertie looked down into her lap and nodded.

'Good. That's real good. Now, Gertie, listen to me. You're hurt. There's blood all over your dress. It looks like it's coming from your legs. Can you tell me what happened to you?'

She opened her mouth, but the words wouldn't come.

'It's okay. You don't have to speak. But can you give me a sign to let me know it's okay for me to check you over?'

She nodded. Aaron instantly knelt before her. He lifted her dress to just above her knees and she watched him wince. 'Jeez, Gertie,' he said. 'You have cuts all over your legs. One of them looks real deep. Have you been in some kind of accident?'

An accident. Was it an accident? She pictured the little red cardigan abandoned on the floor of the bus amidst shattered glass and the conductress slumped in the aisle and… she held herself tighter.

'We need to get you to hospital,' Aaron said.

She shook her head.

'Please, Gertie. You need to see a doctor.'

She shook her head again.

'Okay. All right. But stay right where you are. Promise me that you won't move. I'll be right back.'

Gertie heard the rapid slap of boots grow quieter while the pavement blurred in and out of focus. In what seemed like a few seconds Aaron returned. He placed a jacket around her shoulders and knelt before her. An armful of packets dropped to the ground and Aaron ripped one open with his teeth. Uncorking a bottle, he soaked a wad of cotton wool and dabbed at Gertie's leg. Working quickly, he repeated the process on her right leg, all the while chewing at his bottom lip. Gertie could smell the bitter scent of iodine but she felt no pain, not even when Aaron parted the flesh of her right shin with his thumbs.

'Sorry,' he said as he picked something out. He placed gauze over her shin and wound a crepe bandage around her leg to secure it in place. Finally, he pulled her dress back down before resting back on his haunches and looking up at her.

'There was a piece of glass in the deep wound,' he said. 'I'm worried there might be more in some of the smaller cuts. You really should go to hospital to get checked out properly.'

Aaron rested his hands on Gertie's knees and something about the calmness in his voice gave her the reassurance to speak. 'No,' she said. 'No hospital.'

A little smile smoothed away the crease from Aaron's brow. 'Well thank God for that,' he sighed. 'I thought I was going to spend all day down here talking to myself. But really, Gertie, you should go to hospital. All I've done is patch you up. You need a proper examination. I'd come with you only…'

'No,' she said again. 'No hospital.'

Aaron laughed and shook his head. 'You do know that you are a terrible patient, don't you? By rights, if you're injured, you should do exactly what a medic tells you. But if you won't go to hospital, at least have some of this.' He took a bar of chocolate from his pocket, snapped it in half and held it out to her.

'I'm not hungry.'

'It's for the shock. You need sugar.'

'I couldn't.'

Aaron shook his head and put the chocolate back in his pocket. 'Is there someone I can call for you? Or would you like me to hail a cab to take you home?'

A vision of her empty flat and the empty flat downstairs flashed into Gertie's mind. Or worse, Ted at the parlour window, holding back the curtain, waiting for Sally to push the pram up the street with Brian running ahead, his arms outstretched dipping and weaving, mimicking a Spitfire in a dogfight.

Gertie took hold of Aaron's hand. 'Please don't make me go home. Please.'

'Okay, okay,' he said and squeezed her fingers. 'You don't have to do anything you don't want to. But if you don't want to go home, what do you want?'

She thought for a moment. 'I'd like to go for a walk.'

'I'm not sure that's such a good idea. If you put too much pressure on that wound it might open up even more. And I really should be going. I've got to–'

'Please. I'd like to walk.'

Together they made their way along the corridor of grand, grey buildings lining Northumberland Avenue. It was still the middle of the working day and they were two of only a handful of people heading towards the Thames, passing the embassies and consulates and government offices barricaded by walls of sandbags.

With each step Gertie's right leg throbbed more than she was prepared to let on. What if Aaron tried to make her sit down again? She couldn't face that. The concentration required to put one foot in front of the other to keep up with Aaron was the only thing occupying her mind, leaving less space for other thoughts to creep in.

She gripped the lapels of Aaron's jacket, pulling it tighter around her shoulders, focusing on her best shoes. They were utterly ruined, good only for the rubbish bin now. No matter how hard she scrubbed, she would never be able to clean away the bloodstains. They would be forever engrained into the soft, tan suede.

They came to the end of the avenue and Gertie turned left, leading them into Victoria Embankment Gardens. The grey of the city streets gave way to the green of shrubs and trees. On any other day she would have slipped her feet from her shoes to walk barefoot on the grass. But today, instead of providing a source of pleasure, the grass was a hindrance. It was softer than the pavement, making walking easier, allowing unwanted thoughts to nudge their way in: thoughts of a brilliant flash of light and of blood, thick like treacle, oozing into wooden grooves. Gertie stopped abruptly before the bandstand.

'I came here once, years ago,' she said. 'With my sister. For a concert. Elgar, I think it was. My father's favourite. It was a glorious summer's day and Ruth and I sat in deckchairs under a parasol and drank lemonade. There was an azalea bush there.' She pointed to a tower of sandbags surrounding a searchlight trained on the sky. 'I remember Ruth commenting on it because the flowers were so very pink. And now…'

Aaron took a step closer to her. 'There'll be an azalea bush there again one day soon for you and your sister. You just wait and see if there isn't.'

Gertie looked at the rough, dark bags stacked at least ten high. A number of them had split open, spilling sand onto the grass. 'I wish I could share your optimism,' she said. 'I can't help thinking that this awfulness will go on forever.'

'It's not optimism,' Aaron said softly. 'We have to believe that this suffering is going to make a difference, that all of the sacrifices are for *something*. Otherwise where's the point in any of this?' As Aaron spoke, his voice grew quieter and for the very first time Gertie thought she detected a note of something other than cheerfulness in his tone.

'Are you all right?' she asked and turned to find him staring intently at the pile of sand in the grass by his boots. As though his thoughts were somewhere far from this park on the bank of the Thames.

'Me?' he said. 'Am I all right? I suppose I am. I'm better than… that's to say, at least I'm here and not…' He paused and shook his head. 'Sorry. I'm just tired. I got into a game of poker last night and well, you know how it is. It went on late. So,' he said, his voice returning to almost normal. 'What would you like to do now? From the look of those clouds, I'd say there's a storm coming in.'

Gertie looked up at the steely-grey sky. The first spots of drizzle were falling as dark pinpricks on the path. She pulled the collar of Aaron's jacket tighter round her neck. 'If you wouldn't mind, I'd quite like to walk a little more.'

The crease appeared in Aaron's brow again. 'Wouldn't you rather rest your legs? I think I saw a little café back there a way...'

'No. Please, I'd like to walk. Perhaps just across the bridge. Unless... oh, I'm sorry. I didn't even think to ask if you had somewhere else you should be. How rude of me. I'm so sorry.'

'Don't be,' he said. 'There's nowhere else I want to be.'

Gertie walked by Aaron's side out of the park gates and along the Embankment. She kept up with him until he began to climb the stone steps up to Waterloo Bridge. She fell behind so he wouldn't see how she struggled.

When Aaron stopped at the top to look over the side of the bridge, Gertie knew it was for her benefit. He clearly had the strength to take the steps two at a time and the stamina to walk a hundred miles if he had to. She was grateful for his thoughtfulness and tact. She joined him and leant against the bridge, looking down at the dark water of the Thames; at the oil slicks on the surface of the waves breaking against the supports below, at the black hulks of vessels further upstream, at the barrage balloons stretching around the bend in the river. The ropes securing them to the ground criss-crossed the horizon like scars in the sky.

'Tell me more about Canada,' she said.

'What do you want to know?'

'Anything. Everything. It all sounds so wonderful.' She wanted the distraction of listening to him talk but also hoped it might cheer him up. He still seemed distracted. Perhaps her talk of Ruth had made him think of his own home so far away.

'Do you have any brothers or sisters?' she asked. At last Aaron smiled.

'One of each,' he said. 'Twins. They're thirteen now and they drive my mom mad.'

He continued slowly over the bridge and Gertie tried her best not to limp as she walked beside him. He told her all about the mischief that Ed and Eliza got into on the farm. How they both liked to collect bugs and keep them in jars on the windowsill, much to the dismay of his mother and grandmother. And he told her about the sprawling farmhouse his father and grandfather had built for the three generations of Duksztas to live in with three dogs, two cats, 'And any number of bugs, of course.'

He spoke with such passion and in such vivid detail about his home that it came to life for Gertie. His soft voice took her to a safe place where she was no longer crossing a bridge over the Thames with the drizzle making her hair and face damp; she was on the porch of a white farmhouse, rocking on a swing, watching a bird spread its wings and soar over meadows of long grass and wildflowers.

'Our farm's in the shadow of the Rocky Mountains,' Aaron said. 'And every winter my dad and grandpa take my brother and me on a trip up there. It's a sort of pilgrimage, I guess. We stay in this tiny lodge, just the four of us. And we go hiking and skiing and fishing and we eat jacket potatoes cooked over an open fire. My grandpa lived out in the countryside in Poland, you see, and he wants to teach Ed and me all about nature. You should see it up there, Gertie, you can't help but fall in love with the place. We stay on the shores of a lake called Lake Louise. Only when we go, it's frozen solid so that you can walk right across from one side to the other. The whole world is white and you can't tell the land from the water. We make holes in the ice so we can fish. And the air is so pure and clean that lichens grow up in the trees there that you just don't see anywhere else.'

At the end of the bridge, they headed east along the bank of the river, down a network of streets with the dark factories and warehouses of the docks looming in the distance.

'Last summer Ed and I had a notion to ride out to Lake Louise. We'd heard that when the water isn't frozen, it's as green as an emerald and we were determined to see it for ourselves. We were convinced that we could ride there and back in one day so we saddled up our horses and rode all day, but d'you know what? We never seemed to get any closer. Those mountains were always just a bit out of our grasp and–'

The whine of the air-raid siren interrupted Aaron's story. The look on his face changed immediately. 'Where are we, Gertie?' he asked, all the fun gone from his voice. 'Where's the nearest shelter?'

Gertie looked around, searching for a familiar landmark. But the street looked like any other bombed-out street of terraced houses. Every front door and all of the windows on the ground floors had been covered with rough wooden boards. Most of the roofs were missing, their blackened rafters exposed like skeletons of burnt chickens. A few lonely chimneystacks jutted defiantly into the grey sky and where gutters clung on, they were full of dead weeds. There wasn't a sign of life. Not even a rat. Even the trees lining the street were nothing more than burnt stubs; deep scars the only sign that leaves and boughs had once sprung from the wide trunks.

'I think Waterloo is close by, but I couldn't say where exactly,' Gertie said.

Aaron frowned and ran his fingers through his hair as he looked up and down the length of the deserted street.

'I'm so sorry,' she said. 'It was stupid of me to get carried away and bring us to somewhere I don't know.'

The siren blared insistently.

'It's not your fault,' Aaron said, but his voice took on a more urgent tone. 'I should've kept an eye on where we were instead of running my mouth off. Come on.'

He headed for the first house in the row, picking his way over the rubble on the pavement. He grabbed the corner of the hoarding covering the front door and pulled. It refused to move.

'Fuck,' he muttered under his breath and moved onto the next house. Gertie followed him. Again he gripped the hoarding and tried to prise it away, his face growing red with the effort. 'Move you bastard! Move!'

But just like the hoarding on the first house, it wouldn't shift. He kicked the board and moved onto the third house where he took hold of the top corner of the hoarding. This time when he pulled, the nails holding it to the doorframe came free.

'Ha, ha,' he laughed and turned to Gertie with a satisfied grin. With a final yank and a yell, Aaron pulled the whole of the hoarding free and chucked it to the ground. Gripping either side of the doorframe, he gave the door a single, hard kick and it flew open.

'Go on,' he said and nodded to Gertie. With the siren blaring, she crossed the threshold into the blackness. But immediately wished she hadn't.

Part 3

Chapter 18

'Russell! Russell! Phone!'

Abi came to, lying on top of the duvet, convinced that the pounding in her head was her shrivelled brain crashing against the inside of her skull.

'Are you deaf, Russell? I said phone!'

Okay, so it wasn't in her head; it was someone bashing on her door. 'Keep your wig on,' Abi tried to shout. But the words came out as a garbled croak. That wasn't good; speaking shouldn't hurt.

'You're lucky they said it was important,' the voice on the other side of the door said, 'or I wouldn't have bothered. It *is* 4.30 in the morning you know, and some of us *do* actually get up for lectures.'

Finally Abi recognised the nasally, patronising tone. It belonged to Emma – or was it Emily? – the girl with the room by the payphone. She studied something pointless like political science.

'Fuck off,' Abi croaked.

The door shook with what she guessed was a swift kick.

'Fuck off yourself,' Emma-Emily said.

A few seconds later the sound of a door slamming echoed up the corridor. Abi would have smiled if she hadn't been afraid that the action of moving even a single facial muscle might cause pain. It did sooth her aching head just a bit to know that she had finally managed to get a rise out of Miss Broom-Up-The-Arse 1988. Touché.

She prised open her eyes. What normal person phoned at 4.30 and on a weekday? She scrabbled around in her brain and drew out a culprit. Rob. He had probably only just shoehorned the last straggler out of the club after a lock-in. He would have emptied the ashtrays and loaded the glass washer (if he could be bothered), poured himself a quadruple Jack Daniels, and settled down with a joint to indulge in a session of *Dark Side of the Moon* on the club's sound system. Abi had joined him more than once after a shift, more for the free weed than any appreciation of David Gilmour's guitar skills.

She should have phoned Rob. It took a special kind of coward to just not show up for work. Rob was a good bloke, he would understand if only she had had the guts to explain that she had to resign because her tutors were on her case again. As fun as it was to spend every night behind the bar of his alternative club in a dingy basement, serving pints of real ale to balding middle-aged bikers and halves of snakebite to skinny students in Smiths T-shirts, she really did have to knuckle down if she stood any chance of leaving Leeds with a degree at the end of three years.

She dragged her head up and wiped away the trail of spit connecting her like an umbilical cord to the pillow. Slowly, very slowly, she lifted the rest of her body and sat on the edge of the bed. So much for the plan to stay in at least two nights a week to save money – not to mention her liver – and turn over a new, studious leaf. The events of the previous night gradually began to filter back. After precisely half an hour of hitting the art history textbooks she had given in to the call of triples for a quid at *The Sunset and Vine* and had spent the rest of the evening propping up the bar. She was pretty sure that it had ended with an exploration of the liqueur list with a couple of geology students. She licked her dry lips. Surely it wasn't normal to still taste flaming sambucas hours after drinking them.

Fumbling to switch on the lamp beside her bed, she squinted at the sea of crap on the floor, waiting for it to stop swirling like the contents of an art shop and a jumble sale caught in the eye of a cyclone. Tubes of squeezed oil paint missing their lids, scattered amongst pencils, pastels and paintbrushes. A sketchbook open at a charcoal drawing of a female nude from life class. Off-cuts of fabric hoarded to make a collage. From amongst the mess, Abi wrestled her latest Oxfam purchase – a baggy old man's jumper – it was black, two sizes too big, fraying at the cuffs and a bit loose at the seams, but Abi loved it.

She yanked the jumper over her head, slowly stood up and began to pick her way towards the door, stepping carefully over a sculpture of a horse constructed from twisted wire coat hangers. That's all she needed, to fall over and crush the only assignment she had completed. Well, nearly completed. She watched her feet as she placed them amongst the chaos. Why had she gone to bed wearing her DMs? Maybe she should be more worried that she had no memory whatsoever of getting back to her room than why she hadn't removed her boots before passing out.

The corridor outside her room was dimly lit and eerily quiet. It was too early for anybody to be roaming Boddington Hall. Abi weaved down the corridor. She picked up the receiver dangling from the payphone on the wall. It smelled of bad breath and patchouli. 'Rob. Yeah, sorry and all that,' she said, bracing herself against the wall. 'But I'm like, not coming back.'

There was a pause before the person on the other end spoke. 'Abigail? Is that you?'

Suddenly the corridor stopped spinning. 'Dad?'

***

Abi shared a carriage on the 6.08 from Leeds to Bristol with a couple of men in suits. One had fallen asleep within minutes of pulling out of the station – tie loose, jaw slack, breathing deeply – while the other had spread papers out over his table and was tapping frantically at a calculator.

Abi gazed out at the world passing by the window. It was still the middle of the night. A hard November frost glittered on the grass and trees in parks and gardens. Dull smudges of light glowed from the occasional window. Eyeing up her cigarettes and lighter on the table, Abi decided against expending the energy it would take to wander along to the smoking carriage. She took a can of cola from her duffle bag, forced back the ring pull and slurped at the fizzy brown foam collecting in the rim.

At least she wasn't pissed any more. It turned out that being woken by a phone call in the middle of the night, shoving a pair of knickers and a toothbrush into a duffle bag, stepping out into a freezing Yorkshire morning, and following a milk float down the hill to the station, was a far more effective method of sobering up than drinking a gallon of black coffee and downing two paracetamol.

She took another slurp of cola and swilled it around her mouth. Thank God she had given Dad the payphone number to contact her in an emergency. If she had waited to hear about Nan's accident through the normal channel of communicating with her family – a brusque five-minute phone call she made from Rob's club every other Sunday just to let them know she was still alive – then Nan would have been discharged from hospital before Abi even knew she had been admitted. She still wasn't entirely sure why Dad had felt the need to call her at 4.30 in the morning to ask her to go home, especially when he said Nan's condition wasn't serious. The doctors were only keeping her in hospital to run a few tests. But he knew she would want to know. He was right. She may have made a promise to herself never to return to Cliff Cottage once she had made her escape, but she always knew there would be one exception – if Nan needed her. Because no matter how surly, obnoxious and downright rude Abi had forced herself to be over the last two years, trying her damnedest to make her family hate her, Nan had refused to give up on her.

'Now I know that's not my Abi talking,' she would say, making an excuse whenever Abi said something intentionally provocative. 'It's just those nasty hormones.' And even when Abi tried to shrug her off, Nan persisted until Abi accepted a kiss and a hug.

Abi took another swig of cola, hoping to swallow down the lump in her throat. Nan never knew it, of course, but she had lived for those moments of tenderness. Because for a brief second, when Nan slipped her arms around her, Abi was prepared to let her guard down and allow someone in. But as soon as Nan drew her arms away, Abi slammed the shutters back up. It was the only protection she had, the only way she could put the distance she needed between her and the world.

She looked out of the window. When she saw her watery reflection staring back at her, she turned away. Why hadn't she packed a book along with her knickers and toothbrush? At least then she would have something to drag her mind back from where it was trying to take her. She began to run through the projects she still had to hand in before Christmas – the horse sculpture with accompanying sketches, the essay demonstrating the influence of Andy Warhol on popular culture, the study of the naked female form – but it wasn't enough. With each mile the train took towards Cliff Cottage, images lodged in the dark recesses of her mind came creeping out; Dad with his arm in plaster laughing as he tried to eat a plate of fish and chips one-handed, Nan in the kitchen smiling as she juiced a dozen lemons to make a batch of lemonade, Mum and Tony kissing on the beach, Penny standing by the bins behind the school canteen, tears streaming down her face.

With the can of worms of her past open, Abi was powerless to slam the lid back on. Vivid memories of Penny pursuing her for weeks flooded back; Penny cornering her in classrooms, phoning her at home, tracking her down to the library – 'Please, Abi, please tell me what I did wrong? Whatever it was, I'm sorry. Please can we be friends again? I don't care that you didn't tell me what you did with Thug. Look, I've got a new map of France and I sent away for this prospectus for you from Saint Martin's. Here take it.' – until Abi could bear it no longer.

'What do you mean you want to change schools? You're taking your exams in a few weeks,' Dad said when Abi came home from school one day and announced she was leaving West Hill to enrol at the technical college. 'The tech's miles away in the wrong direction. It must be at least three buses there and back.'

She was sure Mr Munro had tears in his eyes when she unpinned her paintings from the walls in the art room and slipped them into a folder. 'I'll give you a reference anytime you need one. Here, take this,' he said, handing her a piece of paper. 'It's my address and phone number. Call me any time, even if you just want to talk. I'm going to miss you, Abi.'

As always it was left to Nan to cut through the half-truths and get to the heart of the matter. 'Have you had a falling out with Penny?' Nan asked, taking hold of Abi's hand. 'We haven't seen her in weeks. Listen, sweetheart, I know how close girls of your age grow to their friends and how a tiff can seem like the end of the world. But I'm sure if you talk to her you can patch things up.'

But she couldn't talk to Penny, could she? They could never patch things up because there was a huge black lie splitting them in two. And *someone* else knew that too. The same *someone* who didn't question any of Abi's motivations or challenge her odd behaviour, even though that *someone* had never been able to keep her nose out of Abi's business before.

'Abi's old enough to make her own decisions,' Mum had said. 'If she wants to change schools then we should respect that. And we shouldn't pry into her business. She's nearly sixteen now, that's old enough to choose her own friends.'

Mum didn't even complain when she started to wear black and took to locking herself in the attic whenever she was at Cliff Cottage. She didn't comment when Abi fell in with the goths from her art class at the tech and began spending every weekend with them. Of course, Mum didn't know that Abi was sitting in bedrooms behind closed curtains, listening to Bauhaus, Siouxsie and the Banshees and The Cure, downing so much cider and smoking so much blow that she could barely stand. The goths didn't ask questions. They didn't pry. They simply accepted her as a kindred spirit, as though they could see inside her and see the blackness in her core. And it didn't matter that Abi was always short of cash, she was able to trade her talent for recreating the cover of *A Clockwork Orange* in black emulsion on bedroom walls in exchange for bottles of cider, which she downed before crashing out on the floor of whatever room she found herself in. Anything so she didn't have to go back to Cliff Cottage and face the person responsible for turning her into a half-person, incapable of conducting a meaningful relationship with anyone or anything other than a bottle of Merrydown and twenty B&H. The person with whom she had an unspoken understanding: for as long as she kept her mouth shut about Mum's disgusting secret then Mum would keep her nose out of Abi's life.

'Tickets please.'

Abi fumbled in her bag and located her ticket, which she handed to the conductor. He punched a hole in the ticket before handing it back to her. 'The buffet car's open if you're interested. And the smoking carriage is the next one along,' he said, nodding to her cigarettes.

As the conductor weaved his way along the aisle and nudged the shoulder of the sleeping businessman, Abi flicked someone else's crumbs off the table. Outside, a glimmer of hazy pink daylight hovered above the mist on a hill. Would it be so bad if she got off at the next station, caught a train back to Leeds, and posted a 'Get Well Soon' card to Nan? Of course it would. It would be very bad. But as soon as she was sure Nan was on the mend, she would be on the next train out of there. Grabbing her fags, she headed off for the smoking carriage.

***

A flock of sheep wandering on the line somewhere north of Oxford meant Abi only just made her connection at Bristol. She had to sprint the length of the concourse, barging through a crowd of school kids, to jump on the train to Dorchester with the guard's whistle shrieking in her ears.

It was almost midday by the time she arrived at Dorset County Hospital. Before heading off in search of the ward, she made a detour to the ladies. She filled a basin to the brim with ice cold water, submerged her face and held it under for a few seconds before emerging, coughing and gasping. She grabbed a handful of scratchy towels, scrubbed her face dry and forced her fingers through her stiff mess of hair. Mental note: do not backcomb your hair and set it with sugar water on the eve of a family emergency, but if you do, be sure to pack a hairbrush. Mind you, she could show up wearing a raincoat and waders, with a Union Jack tattooed on her forehead, and Nan would still look her up and down and smile. 'Is that the new fashion? Isn't it smashing?'

Abi stopped in at the little gift shop and pulled a pitiful handful of coins from her pocket – all that was left after buying the train ticket. It wasn't nearly enough for one of the bunches of carnations wrapped in cellophane, but it was just enough for a tube of Polos. She paid the cashier and slipped the tube of sweets into her pocket. Outside the shop, she pulled a piece of paper from her bag. A porter helped her decipher her hurriedly scrawled hieroglyphics and after ten minutes in the rabbit warren of corridors and a couple of wrong turns, Abi found herself at the end of a long corridor.

She screwed up the scrap of paper and forced it into her back pocket but instead of making her way down the corridor, she stood to one side. Any normal person would have rushed down without a second thought, to be with their family. But she had spent so long trying to put distance between her and them that she felt like an intruder in her own life. It was then that she saw a man sitting outside a door further down. He was alone, his back rounded, elbows resting on his knees, his face buried in his hands. The collar of his shirt was only half tucked into the neck of his jumper and, with the legs of his jeans hitched up slightly, Abi could see he was wearing no socks with his trainers. Abi took a step towards the man. At the sound of her DMs squeaking on the lino floor, he looked up.

'Abi,' her dad sighed and got to his feet. 'Are you a sight for sore eyes?' Before she could respond, his arms were around her, holding her so close that the buckle of her duffle bag dug into her back. When he pulled away, she saw that his eyes were bloodshot. Keeping hold of her arms just above the elbows he looked at her. 'Good trip?' he asked.

'All right. Are you okay, Dad? You look terrible.'

He laughed, a little laugh. 'Thanks for the vote of confidence. I'm fine. It's been quite a night.'

'Where's Nan?'

Dad let go of her arms and ran his fingers through his fringe. 'Are you hungry? I don't imagine you had any breakfast on the train. There's a café around here somewhere.' He looked around as though half expecting a café to appear in the corridor. 'I could get you a sandwich or a doughnut or something. You always liked doughnuts. Those ones with jam in the middle.'

'I'm not hungry,' she fibbed. 'Is Nan in there?' She nodded to the door closest to them.

'They put her in a private room. It's quieter. The nurse is in with her at the moment. Your mum went home to pick up a few bits and pieces for your nan. I offered to go but she insisted, and you know what your mum's like when she sets her mind on something. Are you sure you don't want that doughnut?'

Abi shook her head. She watched a frown furrow Dad's brow. 'Sit down, love,' he said. Something about the way his voice took on a serious tone set an alarm ringing in Abi's head.

'I don't want to sit down.'

'Please, Abi, sit down,' he insisted.

Abi gave in. She dropped her bag to the floor and sat on one of the plastic chairs. Dad sat beside her. He took hold of her hands.

'What I told you on the phone,' he said. 'It wasn't the whole truth. I didn't want you sitting on that train all by yourself worrying when there was nothing you could do. You see, Abi… your nan, she didn't just have a fall. The doctors think there's more to it than that. They think she had a stroke. I don't understand exactly what it means but the doctor said it's when a blood vessel bursts in the brain.'

Abi tried to free her hands. She didn't want to hear this. She didn't want to know. Her dad gripped her hands so that it was impossible to shake him free. 'Please, love. I know it's hard but you have to hear me out. I have to know that you understand.'

Abi willed him to say that it wasn't serious. Instead he took a deep breath and fixed his gaze on her. 'It's serious, love. But we won't know the full extent of the damage to your Nan's brain until the doctors run some tests later today. We have to prepare ourselves that she might be in hospital for some time or… But the doctor said that some people make a full recovery. And your nan has always been strong, hasn't she? We've got Cyril to thank for raising the alarm. Me and your mum were fast asleep when he woke us in the early hours with his barking and crying fit to bring the house down. Your mum thought that a noise outside might have spooked him, so she went downstairs to calm him and… well… that's when she found your Nan, collapsed in the kitchen. Your mum said it looked like she had gone down to make a cup of tea. The milk was out and the fridge door was wide open. And Cyril was standing beside your nan, refusing to leave her. He was crying and whimpering and nudging her. It's a good job he was there, wasn't it? To raise the alarm.'

Abi couldn't respond. She wanted to run away; to sprint all the way to the station without stopping. She didn't *do* this. Caring. She couldn't do it. Before she could do anything the door to Nan's room opened. A nurse came out and closed it gently behind her. 'Is this Mrs Smith's granddaughter?' she asked Dad.

'Yes,' Dad said, getting to his feet and pulling Abi up to stand beside him. 'This is my daughter, Abigail.'

'Abigail, now isn't that a beautiful name?' the nurse said in a soft Scottish accent. 'Well, Abigail, your granny's sleeping at the moment. Has your dad explained that the doctor's going to run some tests later?'

Abi nodded.

'Good. So why don't you go and sit with your granny for a while? I'm sure she'd like to hear all your news. Your dad tells me you've been away to university. In Sheffield is it?'

'Leeds,' Abi corrected. 'But if she's sleeping, she won't hear me.'

'Och, don't let that stop you. You see, it's a medically-induced sleep to keep your granny comfortable. It's highly probable that she'll be able to hear you. And it's important that she has her family around her.'

Abi looked at her dad. He smiled. 'Go on,' he said and gave her hand a squeeze. 'You two have never been short of anything to say to each other. Just sit with your nan. Talk to her.'

When Abi stepped into the room and the door closed behind her, she felt her stomach slump into her feet. She clamped her hands to her mouth to hold in a cry.

Nan was lying in the bed, her eyes closed, her arms resting by her sides on top of the tightly tucked blanket. An oxygen mask covered her nose and mouth. Her white hair was parted in all sorts of odd ways revealing her baby pink scalp beneath.

Unable to move from the safety of the doorway, Abi let her eyes travel the length of the bed, taking in the mound of Nan beneath the covers. She looked at Nan's face and saw how it seemed to droop to one side, as though her cheek and mouth had turned to melted wax. Dad should have warned her what to expect. That way, she could have spent the last six hours preparing for this moment rather than imagining turning up at the hospital to find Nan being saucy with a young doctor trying to take her pulse – 'Do you know how long it's been since a young man held my hand? You've got my heart going like a racehorse. I bet it's off the scale!'

Abi took a step towards the bed. She had to speak; she had to be normal. Digging in her pocket, she pulled out the tube of Polos.

'Hello, Nan.' She tried to sound cheerful. Instead her voice cracked. She ran her fingernail along the green and blue paper wrapper, feeling the ridges of the mints beneath. 'I've brought you these.' She held out the Polos. Her hand began to tremble. The sweets fell to the floor and smashed.

'I'm so sorry,' she whispered. 'I wish I'd been there to make you a cup of tea. I wish you hadn't been on your own. On the kitchen floor…' She clamped her hand to her mouth again. She couldn't cry. She had to be strong. She blew out her cheeks and took a final step to the bed. She placed her fingertips to the back of Nan's hand and brushed her skin. It was warm and soft but fragile too, like a piece of antique silk scattered with dark patches. She ran her fingers across the pronounced knuckles. For the first time in Abi's life, her nan didn't respond to her. The woman who had cuddled her and promised her that even when her world was falling apart, everything would be all right; the woman who had carried on loving her when she couldn't love herself, was now an old lady in a hospital bed.

Abi watched Nan's chest gently rise and fall and listened to the hiss of the oxygen tank and the muffled sound of voices outside in the corridor. 'It's all right, Nan. You're in hospital. The doctors and nurses are looking after you. Keep breathing, Nan. Just keep breathing because you have to get better. Do you hear me? You have to get better.'

Abi slipped her hand around Nan's. She sat in the chair beside the bed and raised Nan's hand and pressed the palm to her cheek. She closed her eyes, feeling the warm fingers on her face. 'I'm so sorry, Nan. I'm so sorry if I hurt you. I should never have shut you out. But I was so scared. I didn't want to hurt you. If I'd told you, I would have broken your heart. And I couldn't do that to you or to Dad.'

She kissed her Nan's hand and somewhere behind the smell of antiseptic she detected a faint hint of coal tar soap and *Yardley's* talcum powder. 'Please don't leave me. You're the only person who ever understood me. Please don't go. Please.'

***

'Abi… Abi… come on love, wake up.'

Abi prised open her eyes. It took a moment but as the cloying smell of hospital filled her nostrils, she realised where she was.

'You fell asleep,' Dad said. 'You must be exhausted.'

Abi looked towards the bed. Nan was still there, eyes closed, chest gently rising and falling. If it wasn't for the mask covering her nose and her drooping face, she could have been asleep.

'I'm going to take you home,' Dad said quietly. 'To get some proper sleep.'

'But Nan?'

'Your mum's outside. She's going to come and sit with her.'

'But we can come back later?'

'Of course. Once you've had some sleep and something to eat. It's been a long day. Come on,' he said, holding his hand out to her. 'Let's get you home.'

'Just a minute,' she said. She got up from the chair and leant over the bed. She pressed her lips to Nan's forehead and breathed in deeply. The scent of soap and talc was gone. All she could smell was hospital. She closed her eyes and felt Nan's warmth seep into her cheek. 'I love you, Nan,' she whispered.

Abi followed Dad out of the room, looking down at the toes of her DMs, shuffling one in front of the other. They stopped when the nurse's bright white clogs stepped into view. A hand squeezed Abi's arm and a voice said something about being brave, before the clogs disappeared followed by the sound of a door closing. Abi watched Dad's trainers walk along the corridor. 'Rose. Look who's here,' he said.

A pair of blue flat pumps walked into Abi's field of vision; Mum's driving shoes.

'Oh, Abi. I'm so glad you came,' Mum said. Abi let herself be hugged. Half of her wanted to collapse onto Mum's shoulder but the other half stopped her. When she felt Mum's hands slip from her, she looked up to see Mum pick up a carrier bag from one of the plastic chairs and look inside.

'It's awful,' Mum said, addressing her words to the contents of the bag. 'Mum would be mortified if she knew I'd brought her smalls in a supermarket bag. But I couldn't find her overnight case. You know, the red one that she was so fond of. I should have looked harder, shouldn't I? It was probably under the bed, wasn't it?' She looked up and Abi saw the inky circles beneath her eyes. 'I forgot her bed jacket. Oh, Mick, I forgot Mum's bed jacket.' Her hands began to tremble making the carrier bag rustle. Dad stepped towards her and put his arms around her.

'Come on now, try and calm down. Abi and I will bring the bed jacket when we come back later. If you remember anything else, just call us from the payphone.' He dug his hand into his pocket and pulled out a handful of change, which he pressed into Mum's palm. 'You're not to worry about anything apart from sitting with Gertie. Okay?'

'Okay,' Mum said, clutching the change and twisting the handles of the bag.

The door to the small room opened and the nurse came out. She put her arm around Mum. 'Are you coming in?' she said. Mum gave Abi and Dad a small smile before heading inside.

By the time they got back to Cliff Cottage, it was after four o'clock. Abi was too tired to care where she was. The wind that whipped around the side of the house was full of ice, but as she stepped into the kitchen, she got a warm welcome from Cyril. He leapt into her arms and licked her face like she had been gone for two years rather than two months. Dad tried to steer her up to her old bedroom, but she insisted on curling up on the sofa in the parlour. The house was bitterly cold so Dad made up a fire in the grate and Cyril jumped up onto the sofa and tucked into her. He deserved it. He was a hero. The logs began to crackle and Abi looked into the glowing flames. She closed her eyes and ran her fingers over Cyril's silky ears.

At some point she became vaguely aware of the phone ringing in the hall, but it didn't disturb her enough to drag her into consciousness. She turned over and buried her face into a cushion.

She felt something touch her back. She opened her eyes. The room was in darkness. Outside, the last remnants of pale winter sunlight dipped lower in the sky. The fire had burned itself out so that just embers glowed in the hearth and Cyril had slipped away in search of a warmer spot and was curled up on the rug.

'You're awake then,' her dad said.

Abi sat up. 'Just about.'

'Sorry, love. I didn't want to wake you. But we need to go back to the hospital.'

Abi pulled her cuffs over her hands. 'Shall I go and get Nan's bed jacket?'

'Don't worry about that now.'

'It's all right, I know where she keeps it. I won't be a minute.' She made to stand but Dad sat on the sofa beside her.

'There's no need.' He took hold of her hand. 'Love,' he said, 'I have something to tell you. It's your nan.' He paused, and Abi heard him swallow. 'I'm so sorry, sweetheart. But she's gone.'

'Gone?' Abi repeated the word like she didn't know what he meant.

'The hospital just phoned. Your mum was with her.'

'My nan,' Abi whispered.

Dad put his arms around her and pulled her to him. 'I know,' he said. 'I know.'

Abi sat rigid. Nan wasn't gone. She couldn't be. She wanted to tell Dad that he'd made a mistake. It was someone else. Not her lovely, lovely nan. But she couldn't move. Couldn't move and couldn't speak.

Chapter 19

T he church was packed, the pews crowded with old men in dark overcoats and ladies in black dresses and hats. The verger closed the heavy doors, but a cold breeze still whistled around the ankles of the congregation, disturbing the petals of the lilies arranged on the altar and worrying the hem of Father Pearson's cassock as he took his place at the pulpit, his nose and cheeks nipped red.

Abi sat in the family pew on one side of Mum, Dad on the other side, nearest the aisle. Abi kept her eyes firmly forward and her coat buttoned to her chin. When Father Pearson began the service by saying that Gertie Smith had touched so many lives, Abi unravelled a row of stitches from the cuff of her jumper. When he talked about Gertie's unswerving joy of life, her energy, her ready smile, her love for her family, and the strength they had given her when she lost her beloved husband Sid, Abi focused on a patch of ceiling way up in the rafters where a heavy wooden joist met the thick stone wall. When the organ whined as it warmed, and the choir and congregation rose to sing *All things Bright and Beautiful*, Abi stood and listened.

The creak of wood signalled the congregation retaking their seats at the end of the hymn. As the rustle of clothes died down, Abi felt the pew move. From the corner of her eye, she saw Dad stand up and make his way slowly to the open Bible before the altar. He coughed, and Abi stared at the embroidered prayer cushion by her feet.

'To every thing there is a season,' Dad began. 'And a time to every purpose under the heaven. A time to be born, and a time to die.' He paused and coughed. While Dad read the rest of the passage he had chosen himself, Abi counted the white cross-stitches forming the body of a dove embroidered onto the prayer cushion. Then she counted the brown and green stitches forming the olive branch in its beak. She only raised her eyes when Dad finished his reading and the sound of heavy footsteps echoed from the back of the church down the aisle.

The crisp winter sun shone through the vast stained-glass window depicting St Francis, two lambs at his feet and a bird perched on his finger. Shards of gold, blue, green and red reflected on the lid of the pale wooden coffin and Dad took his position amongst five other men. He took hold of the brass handle at the top end and, linking arms at shoulder-level with the man beside him, gently hoisted the coffin up onto his shoulder. Head bowed, hand pressed gently to the side of the coffin, Dad helped bear Nan on her final journey down the aisle.

In the cemetery, Abi kicked at the mud frozen into ripples around the open hole in the ground. When she heard Mum sobbing, something inside her – and she wasn't sure what – made her step closer and reach for her hand. Mum gripped Abi's fingers as though holding onto her daughter was the only thing keeping her upright. When Nan's coffin was lowered into the cold November ground to lie beside Granddad, Mum collapsed, and Abi helped Dad keep her on her feet.

***

People squeezed into every corner of Cliff Cottage. The women of the WI and the men of the village football team took up most of the space in the parlour. Out in the hall, the barman of The Red Lion was deep in conversation with Father Pearson, the newsagent, and the fishmonger. In the kitchen, members of the choir jostled for space with the other villagers, all sipping glasses of sweet sherry, cups of tea, or pints of Dad's homebrew.

Abi eased her way between the various groups, offering trays of ham sandwiches. When there was nothing left but lettuce garnishes, she returned to the kitchen and filled the tray with sausage rolls, still warm from the oven. Every sandwich or sausage roll taken from the tray came with a question or comment. 'There'll be such a gap at church now.' 'Gertie was a terrific friend.' 'We'll miss her flower arranging. What she couldn't do with a handful of peonies was nobody's business.' 'It was a lovely service.' 'Gertie was so proud of you. It was Abigail this and Abigail that.' 'I expect you'll miss her terribly, won't you, dear?'

Abi had to fight the urge to abandon the tray and push through the crowd to make her way up the stairs. Instead, she smiled as best she could and thanked everyone quietly.

***

That night Abi lay in bed with only Cyril's snoring for company. She had been at the funeral; heard Father Pearson's eulogy; seen the ladies of the WI dressed in black, sobbing into hankies; watched as the coffin was lowered.

Why, when she finished drying the last of the dishes earlier, had she turned around expecting to find Nan sitting at the table, patting the chair beside her, saying, 'Come on then. Tell me all about your day.' Why, when she opened the parlour door, had she expected to find Nan sitting on the sofa, a box of York Fruits open on her lap, waiting for the trumpet to signal the start of *Coronation Street*? And why, when she was pouring biscuits into Cyril's bowl, had she expected Nan to push through the kitchen door, stamping her feet and patting her hands together, saying, 'It's brass monkeys out there!'

Abi turned onto her back and stared up into the darkness. She couldn't cry. Mum had. Dad had. The old ladies had. Even some of the old men had. What was wrong with her? Was she a robot? Or just a cold, heartless cow?

Pushing back the covers, she pulled on her jumper, shoved her feet into her slippers, and grabbed her cigarettes and lighter. Cyril didn't move so much as a whisker, staying curled up in his nice, warm spot on the bed.

Abi crept down the stairs but didn't bother to switch on the kitchen light – there was just enough moonlight to see what she needed. She took a glass from the draining board, filled it from the tap, leant against the sink and sipped the freezing water, looking out of the window.

Everything in the colourless garden – the grass, the earth, the stones in the rockery, the shed down by the fence – shimmered with a fresh coat of frost. Abi shivered and curled her toes inside her slippers. If she had any sense at all, she would head straight back to bed and crawl under the warm covers. Instead she picked up her cigarettes. She was on the way to the back door when a voice stopped her in her tracks.

'You couldn't sleep either then?'

Abi spun around. 'Jesus!' she said to the dark shape in the doorway.

'Sorry, love,' Mum said, stepping into the kitchen. 'I didn't mean to make you jump. I heard you on the stairs. I thought I'd come down and put the kettle on.' She crossed to the cooker, picked up the kettle, filled it from the tap, placed it back on the ring, and lit the gas beneath it. She took two mugs and a cup and saucer down from the shelf and arranged them on the side. She removed the lid from the caddy and heaped four spoons of tea into the pot – one for each person and one for the pot. And then she stopped. From the way her head moved from side to side, Abi could tell she was looking from the teaspoon in her hand to the bone china teacup and saucer on the side.

'What am I doing?' she said.

The kettle rumbled, coming to the boil. Mum showed no sign of moving, so Abi leant past her to turn off the gas. She prised the spoon from her mum's hand. 'Sit down. I'll make the tea.'

With no further encouragement, Mum sat down. Abi carefully returned Nan's cup and saucer – decorated with a little house on a hill – to the shelf, before pouring the boiling water onto the tealeaves. She opened the fridge and used the opportunity of taking the milk from the door to study Mum in the pale-yellow light.

Her hair was tangled at the back, her eyes fixed on the tabletop, her hands preoccupied with the task of trying, and failing, to tie the belt of her dressing gown. The shadows cast by the dull light made the dark circles under her eyes appear even darker. The creases running from her nose to the edges of her mouth, deeper. She looked... broken.

Abi closed the fridge door, returning Mum to the more forgiving darkness. 'Aren't you cold?' she asked. 'You've got nothing on your feet.'

'Hmmm?' Mum said, only briefly pausing in her attempt to tie a bow. 'Oh no, I'm fine. And you, love. Are you all right?'

Abi added a splash of milk to each mug. 'I'm okay.'

'Good. That's good.'

Abi poured the tea, heaping an extra sugar into Mum's, and placed the two mugs on the table. 'Here,' she said, taking the seat opposite Mum. 'Drink this while it's hot.'

'Oh, right. Yes I will. Thank you.'

Her mum made no move to touch her tea. They sat in silence for a few minutes with just the faint sound of the waves breaking on the shore below and the creak of the central heating pipes settling down for the night. Abi searched her mind for something to say. What could she say to someone she hadn't made small talk with for two years?

'I used to come down here sometimes in the middle of the night to make Mum a cuppa,' Mum said. 'I told her so many times, "Don't catnap during the day otherwise you won't sleep at night." But would she listen? I never liked to think of her lying awake all alone in her bedroom. She was always so grateful when I knocked on the door and took her in a hot drink and a couple of digestives. I'd sit on the edge of her bed and we'd chat and look through her photo albums. She never got bored of looking through those old photos and telling me the stories from her life over and over... But that night, I didn't go in to see her. I was so tired, you see. I'd been busy in the garden all day helping your dad fix the shed roof after the tarpaulin blew off in a storm. I had a bath and then collapsed into bed… And then… there was all that commotion with Cyril. I came down and she was there, lying on the floor.' She looked at a point on the floor in front of the fridge. 'It was so bitterly cold. I shook her but she wouldn't wake up. I tried. But she wouldn't… Oh God. What was she doing? Why didn't she call for me? If only I'd been there–'

'It's not your fault,' Abi interrupted. 'The doctors said there was nothing anyone could have done.'

Mum turned back to look at her. Even in the half-light, Abi could see the frown crease her brow. 'We gave her a good send-off, didn't we? The hymns were the right ones, weren't they? And everyone had enough to eat?'

Abi glanced at the stack of Tupperware boxes on the side, stuffed with enough leftovers to keep Dad in packed lunches for days. 'I think so.'

Mum sniffed. She fumbled in her pocket and produced an envelope, which she placed on the table. 'It's a telegram,' she said, 'from Arthur. It came this morning, just before we left for the church. He says he was so sorry that he couldn't be with us. He had his ticket booked but the doctor advised him against flying. It's a long way from Brazil and he's had a few dizzy spells lately.' She picked up the envelope. 'I hope he's all right. It's just me and him now, isn't it? Everyone else has gone.'

Abi cupped her hands around her warm mug. 'Why don't you phone him in the morning? You could tell him how everything went today.'

'What a good idea, I might just do that. It'll be good to speak to him.' She turned the envelope around. 'Before I heard you on the stairs, I was lying in bed thinking about all the happy times we had together as a family when I was a girl. Mum, Dad, Auntie Ruth, Uncle Henry, Arthur and me – we were all so close. We went on outings, we had picnics and birthday parties and we spent every Christmas together. And, of course, we came here for a fortnight every summer. This creaking old cottage is so full of wonderful memories.' Her voice momentarily brightened. 'We spent whole days down on the beach. There were beef paste sandwiches and ice cream and fish and chips. It was all so easy, so innocent. At least it was until… until…' Her voice trailed away.

'Mum?' Abi said.

'Hmmm?'

'You were saying something about innocent holidays. And then you stopped.'

'Did I? Yes, I did, didn't I?' She turned the envelope over and over before finally placing it back on the table and pushing it away. 'There are things I should tell you… things from those times you don't know… about me… things that might make you feel differently about me.'

Abi pulled at the loose thread hanging from her cuff. It was a strange enough sensation to spend time in Mum's company without feeling the overwhelming urge to run away. 'You don't have to tell me anything.'

'I wish that was true, love. You have no idea how much I wish that was the case.'

Imagining that Mum wanted to offload about something like getting tipsy on a glass of scrumpy, Abi squirmed in her seat. 'Honestly, Mum. I *really* don't need to know.'

'I know you see me as old fuddy-duddy and can't imagine that I was ever young like you…'

Here we go, Abi thought.

'But I was. I was the same age as you when we came on our last family holiday here. Oh and you should have seen me! I thought I was the bees' knees. I imagined that I was the most sophisticated creature ever to have graced the Earth. I had my whole life mapped out and nothing was going to stop me from achieving my dreams. I was so ambitious. I'd worked hard to get a place at grammar school then worked hard to get the best grades in all of my exams. I was determined that I was going to be a success, that I would never have to struggle like my parents, living from one month to the next, waiting for the next pay packet, never sure whether it would cover all of the bills. I wanted a better life.' She looked around the kitchen. 'But they didn't do too badly in the end, did they? Not that I would have admitted it back then. I was just so desperate to rush out and grab the world by the scruff of the neck and drag it along behind me. I was so full of ridiculous pride.'

With a sudden burst of energy, Abi's mum pushed her chair away from the table and stood up. She turned her back to Abi and leant against the sink, wrapping her arms around her waist. 'Look at me,' she said. 'Twenty-five years later and I still feel the shame as though it all happened yesterday.'

Shame? Abi curled her toes. 'You don't have to tell me any of this. Really. It's none of my business what you did.'

'Please, Abi.' Mum held up her hand. 'If I don't tell you now then I might never find the courage again. And I have to. I don't want to keep secrets from you any more.' Her shoulders rose and fell. 'When I was eighteen, I let myself and my family down. I made a mistake on that last holiday. I let myself get carried away. A boy paid me attention. He noticed me in a way nobody ever had before. He made me feel so special. He treated me like a woman when all I'd ever wanted was for someone to see me as a grown up. Before him, I'd never even kissed a boy.'

Abi had to fight the urge to stick her fingers in her ears.

'When I went up to Edinburgh,' Mum continued, 'I managed to fool myself into believing that my body was a mess because I wasn't eating properly. I was drinking too much and staying out late – doing all the things a teenager does when they have their first taste of freedom. Only… I'd had my first taste of freedom while I was still on holiday. I was hundreds of miles from home and pregnant.'

Abi stared at the back of Mum's head. 'Pregnant!'

From the way Mum's head moved, Abi could tell she was nodding. 'Eighteen, unmarried and pregnant. It was so stupid, so irresponsible. I didn't even have the excuse that I was ignorant of biology. For Christ's sake, I was in Edinburgh training to become a doctor.'

'A doctor? What do you mean you were training to become a doctor?'

'I was in Edinburgh on a scholarship to study medicine. I wanted to be a surgeon. God, that sounds ridiculous now, doesn't it?'

Abi rocked back in her chair. 'I had no idea.'

'Why would you? My medical career only lasted two months. I never told you because I didn't want you to see me as a failure. Once I left Edinburgh and returned home I put those dreams behind me. I told Mum and Dad I'd given up on uni because I was homesick. I'd never given them a minute's trouble before, so they had no reason to doubt my honesty. But I'm sure Mum knew there was something I wasn't telling them. She tried to wheedle it out of me but I kept my mouth shut. It was better that they never knew. It was shameful, you see. In those days. If it had come out, people would have stared at us in the street, neighbours would have whispered behind our backs. I couldn't do that to Mum and Dad. They would never have understood. In their eyes I would have been dirty, and I couldn't bear to have them think of me like that. I tried to get back to normal. I helped Mum around the house, became the dutiful daughter they had always known.

'And then I met your Dad. I didn't think I deserved to be happy again, but Mick made me so very happy. I wanted to tell him the truth but, how could I? I was convinced he'd run a mile and I couldn't face that. I had finally found a man I loved and who loved me back and I just couldn't bear to lose him, I just couldn't.'

'But the baby, Mum. Where's the baby?'

Mum's shoulders slumped. 'I'm sorry, love. I should have said. I lost it. I had a miscarriage while I was still in Edinburgh…' Her words trailed away in a sob.

Abi pushed her chair back from the table and crossed the short distance to the sink. She looked at the side of her mum's face.

'Mum…' she said, gently. 'I'm so sorry. It must have been horrible.'

Abi's mum turned to her and smiled as a tear slipped down her cheek. Her hand was warm when she put it to Abi's cheek.

'There she is. My beautiful, sensitive little Abigail. But you're not to worry. It happened a long time ago and I miscarried early in the pregnancy so there really was no fuss. It was no worse than a heavy period. I'm only crying now because I'm a soppy fool. But you do see why I couldn't tell anyone? Why I had to wait until after… until there was no chance of upsetting Mum.'

'Does Dad know?'

Mum nodded. 'I told him a couple of days ago. I worried myself sick about how he would react. Imagine finding out that your wife of over twenty years has kept such a secret from you. Do you know what he did? He held me and said that keeping it from Mum and Dad had been the kindest thing to do. He said that since it had happened before we met, it wasn't his place to stand in judgement. Do you have any idea how many men would be so forgiving, so understanding? Especially after I told him the rest.' Her hand slipped from Abi's face.

'Mum?' Abi said. 'What do you mean "the rest"?'

'You don't have a spare cigarette, do you?'

'What? I… I don't smoke.'

Mum nodded to the cigarettes on the table. 'Don't look so surprised. I'm your mum. I know you better than you think I do.'

Abi really hoped that wasn't true. 'But *you* don't smoke. You hate smoking.'

'I'll make an exception, just this once. Come on.'

It was bitter outside and even though Mum had insisted she put on Dad's huge parka and his even huger Wellington boots, Abi still trembled as she shook two cigarettes from the packet. She cupped her free hand around the lighter and Mum held her hair back from her face as she hovered over the tiny white flame. They stood side-by-side, their backs to the kitchen wall. Abi lit her own cigarette, and glanced across as Mum inhaled and drew the smoke deep into her lungs, before blowing it out in a single long stream without coughing even once. Where had she learned to smoke like an expert?

Mum held the cigarette away from her face, studying the glowing tip. 'First ciggie in over eighteen years, this is. The tobacco's milder than I remember.'

Abi self-consciously blew her smoke away from Mum. Who was this woman leaning on the wall beside her, wearing Nan's old anorak, exhaling a cloud of white smoke? If anyone had asked Abi that morning, she would have said she knew everything there was to know about her mum. But standing there in the freezing cold, it was clear she didn't really know her at all.

Abi took a final drag of her cigarette, stubbed it out under the sole of her dad's Wellie and chucked it down the drain. When she looked up, she found Mum chuckling quietly to herself.

'What?' Abi said.

'Just look at us,' Mum giggled. 'Sneaking around outside for a crafty fag like a couple of teenagers. And what do we look like? You in your dad's coat and wellies with your old Snoopy pyjamas and me in my nightie and your Nan's anorak.'

Abi grinned. 'We do look a bit bonkers.'

The simple observation was enough to set Mum off. She laughed so hard that tears rolled down her cheeks and when she snorted, Abi burst out laughing too.

'Oh, I feel as giddy as a kipper,' Mum howled, the cigarette dangling from the corner of her mouth as she grabbed onto Abi's arm to steady herself. Abi laughed so hard her stomach ached although she really didn't know what she was finding so funny.

It took a few minutes but gradually they calmed enough so that they could look at each other without laughing.

'Come on,' Mum said, wiping her tears on Nan's sleeve. 'We deserve a proper drink.'

She stubbed the cigarette out on the wall, dropped it into the drain and took hold of Abi's hand.

While Abi kicked off Dad's wellies and hung his parka on the hook behind the back door, Mum tipped their cold tea down the plughole. She left the two mugs in the sink, took a bottle of brandy and two glasses down from the shelf, and placed them on the table.

'Here,' she said, opening the bottle and pouring two large measures. She draped Nan's anorak over the back of one of the empty chairs and simultaneously kicked off her boots, leaving them where they landed. 'This'll warm you up.'

Abi sat down and picked up her glass.

'Cheers,' Mum said. She took a large swig of her brandy, relaxed back into the chair, closed her eyes, and sighed.

'Cheers,' Abi replied and took a slug of the brandy. The marzipan warmth crept down her throat, heating her from the inside out. It gave her the Dutch courage to pick up the conversation where they had left off. Because if Mum had another surprise for her then they might as well get it over with. 'Well?' she said.

Mum kept her eyes closed, her face turned up to the ceiling. 'Well what?'

'You were going to tell me something else.'

Slowly Mum opened her eyes and took her time to sit upright. 'Are you hungry? There's some Victoria sponge in the cake tin or I could put a couple of those leftover ham sandwiches under the grill.'

'I'm fine. What did you want to tell me?' Whatever it was, Abi was pretty sure it couldn't be any more shocking than finding out that Mum had been a medical student and had lost a baby.

Mum picked up her brandy and with a swift flick of her head downed what was left. She refilled her glass and topped up Abi's glass.

'Have another drink,' Mum said.

'Why?'

'Because.'

Under Mum's watchful gaze, Abi picked up her glass and took another mouthful. It was only when she placed the glass back down on the table that Mum opened her mouth to speak.

'You have to understand,' she said, every drop of laughter gone from her voice, 'that I never thought I'd see the boy from that last holiday again. When we came here to live with Mum, I expected that he would be long gone. When I knew him, he didn't seem the type to stay put in one place for his whole life.' She paused and rolled the glass backwards and forwards between her palms so that it chinked against her wedding ring.

'If I'd thought for one second that he would still be here, I would never have brought us to live here. The day I saw him, it was like a door to my past was thrown open. No matter how hard I tried, I just couldn't close it.'

She raised the glass to her lips and drained the remainder of the second brandy. 'Until then I'd managed to keep that part of my life to myself. Sometimes I could even pretend it was all a bad dream or that it had happened to someone else, but seeing him again made it all real. In the end it got too much to bear. It was his baby after all. He had a right to know. I needed to talk to somebody and he was the only person I could talk to.' She paused but this time, instead of reaching for her glass, she looked across the table at Abi.

'So, one day I summoned up the courage and arranged to meet him. It was such a relief to finally tell someone about the miscarriage. And he was so sweet about it, so upset that I'd had to go through it on my own. But we also agreed that we needed to keep it to ourselves. There was nothing to be gained from raking over the past and upsetting his family and mine. Your dad was still recovering from his illness and I didn't want to tip him over the edge when he was on the mend. And I couldn't bear to hurt you and your Nan. So, you see, it was all for the best. You do understand why I did what I did, don't you?'

Abi shifted in her seat. 'I suppose so.'

Mum breathed out heavily. 'Thank God. You can't imagine how that has been hanging over me. I hated not telling you the truth that day.'

'What day?'

'The day you saw me talking to him.'

'To who? Mum, you're not making any sense.'

'I thought you realised. You saw us sitting together up on the cliff by the car park that day. Remember? The day your dad had his accident at work and broke his arm.'

The memory hit Abi like a juggernaut. She saw the scene as clearly as if she were once again crouching in the long grass, the coarse weeds scratching her legs. 'Tony,' she whispered. 'The boy you were *pregnant* to was Tony. Penny's dad, Tony.'

'Yes. But don't you see, we were so young when it happened. What we did came out of a moment of craziness. Of being young and reckless.'

'But when I saw you together on the bench that day, I thought you were having an affair *then* not when you were young... I thought—'

'I know what you thought. But it wasn't what it looked like.'

'He was all over you.'

'We held each other. That's all. You were young. It probably looked like more. I promise it was completely innocent. You're old enough now to understand that after something like that anyone would need a moment of comfort. That's all it was. I would never cheat on your dad. But you can see why I couldn't admit at the time that you had seen Tony and me together. Why I had to make you believe you had been mistaken. There would have been too many questions. And your dad was so delicate and there was Shirley and Penny to consider. And you and Mum. So many people would have been hurt and I couldn't risk breaking up two families for something that happened so many years earlier when Tony and I were young and foolish.'

'But all this time, all this time I...'

'I wish I could have told you sooner, love. But I had to wait until the time was right. Until your nan... You see why I couldn't talk about it at the time. And I explained. Remember? In the kitchen that day. Just before that nasty business when you tripped over Cyril. I said you had been mistaken when you thought you saw me with Tony. You never mentioned it again, so I knew you believed me and had put it out of your mind.'

'You think I forgot what I saw?'

'Of course.'

'You don't think I changed at all after that day?'

'Well, yes. But you were changing all the time. You were sixteen and growing into a young woman. I was just pleased when you started to make decisions for yourself about your school and university. I took a step back because I wanted you to blaze your own trail.'

Abi wrapped one arm around her waist and covered her face with her other hand.

'Abi… Abi… What is it?'

She felt Mum try to prise her hand away from her face but she kept it clamped in place and turned away.

'Talk to me,' Mum begged. 'Oh, sweetheart, what have I done? Don't go quiet on me now. Please, Abi. Speak to me.'

Chapter 20

Rose – Thursday 5 December 1963

'So,' Marina said, leaning over Rose to see what she was reading. 'Are you coming or not?'

'Not,' Rose said without looking up from the textbook on her desk. 'I told you, I have to revise this section before path class on Monday.'

Rose had already spent most of the afternoon in the small room they shared acting as the audience for Marina's fashion parade. Every surface was covered with evidence of Marina's preparations for the medical school's Christmas Ball; dresses laid out on both beds, stockings hanging like flaccid sausage skins over the backs of the chairs, shoes and handbags strewn across the floor and Marina's desk.

As the daughter of a minor Italian aristocrat and an English MP, Marina had arrived at Edinburgh with a trousseau of clothes and accessories, quite putting Rose's single suitcase to shame. Not that Marina had ever mentioned it. She was too well-bred to gloat; in fact, her generosity to Rose with her wardrobe was only surpassed by the generosity of her friendship.

Wearing nothing but a coral-coloured silk slip and a frown, Marina rested her chin on Rose's shoulder. 'What happened to the girl I met when we first arrived?' She pouted. 'The girl who I could rely on to come to all of the parties? She used to dance and drink gin and be such fun. I liked her.'

Rose nudged Marina's chin away and, pretending to be stern said, 'She woke up and realised that she actually had to study if she wanted to qualify. Because – and as much as it may surprise you to learn this – not all of us have a father who is best friends with the Dean and can afford to donate all of the equipment for the new lab.'

Rose enjoyed this banter with Marina. It was like a game of good-natured insult table tennis. She picked a blue silk scarf from her desk and handed it to Marina. 'Yours, I believe.'

Marina took the scarf and let it drop to the floor. She made a huffing sound and Rose twisted in her seat to watch her cross the room and take a cigarette from her silver case on the mantelpiece. She favoured cocktail cigarettes wrapped in coloured paper. Today they were pink. She placed the gold tip of the cigarette between her red lips and knelt to light it from a bar of the electric heater; she was forever misplacing her lighter. She held back her long dark hair and, in the orange glow, Rose looked at her face. Her features were large; full lips, wide hazel eyes and a pronounced nose. Marina was attractive rather than pretty and amongst the pasty, sun-starved students and locals, her exotic, olive skin had proved an instant hit. Especially with the men.

Marina sat on the edge of her bed and clamped the cigarette between her teeth. As she rolled a sheer stocking up her long leg, a tendril of smoke wound its way to her eye. She blinked it away. 'Why did my best friend have to go and get all dull?' She removed the cigarette from her mouth and blew smoke in Rose's direction. Rose batted it away and coughed exaggeratedly.

'Stop blowing that filth at me. And stop talking about me in the third person. I am here you know.'

'My point precisely,' Marina said, emphasising her words by stabbing the air with her cigarette. 'Aside from lectures, you've hardly left this room in weeks. And tonight you're lumbering me with that awful Alice girl again. She doesn't stop yakking about her extracurricular study of psoriasis. It's enough to put one off one's lamb chops.'

Rose laughed. 'So you want me to come to the Ball just so I can save you from a discussion on flaking skin?'

'And because it's the Christmas Ball.' Marina ground out her barely-smoked cigarette in the ashtray on the floor before sliding on her second stocking and clipping it to her suspender belt. 'You know, *the* Christmas Ball. Everyone's going. There's a jazz band and dancing and there'll be champagne. Lots and lots of champagne. There's still time. You can borrow one of my frocks if you like. The red one would look simply stunning on you.'

Rose smoothed out her flannel skirt and pulled at her sweater, which of late had developed a habit of riding up. 'Sorry, but these pages of Grey's Anatomy won't read themselves.'

Marina sighed. 'Don't you think that university would be so much more *fun* without the study? It's such a bore and really does get in the way of a good party.'

Rose shook her head. 'Tell me again why you chose to study medicine.'

'How many times?' Marina said, twisting her hair into a long dark coil and securing it at the back with a silver clip. 'I'm here because I have a thing about men with stethoscopes. I really have no intention of becoming a doctor myself.' She winked at Rose. They both knew the truth. The investment Marina's parents had made in her private education had not gone to waste. 'Anyway, I can always catch up next term. It's Christmas. And like any normal person I intend to go out and enjoy myself rather than hide away in the dark like a mushroom.'

'Since when have you needed Christmas as an excuse to dress up and drink champagne?'

Marina smiled. 'Perhaps you're right. But can I really not twist your arm? Come on. You know it'll break Graham Thompson's heart if you're not there. He's carrying one hell of a torch for you.'

'It's a good job it's snowing then. It'll snuff it out.'

Marina laughed. 'Have it your way. I know when I'm beaten. But the least you can do is help me into this.'

Rose stood and took a deep blue cocktail dress from its hanger. She held it open for Marina to step into and slid it up her body. While she fastened the zip, she looked at Marina's narrow waist. When Marina turned to face her, she quickly diverted her attention to adjusting the neckline.

'So,' Marina said, holding out her arms. 'How do I look?'

Rose took a step back and looked her up and down. 'Truthfully? Bloody awful.'

Marina laughed. 'Cow. I'm really not sure why I bothered now, since you're always so rotten to me, but I spoke to my mother earlier. The offer's still open. If you'd like to come and spend Christmas with us in our little log cabin, then you're more than welcome.'

By little log cabin, Rose knew Marina meant a ten-bedroomed chalet in the Pyrenees with a permanent staff. 'I can't ski,' she said.

'That's no problem. There's an excellent instructor in the village. Mario. Legs like tree trunks.'

Rose chose to ignore Marina's eyebrow waggle. 'And my parents would never forgive me if I didn't go home.'

'Suit yourself.' Marina dropped a lipstick into a bag then leant in to hug Rose. 'Oh my,' she said, her eyes widening. 'Has someone been sneaking one too many mince pies behind my back?'

Rose sucked in her stomach and puffed out her cheeks. 'It's indigestion,' she said. 'I'm just a bit bloated. I think it was that shepherd's pie at lunch.'

'Oh, yes. Ghastly grey mash.' Marina grimaced. 'Well as your personal physician, I prescribe a dose of Epsom salts followed by an early night. Okay?'

'Okay,' Rose said.

Marina grabbed her wrap. 'I can't afford to hang around here with Cinderella any longer. This princess really must go to the Ball.' She tucked her bag under her arm and opened the door. 'Who knows, I might even find my prince with a stethoscope tonight. Don't wait up,' she said, briefly curling her leg suggestively around the doorframe before disappearing into the hall.

Long after Marina's heels had echoed away along the long corridor of the halls of residence, Rose was still smiling. Marina may have left, but the room was still full of her; her perfume, her presence, her mess.

Rose went around the room, collecting up stockings, scarves, a discarded set of eyelash curlers, and all manner of make-up items. She placed everything neatly on Marina's desk. She folded clothes and lined shoes up in pairs beside the fireplace and placed dresses back on hangers. But it was when she opened Marina's wardrobe and caught sight of her reflection in the full-length mirror that she stopped. Was Marina right? Did it look like she was putting on weight? She placed the hangers on the rail before pulling her sweater up over her head and slipping out of her skirt. Then came the slow process of rolling the girdle down her body, easing the tight, flesh-coloured fabric over her stomach, down her hips, prising it over her buttocks, until finally it fell to the floor, a misshapen sheath of cotton.

After eleven hours trussed up in the contraption, the blood rushed back to the surface of her skin and she sighed with the pleasure of feeling the cool air on her bare flesh. Now that she was down to just her bra and knickers, she turned slowly to the side. She looked at her reflection and ran her hands over her swollen stomach.

Almost from the moment she had stepped down from the train at Waverley Station, Rose had thrown herself whole-heartedly into every aspect of student life. She had roamed the bustling corridors of the medical school taking in all the new sights, sounds and smells. She sat with her pen poised over her notepad in the lecture halls and, wherever she went, her nostrils were alive with the woody scent of oak panelling mixed with surgical spirit. She soaked up the history of the glorious buildings and of her distinguished predecessors and she knew that to be a success at university depended not just on her academic achievements but on moving in the right circles. She joined both the chess club and the debating society and was an enthusiastic participant until Marina convinced her that her time would be better spent with the second years on their almost nightly forays into Edinburgh. They went to only the coolest of bars on the Royal Mile and descended ancient, worn stone steps into smoky basement clubs in the wynds just off The Cowgate where Rose soon developed a taste for jazz and dancing and gin.

When she first started to feel ill she hadn't been wholly surprised. She couldn't pretend that she had been taking care of herself. It began as a general sense of feeling not quite right; a headache, tiredness, a tenderness in her stomach. She put it down to burning the candle not just at both ends but, in the middle, too. Until the morning when she began to vomit. She couldn't blame the alcohol on that occasion since she had spent the previous evening in the library researching an anatomy paper. When she was sick again the following morning, she made an appointment to see the nurse. 'I'm sure it's nothing sinister,' the nurse said, taking a thermometer from under Rose's tongue. She consulted the reading then flicked her wrist and popped it back in her top pocket. 'It's probably just a bout of freshers' flu. Nothing to worry about, lots of new students get it. It's just your body adjusting to being away from home for the first time. Take better care of yourself and be sure to eat properly and get enough sleep. But do come back to see me if you don't feel better in a week or so.'

Mercifully after another week, in which Rose ate little but dry toast and sipped weak tea, the sickness subsided. Finally, she was able to throw herself back into her studies and resume her late nights in the library and even later nights out on the Royal Mile. She was so busy that she didn't even realise when she missed her first period. When she missed her second, she put it down to the mysterious freshers' flu. She wasn't concerned; her body would find its equilibrium soon enough.

But all the while she had been convincing herself that everything was normal, things were happening inside her body. The lining of her uterus was thickening, cells were dividing and multiplying and somehow, the secret inside her was weathering the tidal wave of alcohol and late nights and growing stronger each day.

When she finally let herself believe the unbelievable, she cried. For days, she locked herself in the toilet and sobbed so hard that she had to cover her face so nobody would hear. How had this happened to her? This kind of thing only happened to silly girls with no sense, not girls who were going to be doctors. And what would her parents say? Her parents who had channelled all of their hopes and dreams into her, not to mention every spare penny. How would she ever find the words to tell them? She would have to leave Edinburgh, of course, and all of her dreams behind, and for what? The shameful life of an unmarried mother, begging for handouts at the council offices, facing the neighbours and people whispering and pointing. 'There she goes. *That* girl. The one who thought she was so clever. Going to be a doctor. Look at her now. Taken down a peg or two. She's no better than she ought to be.'

When she finally stopped crying for long enough to leave the halls, she paid a visit to the lingerie department in Jenners on Princes Street where she bought the tightest girdle she could fit into. She let out her skirts and replaced her tight sweaters with loose-fitting jumpers. Until she worked out what she was going to do, she couldn't risk anybody finding out. In her darkest moments she even considered creeping down to a lecture room late at night to help herself to a tray of instruments. She knew the procedure. But it transpired that possessing the knowledge and having the courage to carry it out on herself were two very different things.

Rose closed her eyes and ran her hands over her swollen stomach. How could she have even contemplated doing such an horrific thing. It was illegal. Did she really want to add criminal to the long list of new things that she was discovering about herself? She took her dressing gown down from the back of the door, pulled it on and held her hands over the whisper of warmth radiating from the orange bars of the heater. That's when she spotted Marina's cigarette case on the mantelpiece. Pilfering Marina's cigarettes to smoke in secret and sate her craving had become a daily occurrence. So she could add thief to that growing list. And not just any old thief, but a desperate thief, who often resorted to unfurling the dog-ends Marina had discarded in the ashtray to feed her newly-discovered craving.

Rose popped the clasp on the case and helped herself to one of the pink cigarettes. Kneeling down, she lit the tip on the glowing orange bar and then sat back on her haunches. She drew the smoke deep into her lungs, letting its calming tendrils filter into her blood stream before she exhaled slowly. Using Marina's bed for support she hauled herself up and wandered across the room to the window where she wiped the glass with the side of her hand and looked out through the gap in the condensation.

It was dark and, up on the hill, the lights of Edinburgh Castle were little more than yellow smudges amongst the heavy snow. Down on the pavement, people hurried along, collars up, scarves wrapped tightly around their necks, hats pulled low, a cloud of warm breath preceding each of them. No doubt they were all on their way home. To gather around a fire with family; to enjoy a conversation around the dinner table; to sit in an armchair and read a book or watch the television. Everyone else had a simple, normal, uncomplicated life. And she could have that too, one day, if only she could summon the courage to set her plan in motion and see it through. But for now, she couldn't think beyond a long, hot soak. She took a final drag of the cigarette, stubbed it out, collected her sponge bag and towel, and headed for the door.

With everyone at the party, the sound of Rose's bare feet slapping on the wooden floor echoed up the deserted corridor towards the bathroom.

There were five baths lined up along the far wall, all separated by wooden panels. She chose the stall in the farthest corner and turned on the taps. With no competition, the water that gurgled from the tap was unusually hot and the room soon filled with steam. She added a splash of bubble bath, let her dressing gown fall to the floor and stepped into the frothy water, hopping from one foot to the other until her skin grew accustomed to the heat.

She submerged her whole body, rested her head against the back of the bath, closed her eyes, and ran her hands over her stomach, now soft and slippery from the bubbles. She would kick start her plan tomorrow when Marina was nursing a hangover.

She would go to Waverley Station, enquire about the timetables, book her ticket and be back in their room before Marina could ask where she had snuck off to all alone. Then on Friday, when everyone else was boarding trains to take them straight home for the Christmas holiday, she would make a detour. Her parents thought she was going to spend a couple of days with Marina before arriving home on Monday. What they didn't realise was that Marina would be boarding her plane to Turin on Friday, at roughly the same time she was boarding a train to Dorchester.

It really was the only decision that made any sense. She had to get to him. To Tony. He had a right to know and once he got over the initial shock, they would be able to face this together. Of course, when they had parted, he had said that a clean break was for the best; that there was no point pining for each other when they were hundreds of miles apart. She needed to be free to focus on her studies. He had said it was the mature way to part. But that was before he knew about the baby. Everything was different now. She could hardly wait for him to hold her and whisper that he loved her, just like he had that night. He was a gentleman; he would do the right thing, the honourable thing. They could travel together to see her parents. With Tony by her side, she would find the strength to tell her parents and they would see how much she loved Tony and how much he loved her. In time they would come to understand. And with Tony, she would be able to face the future. In truth, she had never wanted to leave him. She would have been happy with the letters and the long-distance phone calls and the visits in the holidays.

She ran her hands down her sides. They were still slim; she was carrying her pregnancy all at the front. It was still quite small and neat but without the benefit of a girdle it would have been quite obvious beneath her clothes. She ran her fingertips across the bump. Her baby would have ears and fingernails now. It really was a miracle.

If anyone had told her just a few weeks ago that she could be happy about this situation, she would have called them mad. Now her every thought, every decision, and every breath, was wrapped up with the life inside her. All of the energy she would have put into becoming a doctor she would now put into becoming a mother. Maybe one day she could go to college and study to be a nurse or a midwife. 'We'll be all right, little one. You'll see,' she said in a whisper even though there was nobody to overhear.

When the water cooled, Rose reluctantly stepped from the bath into the chilly air. She wrapped herself in her towel and hopped from foot to foot to minimise contact with the freezing cold tiles. She rubbed her body roughly, all the while thinking about what she would have for dinner. If she was quick, she might just make it to the café on the corner for a plate of liver and onions. These days she was as partial to a plate of liver as she was to a sneaky cigarette.

She took the talcum powder from her sponge bag but at the very moment she was about to dispense a pile into her palm, a pain in her side caught her off guard, and she dropped the bottle to the floor. She gasped, and the pain struck again, making her bend double. She clutched her stomach. *Stay calm, you have to stay calm.* The pain struck again, worse this time, like a hand grasping and twisting her insides. Rose screamed out and sank to her knees. There was thick, dark blood smeared all over the insides of her thighs.

'Help,' she called. There was nobody to hear. She tried to drag herself to her feet but again her stomach went into spasm. *What was happening to her, oh God, what was happening?*

'Are you in that bloody bath again?' A voice called from the hallway. It was accompanied by the click-clack of high heels. 'You've practically taken up residence in there,' the voice said, approaching her cubicle. 'I only went and forgot my ciggies, didn't I. And I didn't fancy poncing off the blokes all night. You know what they're like. One good turn and all that. I thought, while I'm here, I might as well pop my head around the door and see how the killjoy is getting on and… Rose! Oh my God. Rose!'

Rose looked up to see a look of utter horror in Marina's eyes. She kicked off her shoes, dropped her bag and fell to her knees. 'Jesus Christ. What's happened to you?'

'I'm bleeding,' Rose whimpered. She felt Marina's hands all over her.

'Where's it coming from? Have you fallen?'

'It's coming from there.' Rose nodded to her privates.

'Come on, let me look at you. Lie on your back for me.' Marina's voice was slow and measured and Rose tried to do what she asked but as she lay back and parted her legs another spasm made her curl her knees into her chest. As it subsided Marina gently prised Rose's legs apart.

'Rose,' she said calmly. 'Try and relax. I need to examine you.' It didn't take long. Marina's hand pressed down on her belly and stopped there. She sat back on her heels, wrapped the towel around Rose and helped her sit up. 'How far gone are you?'

'Please don't tell anybody,' Rose cried. 'Nobody can find out. Not yet.'

'We'll worry about that later. How far gone are you?'

'Seventeen weeks,' she said.

'Seventeen weeks! Shit.'

'My baby. Marina… my baby…'

'Listen, Rose, don't push. Just don't push. Okay? We have to get you to hospital.' She draped Rose's dressing gown around her shoulders. But when she made to stand, Rose grabbed her hand.

'Don't leave me. Please.'

'I'll be right back,' Marina said, giving Rose's fingers a gentle squeeze. 'I promise.' She stood up and that's when Rose saw her mess smeared on Marina's legs and soaked into the hem of her blue satin. 'Your dress. I'm so sorry,' Rose sobbed. 'It's ruined.'

Marina kicked her shoes out of the way as she headed for the door. 'Fuck the dress. You're my priority right now.'

Chapter 21

Abi – Thursday 17 November 1988

Still cocooned in her blankets, Abi jabbed at the button on the side of her watch. A murky green light illuminated the numbers: 07:00. It was dark outside and ice crystals glistened on the inside of the glass. Abi kicked the now redundant hot water bottle from the bed and it slipped to the floor, splatting like a pink, swollen bladder. Cyril, who had been fast asleep on top of the bed, raised his head briefly before tucking himself back into a nose-to-tail ball. He had been snoring ever since she crawled back into bed in the wee small hours and had lain there, feeling the hot water bottle her mum had insisted on her taking up, grow cold while the seconds turned to minutes and the minutes turned to hours.

She couldn't sleep, not with the thoughts in her head going around and around like a washing machine on full spin. Had Mum been able to sleep or was her brain churning over and over, replaying every word of their late-night conversation? Maybe not. Because none of the information was new to Mum. She had lived with the knowledge that she had lost a baby for over twenty years. Tony's baby. Penny's dad's baby. It made sense of everything; why Mum had behaved so strangely around Tony when he used to drive Penny out to Cliff Cottage and why she had spent so much time staring at Penny. Perhaps she had been trying to work out what her baby might have looked like if it had survived.

How had Mum felt when she had pushed her to admit that she was having an affair with Tony? She must have been terrified that her secret would come out too soon. She must have been desperate to do anything, say anything, to save not just her family but Tony's too. Mum had done nothing wrong apart from have a holiday romance. It was before she met Dad. If she was guilty of doing anything, it was having unprotected sex. It was hardly the crime of the century.

Abi kicked out her legs but immediately recoiled to the warm core of the bed. If only she hadn't been such a stubborn sixteen-year-old. If only she had listened to Mum and let the subject drop back then, she wouldn't have carried around this hatred for so long, driving a wedge between her and everyone she loved. Her mum wasn't a monster. She was a human being. With all the faults and imperfections of any human being.

It would have been so easy to share a few home truths with her but what was the point? And Mum had looked so relieved when Abi finally pulled herself together enough to say that she had forgotten all about seeing Mum and Tony on the beach that day. That Mum had been right to think all of the changes she went through after that day were because of her age. Nothing else.

Pushing back the sheets and blankets, Abi sat on the edge of the bed. She hugged herself against the cold. Who was she trying to kid? Everything changed that day. She willed it not to, but a memory pushed its way forward: a barn, a floor covered in straw, a feed sack sliding beneath her backside, Thug over her.

She shoved her feet into her slippers, pulled her jumper over her pyjamas, grabbed her cigarettes, and headed for the door.

Down on the first-floor landing, Abi found the door to her parents' room open, the bedspread in a heap at the end of the bed. She loitered with her foot on the top stair, listening to the low rumble of voices coming from the kitchen below. If she went down and Mum and Dad decided to drop another bombshell over the cornflakes – an adopted child, perhaps, or a mad aunt locked up in an asylum somewhere – she might actually go crazy. At the very least they would probably want to talk about Mum's confession. And Abi wasn't ready for that. Not yet.

She looked at the bedroom next to her parents'. A warm light glowed from within. Abi didn't have to think twice before tiptoeing across the landing and slipping quietly inside.

Mum had insisted they leave the lamp on in Nan's bedroom every night, so when Abi stepped inside, she found everything just as Nan had left it – bedspread smoothed out over plumped pillows, quilted dressing gown hanging on a hook behind the door, a two-week-old *Radio Times* open on the bedside table with a pen and Nan's glasses balanced on top.

Abi picked up a tub of *Yardley's* talc from the dressing table. She unscrewed the cap and sprinkled a small pile into her hand. Rubbing her hands together, she held her palms to her nose and smiled. Lily of the Valley. It was the smell of Nan in a bottle.

Easing past the bed, Abi opened the wardrobe doors and ran her hands along the familiar clothes ordered neatly by season. There were pastel-coloured blouses and sundresses at one end, cardigans and winter coats at the other. Abi gathered up an armful and pressed her face into the cotton and silk and polyester. At the bottom of the wardrobe Nan's collection of boxed shoes was stacked three high and two deep. She was a great believer that every outfit needed just the right pair of shoes.

Abi knelt on the floor, pulled the top box from the pile and lifted the lid. Snuggled inside, toe to heel, were Nan's brown pumps, the sensible, everyday shoes she wore with slacks and a blouse or jumper for a trip out to the shops or to a WI meeting. Abi opened another box. It contained Nan's navy-blue court shoes; her church shoes. In the third, Abi found the Scholl sandals Nan wore around the house in the summer and in the fourth, the black patent heels that she used to let Abi clomp around in when she was little.

Ploughing through the boxes, Abi couldn't help but smile. Each one was a time capsule, bringing Nan back to her through the medium of shoes. Slingbacks, sandals, sensible flats; leather, patent and even sequined. Whatever the style and material, Abi could see her nan in each pair, at birthday parties, at Christmases, on the beach, flower arranging at the church, or spring-cleaning at Cliff Cottage. Once Abi started to relive the memories, she couldn't stop. Soon there were so many boxes open on the floor that she could hardly see the pink carpet. Just when she thought she had come to the last item of footwear – a pair of fur-lined winter boots in an over-sized green box – she spotted one final box. It was tucked at the very back of the wardrobe, pushed so far into the corner that she had to part the hems of Nan's long winter coats to reach it. She pulled the box towards her, sat back on her heels, and balanced it in her lap.

This box was different to the others. It was old and delicate and made of faded beige-coloured papery-board, rather than sturdy, colourful cardboard. It was no wonder that Nan had kept this box separate; it would never have survived under the weight of the tougher cardboard boxes. There was a paper label pasted to the lid, curling at the edges: *Harrison's Fine Shoes, Regent Street, W1.* Abi ran her fingers over the lid. It was so soft that it felt like fabric. When she lifted it, the musty scent of something left shut away for a long time escaped. Carefully peeling back a layer of tissue paper, Abi revealed a pair of tan suede stilettos. They were the shoes of a young woman, not a grandmother. When Abi gently prised the first and then the second shoe from their paper nest, her heart sank. The shoes were ruined. They were streaked with brown stains that had even dripped down the insides and soiled the linings.

Abi was about to place the shoes back in their box when she spotted something else nestled in the tissue paper. Putting the shoes to one side, she pulled out an envelope. Like the label, it had yellowed with age. The address '*Mrs Gertrude Smith, Miller and Miller Solicitors, The Strand, London, England,*' had been crossed through and the letter redirected to an address in Brixton. There was a postmark over the stamp of a king's head bearing the word CANADA. It was faint, but she could just make out *May 1945.* The top corner of the envelope was blackened, charred like it had been held to a flame. Why did Nan have a burned envelope tucked beneath her stained shoes? Abi shook her head. It was a question that would now never be answered.

Abi turned the envelope over but as she lifted the flap, she stopped. Snooping around Nan's court shoes and talcum powder was one thing, but snooping in her private letters? Abi looked over her shoulder then back to the envelope. What harm could it do? If Nan hadn't wanted anyone to read it then she surely wouldn't have left it lying around for anyone to stumble across. Abi pulled the letter from the envelope and unfolded the single sheet. It was singed on both the top and bottom right-hand corners to match the envelope. She began to read:

Alberta, March 1945
Canada
My Dear Gertie,
I hope this letter reaches you and finds you well. As I do not have another address, I have taken a chance on remembering your work address correctly.

I know that some time has passed and since our friendship was brief, it is perhaps just a distant memory to you now. But I have often thought of you and have recalled the kindness you showed me, a young man so far from home.

I remember how you listened to the stories of my family and our farm and it is for that reason that I so wanted to send something to you. I found it today when I was riding out to check on the herd. Even when I was still a way off, I spotted a clutch of colour amongst the patches of melting snow and rough grass. It's called a Prairie Crocus and it's the first flower to blossom when the snow melts.

As I write, I have the flower on the desk beside my hand. It is so fresh that the dew is still on its lilac petals. It survived a long winter under snow and I just hope that it survives the journey to you and that when you see it, you can in some way share this moment with me.

I hope you don't think me too sentimental, but I am also sending you this photograph as a reminder that even in the worst days, there is always a glimmer of joy.

Do you remember that I told you about Peggy? Well, we are to be married in June. I was sent home after my wounds failed to heal when I was posted back to France. I'm determined to be a good man and a good husband. More worthy men than I never came home, and it is my duty to live each day for them and for the lives they should have had.

I thank God that He spared me, and I thank Him for giving me you, Gertie. You were a true friend when I so needed one. I was lost and without you I am sure I would never have found my way through the darkness. I can never thank you enough.

I wish you only eternal happiness and hope that if you sometimes recall our friendship then you will remember me fondly, as I do you. Your friend, always,
Aaron

Aaron? Abi wracked her memory but couldn't remember Nan ever mentioning anyone called Aaron. She used to write to a friend, Ivy, in an Old Folk's Home in Sussex, but she had died a few years back. Perhaps this Aaron was a friend of Granddad's. But if he had known Granddad then why hadn't he addressed the letter to him too or even mentioned him? And why had the letter been sent to Nan somewhere that she used to work?

Abi prised open the envelope and peered inside. There was no sign of the flower or photograph; at least not an intact photograph. She upended the envelope and fragments of a photograph scattered to the floor. Abi pieced them together and an image took shape on the carpet of a man in uniform with what looked like a huge stone paw behind his shoulder. But there was one piece of the jigsaw missing – the man's face. Abi checked the envelope but it was empty. Someone had cut this photograph into pieces and removed the man's head. Abi looked from the letter back to the photograph. There was something familiar about the shape of the hole where the man's head should have been. It was oval and had been cut out quite precisely and as she looked, a thought began to take shape. It made no sense. Even so…

Placing the letter and envelope back into the box, Abi pulled herself to her feet. She opened the dressing table drawer and took out a small box. Kneeling back down, she prised it open, removed Nan's locket, and held it over the hole in the photograph. It was a perfect match. A sensation like a gust of wind ran through Abi. Perhaps she should put everything back as she had found it. Almost in spite of herself, she unfurled her fingers from around the locket and flicked it open. There was a photograph of her as a baby on one side and a photograph of Mum as a teenager on the other.

She ran her fingernail under the glass holding her baby photo in place and popped the glass and photograph out. Tucked into the gold casing was a tiny sepia-tinted photograph of an old man and woman who she knew to be her great grandparents. But when she tried to do the same with the glass and photograph of Mum, it wouldn't budge. It felt like it had been glued in place. She began scratching away until finally the glass came free. When she picked out the photograph of Mum, she almost dropped the locket to the floor.

Wedged into the concave casing was a dried flower and behind it, an oval of white. Something in Abi's head screamed at her to stop, to put it all back together. But her fingers refused to listen. They turned the locket over and gave it a shake. The oval of paper fell to her knee. She picked it from her pyjamas, turned it over and found herself looking into the face of a young man. He was smiling and behind him, she could just make out the haunch of a stone lion. But this man was no stranger. She scrabbled to collect up the photograph of Mum and compared it to the young man. The same pale eyes looked out at her from both, the same heart-shaped face with the same blonde hair. *Oh, God.*

'Abi is that you? Are you up?'

Abi jumped to her feet. 'Yes, Mum… Yes. I'm up here.'

The bottom stair and then the second stair creaked as they took Mum's weight. 'Do you want a cuppa? The kettle's on.'

'Yes. A cup of tea. Yes, that would be great.' Abi ran out onto the landing and looked over the banister. 'I'll be down in a minute.'

'Shall I make you some porridge?' Mum took the third step. 'You know you really should try to eat something, it's not good to—'

'Yes, porridge. And toast! Two pieces of toast. And an egg, yes, an egg. I'm starving. I'll be right down.' Abi realised she was still holding the man's face and wrapped her fingers tightly around it as Mum smiled up at her.

'A boiled egg and soldiers coming right up,' Mum said and turned to head back down the stairs.

Abi waited for her to disappear into the kitchen before running back into Nan's room. She hurried to shove all of the normal shoes back into their boxes, pile them up in the bottom of the wardrobe, and close the door. Then more carefully, she collected up the bits of photograph, the locket and the flower, and placed them all into the box with the stained shoes. She replaced the lid and rushed out onto the landing where she took the steps up to the attic two at a time with the shoebox tucked under her arm.

Chapter 22

Gertie – Friday 28 July 1944 – Evening

Mould. Damp. Blasted brick dust. Just two steps inside the boarded-up house, Gertie was engulfed by the smell of destruction and decay. Outside, the warning siren kept up its insistent wail. She took another tentative step inside but lost her footing on the debris covering the floor. Aaron jammed the front door back into its frame, shutting out the last hint of pale daylight. In an instant, the hallway was plunged into darkness. It was black. Black like suffocation. Black like being pinned down, a deadweight crushing the last breath from her chest. 'I can't, I just can't,' Gertie said and stepped back, stumbling into Aaron.

'Hey, it's okay,' he said. He sought out her hand and gave it a gentle squeeze. 'I won't let anything happen to you. Trust me.'

Gertie gripped Aaron's hand, his warm fingers around hers. She felt him pat at his clothes with his free hand. There was a click followed by the oily scent of fuel. A tiny chink of light broke through the darkness. Aaron smiled, the whites of his eyes bright in the small flame of a cigarette lighter.

'See,' he said, 'you can always trust an old boy scout. We come prepared.'

Holding the lighter aloft, Aaron eased past Gertie and picked his way slowly along the hall, his boots crunching on the shifting debris. Gertie followed close behind as he moved the small flame from side to side, bringing details of the hallway briefly into view before they disappeared once again into the gloom: a staircase missing its banister, most of the steps smashed like a smile without its teeth; a wooden frame suspended at a perilous angle on the wall, shards of charred mirror clinging to the outer edges. And, at the end of the hall, a doorway, the lintel broken and hanging loose, barring the path into the room beyond.

Aaron held the flame up to a small door beneath the staircase. 'We should sit out the raid in there, the space beneath the stairs is the strongest part of a building.' He nodded to the handle. 'Could you get that? I've kinda got my hands full.'

Gertie reached for the handle but as she grasped the cold metal, the boom of an anti-aircraft gun sounded close by. The floorboards beneath them shuddered. The small flame flickered. The broken lintel swung, like the pendulum of a grandfather clock keeping slow time. Gertie took a step back, straining Aaron's hold on her. What if they got inside the cupboard and closed the door only for another explosion to bring what was left of the house crashing down on them? What if the lighter ran out of fuel and they were plunged into darkness, buried alive, crushed beneath rubble, with no chance of escape?

'Please no,' she said, shaking her head. 'Please don't make me go in there. I couldn't… Not after…'

'We need to take shelter,' Aaron said. Another thud brought a shower of plaster down around them.

'I can't. I just can't. Please…'

Aaron stepped towards her. 'It's okay. I won't force you. But I need you to stay calm. Can you do that for me, Gertie?'

For the first time, Gertie detected a hint of frustration in his voice. She had to at least attempt to be brave. It was unfair to let this boy shoulder the responsibility for them both. 'I'll try,' she said but immediately corrected herself. 'I mean yes, I'll stay calm.'

Aaron sighed. 'Good. That's real good, Gertie.' He held the flame up to a doorway in the opposite wall. 'How about in there?'

Gertie peered past him into a small parlour at the front of the house. 'All right,' she said, hoping that she sounded confident. But as she followed Aaron over the threshold, she committed the layout of the house to memory, just in case she needed to find her way back out in the dark.

After closing the door behind them, Aaron held the lighter aloft and moved the smudge of light in an arc around the room. The parlour hadn't fared any better than the rest of the house. Rain-soaked lining paper hung in limp strips from the walls, plaster and smashed masonry littered the bare floorboards and a gaping hole in the ceiling revealed the wooden struts supporting the floor above. A single dining chair sat at the hearth with a stack of newspapers piled beside it, as though waiting for someone to return to warm their feet by the grate and have a good read.

Gertie's heart sank. Nobody would ever come back to this sorry little house. It had been abandoned, its residents long gone, taking all of their possessions – except for this lonely little chair – with them. She imagined the birthdays and Christmases that might have been enjoyed in this parlour. The candles on a cake casting a ruddy hue on the festivities and the laughter. Perhaps there had been a piano in the corner, like there had been in the vicarage when she was a girl. She had never had the patience to learn to play of course. It was Ruth who had provided the musical entertainment at gatherings of family and friends, impressing everyone with her skills. As children Ruth had been a more accomplished daughter than Gertie, just as she was a better woman and wife now.

Aaron loosened his grip. Gertie shivered, certain the ghosts of this dark house were standing at her elbow. She groped for Aaron's hand but it was too late, he had released her.

'Here, take hold of this,' he said, clearly focused on practicalities. 'Keep it high, that's it, so I can see what I'm doing.'

Gertie cupped the lighter in both hands, trying her best to keep the flame steady as she followed Aaron to the fireplace. Their elongated shadows inched along the wall.

'Stay behind me,' Aaron shouted over another barrage of anti-aircraft fire. He waved Gertie back but gave no further warning before picking up the chair and smashing it against the wall. Gertie flinched as shattered legs and spindles clattered to the floor. Aaron sank to his knees. He collected up an armful of the spindles and piled them into the hearth then grabbed a newspaper from the centre of the stack, screwed the pages into tight balls, and forced the balls between the spindles. He twisted one page into a long taper and held it to Gertie. She put the lighter to the paper and the flame licked rapidly up the tight coil in a curl of orange. Burning smuts floated through the air and Aaron turned quickly back to the grate. He touched the taper to each of the paper balls and flames began to glow around the wood. Finally, he stabbed the taper into the centre of the fire and looked up the flue.

'We're lucky that chimney's still intact,' he said, smiling at his handiwork. 'Otherwise we'd be about smoked out by now.' He stood up, wiped his hands on his trousers, took the lighter from Gertie and snapped it shut before returning it to his pocket. He looked at her and in the new light from the fire and Gertie saw his contented smile dip to a concerned frown.

'Are you warm enough?' he asked.

Gertie ran her fingertips alongside the inside cuff of Aaron's jacket which she still wore. 'Yes, thank you.'

'How do your legs feel?'

'My legs?' Gertie glanced down at the bandages wrapped around her shins. Somehow the pain had quite disappeared. 'Fine, thank you.'

A breeze whistled down the chimney, fanning the flames so they rose and fell. Gertie clutched the collar of Aaron's jacket tighter around her neck. 'This was someone's home once.'

'I guess.' Aaron surveyed the room as though seeing it for the first time. 'Not for a while. But this is a good fire though.' He crouched and piled another bundle of spindles into the flames. Gertie watched him, his skin glowing in the light with the newness of youth, his cheekbones and jaw firm, not sagging and shadowed by the heaviness of time and life.

The anti-aircraft gun started up again and Aaron stood up. 'Come on,' he said and took hold of Gertie's hand. 'We'd better get away from the window, you never know what might—'

Aaron's words were lost; drowned by an explosion so loud it could have been on the street outside. Thousands of shards of dazzling light burst through the gaps in the hoarding covering the window. The floor heaved. A terrible groan and creek of wood came from above. Gertie looked up to the gaping hole in the ceiling. Any second now the precarious chimney stack, the burnt rafters and what was left of the roof, was going to come crashing down on top of her. Sid's words raced through her mind. *Fight to get out and don't stop fighting till you're free.*

She yanked her hand from Aaron's, ran to the door, and fumbled for the handle. The door refused to open. She tried the handle again but the door refused to move. It wasn't until she tried for a third time that she became aware of Aaron's hand on the door above her head.

'Jesus Christ,' he yelled over another explosion. 'What in hell's name's gotten into you?'

Gertie dipped below the crook of his arm and ran to the window. She balled her hands into tight fists and pounded at the hoarding. Again, Aaron was behind her, this time with his arms around her waist, pulling her back as another explosion rattled the window frame.

'You're gonna get yourself killed,' he yelled over the thud of the gun. He dragged her to the far corner of the room, her heels scraping across the floorboards.

'Let me go!' Gertie screamed and tried to slap his hands away. 'Let me out!' She hit him as hard as she was able.

'You're talking crazy. It's not safe out there.'

'Nowhere's safe. Don't you understand?'

'Is this about what happened to you today?' Aaron demanded. Gertie hit his hands again. It did no good; his grip was too firm.

'Talk to me,' he shouted.

'You wouldn't understand.'

'Try me.'

In that instant, Gertie's frustration burst. Who was this boy to shout at her in the midst of an air raid and keep her here against her will? 'Sally is never late,' she yelled. 'Do you understand? Never! She was there. I know it. With Enid and Brian and...

and… oh God, Rosemary.' As she said the names, the paper-thin wall keeping the truth at bay tumbled down and she collapsed like a rag doll in Aaron's arms. Only his strength kept her from falling to the floor.

'Who are those people, Gertie?'

'My friend and her sister and her children.' She hid her face in her hands and sobbed. 'I was on a bus… with a cardigan… but there was a bomb… so much glass and blood and… and the conductress, she fell on me… and then they said… in the park… they said it was gone… Woolworths.'

'Woolworths?'

'The café…. they were waiting for me. A doodlebug… the whole lot gone… no chance of survivors.' Gertie drew in breath and choked on the air.

'Oh God, Gertie. I'm so sorry,' Aaron whispered into her hair and pulled her closer.

'It should have been me.'

'Don't say that.'

'They'll all be missed. Right now people will be wondering where they are. Worrying. I could have died today and nobody would know until Monday when I didn't turn up for work.'

'Of course they would–'

'No! I don't mean enough to anyone.'

'But your husband?'

Gertie's tears caught in her throat. 'He has his fires to keep him warm.'

The moment the disloyal words left her mouth, Gertie became aware of Aaron's presence, his closeness. Standing up straight, she swiped at her eyes. 'Would you please be kind enough to release me?'

Aaron hesitated then let his arms slip from around her waist. 'I'm sorry,' he said. 'I didn't mean to pry. Shock does funny things to people. Makes them say… You're upset and not thinking–'

'Do not tell me how I feel or what I'm thinking.' Gertie spun around. 'You know nothing about my life. When this is all over you'll go back to Canada. You'll get married and live a perfect life in your house on the farm. But life's not that like that for all of us. For some of us every day is a struggle, another day to endure with no hope of an end to it all.'

'I do know something of suffering. I–'

'What could you possibly know about anything? You're little more than a child.' Gertie spat out the words with such force that Aaron took a step away from her. He opened his mouth to speak but closed it again. The look on his face changed as though someone was slowly turning a handle inside him. All sign of compassion and caring disappeared and he glared at her, clenching his fists. She had gone too far. For a moment she was more afraid of Aaron than the battle outside.

The walls of the house rocked as the guns let off another barrage and without a word, Aaron turned on the spot and marched to the door. He yanked it open with such force Gertie thought the handle might come away in his hand.

'Go on then. Leave. Don't let me stop you,' he said, his voice hard. 'Well? What are you waiting for?' He stared at her, his face half in shadow and half aglow from the light of the fire which now blazed in the hearth. 'Do you think I'm here because the army wanted me to have a holiday in London? Do you want to know why I'm really here? Well do you?'

Aaron grabbed either side of his shirt and pulled. The threads holding the buttons gave under the strain. He ripped his shirt open, scattering buttons to the floor. Gertie gasped. From navel to armpits, Aaron's torso was wrapped in bandages.

'Is that enough suffering for you? Enough real life?' The boom of the anti-aircraft gun outside subsided, leaving Aaron's raised voice echoing around the empty room.

Gertie took a step towards him, ashamed to hear her words thrown back at her. 'I'm so sorry,' she said, taking in the raw pink scars scattered across his shoulders, unable to imagine what injuries the bandages covered.

'What do you care?' Aaron turned from her, his shoulders rising and falling, his anger making his breath heavy.

Gertie placed her hand on his shoulder, but he shrugged it away. 'Please look at me,' she coaxed. 'You've been so very kind and I've repaid you by behaving so badly. I'd like to help, if you'll let me. Please.' Finally, her persistence paid off and Aaron turned around. When he slowly lifted his head, Gertie saw why he had tried to hide from her. Her heart broke for him. 'What happened to you?' she asked, trying to hide her shock at seeing a man with tears creeping down his cheeks.

'I...' Aaron wiped his eyes on the heels of his hands. 'It's...' He held out his right hand and flexed his fingers. In the quiet left by the retreating explosions, he stared as though transfixed by the movement of the muscles and bone beneath the surface of his flesh. 'Do you know why I enlisted?'

'Tell me.'

'Ever since I was a kid I've been obsessed with fixing things. Trucks. Cars,' he said, addressing his words to his palms as he sniffed back the tears. 'Then animals on the farm, helping my dad and grandpa treat the herd if one of them got sick. At weekends I volunteered at the local hospital and when it came time to enlist, Doctor Cartwright put in a word with the board. That's why they made me a medic.'

Aaron fanned out his fingers, curled them into his palms and unfurled them again before turning his hands over and staring at his palms. He wiped his face roughly on the back of his hand.

'When we got to England they set to teaching us how to be soldiers. We marched and drilled and learned how to load our rifles, clean our rifles, fire our rifles. Other days we were put on boats, which took us out to sea and we had to get off the boats, wade onto the beach and run in full uniform. And then one day we were circling around the English Channel cooped up below decks, the rain like bullets on the metal of the ship.'

Aaron paused. He looked towards the fire.

'The sky was so grey, and it was raining when they lowered us into the sea. The water was full of boats. We were tossed around and the waves came crashing over the sides. Men were puking and the stink of it mixed with the stink of diesel. Anderson was sitting next to me. He came over on the boat from Halifax with me. He had this crooked sort of smile from where his front teeth had been knocked out in a bar brawl in Montreal, he said. He caught me staring at him and smiled. "You okay, Duckman?" he asked. I nodded. I didn't like the way he was holding his rabbit paw real tight. He usually made a joke of how his kid sister had given it to him. Said he'd rather put his trust in Lee-Enfield than a bit of dead rodent. But that day he held that little bit of fur and bone so tight, like his life depended on it.'

Aaron began to tremble. Gertie took hold of his hands. 'Aaron?' she said but he appeared not to hear.

'We were still a mile out at sea when the shelling started,' he said, the yellow flames from the fire reflecting in his eyes. 'Our ships bombarded the beaches and we were stuck out there with so many explosions above us, it felt like the air we were breathing was on fire. When we got closer, the Germans opened up with gunfire so we had to duck and the bullets split the air around us. "On your feet," the sergeant shouted. "Fall in line! But keep your heads down! Keep your fucking heads down." I got up but with the waves and all, I stumbled into Anderson. He was too busy slipping his rabbit foot in his pocket to notice. And then they dropped the door at the end.'

Aaron gripped Gertie's hands so tight that they hurt but she said nothing.

'The guys up front were cut down. They didn't stand a chance. The Germans picked them off before they could get into the water. Some guys on the second line managed to make it into the water and pushed forward. I followed Anderson into the water. It was so cold. It took my breath away. But I knew I had to get to the beach. I held my medical pack and rifle above my head. My arms and legs ached from the water weighing down my uniform.

Water exploded all around. I could hardly see. I knew there would be injured men on the beach and I was desperate to get to them. But when the water was up to my waist, I saw this guy. He was lying on his back, his pack acting as some kind of buoy, keeping him afloat. He was sort of staring up at the sky. I recognised him from the train from Calgary. I grabbed hold of the strap of his pack and tried to pull him behind me only he was so heavy. I thought maybe I would have to leave him when suddenly he got lighter. "Go on, Duckman!" Anderson yelled in my ear. He had hold of the other side of the guy and was helping me drag him up onto the beach. We managed to get to shelter behind one of the metal defences the Germans had put up to stop boats getting to the beach. I fell to me knees. Sand exploded like fountains everywhere and everywhere people were yelling for medics. "I'd stay to help, only..." Anderson shouted and pointed to an officer further up the beach yelling at men to go forward. Anderson got to his feet. "Good luck, buddy," he shouted. "I'll stand you a beer when we get to Paris." From the corner of my eye I saw him get to his feet but the next second he collapsed face down on the sand beside me. When I turned him over I saw...I saw...Oh God, his stomach was split clean open. His guts, they were hanging out. I grabbed my pack and I pulled out dressings, bandages, anything I could find. He was screaming and kicking but as fast as I pressed those dressings into his belly, they were soaked with blood. I was up to my elbows in Anderson's blood, trying to force his guts back inside. He grabbed my arm and when he tried to speak, he coughed up blood. "Hold on, buddy." I shouted. "Don't try to speak. We'll get you to hospital and get you fixed up. Don't close your eyes, Anderson! Don't you dare close your fucking eyes. Look at me! Keep looking at me! Stay with me. Don't leave me." But I knew. From the look in his eyes. This bubble of blood like foam was coming out of his mouth. And he was in pain. So much pain. "I'm gonna give you a shot," I shouted. "Nod if you understand." He gripped my arm and nodded and that's when I gave him the first shot in his leg. After the second, he stopped kicking. After the third, his grip loosened on my arm. He started sort of panting like he couldn't get his breath. After the fourth I took hold of his hand and held it until his chest stopped moving altogether.'

Aaron pulled his hands free of Gertie's and buried his face in the crook of his arm.

'Oh, Aaron,' Gertie said, 'I'm so very sorry.'

'When I woke up a few days later in hospital, they said a shell had exploded just yards from me,' Aaron sobbed. 'I was lucky to escape with just burns and flesh wounds. Lucky!'

'Aaron–'

'I killed Anderson. Do you understand? Me. Not the Germans. What right did I have to play God like that?'

'You did your best.'

'My best? I didn't save anyone. I don't even know what happened to that other guy we dragged onto the beach. I should be on a train going back to the hospital now. They're going to send me back to my unit tomorrow. They say I'm all fixed. But what about the things I see when I close my eyes? When are they going to fix that?'

Aaron's chest heaved as he struggled to catch his breath. Gertie reached to tuck in the edge of the bandage, which had worked loose. She let her eyes take in the angles of his strong frame, the muscles curving below smooth skin. It was too awful to imagine that a violent event might take the breath from this strong, vital body.

Gertie moved to take her hand away but she was too slow. Aaron covered her hand with his. His fingers closed around hers.

'Thank you,' he said.

'I really haven't done anything.'

'You listened. And I'm sorry… for how I spoke to you before. I was raised better than to talk to a lady like that.'

Gertie looked up at him and smiled. 'Well, I'll say nothing more about it if you don't.'

Despite the tears still in his blue eyes, Aaron smiled back. 'I don't think I've ever met anyone as kind as you. Or as beautiful,' he said.

Gertie tried to pull her hand away, but Aaron kept it pressed to his chest. 'You shouldn't say things like that,' she said and looked towards the floor, desperate to break whatever spell was being cast over her.

'Because I'm too young?'

'Because it's wrong.'

Aaron put his finger beneath her chin and lifted her face so that she had no choice but to look at him. He pressed his lips to hers and Gertie didn't try to stop him. Aaron's kiss woke something inside her that had been asleep for so long. For the first time in so many years, she felt a spark inside her, in her chest, in her core. He kissed her neck, her shoulders. Pushing aside the collar of her dress, he kissed along the length of her collarbone.

'Don't stop,' she murmured.

'Are you sure?'

'Yes.'

She unfastened the buttons of her dress and let it fall to the floor. Together they freed her underclothes so that she stood naked to the waist, only her thin cotton slip covering her from the waist down. Aaron looked at her, his eyes taking in every part of her pale skin as though surveying something miraculous.

'You are so beautiful,' he said, his voice low and thick. He ran his fingertips down her arms, across her stomach, and over her breasts.

Gertie closed her eyes. 'You darling boy,' she said. 'You beautiful darling boy.'

Aaron explored her body with his mouth and his hands, touching, stroking, brushing, until Gertie felt she might explode. In that moment, there was only the two of them. There was no war, no grey London street outside. The whole world was reduced to a pinpoint of sensation, existing only in the warmth of the fire pricking them with sweat, making Gertie's throat dry and her heart race. She pushed Aaron's shirt down, forcing it over his hands. With him naked to the waist like her, she pressed her lips to a small mole on his neck before kissing each of the pink scars along his shoulders while running her nails down the ridges of his spine. Aaron sighed and when he put his hands beneath her backside and lifted her so her feet no longer touched the floor, she wrapped her legs around him and crossed them behind his thighs. He spun her around. Her back was to the wall. With the warmth from his chest pressing against her bare breasts, she felt she might melt into the wall.

'Gertie,' he breathed into her ear, 'tell me you want me.'

'I want you,' Gertie gasped. 'I want you more than I've ever wanted anything in my life.'

As he kissed her again, the all-clear sounded outside.

Chapter 23

Abi – Thursday 17 November 1988 – Morning

The wind churned the sea into filthy brown peaks. Abi stumbled through the unforgiving pebbles, fighting against the direction of the gale and the November rain spitting icy shards into her face. Drowned by Dad's heavy parka, she could barely feel her hands or feet and had long since lost any sensation in the tip of her nose. Beside her, Cyril soldiered on, fur ruffled, ears pinned back to his head. For the first time Abi could remember, he didn't seem overly keen on his walk. More than once he turned for home. It was only Abi's determination to press on that brought him back to heel.

Abi shoved her hands deep into her pockets and bent her head into the wind. When Cyril was pissed off, he growled. When he was happy, he wagged his tail. When he was hungry, he nudged her ankles until she gave in and reached for a packet of ham. He would never save up a mountain of emotional bombshells to drop on her. He would tell her straight, 'You once had a sort of half brother or sister and now you've possibly got a new granddad, all right? Now where's that tennis ball?'

A strong gust blew the hood from Abi's head. She pulled it up and tried to tighten the cord but when it blew down again, she gave in and let her hair whip around her face. She patted the bulge in the pocket of her jeans. It was one thing to leave the shoebox unattended in the attic – if for some bizarre reason Mum or Dad decided to rummage under her bed, all they would find was a pair of old shoes in a battered shoebox – but the letter and Nan's locket were another matter altogether. For now, the ticking time bombs primed to blow a hole right through her family were tucked safely inside the pocket of her jeans.

A crab scuttled over the pebbles and Abi paused to let it cross her path. 'Aaron Dukszta, London, July 1944', she silently recited. The decapitated solider had a name. She had found it written on the back of one of the larger fragments of photograph when, after breakfast, she had lain the contents of the envelope and locket out on the blanket in the safety of the attic. With a name the handsome man in uniform was no longer a stranger; he was transforming into a real person. Abi couldn't decide whether that was worse. The only thing she *was* sure of was the significance of the date – July 1944. Mum was born in May 1945. She had been late – Nan had always said so. Mum had made her wait.

Abi watched the crab disappear beneath a rock. A few words from her now and she could crush Mum just as easily as she could smash the delicate shell of that crab under her trainer. Two weeks ago – one week ago even – and she might have been tempted. But after last night… She stooped, picked up a pebble, and ran her finger along the smooth surface before flicking her wrist and sending it skittering across the shingle. Nan had always said to tell the truth and shame the devil. How then could Nan have kept this massive secret from Mum? Perhaps she hadn't kept a secret at all. Perhaps this Aaron had been an innocent friend after all. Yeah, and Abi was the Queen of Sheba. There would have been no need to hide a letter from an innocent friend and conceal a photograph and flower they sent in the casing of the locket. And Abi's mum wouldn't have his eyes and his hair.

Last night Mum had been mortified at the prospect of Nan finding out about her pregnancy. Would it ease Mum's conscience to know that Nan might have had some kind of wartime affair with a Canadian soldier? Abi kicked at a tangle of seaweed. How could finding out that your dad might not be your dad, help anyone? And what if Abi had put two and two together and come up with fifty? Nan wasn't here to explain or defend herself. If she told, it would taint the memory of Nan and Granddad forever. But how could it be right not to tell Mum?

'Oh, Cyril, what should I do?' Abi said. 'How can I keep quiet about *this*?' She looked down, expecting to find a pair of friendly brown eyes looking up at her. Instead she found an empty patch of pebbles. She spun around and spotted Cyril some way back, cowering beside the rock the crab had taken shelter beneath. 'Oi, lazy!' she called. 'Get your butt here.' Cyril turned his face even further from her. 'Come on,' she begged. 'There'll be another slice of ham in it for you.' Her attempts at bribery fell on deaf ears. Accepting defeat, she slowly waded back through the pebbles.

'Have you had enough then?' she said. Scooping Cyril up, she unzipped the parka, tucked him inside, and zipped the coat back up so that just his head was exposed. His fur was damp but his little body was warm and she kissed the patch of brown fur between his ears. 'Eurgh, you filthy hound,' she said. 'You taste like salt!' She held Cyril a little tighter and nuzzled his fur. 'I wish you could talk. You'd tell me what to do, wouldn't you, boy? You wouldn't let me down.' She laughed sadly. 'How tragic am I? The only person in the whole world I have to talk to is a dog. Sorry, no offence intended.'

If Cyril took any offence, he didn't show it. He just turned around and licked her on the nose.

***

'Hello, love. Good walk?' Mum asked as Abi slammed the back door and placed Cyril on the kitchen floor. She wiped his sandy paws with a towel before he squirmed free.

'It was all right. A bit cold,' Abi said and kicked her soggy trainers off on the mat while Cyril made a beeline for the table, which was laden down with plates of fairy cakes, cheese flans still in their tins and Tupperware boxes stuffed full of shortbread. Abi shrugged off the parka, hung it behind the back door and pushed Cyril away from the table with her foot. 'What's with all the baking?'

Mum slid a tray from a shelf in the oven before pushing the door closed with her knee. 'I know it sounds silly,' she said, picking up a spatula and nudging a fresh batch of sausage rolls from the tray onto a cooling rack on the table. 'And they told me not to trouble myself, but it was your nan's turn to make the refreshments for the WI meeting tonight. I didn't have anything else to do and, well, I didn't like to let them down. I was going to make some shortbread for this afternoon anyway. The solicitor's coming to sort out the wi… to sort out the paperwork.'

'Oh yeah. Sorry.'

'For what?'

Abi shrugged self-consciously.

Mum slipped off her oven gloves and placed them on the side. 'It's okay, love. Really. I don't want you ever to feel like you have to tread on eggshells around me. Sometimes when we talk about Nan, I'll get upset. Sometimes you'll get upset. So don't feel you have to hide how you feel from me. We wouldn't be human if we didn't feel sad and shed a tear. Okay?' She smiled.

Abi nodded and snagged the inside of her socks with her toes. Maybe Mum had hit the nail on the head. Maybe the reason she hadn't been able to cry for Nan was not because she was heartless, but because she wasn't a human at all.

Mum took a sausage roll from the cooling rack and broke it in half, releasing a small waft of steam. While she pursed her lips and blew on each half, Abi studied her face in profile; the delicate nose that turned up slightly at the end, the fair eyelashes and the fine blonde hair free from any kink. There was no trace of Granddad Sid in the photographs of his younger days. Of his thick, dark hair and heavyset features. Or of Nan and her mousey waves that used to tumble to her shoulders.

'Here you go,' Mum said, crouching down to feed the first half of sausage roll to Cyril. Abi watched on in surprise. Mum hardly ever paid Cyril attention, except to chase him out of the kitchen with a mop, never mind feed him one of her sausage rolls.

'Look at him, isn't he a sweetheart,' Mum said and handed him the second half, which he wolfed down in one gulp, his little stump of a tail wagging so fast it was little more than a blur. Mum brushed the crumbs from her hands and Cyril snuffled around the floor, leaving damp tongue-shaped patches on the tiles as he licked up every last trace of pastry.

'Who needs a Hoover when you've got a Cyril?' Mum said, still smiling down at him. 'Why don't you take him through to the parlour and get warmed up? Your dad's popped into town to pick up a box of tea bags and a couple of pints of milk, but he lit a fire before he left. It'll be toasty in there by now. Go on, I'll be through in a minute, the kettle's just boiled and the pot's warming.'

Cyril made the most of the unexpected invitation into the parlour and curled up on the rug in front of the fire. He closed his eyes and began to snore. Abi sat at the far end of the sofa, her legs tucked beneath her, running the tip of her index finger along the ridge in her pocket. Should she tell, or shouldn't she? Was she putting two and two together and coming up with fifty, or wasn't she?

'Here we are,' Mum said, pushing through the door. She placed the chinking tray down on the coffee table and Abi pulled the hem of her jumper down to cover her pockets.

Mum sat down on the sofa beside Abi, poured the tea and placed a mug on the table before Abi. 'Do you remember when you were a little girl,' she said, taking a plate of fairy cakes from the tray and holding them out to Abi, 'and you insisted on purple icing on the cakes for your birthday parties? Yellow at a push.'

Abi smiled. 'I remember.'

Mum held the plate further towards Abi. 'Go on.'

Abi chose a cake, pulled back the paper case and took a bite.

'Have another. Go on,' Mum encouraged. Abi took another cake and balanced it on the arm of the sofa. She chewed slowly, staring into the orange light of the fire, all the while sensing Mum's eyes on her. Her cheeks began to glow, and a log crackled in the hearth. Mum placed the plate down on the table.

'How are you, love? Really?' she asked.

Abi picked at the paper around her cake. 'All right.'

'Sure?'

Abi managed to cross the fingers of her free hand before she nodded.

'Because I was worried that I had dropped too much on you last night. I shouldn't have let it all come out like that. But I wasn't thinking straight. It must have been a shock to hear all about me and Tony on top of… well, on top of everything else yesterday.'

'It was all right.' Abi shrugged.

'I didn't get a wink of sleep after you went to bed. I was tossing and turning all night thinking that it had been selfish to unburden on you like that. If you want to talk about it, if you've got any questions, I'll do my best to answer them.'

Do you know who your dad is? Abi thought, staring into the flames. 'There's nothing.'

'I remember how I felt when my dad passed away.' The sadness in Mum's voice made Abi turn to look at her. She was staring into the fire, a distant look in her eyes as though she was somehow viewing the past in the flames. 'I couldn't bear to talk about him for weeks,' she said quietly. 'Just thinking about him made me burst into tears. I tried to hide it from you and Mum. I didn't want either of you to see me so upset. Your dad was the only one who knew. I could hardly keep it from him, not when I sobbed into my pillow every night.

'And then one day, when you were at school, your dad took the day off work. He drove me out into the country and we went for a long walk. It was a quiet spot so we didn't bump into anyone and as we walked, your dad encouraged me to talk about my dad. About happy times and good memories. I refused at first. I didn't think it would help. How could it make me feel better to cry? But your dad persisted and gradually wore me down. Once I started, I found I couldn't stop. We walked for miles with me jabbering on. I cried and laughed, all at the same time, remembering memories from when I was little with Mum and Dad. And all the while your dad held my hand and listened. He was right, you know. It was such a relief to talk. It made my dad feel real again as though he was solid rather than just a thought or a fading memory. I felt close to him again and it was wonderful. Sad but wonderful. And that's when I realised how unhealthy it is to bottle up your feelings. You need to let them out or they drive you mad. Do you know what I mean?'

Abi shifted. 'Do you, you know, still miss him? Granddad?'

Mum picked up her mug. 'You never stop missing someone you love, not really,' she said directing her words to her tea. 'How can you if someone has been so important in your life? If you've loved someone so very much, then that love can't die. It stays with you, in here.' She placed her mug back down on the table and put her hand to her chest. 'And my dad was the very best of men. So sweet and kind,' she said, smiling to herself. 'But you know that better than anyone, don't you? He loved you so very much.' She turned to face Abi, still smiling. 'Have I ever told you about the first time he came to see you when we were still in the hospital?'

Abi shook her head.

'He drove Mum to the hospital but refused to come onto the ward. He was coming to the end of a nasty head cold and was afraid of giving it to you or me. But I wouldn't hear of him missing out on meeting you. You were so perfect, so beautiful and I wanted him to see you. I sent your dad out to talk to him and in the end, he caved in. It was naughty of me really, I'm afraid I had a knack of wrapping your granddad around my little finger. But when I placed you in his arms, I knew I had been right to insist. He took you so gently and looked down at you so softly with tears in his eyes. I don't think I've ever seen so much love in a person's eyes. My big, strong dad was crying because of you. Because of the love he had in his heart for you. And you were so tiny in those big hands of his. Do you remember his fingers? Like thick pork sausages?'

Abi couldn't help but smile at the memory of her granddad's hands, always muddy with soil from his vegetable patch or flower borders. 'I always thought they looked like bunches of bananas.'

'See?' Mum said. 'We can remember your granddad now and talk about him without feeling sad. One day we'll be able to talk about your nan without feeling...' Mum's voice caught in her throat but she swallowed hard. 'But I'm lucky. I've got a daily reminder of her.'

'What?'

'Not "what". Who. You, love. You're so like her. You've got her eyes, her smile and so many of her ways. All I have to do is look at you and I see her.'

'Really?'

Mum nodded. 'And I'm so glad that you had her. Especially when I...' She paused and looked into the fire again. 'Sorry. It's just that it's so hard to say, to admit.' Her shoulders heaved as she took a deep breath. 'I still feel so guilty about how Mum had to step in to take care of you when we first moved here. I was so wrapped up in myself, trying to sort out your dad and money, that I let my job as your mum fall down the cracks. I was a mess and I let you down. If it hadn't been for your nan... if she hadn't been there to pick up the pieces... I don't think I ever thanked her properly. I took her for granted. And now...'

A tear slipped down Mum's cheek. She wiped it away with the back of her hand. She was sitting so close to Abi that their knees were touching, and Abi knew what she had to do. She put her cake down on the table and reached for Mum's hands. 'Don't cry. I'm sure Nan knew how grateful you were. And you don't need to worry about me. You didn't let me down.'

'Are you sure?' Mum looked into Abi's eyes, a crease in her brow.

'I'm sure.'

'Promise?'

'Promise,' Abi said. 'You were a good mum. It was just a shit time.'

In spite of her tears, Mum laughed. The crease smoothed away and her cheeks glowed in the light from the fire. She gripped Abi's hands. 'Yes, it was rather, wasn't it?'

She looked like she was about to say something else but the sound of the back door opening interrupted whatever it was.

'That'll be your dad,' Mum said letting go of Abi's hands, but not before giving them a final squeeze. She wiped her eyes roughly on the sleeve of her blouse. 'Oh, would you look at the time! The solicitor will be here in just over an hour. I need to put my face on and tidy that kitchen.' But as she stood up, she pointed to Abi's pocket. 'What's that?' she asked.

Abi looked down and saw that her jumper had ridden up to expose a corner of the envelope. She yanked her jumper down. 'It's nothing. Just something I'm working through.'

'For uni?'

'Something like that.'

Mum placed her hand on Abi's face and cupped her cheek. 'And you're sure you're all right, love?'

'I'm fine,' Abi said, leaning into Mum's warm palm. 'You don't need to worry about me.'

Chapter 24

Rose held back the bedroom curtains and blew cigarette smoke out of the open window. Overnight, the world outside the bungalow had turned white. Snow weighed heavy on the bare branches of the shrubs in the front garden and, although it was almost eleven o'clock, a thick fog still cloaked the street. Rose could just make out the soft glow of the multicoloured bulbs decorating the Christmas tree in the Thompsons' front room opposite. The Thompsons had three children. Once upon a time, in a different lifetime, she had been their babysitter.

She took a last drag of the cigarette, flicked it out of the window, and watched a robin appear from amongst the tangled branches of her father's privet. It hopped around, pecking fruitlessly at the ground, leaving a trail of tiny prints in its wake. Taking pity on the poor thing, Rose tore the crust from the cold slice of toast on her dressing table and threw it into the garden. She closed the window and watched the robin jerk its tiny head from side to side. It looked from Rose to the bread and back again. In the end it took the plunge. With one hop, it grabbed the crust and flew away into the tangled branches of the privet.

Rose sat down at her dressing table and pushed the plate of toast away. Her mother had insisted on leaving it for her. 'It's a big day. You need to keep your strength up,' Mother had said. Rose had smiled, thanked her and even managed to nibble a corner, waiting for Mother to leave so she could spit it into a hankie. Over the last year, she had become well practised in the art of subterfuge. The last thing she needed today was questions. She was only just holding it together.

So many times, over the last year, she had been tempted to unburden to Mother. Her mother wasn't stupid; she knew that her story about returning from Edinburgh because she was homesick hadn't rung true. But to her credit, Mother had never tackled her in front of her father. She always waited until they were alone – washing up or peeling and chopping vegetables – to comment on how tired she thought Rose was looking. She looked so sad. Where had her sparkle gone? Mother had tried every trick in the book to tease the truth from Rose; cajoling, reassuring, hugging. But Rose just couldn't say the words. Her mother would never understand what had made her daughter have sex outside of marriage. She would think Rose was dirty and disgusting. And she couldn't bear that. And Father. She couldn't stand to imagine how he would look at her if he ever found out. There was only one other person in the world who knew the truth and Rose was determined that was the way it would stay.

Marina had travelled with her in the ambulance that awful night and had made quite a scene in the delivery room until the doctor firmly insisted that unless she take herself outside, he would carry her out.

With Marina dispatched, a young nurse and a midwife stood by as the doctor gave Rose an injection. She was told to bend her knees and part her legs. They poked her and prodded, and she gritted her teeth, squeezing her eyes tight to shut out the bright light in the ceiling above. There had been no gentleness. No tenderness. The medical team had seemed determined to perform a process with the minimum of fuss or ceremony. With her legs bent, Rose couldn't see what was happening. When it was over, she couldn't see what the midwife was wrapping up in a towel. She struggled to sit up, but the nurse pressed her back by the shoulders. She only wanted to see her baby, she begged.

'Please, just once. To say goodbye.'

The doctor pinned her down while the young midwife hurried towards the door with the towel. Rose screamed after her. She screamed until her lungs ached. The doctor forced a mask onto her face and held it in place until she stopped kicking.

When she woke it was morning. She was on a general ward with a curtain pulled around her and the sides of the bed pulled up. She ran her fingers along the bars of the bed. Someone took hold of her hand and kissed it. Marina, still in her blue dress, mascara smudged, eyes rimmed in red, looked down at her. She stroked Rose's hair, telling her that it would all be all right. In time.

If anyone from the hospital asked, Rose was to say that they were visiting Edinburgh to do some Christmas shopping. That their husbands were in Italy on business. If anyone telephoned Italy to check, Marina had made arrangements for the story to be verified. She had also arranged for the caretaker to clean the bathroom in the halls. Nobody would ever know.

Marina let the side of the bed down and sat beside Rose. She slipped her arm around her shoulders and moved in closer. Marina held her while she sobbed onto her shoulder.

Three days later, when the doctor finally discharged Rose, Marina was waiting at the hospital door with a taxi. Rose's suitcase was packed and in the boot and Marina offered to check them into a hotel for a few days so that Rose could travel when she felt stronger. But Rose just wanted to get home.

The taxi drove slowly through the crowds of Christmas shoppers spilling from the pavement along Princes Street into the road. When they reached Waverley Station, Marina insisted on buying her a first-class ticket and settling her into the carriage.

'Promise me,' she said clasping Rose's hands through the open train window, 'that you'll stay in touch. You have my address. You've nothing to rebuke yourself for. Nobody knows. And if you want to come back next term, then I'd love to have my roommate back.'

The train pulled away from the platform and Rose leant out of the window to watch Marina waving until she disappeared from view.

Rose looked at her reflection in the mirror. Perhaps she should have contacted Marina again. If for no other reason than to say thank you. But there had never seemed to be a good time.

She curled a strand of hair around her finger. Maggie from the salon had visited earlier that morning to curl her hair and do her make-up; a faint dusting of powder, a touch of pale brown eye shadow; a wipe of mascara. It was demure. Virginal. Looking at her now, nobody would ever guess what she had been doing a year ago today.

When they had set the date, she hadn't realised the significance. The anniversary of her miscarriage wasn't a date she had circled in her diary. By the time she realised, it was too late. Arrangements had been made, deposits paid. There was no conceivable reason that she could give for changing the date. She couldn't tell anyone that by rights, she should have a baby just two days off being seven months old. That in her dreams, she had a baby girl with chubby cheeks and bright hazel eyes and the most beautiful, beautiful smile.

If only she hadn't drunk so much gin and worn a tight girdle. If only she hadn't been ashamed of the life growing inside her. If she had let her breathe instead of crushing the life from her tiny form. If she had wanted her baby from the start rather than when it was too late.

Sometimes she sat and looked out of the window, watching Mrs Thompson with her three girls, imagining walking her own little girl to school. Holding her hand as she skipped beside her, her brown curls tied up in red ribbons. Emily. She had named her daughter Emily.

Rose pressed her palms to her stomach. She had no need for a girdle; her stomach was as flat as it had always been. There were no outward signs that it had ever been otherwise. No stretch marks. No sagging skin. No clue that would give her away. She had wanted to go to the family doctor to see if she was still capable of having children. But she had known him since she was a baby and he would be sure to tell her parents. So, instead of medicine, she turned to silent prayers. If she were ever blessed with another child, she would love it so much. She would protect it and never let it come to harm. Another child would never replace Emily, but it would be a new life, fresh and unspoilt. Born as it should be; from a loving marriage.

She had hardly dared to believe that she would be given a second chance. Had her father not sent her on an errand one Monday to collect a bag of nails from the hardware shop, then she would never have met Mick. Each day for a week, her father had sent her for another small item from the shop and each day Mick had chatted to her. He did the impossible and made her laugh with his silly jokes. He was fair and slim and funny and when he invited her for coffee, there had seemed no harm. Gradually he had worked his way into her life with his cheeky grin. They had gone to the cinema where he always bought her chocolates and ice cream. She had cheered from the side-line when he scored at five-a-side football. When he first came to tea, he brought her mother a bunch of flowers and her father a bottle of whisky. And that night when he left, he had paused on the doorstep, slipped his arm around her waist and pulled her to him. There were no rockets or stars, just soft, gentle, slightly embarrassed lips. She knew then that he would look after her. And she would protect him.

Mick would never know the shame she had brought on herself before she met him. How she had succumbed to hot breath whispering into her ear. She closed her eyes and imagined the smell of leather. For a moment she was back on that beach on a hot summer's night.

There was a knock on the door and Rose jumped.

'Are you ready?' her father said on the other side. 'The car's here.'

'Just a minute, Dad,' she said, struggling to catch her breath. The past was the past and that's where it should stay. Today was a fresh slate. In less than an hour she would be respectable again. She smoothed out the crushed ivory velvet of her dress then took Mother's locket from its box and slipped it over her neck. She ran her fingernail over the rosebud. Something old and borrowed. She took a final deep breath and pulled her veil over her face.

Chapter 25

Abi – Thursday 17 November 1988 – Afternoon

'I think that's everything, Mrs Russell. Your mother and father made good provisions for you. It was their wish that you and your family should be comfortable.'

Mr Anderson, Nan's solicitor, directed his words across the kitchen table to Mum while he collected together his papers, forced them into a buff-coloured folder, and placed them back inside his briefcase. 'I'll be in touch again once the probate is in order so that we can transfer the house into your name. The first of the savings bonds is due to mature early next year and the final one five years later. I'll contact the bank and ask them to set up a meeting with you to arrange the requisite paperwork. Do any of you have any questions?' He looked at Abi who was seated to his right, with her back to the sink, but she shook her head. Dad shook his head too when Mr Anderson turned to him.

For the last half an hour neither of them had said much at all; Dad's silence indicating to Abi that, like her, he felt any talking should be left to Mum.

'You've been very thorough,' Mum said. 'I had no idea that my parents had managed to squirrel away so much. But they were always so careful, so thoughtful.' For the first time since Mr Anderson had commenced the reading of Nan's will, Mum let go of Abi and Dad's hands. She took a tissue from her pocket and dabbed at her nose. 'And thank you again for coming all the way out here in this awful weather. It really wasn't necessary, we could have come to your office.'

'Think nothing of it,' Mr Anderson said. 'Besides, Mrs Smith was very specific in her instructions that, as and when the situation required, I should come out to Cliff Cottage rather than conduct matters in my office. She was keen that I see her home for myself. I'm sure that in more clement weather, it's a lovely spot. I can certainly see why it held such an attraction for her. And for your late father.'

'Yes,' Mum said, looking around the kitchen. 'My parents loved it here. It was their little piece of heaven.' She wiped away the trail of mascara inching down her cheek. 'Won't you have another cup of tea before you go? Or another piece of shortbread?'

'Oh no, thank you.' Mr Anderson puffed out his cheeks and patted his stomach, which strained the buttons of his pinstriped waistcoat. 'It's very more-ish but I'm supposed to be watching my waistline. My wife has put me on a strict diet.'

'At least take some back for the other people in your office.' Without waiting for a response, Mum stood up and took a roll of cling film down from the shelf beside the fridge. She wrapped up enough shortbread to feed a small army and Mr Anderson slipped the parcel of biscuits inside his briefcase.

'Most kind. It will be very much appreciated at teatime, I'm sure.' He smiled at Mum. 'I can see that your mother's generosity lives on in her daughter. I would like to say again how truly sorry I am for your loss. Mrs Smith was a wonderful woman, a real live-wire. Her presence will be much missed in the local community.'

'Thank you,' Mum said. 'She meant the world to me. To all of us.'

'Quite right.'

With his business clearly concluded, Mr Anderson closed the brass-coloured clasps of his briefcase with a snap before easing his bulk up from the chair. He took his pale rain mac from the back of the chair and shrugged it on over his dark suit. 'Now I'll take my leave and let you good people alone to get on with your day.'

Dad got to his feet and shook Mr Anderson's hand. 'Thank you again for coming. I'll see you out.'

'No trouble. No trouble at all. But – and I don't mean to appear rude – but I was rather hoping that Abigail might do me the honour of escorting me from the premises.' Mr Anderson took hold of the handle of his briefcase and slipped it from the table before looking down at Abi. 'Your grandmother told me about a wonderful azalea in the front garden. I thought you might point it out to me.'

Abi looked up at Mum who nodded for her to do it.

'Okay,' she said and pushed her chair away from the table.

After waiting for Mum to thank Mr Anderson again for coming all the way out to Cliff Cottage and Mr Anderson to thank Mum again for her hospitality and the biscuits, Abi led him out into the hall. She held the front door open while he stood on the doorstep, his shoulders hunched, his collar turned up against the sleet.

'It's that one,' she said, folding her free arm over her chest and tucking her hand into the warmth of her armpit. She nodded to a bush of uninspiring bare twigs rattling in the wind. 'It looks better in the summer.'

'Very good,' Mr Anderson said. Without so much as a passing glance at the bush, he dipped his hand inside the breast pocket of his suit jacket. He pulled out an envelope. 'This is for you.'

Abi withdrew her hand from the warmth of her armpit and took the envelope.

'There, I have discharged my final instruction.' Mr Anderson smiled. 'It was a pleasure to meet you, Abigail. You are just as your grandmother described. Goodbye to you, my dear.' He fought his way against the wind to his car, the flap of his overcoat billowing like the sail of a yacht tossed around on a stormy sea.

***

The window rattled in its frame, wind whistled down the chimney, and Abi sat cross-legged on her bed, staring down at the pink envelope resting on her blanket. Her full name *Abigail Gertrude Russell* was written on the front in Nan's distinctive copperplate hand. Abi picked up the envelope, twisted it around, then put it down again. Why had Nan written to her? And why had she given it to her solicitor to deliver when all of her official business was wrapped up in her will? Everything, quite rightly, had been left to Mum. There could be nothing else left to say.

The sea crashing on the rocks outside had nothing on the tidal wave of nerves battering Abi's insides. She sank to the floor and felt around under the bed until she found the old shoebox. She pulled it out, lifted the lid, eased the charred letter from beneath the shoes and placed it on the blanket. Still kneeling on the floor, she looked from the pink envelope to the burnt envelope. It was official. She was going mad. There was no other explanation for why her brain was trying to convince her that there was a connection between these two letters. There was no way in the world that Nan could have known she would stumble across the shoebox and be left looking for some kind of clue to unlock the tangled mysteries inside. It was just a coincidence.

'Oh, sod it,' she said under breath. 'Abigail Gertrude Russell, if you think this letter from Nan is anything to do with that photo and those shoes, then you are seriously losing the plot.'

Before she could talk herself out of it, she picked up the envelope, ran her finger under the flap and pulled out a white card decorated with a single red rose. Inside the card was a letter. She opened it and began to read.

My darling Abigail,

Well, if you are reading this then I am no longer there with you. Since I can't even begin to imagine that, I will move quickly on and think only happy thoughts.

I am sitting here in the kitchen, watching you through the open window. It is a glorious spring day and the air is warm and tinged with salt and the scent of the first blooms of the year. You're out in the garden, throwing a ball for Cyril. I have never told anyone this before, but after your granddad died, I worried that I might lose Cyril too; he cried and pined so very much. But then you came to live with us and gave him a reason to live again.

It fills my heart with joy to have the chance to see you every day and watch you blossom into a lovely young woman. I know that the circumstances of your moving here weren't the happiest and I know how hard it was for you at the time, but I believe that God makes each of our journeys difficult and puts obstacles in our way so that when we eventually receive our rewards, we can appreciate them all the more for the struggles we have faced.

Now, I should probably get to my reasons for writing to you, there's only so much space on this paper, after all. I wanted to let you know that I would like you to have my locket. You're not to worry, I have talked it through with your mum and she is happy for it to be your inheritance. It once belonged to my mother and her mother before her and has always been precious to me. I know that you will treasure it as I have and that in your hands it will be safe.

And now to my other reason for wanting to write to you. But I hardly know where to begin. You see, none of us knows how long we will have in this life and I have often wondered what the people who have left us might have wanted to say, what advice or pearl of wisdom they might have wished to share but never got the chance. I'm not clever or wise but I have lived a long and happy life and I've learned so many lessons along the way. I want to share with you the most important lesson of all, and it is this – that the past is a dry and dusty place. Life is too short to constantly look back and regret what we cannot change. We should live always in the present and look to the future, seeking out the light and the colour in life. Because, sweetheart, that is what you have been to me. Since the day you were born, you have brought me nothing but joy. And you see, I have been one of the lucky ones. I have loved and been loved. So when you think of me now, don't be sad. Smile for me, just as I am smiling at you now.

I want you to remember that wherever you go and whatever you do, you will always have my love and your granddad's love with you. So, my darling, go forward and live your life unburdened and free from worry. Do your best every day and above all, be happy.

I won't say goodbye, just ta ta for now.
Until we meet again my beautiful girl,
Your loving Nan xxxx

A tear dripped from Abi's cheek. It fell onto the letter, smearing the blue ink of Nan's final kiss. She closed the card, placed it on the bed and buried her face in the crook of her arm. The tears she had been waiting so long for finally came and with such a force that her whole body shook. Nan was gone; she was never coming back.

Abi wiped her eyes on her sleeve. She rocked backwards and forwards, the floorboards creaking beneath her. Her cries were muffled in the folds of her jumper. When she thought she had cried herself dry, another sob caught in her throat and the tears came all over again.

Eventually, and summoning every ounce of strength she had left, she dragged herself onto her feet and crawled into bed. She pulled the sheets and blankets over her head, curled into a ball and buried her face in the pillow. What she had found in that stupid shoebox yesterday meant nothing. There was no great mystery to unravel. No secrets to uncover. Gertie and Sid Smith were her nan and granddad. They were the best and kindest people in the world. And she loved them more than her heart could take. That's all she or anyone else needed to know. Ever.

Chapter 26

'We're popping into the village,' Mum called up the stairs. 'I said I'd drop this organza off to Mrs Williams so she can make a start on the arrangements for the wedding on Saturday. Do you want anything from the shop?'

Abi placed a pile of freshly ironed laundry into the new suitcase open on her bed. Mum had insisted on buying the red case for her on their previous day's shopping trip, along with a new jumper, a pair of jeans, three T-shirts, two bras, a vest, and ten pairs of M&S knickers. They'd only gone into Weymouth to pick up some flower arranging supplies but in the cash-and-carry car park, Mum had 'suddenly' remembered she needed a few things from town. She was a clever woman, Abi's mum. Clever and slightly devious.

Abi looked at the new knickers, bought to replace the threadbare grey pairs Mum had wrestled from Abi's duffle bag a few days earlier and dumped unceremoniously into the bin. The neatly folded knickers in white and pastel shades, smelling of lavender fabric softener, were tucked into the side pocket of the case.

'I've got everything I need, thanks,' Abi called out.

'What was that, love?'

Abi opened the door and stepped out on to the landing. She looked down at Mum on the first floor.

'I said I'm okay, thanks.'

'I'll get you a nice fresh loaf. The shop gets them delivered from the baker in town every morning now. You can have beans on toast for your tea when you get back to the halls.'

'But I've got that leftover flan and half a Madeira cake you wrapped in foil.'

'That's just a snack for the journey! I'll get your dad to stop at Parr's Farm on the way back and pick up half a dozen eggs. They'll poach up a treat and–'

'If you two don't stop your yakking,' Dad called out, his voice echoing up from the hallway downstairs, 'we'll hit that traffic on the bypass. She'll be back in two weeks for Christmas and there's always the phone, you know. Oh, bloody hell… I'll see you in the car.'

The icy blast whipping to the top of the house and the impatient jangling of Dad's car keys signalled his exit from the house.

Mum looked heavenwards and tied a pink scarf around her neck. 'I don't know what he's fussing about. It's not even nine yet. There's plenty of time to get to the village and back and still have time for a cuppa before we have to get going. I'll get him a custard tart, that'll keep him quiet, won't it?'

Abi watched as Mum straightened the knot in her scarf and took a pair of gloves from her coat pocket. In the pale winter light, Abi was sure she could see a hint of Nan in Mum's cheeks and eyes.

'You okay, love?' Mum looked up at her again and smiled. 'You're a million miles away.'

'I was just thinking about something.'

'Anything you want to share.'

'Nothing important. And thanks, Mum, you know, for all my new clothes and well, for everything.'

'Get away with you,' Mum said, slipping her hands into her gloves. 'What's the point in having a bit of cash if I can't treat you once in a while. It's what your nan would have wanted.'

They stood and looked at each other for a moment until they were interrupted by the honk of the car horn outside. Mum raised her eyebrows again. 'Honestly, I've never known anyone get their knickers in such a twist over a little bit of traffic. Do us all a favour and have your case packed by the time we get back. It'll be one less thing for your dad to fuss about.' She winked at Abi. 'We'll be twenty minutes. Twenty-five tops.'

Abi crossed her fingers behind her back. 'I won't leave this room till I'm packed.'

'Right-o. See you soon, sweetheart.'

Abi stood on the top landing, watching Mum make her way down the stairs. Twenty minutes. Was that long enough? It would have to be. She listened to the noises of Mum preparing to leave the house; the zip on her handbag as she checked for her purse; a quick goodbye to Cyril; the rattle of teacups placed in the sink. The moment she heard the back door latch and felt the cold breeze whip up the stairs, she left the top step, like a sprinter leaving the starting blocks. She ran down the two flights of stairs and was in the hall in time to hear the Cortina roar to life and pull away up the lane.

She ran through the kitchen, yanked open the back door, flew outside and sprinted down the garden to the shed. Opening the shed door, she rushed inside and breathed a sigh of relief to find the carrier bag she had carefully prepared last night, just where she had left it on Granddad's old workbench. She grabbed the bag, closed the shed door and ran back into the house.

On her way back past the parlour she picked up a tail. Cyril raced up the stairs behind her, a string of squeaky plastic sausages dangling from his mouth.

Abi dropped the carrier bag to the attic floor. It landed with a heavy clunk. Cyril deposited his string of sausages at her feet and looked up at her expectantly, one foot off the ground, ears cocked.

'There's no time for games now, mutt,' she spluttered and sank to her knees, trying to catch her breath. Maybe she should knock the fags on the head. Taking hold of the matted tassels at one end of the old rug, she pulled it back to reveal the floorboards beneath. She forced her finger into a knot in one of the boards and pulled.

'Bingo!' She smiled at Cyril and he wagged his tail. She pulled the board free and an icy blast of air shot from the hole, carrying with it a shower of dust. It landed on her jeans and made Cyril sneeze. Putting the board aside, she looked down into the dark void, at the criss-crossing wooden joists supporting the attic floor, which separated it from the ceiling of Mum and Dad's bedroom below. She had expected to find her old hiding place empty.

'Bloody hell,' she said, reaching in, freeing a small box from a network of spiders' webs. The metal was cold to the touch. With the cuff of her jumper, Abi wiped away a layer of thick dust to reveal the gold and yellow Chinese ladies still there, still picking tea, with a pagoda and lotus tree in the background. Beneath the grime the old tea caddy still gleamed as brightly as it had on the day Nan had given it to her to use as a moneybox.

She shook it, but it was empty. She knew it would be. A bender two years earlier had emptied the caddy of her hard-saved Christmas and birthday money. Abi sat back on her heels. Cyril gave the caddy a good sniff.

'It was supposed to be for Europe,' she said. Cyril put his paws on her thigh and licked her cheek. Abi stroked the fur on his ears. It was turning grey, like the fur around his muzzle. Abi pulled him a little closer and kissed him on the head.

'Come on then,' she said. 'Let's get this over with.'

Putting the caddy aside, she groped around under her bed, and pulled out the old shoebox. She lifted the lid. Everything was back exactly as she had found it: the scraps of photo tucked into the folds of the letter inside the envelope; the shoes wrapped in the delicate tissue paper. Abi freed Nan's locket from beneath her jumper and ran her nail along the ridges of the engraved rosebud. The soldier's face and what was left of the flower were back in the gold casing, covered over by Mum's photo with the glass glued in place. Back where they belonged.

Replacing the lid, Abi placed the shoebox into the void, easing it into the gap between the joists. Somehow the box looked lonely. Abandoned. Abi grabbed her old black Oxfam jumper from the suitcase on her bed. Mum had washed it so that it smelled of lavender. With great care she tucked it around the delicate cardboard box. 'I don't know who you are, Aaron Dukszta,' she said. 'But Nan thought enough of you to keep your letter.' She withdrew her hand and took a final look at the bundle before replacing the floorboard. She tipped the contents of the carrier bag onto the floor. She took up the hammer and positioned one of the nails over the board, judging where the joist was beneath.

'Stand back,' she said to Cyril who had come to investigate. She nudged him aside, swung the hammer above her head and brought it down with a thump on the nail. Cyril sprang back and ran from the room. Abi picked up another nail and another, repeating the process until she had hammered a dozen nails into the floorboard. She hooked her finger into the knot and waggled it. The floorboard didn't move at all. There was no way it would ever move again.

Abi repositioned the rug. She collected together the hammer and remaining nails and shoved them back into the bag. Picking up the caddy, she sat on the edge of the bed. She turned the caddy around in her hands. Once upon a time this cold metal box had held all of her dreams.

'I got it all wrong, didn't I?' she said to the Chinese ladies. They didn't respond, they just carried on picking their tea. Abi laughed. She was going mad. Talking to herself like that. There was one person who would have understood her. She looked at Nan's card. It was on the mantelpiece where it had been since the day the solicitor gave it to her. She had read Nan's words so many times that she knew most of them by heart.

The past is a dry and dusty place
Live your life unburdened
Do your best every day and above all, be happy.

She looked down at the tea caddy. It had been so long. So much had happened. As hard as she tried to talk herself out of it, Nan's words came back to her: Be happy.

She leapt to her feet and raced down the two flights of stairs. In the hall, she picked up the phone and dialled the number she still remembered by heart. Her heart pounded in her chest as the ring tone sounded. What's the worst that could happen? The person on the other end could hang up on her or...

'Hello,' the voice at the other end said.

Abi's heart jumped into her throat. More than two years melted away. She was fifteen again.

'Hello. Is there anybody there?' the voice said again.

Abi swallowed. 'Penny,' she said. 'It's me. It's Abi.'

Chapter 26

It was almost eight o'clock. The evening had chased the last finger-width of daylight from the sky, but a ruddy glow hovered over the rooftops of London from Buckingham Palace to the most modest one-roomed charitable foundation flat in Mile End, and everything in between. Every streetlamp was lit, and every home and business had thrown open their doors and windows. The inside world had turned to the outside, friends and neighbours, strangers and new lovers, all came together to celebrate on this mild spring evening. The lights that burned bright that night could never be snuffed out again.

From her bed, Gertie could see down onto the street below and her friends and neighbours enjoying the festivities. The tables, which had earlier lined the road, had been moved aside, clearing space for a makeshift dance floor. Men held women close or spun them around to the music provided by the piano from the public bar of The Royal Oak, which had been brought out onto the pavement. Girls laughed as their skirts twirled and their dance partners tried to steal kisses. Children, wearing newspaper crowns and full of precious sugar, squealed as they wove in and out of the legs of the dancers.

From amongst the cacophony of music and singing, Gertie's ears tuned into a softer sound: a small mew. She looked down into the crib beside her bed. A breath caught in her throat. Beneath a blanket, crocheted by her mother, a tiny baby girl squirmed. Gertie pulled back the blanket, placed one hand under the baby's head and the other beneath her back, and eased her ever so gently from her bed. The baby grizzled briefly.

'Shhh,' Gertie whispered. She brought the baby into the crook of her arm and looked down into the baby's delicate features. 'Mummy's got you now. Mummy's got you now.'

A sensation of joy flooded every part of Gertie's brain and body. No longer did those words belong just to other women. Now they were hers to use. She was someone's mummy. Gertie held her daughter close, feeling the rise and fall of the tiny chest, full of new life. She smiled through her tears. This perfect, warm, soft little girl feathering her neck with her new breath was hers. She had created those lungs for God to put breath into. She rocked her baby. *Her baby.*

'Did you know,' she whispered, 'that the whole world is having a party just to welcome you? Everyone is waiting to say hello. Your cousin Arthur is desperate to meet you.' Gertie smiled. 'He's promised to look after you and be just like a big brother. Because, you see my love, you won't have another brother or sister. You see…'

She glanced at the closed bedroom door. It was the first time she had been alone since Mother and Ruth had rushed halfway across London, fighting through the crowds to be with her.

She reached under her pillow and pulled out an envelope. It was charred in one corner where the flame had taken briefly before she had blown it out. Even now, the memory of Sid's face when he had found her doubled up beside the fireplace made her briefly reconsider what she was about to do. The colour had drained from his face as he knelt beside her, not wanting to leave her to go to the pub to telephone her mother, but knowing he had to. It was when she heard his footsteps pound down the stairs, that she slipped the envelope into the pocket of her dressing gown.

For nine months she had constructed a truth, wrapped herself in a cloak of lies to protect her, to protect Sid. His convictions had never been in doubt. The baby inside her was his. With his belief, she had managed to convince herself too. The envelope falling onto the mat that morning had whipped away the cloak; left her exposed to the truth.

She eased the photograph from the envelope and held it to her baby's face, her heart fluttering in her throat. 'There's a very special person that I need to introduce you to,' she said, her lips close to her baby's ear. 'This is Aaron. It's important that you meet him now because after today we won't be able to talk about him again. He came from a magical country very far away with mountains so high there's snow on the peaks all year round and lakes of green water. I met him when I was so very sad. He helped me smile again. He was sweet and kind. And just this once, I want you to see what he looks like. Because, sweetheart, he gave me a wonderful gift.' Gertie sniffed back a tear. 'There will always be a little bit of him in there.' She placed two fingers over the baby's heart. 'But it has to be our secret. Just you and me. Nobody else can ever know.'

She rocked her daughter, wondering whether there might be a place in Aaron's heart forever in that bombed-out room, just like there was a place in hers filled with the memory of a boy, his chest wrapped in bandages. A boy who had held her so tight and made her feel alive again.

'I promise that I'll try my hardest to be the very best mummy I can be. And, somehow, I'll make sure Aaron is always with you when it matters. I don't know how yet, but I promise you I will.'

There was a soft knock at the door and Gertie forced the photograph and envelope back under the pillow. 'Come in,' she said.

The door opened and Sid looked in.

'Come in then,' she said.

Sid stepped into the room. He shifted from one foot to the other, twisting his cap in his hands as though he didn't belong in his own bedroom.

'You're making the place look untidy.' Gertie smiled.

'Ruth said it was okay to come up… Are you… Did everything go…' he said, still twisting his cap.

'I'm fine. A bit tired. But fine. Come here.'

'I shouldn't. I've had a few pints, to wet the baby's head, like.'

'We don't mind. Come on.'

Sid walked slowly across the room. He stood beside the bed and stared down at the bundle in Gertie's arms.

'Is she… I mean is she…?'

'Ten perfect fingers and ten perfect toes,' Gertie said. 'Here.' She offered the baby to Sid. He backed away.

'I don't know how.'

'You won't break her,' Gertie said softly. 'She wants to say hello.'

Sid sat on the edge of the bed.

'You'll have to put your cap down,' Gertie said.

'Oh, yeah. Right. Sorry,' he said and placed his cap on the blanket.

'Put one hand under her head to support it,' she said, carefully transferring the baby into his arms. 'Put the other under her back. That's it.'

Sid's hand engulfed the baby's head, but he cupped it so very gently. Gertie watched him look down at her.

'She's beautiful,' he whispered, staring at the baby who had fallen into a deep sleep as he held her, her eyelids fluttering, her little hands balled into tight fists against her face. Sid sniffed and turned to wipe his eyes roughly on his shoulder. 'Gert, I've never seen anything so perfect in my whole life.'

'I thought we might call her Rose. If you don't think Ted will mind.'

'Rose,' Sid repeated. 'Hello, Rose,' he said and lifted the baby to his lips. He kissed her gently on the forehead. A tear slipped down Gertie's cheek. It was a tear of joy and a tear of sadness. For Rose and for Rosemary, the little girl who had died on the day Rose had come into being. The little girl who never got to wear the cardigan lost on the floor of a bus littered with glass and blood. Had she lived then Rose wouldn't be here now.

Gertie threaded her arm through Sid's. He looked at her and smiled. It was a real smile. For the first time in so many years she saw a flicker of the old Sid. The Sid before the filth and grime.

Rose had done that. She had brought Sid back to her. How could that ever be wrong?

Gertie rested her head on Sid's shoulder. The only thing that mattered now was that they were here, together. A family. They had survived, and her baby would be safe in Sid's strong arms. Her life would be her family. From this day on she would be the glue to hold them together. Always.

THE END

Acknowledgements

Somebody once said you should write what you know. With *Keep You By My Side*, I've sort of done that. From a very early age, I was fascinated by snippets of history my family shared of their lives in London in the Second World War and 1960s. This story is not my family's story, but years of listening gave me a rich seam of situations, turns of phrase and historical detail to mine. I thank them with all my heart.

I'm also indebted to the magical stretch of Dorset coastline running from West Bay to Lyme Regis, which inspired the setting for Cliff Cottage.

Thank you to the team at Bombshell Books – Sumaira, Sarah and Alexina – and especially to Betsy and Fred who helped me achieve my dream.

Thanks to my writing pals who helped shape this book – Zoe Antoniades, Sam Hanson, Susie Lynes and John Rogers. Also to my great friend Virginia who has been there with beers and an ear to bend with all of my writing talk.

A book about the 1980s wouldn't be complete without a mention of the special people who made my own 1980s teenage years at once bearable, mad fun, and at times, totally bonkers! Thank you Sharon, Fiona, Suzanne and Karla.

And the biggest thank you goes to Pete, still my cheerleader-in-chief.